INTO ME YOU SEE

H L Potter

ISBN: 9798839211643

CONTENTS

To anyone who has a dream
'Shoot for the stars, even if you miss,
you'll land among the stars'

PROLOGUE

THE FLASHING BLUE LIGHTS *are the first thing I see as I open my eyes, and all I can hear is a buzzing in my ears.*

What happened?

I can't move my head or anything for that matter. I am trapped. I feel like I'm trapped in a vise that's getting tighter with every passing second.

My head is pounding, my head, God it hurts. I can feel something warm running down my face, I think it's blood, but I can't move my arms either. I can hear voices all around me. People are talking and people are shouting frantically in the distance.

"Hello love, can you hear me?" Where's that voice coming from? I move my eyes and I see a man kneeling down next to the upside-down car I'm in. "What's your name?" His voice is calm and gentle.

"Felicity," I reply, my voice barely audible.

"Hello, Felicity, My name is Alan, I'm a fireman, we are going to get you out of the car, ok?"

"Ok" I open my mouth and reply but I don't

think any sound comes out. My eyes are feeling heavy again, they start to close. No, no, no I can't fall asleep. I fight with everything I have left to open them again. I blink over and over again.

What's going on?

"Please don't fall asleep yet," Alan's voice now full of concern and he is pleading. I will try to stay awake, but my eyes are blurry and everything is slightly out of focus, even blinking doesn't clear my vision. I feel so dizzy. Everything hurts. I want to sleep.

"That's it, now try to keep them open ok, Felicity? You've been in a serious collision but everything will be ok,"

A collision? Oh yes, I remember now, I think. The fireman is trying to sound reassuring to make me feel better. But I'm scared. My eyes are closing again, I feel so sleepy. I. Must. Not. Fall. Asleep.

"Felicity, please try and stay awake. We need you awake as we are going to start cutting the car to get you out," Alan's voice is now firm and assertive and my eyes fly open. Come on, stay awake, Felicity.

"Am I going to die?" I ask him, my voice is still barely a whisper as pain explodes around me, in my head and all down my right side.

"Not if we can help it," he replies.

"Good, I have too many plans to die now."

"Ok, Felicity, we are going to start cutting now and then the paramedics will take you to the hospital. But we need you to stay awake, can you do that for me?" I glance over to him and form the word

yes with my mouth. "Felicity, do you understand what I am saying to you?"

"I understand," I breathe.

"There is going to be a lot of noise but stay calm, I know it's scary but you must stay awake, ok?"

"Yes," I know. I'm trying.

There is suddenly screeching noise and the car starts moving. It is being sliced and pulled. Being torn from around me, it's as though it's screaming from the pain. I want to scream from the pain too. The noise, oh the noise. My head. It hurts so much. Every part of my body hurts. I want to close my eyes and rest. I want this pain to stop. I can feel myself giving in, my body is disobeying me. I try to stop my eyes from closing but it's no good. I can't.

1

I LET OUT A sigh as I stared at myself in the mirror while I tried to tame my thick auburn locks. My hair was one of the things I would have changed about myself. Thick, unruly, and unattainable. Once I managed to get it into some sort of style, I looked at the finished product in the reflection in front of me. I knew I wasn't ugly, but I wouldn't have said I was beautiful either. I have an average nose, full lips and hazel-green eyes, nothing to write home about.

As I wiped away an errant strand of hair from my face, I caught sight of my eyes. They looked sad. Tired even. I was sick of looking like that. I was sick from feeling like that, too.

The sounds of sirens outside jerked me back. The sound that still sent shivers down my spine, reminding me of that fateful night I would never forget. That sound would never be just a typical sound of London ever again. I knew I had to get used to it though, as the top floor flat that I shared with my two flat mates was just a short walk away from the Chelsea and Westminster Hospital. It seemed as though all day, every day, people were getting hurt. People were suffering, People were dying. And it's just part of life.

The sirens faded away into the distance and everything was calm again. Turning my back on the mirror, I headed into the kitchen. I boiled the kettle and once it was done, I poured the boiling water into my mug. I watched as the water turned to a copper colour as the cascading water hit the teabag.

"Morning, Fliss," My flatmate Heather said as she walked into the open planned kitchen diner. She shot me one of her megawatt smiles.

Heather Ross is the definition of beautiful. She is in fact so perfect that she doesn't need any make-up to cover her flaws, because she doesn't have any. Even her poker straight natural blonde hair is perfect, which isn't fair.

Heather had been my best friend ever since infant school. She was my rock and my saviour, and she got me through the hardest time of my life. She saved me from myself when I was in a dark place and started to cut the inside of my thigh. I just needed to try and relieve the pain I was in following the death of my fiancé. But, thankfully she was there when I cut too deep, she took me to the hospital. She got me the help I needed to see the wood through the trees.

"Hey," I replied, "want a cuppa?" I grabbed another mug out of the cupboard before she got the chance to reply and dropped a teabag in it.

"Burning the candle at both ends I see," I teased as Heather yawned.

Heather was somewhat famous for her one-night stands and crazy partying. It was surprising to me and Ethan, our other flatmate, that she'd been seeing Isaac for a month or so now.

She rolled her eyes at me and took the mug I handed to her. I took a sip of tea as I sat on the barstool at the breakfast bar.

"He's not like the others, you know. He's the real deal, I really like him," Heather said as she sipped her tea. I looked over at her, she looked genuinely happy as she talked about her latest beau.

"I think it could turn into something really special, I think it could be like what you had with Luke."

The sound of my fiancé's name - my dead fiancé's name - hit me like a ton of bricks. Even eighteen months after his death, I still stopped breathing at the mention of Luke's name. I didn't know if that would ever change. We were childhood sweethearts from the age of fifteen so living without him was painful.

People told me that it got easier over time, I just didn't see how it could. Even some places in the city were off-limits, famous landmarks I couldn't yet bring myself to visit, especially Regents Park as that's where he proposed to me, just by the Triton Fountain. Suddenly the city I loved became loaded with emotional landmines that could go off at any given moment.

"I'm ready now, you know? I want to find 'the one' and be happy. You two were so happy, I want that," Heather said, her voice genuine.

Oh, we certainly looked like we were unbreakable on the outside, but on the inside we were far from it. Happy? Yes, but that happiness changed the moment I found out that he had slept with someone else. And it broke me. It broke us. It broke him. It was never the same between us after that. Our love had changed and, although Luke tried his hardest to bring it back, he never could. No one knew about it, not even Heather. I disguised my hurt well, I got good at disguising things.

"If he is 'the one' then please treasure every moment of it, because once it's gone, you'll miss it," I said, checking my watch and pouring the remaining dregs of tea into the sink.

"I'm going to work now, have a good day," I said as I grabbed my bag off the counter and walked past Heather.

"You too," I heard her say as I closed the door behind me.

As I walked down the steps from the front door that led to the pavement, I took a deep breath and took in my surroundings. The street we live in is in a quaint area of south-west London called West Brompton. The road is filled with beautiful Georgian townhouses, some of which had been converted to flats like ours. I always imagined that the houses were filled with lots of exciting history from the families that lived here over the years gone by.

Our flat was housed in a building that had creamy yellow bricks that were broken up with white sash windows that flooded each room with light. It was a square symmetrical shape, carefully proportioned and had a graceful feel about it. I was so grateful to live in such a breath-taking building which was made possible by Hugh and Meredith Walker - my adoptive parents. They very kindly help us pay our rent as on my salary, even combined with my two flatmates salaries, we would never have been able to afford to live there on our own.

My adoptive parents had taken me in when I was four because I had no other family to care for me. They were amazing and I owed them everything. They gave me a happy childhood, raising me in the town of Richmond.

My birth mother from what I could remember of her was petite, slim and always smelt of smoke. She was also a drug addict, heroin was her poison of choice. She'd tried to make contact with me a few times over the past few years but I didn't want to see or know her. She overdosed despite me being in the house so I had no interest in her whatsoever.

I remember certain things about that night, I

remember her laying on the floor and the marks all over her wrists. I remember sitting next to her cold, rigid body while holding her hand. I faintly recall the man who lived next door calling my name through the letterbox, he must have alerted the Police.

I can remember the nice Police Officer who took care of me until the lady from social services arrived. But the thing I remember most like it was yesterday, was the fear. The fear that my mummy wasn't waking up, that my mummy wasn't cooking my chicken nuggets like she always did. The fear that I was alone. That's why I was so thankful that I was only young and that I got to live most of my life with the two most caring people in the world. It's one of the few things I was thankful for in life.

THE WALK TO THE Tube Station wasn't far. As I walked down roads lined with cars and a few trees, I breathed in the fresh September morning. The season was just starting to change to autumn, and I noticed some red and orange tinges that brushed the tips of the leaves. As I turned into the road where the station was, the hustle and bustle really began. There were people running for buses and running towards the Tube. It always made me smile with amusement. I always wondered why people were in such a hurry in life or why people left things to the last minute.

I marvelled at the delivery and bus drivers who navigated the small streets in bumper-to-bumper traffic while trying to avoid the pedestrians who stepped out in front of them regardless of the red predestination signals.

I walked through the doors of the station and walked onto the platform. I looked around and took in the smell and humidity of the underground. I loved London, despite everything. I loved everything about it. There was always something fresh and exciting happening to take your mind off things even if it was just for a second.

The train arrived and I stepped into the carriage. It was crowded as expected at 07:45 on a Friday morning. There was a vast array of people, different ages and different cultures in the carriage with me. And an array of stories to tell too. I look at the people around me and imagine what their lives were like, did they have children, what did they do for a living and what physical or mental scars did they cover up from the world. We all have them, but some are easier to cover than others.

As I arrived outside the building that housed LuxeLife Magazine, I looked up and admired it. The building was simply magnificent, a sleek tower that looked as though it could almost perforate the clouds. The modern design of the building managed to blend in with the older buildings that surrounded it. I was so grateful to work in such a fantastic building for an equally fantastic company where I had been the Editorial Assistant for the magazine for three years.

I chose to enter the lobby through the revolving door. The lobby was vast with tall walls and tall windows at the front of the building. The tiled floor had been polished to perfection, so shiny you could see your reflection. The whole feel of the building including the lobby was modern but timeless. My heels clicked as I walked past Bob at the security desk and waved, he was always so cheerful it made me smile warmly.

I headed over to the bank of lifts and pressed the call button. Once it arrived, I stepped in. Just as the doors began to close, I heard my name being called.

"Felicity!"

The crowd parted like the Red Sea, revealing Amber, my friend and colleague running towards me. I smiled and pressed the 'hold door' button. She came running in out of breath and placed her hand on her side trying to ease her stitch.

"Good morning," I said, trying to hide my amusement in my voice but failing miserably, "are you ok?" I asked, pointing to her hand that was still placed on her hip.

"Yeah, yeah, I'm fine, just a stitch. Man, I need to start going to the gym!" She replied while bending over trying to catch her breath.

"Well, if you're serious I'll go with you. I've been after a gym buddy for ages as my flatmates have no interest," Honestly, trying to get Heather or Ethan to do any exercise that isn't sex was nigh on impossible.

Amber and I carried on chatting as we rode the lift to the first floor. The doors opened and we stepped out and instantly we were greeted by the heavenly scent of fresh coffee and pastries. That only meant one thing - visitors. As I walked over to my desk, my manager Evelyn collared me.

"Felicity, good morning. I need to ask you a favour. As Beth isn't here today, I will need you to lay out the boardroom in preparation for our meeting," She asked, nervously as she knew hospitality wasn't one of my strong points thanks to my clumsiness.

"Ok, you want me to do it now?"

"Yes please, oh and I will need you to bring the teas and coffee in too when they arrive. This is a very important meeting so I can't stress enough how perfect everything needs to be," Evelyn seemed on edge, which made me nervous as she was usually the definition of cool, calm and collected - especially when it came to the VIP guests we had in for photo shoots for the magazine, and they were very demanding.

As Evelyn walked away, I let out a sigh, it was typical that Beth, the PA, had to be ill the day of a seemingly huge meeting. I got up from my chair and headed over to the kitchen. I gathered the pastries and biscuits and brought them into the boardroom. The table was huge, and Ron, the Managing Director, was sitting in one of the chairs going through some notes. I smiled at him, and he glanced up and said hello without taking his eyes off the piece of paper. He was usually very friendly, and I had the feeling something was off today. Something felt off with everyone.

I went back to my desk once I had finished in the boardroom and turned on my Mac. I checked my emails and started work on some transcripts when I got a call from reception telling me that the guests were here and I was informed of their beverage choices.

I headed back into the kitchen to make some tea and coffee. *Crap, how am I going to carry it all to the boardroom?* I thought to myself as I frantically looked for a tray knowing that I would have to do multiple trips if I couldn't find one. Knowing the guests are probably sitting there patiently waiting for their refreshments, I grabbed two cups and carried them by the saucer. I heard a clunking noise and looked down at my hands, shit - I was shaking. Coffee started to slop over the edge of the cups.

I finally reached the door of the boardroom and peered in through the small window, I caught Ron's eye and he waved me in. I used my hip to open the door and as soon as I walked into the room, I felt all eyes on me. I felt myself blushing as I walked slowly over to the table, trying not to spill anymore of the drinks.

"Erm, the coffee?" I asked, my voice sounding shakier than I had hoped. I could barely look up at the group of people round the table.

"Yes, that's me," The sound of the voice made me stop, I was rooted to the spot. His voice was silky smooth but with a rasp that somehow managed to send tingles down my spine.

I raised my head up from the saucers to see who'd replied . . .

Wow.

I was completely stunned by his sheer beauty as soon as my eyes landed on him. I tried to shake off the dumb struck look on my face before walking over towards him.

As soon as my feet started to move, I stumbled. I tried to place the cup and saucer on the table as carefully as possible, but I completely missed it and the cup fell onto his lap.

The whole thing happened in slow motion, and I didn't even have time to react. I heard gasps and curses coming from the others in the room. The incredibly handsome man jumped up with grace, not showing a hint of anger or frustration, while dabbing his trousers - which were clearly tailor made for him. He lifted his head up so he was standing up straight, all six foot two inches of him, revealing a scorching force of manliness and power.

Oh dear God. I thought as I shamefully picked up the cup that was now on the floor.

He looked down at me, his eyes were an incredibly piercing sapphire blue, bluer than any eyes I had ever seen. His blue tie that he was wearing made his eyes stand out more. I could only stare - stunned. His face and his cheek bones were sculpted so perfectly, like they were carved by angels.

His hair was a beautiful dark chocolate brown, it was long on top, at the sides and at the back, so long in fact that it brushed over his shirt collar at the back. It made my hands twitch with wanting to run my fingers through it, feeling each perfect strand. As he rose up to his feet, a few errant strands flopped onto his forehead, somehow making him seem even more gorgeous.

He stared back at me, and as he did, I felt the air thicken and shift between us. He must have felt it too as he suddenly blinked, looking away from me as he tried to compose himself. I realised, in my clouded haze that I hadn't actually said anything or even apologised, I was too preoccupied gaping at the God that was inches from me.

"I'm, I'm," I stuttered, "I'm so sorry I -,"

What is wrong with me, why can't I speak?

"No apology needed, accidents happen," He interjected, putting his hand up as if to silence me, stopping my shameful apology in its tracks. His reaction was cool and very calm. He looked into my eyes again and smiled at me, but the smile didn't quite reach his eyes.

"Felicity, go and make Mr. Harper another coffee please," Ron said. But I barely registered Ron's voice as we continued to maintain eye contact and for some reason I was unable to look away from him. I felt drawn to his eyes, I couldn't find the will to tear them away.

"Felicity?" Ron said again, this time through gritted teeth. His stern voice jolted me back into the room.

"Yes of course," I turned on my heels and quickly left the room.

Jesus what was that?

I had never experienced a feeling quite like that. I had read about such feelings in various Romantic Novels where the hero would waltz in and turn the heroine's life upside down but, I never for a minute thought it would or could happen to me.

I headed towards the kitchen, almost running. My eyes never leaving the door, I was so intent on reaching my destination. In my peripheral vision I saw Amber get up and follow me. As I pushed my way through the door, I released a breath I didn't know I was holding.

"You ok girl? You look like you're in shock," Amber asked, her voice laced with concern as she suddenly appeared at my side.

"No, I've just made an idiot out of myself!" I said, placing my hand on my forehead. He must have thought I'm incapable of anything.

"Why, what happened?"

Before I even got the chance to open my mouth to explain the embarrassment of what just happened, he walked in. I looked at him and he stared at me, pinning me down with his gaze. He was looking at me in a way no one ever has. It's as if his eyes were burning into me. Amber saw that my eyes were looking past her and she turned to look at what was captivating me. She let out a slight gasp, she was speechless at his raw sexual magnetism.

"Felicity?" Even the way he pronounced my name got me, the way his tongue glided over each syllable. Amber looked from him to me and then back to him again. She cleared her throat and scurried off when she realised that was her queue to leave. He took a step closer to me and I instinctively stepped back, walking into the kitchen worktop, I grabbed hold of it and gripped tightly.

As he approached me, my heartbeat quickened, it was beating with so much force it felt like it was going to beat out of my chest at any moment. My lips parted to accommodate my rapid breaths. He smelt outrageously good, it's almost sinful. It wasn't aftershave, it could have possibly been body wash. But whatever it was, it was intoxicating and delicious, almost as delicious as the man himself.

He held out his left hand to me, willing me to

shake it, exposing his Rolex and onyx cufflinks. Hell, his wrist was worth more than my whole wardrobe. I hesitated before removing my hand from the worktop. It trembled as I brought it up to meet his, I looked him square in the eye as I placed my hand in his. My pulse leapt when he gripped tighter. His touch electric, sending shockwaves all the way up my arm so all the hairs were standing on end. He didn't move his hand, he just stared back at me with a frown that created a little 'V' above his brow. His expression was unreadable and his eyes turned darker. I was sure he could feel whatever the hell I was feeling too.

We stood there staring, hand in hand. He was younger than I'd first thought, younger than thirty-five I would've guessed, but his eyes were full of wisdom and experience and something else I couldn't put my finger on. He was clearly sharp and intelligent.

I felt strangely drawn to him, as if my wrists were tied with a rope that he was slowly, erotically pulling, bounding me to him. Blinking out of my daze, I let go and my hand was freed from his grip. He was just so captivating. He was the kind of man that made women weak at the knees with just a look or a smile. And in that moment, I was that woman, I wanted nothing more than to undo his sky blue tie and rip open his shirt and watch as the buttons scattered over the floor along with my mind and inhibitions.

What is wrong with you, Felicity? Get a grip! I scolded myself. I'd never had those kinds of thoughts before. That wasn't me, I didn't do that.

"Are you ok?" he asked. "You look flushed."

Mortified, I composed myself and smoothed my pencil skirt down over my hips, trying to cover up my shaking hands.

"Yes, I'm fine thank you, I should be asking you that question considering you are the one who had scorching water thrown over your lap," I tried to act like I wasn't flushed, although I could feel the heat in my cheeks rising from the thoughts I had about his shirt. . .and what was underneath . . .

Stop it Felicity! My subconscious roared at me.

"Don't worry about me, I can handle what most women throw at me," he replied with a glint in his eye.

What?!

What was I supposed to do with that comment? Was he just making a joke or was he flirting with me? I couldn't read him at all.

"Right, well I'm glad you are ok," I said, trying to dismiss the comment.

"Well, I wanted to make sure you were *ok*, you seemed embarrassed," He said as his eyes made their way down to my lips. Suddenly I felt like I was on display, I felt vulnerable even. I turned around and faced the kettle. I couldn't deal with the heated look in his eyes. I thought I was going to combust if he carried on.

"I also to tell you that you don't have to worry about the coffee, I'll make do with orange juice so you don't have to go back in there, I wanted to spare you the embarrassment, " I could feel that he had taken a step closer to me, all the hairs on my nape stood up with the sheer proximity of him.

"Ok," I turned back around to face him and all of a sudden he was inches from my body. I could see his powerfully lean body under his suit jacket and shirt. I imagined running my hands and my tongue over each muscle on his chest . . .

STOP IT, WOMAN. I scolded myself.

I shook my head trying to shake away my carnal thoughts. "I'm going to get on with my day now Mr Harper -"

"Please call me Matthew," he interrupted me, as he stared deep into my soul.

"Ok then, Matthew. It was lovely to meet you. Goodbye," I turned and started walking away.

"Is that it?" He called after me.

I paused and closed my eyes, psyching myself up to turn and face him again. My heart skipped at the sight of him standing there with his hands casually his trouser pockets.

"Is there more?" I asked, confused.

"Oh, I really hope so," he replied. His tone was so certain. It sounded like a challenge.

I frowned at him. Why would I see him again?

I decided the best thing to do was to get the hell out of there before I submitted to his raw sexual magnetism. I offered him a polite smile and practically ran out of the kitchen without looking back.

I made a beeline for the Ladies knowing I'll be safe from him and whatever force I just experienced in there. I reached the basin and splashed water on my face to cool my burning cheeks. I looked at my reflection in the mirror, I was definitely flushed. My hazel eyes were bright and hungry. I had seen that look before - it's the look of longing and pure desperation to be touched. What was it doing on my face?! It had no right to be there right now.

Five minutes with him, a man who seemed so certain and sure of himself and I was filled with a hunger I hadn't felt for a very long time, if ever.

I stood in the Ladies for God knows how long trying to compose myself. Finally, I plucked up the courage and composure to move. I opened the door and checked that the coast was clear before leaving and I ran back to my desk unscathed. I unlocked my Mac and tried to get lost in work.

LUNCHTIME SOON ROLLED AROUND and Amber and I left the office to grab some food. The sound of horns blared around us as pedestrians darted in front of black cabs. Hand gestures were made at other drivers. Just a typical day in the Capital.

"So, this gym thing, fancy going tonight?" Amber asked as we took our seats in the booth.

We picked a local deli that had about four or five tables. They made delicious sandwiches, baguettes and salads. It was a popular lunch choice with workers so we were lucky to get a table.

"Yes, let's go tonight. There's a new one not far from my flat, I can meet you there at let's say 6:30pm?" Finally, someone who was keen to go to the gym with me.

"It's a date," Amber smiled as she bit into her chicken tikka baguette.

I picked at my pasta salad not feeling like eating, my thoughts were still stuck on Matthew Harper.

We finished our lunch while talking about men and gossiping about the latest celebrities who had come in for photo shoots and, before we knew it, the hour was up. Just before I got to my desk Evelyn and Ron approached me. They asked me into the meeting room, and as I walked in I saw various employees from other departments sitting at the table already and that the projector was fired up with a presentation titled 'LuxeLife, the future'.

I stood at the back of the room as all the seats had been taken and Amber joined me with her team and manager. Ron started the presentation and we learnt that the magazine had been bought out by another company and the guests that were there in the morning were finalising the details. There was muttering and chatter in the room from my colleagues and we were assured that the new company wanted to keep the same structure so all our jobs were safe.

I watched as the slides changed on the screen. We learnt that the company who bought us out was named MWH Group Holdings. Suddenly, it hit me as I read the name on the screen and I began to piece it all together, *Matthew Harper.* With his tailored suit and Rolex, which both screamed financial success, he had to be the owner of the company, the initials had to be his. I cringed inwardly at the memory of our first encounter. Is that why he said that comment about hoping there was more? I wondered how much I would actually see him.

Hopefully, a lot.

I shook my head and scolded my subconscious as I listened to what Ron had to say. I didn't care if I ever saw him again to be honest. Or so I kept telling myself.

AFTER OUR FIRST WORKOUT session, Amber and I headed to the locker room. We worked out for a full hour so I felt good, if not a little unfit.

"We are definitely doing that again!" Amber said as she pulled up her jeans. I smiled at her in response. Her black curly hair was pulled into a neat ponytail and a few beads of sweat shimmered on her forehead. She still looked good even after a workout. Me on the other hand, well, my wavy hair had been thrown up into a bun, my pale skin was now red and my top was drenched in sweat. But if it made me fitter, it was something I was going to have to get used to.

"So this man who came in the kitchen earlier, he was *hot!* Is he something to do with the takeover?" Amber had been wanting the lowdown ever since she left the kitchen and since I didn't let her get the chance at lunch, she saw her opportunity and took it there and then.

"I think he might be the owner of the company who bought out the magazine, but don't quote me on that, I could be wrong. He just seemed very well dressed for just an employee and his name is Matthew Harper, the same initials as the new company." I replied.

"Oh, I hope he is, I wouldn't mind working for him, on top of him or being under him," she winked.

"Amber!" I gasped, slapping her arm playfully.

She looked at me and shrugged, "What? Are you seriously telling me you wouldn't have a go if the chance presented itself?" I didn't even want to think about it because quite frankly, he was all I could think about that afternoon. Even though I didn't particularly like him and I found him extremely arrogant.

*His tall, dark, lean body on top of me. . .*My mind wondered.

"Fliss?" Amber waved at me, distracting me from my wayward thoughts. God, it had been so long since I'd been kissed or even been looked at by a man. I swallowed and smiled at her.

"Come on, let's go grab a drink at my place."

As we left Alpha Fitness, my phone vibrated in my bag. I fumbled around for it and pulled it out. I frowned as I looked at the screen, I didn't recognise the number so I let it go to voicemail. I threw my phone back into my bag and we continued walking to my flat.

As I opened the door to my flat, I saw Heather and Isaac rather rapidly get up from the settee. Isaac quickly tried to do his fly up while Heather smoothed down her messed up hair. Both had guilt written all over their faces.

"You better wash that cushion or better that, just burn the whole settee," I said, rolling my eyes at them as I headed over to the fridge. That wasn't the first time I'd walked in on Heather with a man. Although it was the first time I'd walked in on her with the *same* man.

"Hev, you have a bedroom through there, why don't you actually use it? We have guests over sometimes and that's the last thing they want to see," I gestured to Amber to try and make a point. Amber, feeling awkward, just smiled and waved shyly. I narrowed my eyes at Heather playfully and shook my head.

"Hi guys!" Ethan called as he walked through the door into the living area.

Heather and I met Ethan at a gallery event where Heather worked. He was a couple of years younger than Heather and I and he was like a younger brother to us. Ethan had moved in with us after he came out gay to his parents, they didn't take it well to say the least.

We all sat in the living room after eating a Chinese takeaway when we said goodbye to Amber. When I returned to my seat Heather looked at me with a questioning look on her face.

"What?" I asked. Why was she looking at me like that?

"How was your day, did anything interesting or unusual happen?" She was smiling ear to ear and it made me feel very uneasy.

"Well, the magazine has been bought out, but apart from that no."

And I met a strikingly handsome man and made a complete dick out of myself.

She got up and went into her room. I looked at Ethan and he shrugged. Then after a minute, she reappeared.

"Well how do you explain these then?" She stood on the threshold of her bedroom, and in her hand was a vase with what looked like a dozen beautiful red roses.

"Whose are they?" I asked, surely they couldn't have been for me.

"Yours!" she replied with glee, jumping from one foot to the other, her long blonde ponytail bouncing as she did, "Oh and I took the liberty of reading the card. Who's M Harper?"

I sighed at her. I wasn't surprised that the tenacious Heather Ross had opened the card. She was always poking her nose in my business. I got up from my seat and walked over to her, I took the card and read it.

Felicity,

It was a pleasure meeting you today, wet trousers aside.

Looking forward to seeing you again soon.

Until then,

M Harper

I stared at the handwritten card. So was this what he meant by more? I suddenly realised that I was smiling, I felt like a giddy school girl. One of the hottest, albeit arrogant men that I'd ever met had sent me flowers. Why and *how* did he send them? How did he get my address? I then remembered that I had a phone call from a number I didn't recognise.

Maybe it was him. I thought.

I looked up at my bag that was sitting on a barstool and walked over and got my phone out of it. I had one new voicemail. I turned on my heels and dashed into my room, shutting the door on the questions I heard being asked. I fell onto my bed with my phone. Sure enough I heard his smooth, sensual, velvet soft voice in my ear. I replayed the message several times before I sat up. He wanted to see me again. Apparently I made an impact on him. Well, he certainly made an impact on me.

I felt excited and I caught my reflection in the mirror, I was smiling ear to ear. I was like a love struck teenager! I got up off my bed and realised that I had been in my room for far too long, Heather would be getting antsy. It was time to get out of my room and face the music. Sure enough as soon as I opened my bedroom door, there she was, ready and waiting with her hands on her hips. Poised to jump in with the questioning.

"Felicity Jayne, if you don't tell me who this mystery man is right now, I swear I will hunt him down and make him tell me himself!" she warned.

I held my hands up in defeat. "Ok, ok, I'll tell you,"

I recalled the events of the day to Heather, Ethan and Isaac. I watched Heather as she practically squealed with delight.

"So, are you going to call him back?" Ethan asked, all bright eyed.

I opened my mouth and closed it again, even just talking about him gave me butterflies. I could picture his breath-taking face with crystal clear clarity and I could still feel the surge of electricity that crackled between us, both in the air and up my arm when he held my hand. Sure, he was successful and so sure of himself but, his face, his beautiful handsome face made me nod in response.

"Yes, I'm going to call him. Maybe not tonight, as for one, it's getting late and two—," I paused thinking about what to say next, "well I don't know what two is to be honest, but I just want to wait," I replied, because that was the truth. But why did I want to wait? What was wrong with me?

"Well baby girl, I can't blame you. You have been out of the game for what, like eleven years?" Ethan said looking at Heather who then nodded. "So, I can see why you are perhaps a little hesitant, but don't wait too long because a rich hottie like that won't be on the market forever," He got up and kissed me on the top of my head.

"I'm hitting the hay now, just sleep on it and then see how you feel in the morning."

Not long after Ethan went to bed, Heather and Isaac followed. I sat alone in the living room with only the glow from the table lamp. What was I going to do? Did I even want to go on a date? Did I want to start anything with Matthew? Was I ready?

It might not even become anything.

Even so, I was allowed to enjoy a little bit of fun, wasn't I?

With thoughts and questions buzzing around my head, I decided to take Ethan's advice and sleep on it. I got into bed and closed my eyes. I started to drift off to sleep and as I did, thoughts of the insanely attractive, blue eyed God filled my mind.

2

I WATCHED ETHAN IN the mirror as he attempted to style my hair into a chignon. I was incapable of styling it myself unless it was down or in a simple ponytail.

"How are you feeling about the whole situation with the billionaire?" Ethan asked.

"We don't know if he's a billionaire Ethan," I replied as Ethan finished my hair and sprayed a little bit of hairspray to hold it in place.

"Course he is, he owns multiple businesses in London and around the UK," I shot him a questioning look in the mirror, "Ok, I Googled him last night," He shrugged. "What can I say, I was curious," He held up a mirror behind me so I was able to see his handiwork.

"Thanks Eth, it's perfect," I smiled.

"Anytime baby girl," He walked over to the door. "I'm heading up West to meet Sam for breakfast now. Have a good day today and let me know what you decide to do about lover boy, the suspense is killing me," he winked and left, closing the door behind him.

As it was Saturday morning, I called my mum for our weekly catch up. We chatted about what we had both done that week and which of my mum's many friends had thrown a cocktail evening. My mum had a very large social circle thanks to my dad's job as a Neurosurgeon. They would always throw parties for absolutely no reason for all their friends, who the majority of were fellow colleagues and ex colleagues.

We chatted about most things from that past week, apart from *him*. The less my mum knew, the better.

“So, honey, how's work?” My mum asked.

“It's ok, the magazine has actually been bought out by another company, MWH Group or something,” I said, trying to act nonchalant.

“Oh, well that sounds interesting, is your job safe?” I could hear the apprehension in her voice. I hated to worry my mum. She had so much to worry about when it came to me, especially with what happened in my past with my fiancé‘s death.

“As far as I know they want to keep the structure of the company as is, so they said we are fine” I said, trying to reassure her.

We ended the phone call after arranging a spa day for the next day, which was well overdue. I made myself a cup of tea and flopped onto the settee, switching the TV on. I wasn't really aware of what I was watching, I just occasionally heard the voices of the characters on the screen.

I laid there playing back the encounter at work in the kitchen. I couldn't deny that there was definitely a connection of some sort. For him to send me expensive and very beautiful roses, he must have felt it too.

Before I made any rash decisions, I decided I needed to do some research. I grabbed my phone and loaded up Google.

I just sat there staring at the screen, not knowing where to begin. Finally after psyching myself up, I typed in 'Matthew Harper, MWH Group' and I watched as the screen flooded with news articles and various interviews that he had done. I saw that the acquisition of LuxeLife magazine was already public knowledge.

I read about Matthew's accomplishments in the business world and how he conquered many markets at a young age. I learnt that he owned many companies in London as well as out of London as Ethan had said. The companies included a prestige hotel chain, an architect firm and publishers to name but a few.

I clicked on 'images' and immediately my heart leapt into my throat as I was bombarded with image after image. There were photos of him from various events and fundraisers, the formal wear he was sporting was the giveaway. Some of them were of him on his own and others were pictures of him with various dates. All of the women in the pictures were blonde and beautiful. The textbook woman that you would put with him. Flawless and stunning.

Why did he contact me, why did *I* make an impact? I was clearly not the type of woman he would have normally gone for, Heather would've certainly have been his type. Maybe he was bored and fancied a new challenge with me?

Mixed in with the fundraiser photos, there were some photoshoots and some candid ones too, walking out of buildings and getting into his car or simply out walking while on his phone.

Each image burnt into my memory. But, I couldn't help myself going back to look at the pictures with him and various women. The more I looked, the more I could feel the jealousness coursing through my veins.

Pushing the jealous thoughts to one side, I clicked on some of the images to enlarge them so that I could see his face more clearly. He was so alluring. The way he held himself was so dominating and assertive, if he were to walk into a room, everyone would stop and take notice.

I couldn't help but stare into his amazing blue eyes, but as I did, the more of him I saw. I could see that deep down he could possibly have a dark side, he looked as though he was haunted by something or *someone*. At a glance, he looked unbreakable. To me, I could see wounds, I could see scars that he tried so hard to hide from the outside world. I could see them because I had wounds too.

Putting my phone face down on the armrest, I sighed. Was I ready to take the leap? Could I leave my fear and the guilt I felt about somehow betraying Luke behind?

He betrayed you. My subconscious snarled at me.

I groaned knowing that I was going to have to do something, and soon. Having been raised with the manners of 'be nice to people and don't put your elbows on the table', I decided to text him to thank him for the flowers and apologise again for the coffee incident.

Matthew,

Thank you for the roses, they are beautiful :)
And again, sorry for yesterday.

Fliss x

P.s. how did you get my number?

As I pressed send, I immediately regretted doing so. I threw my phone onto the armchair next to me and collapsed on the settee with my arm over my eyes and let out a large sigh. After a few minutes my phone vibrated. I debated ignoring it but then realised it might not be him. I leant over and reached for my phone. Yep, sure enough it was him.

Felicity,

You are more than welcome. For someone so beautiful,
you deserve more than just roses.
Meet me today, 2pm La éléments Restaurant, Kensington and I'll tell you how I got your number . . .
Until then,

M Harper

I read his text over and over again. He wanted to go out with me, I couldn't believe it. I glanced up at the clock, it was 11:30am. I had some time. I decided to go shopping and get myself something nice. I replied to him before I left.

Matthew,
It's a date ;)
See you then.
Fliss x

I heard the cab pull up outside and I grabbed my bag and closed the door behind me.

AS I WALKED DOWN OXFORD Street, I marvelled at all the dresses that were in the windows of the various clothing shops. Some of the dresses and clothes were garish, others were more like my style - plain and simple. I would never have been brave enough to wear half of the things that were in the shops.

I had so many questions going around in my head, what should I wear for this date? Do I go smart casual or really smart and buy a new dress? La éléments Restaurant was posh from what I had seen and heard, so maybe I should get a dress. I really needed Heather as she was a fashion guru.

Finally after some time, I found a dress that I liked. It was cobalt blue, just tight enough to hug my curves in all the right places and sat just above the knee so I felt comfortable with the fact that it was long enough to cover the scars that were on my thighs. It was a V neckline which just about showed the top of my breasts, I wanted the right look, sexy yet classy. Feeling proud of my purchase, I headed home to get ready.

As I stepped out of the cab and onto the pavement, I was suddenly overwhelmed with nerves and emotions. Ethan was right, I hadn't been on a date in eleven years up until now. Was I ready for this? I looked up at the beautiful old building that the restaurant was in and I took a deep breath before walking through the door.

I was greeted by the Maître d' and I followed him to the table. As I walked through the restaurant, the butterflies that I already felt in my chest doubled. I could see that Matthew was already seated at the table in the far corner of the restaurant away from all the other diners.

God, I forgot how handsome he was. I thought.

He looked up as I approached and beamed at me and I could have sworn that my steps faltered.

Matthew got up from his seat and walked over to me, his confidence was evident with every graceful step he took. He began to lean in closer to me and I released he was going to kiss my cheek. I held my breath and as he got closer, I felt the air shift just as it did before. As his lips caressed my cheek, I shut my eyes to savour his touch. I didn't realise how much I was craving it until he touched my skin. He smiled down at me with warm eyes and pulled out the chair for me to sit.

"Thank you," I said shyly.

"You're welcome, Miss. Walker,"

I was taken aback by how he knew my last name, not to mention my address to send the roses.

As he sat down, he unbuttoned his suit jacket, removing it from his broad shoulders. I looked around at the other diners in the restaurant and noticed that they were all dressed up in suits and dresses. Thankfully I didn't look out of place.

"You look beautiful by the way," he said as he rolled his sleeves up to his elbows, exposing his dark arm hair and forearms.

I blushed and looked down at my hands, I was not used to this.

"So, thank you for agreeing to meet with me," he began.

I smiled at him, suddenly feeling very awkward. It felt more like a business meeting than a date, or were they usually like that and I was so out of touch?

"How are you, have you had a good day?" He asked.

Ah small talk, now it feels like a date.

I felt a slight smile brush my lips, but not enough for him to notice.

"Yes, I went shopping. How about you?" I asked, and I realised that my voice was a little more nervous than I wanted it to sound.

"It was average but has just taken a turn for the better," he replied with a boyish grin that made my heart flutter.

I couldn't help but smile at his optimism. Before I got a chance to reply, the waitress came over and took our drinks order. I opted for lemonade and Matthew ordered a glass of Merlot. Once the waitress disappeared, I looked down at the menu and nearly passed out looking at the prices. I couldn't even afford the starters!

I continued to look down at the menu without looking up as I felt Matthew's eyes burning into me. We sat in silence for what felt like eternity before Matthew spoke.

"How do you feel about the news yesterday?"

I looked up at him and realised he was talking about the magazine being taken over.

"Erm, ok I suppose. I knew something was going on when I got to reception and could smell fresh coffee and pastries," I said, offering him a shrug.

"You're quite intuitive then, Miss. Walker?"

Me, intuitive? No way. I shook my head.

"You just pick up on these sorts of things when you have worked there for a while," I paused and then continued, "speaking of intuition, how do you know my phone number, address and last name?"

He glanced up from his menu and looked at me, his expression unreadable. The waitress then returned with our drinks. He continued to look at me while she placed our drinks on the table.

"Are you ready to order?" The waitress asked without actually looking at me. She was too engrossed with looking at Mr. Good Looking sitting in front of me. She may as well have twirled her hair around her finger.

I looked from Matthew to the waitress and then back to Matthew who was still staring at me.

"Yes, I'll have the chicken breast with the braised potatoes please," I said, narrowing my eyes at her.

I heard Matthew let out a small chuckle and then he ordered. I took the moment to study him closely while he wasn't looking at me. He was ridiculously handsome. He was clean shaven the last time I saw him but today, his jaw sported a day or two's growth which highlighted his strong profile even more so. He was the definition of sexy.

Once Matthew had finished ordering, Little Miss. Flirtatious sauntered off and I instinctively rolled my eyes.

"Was that jealousy I just witnessed there?" he teased.

"What? No! I just think it's rude to ignore the other people at the table,"

Yes I was jealous. I am on a date with you, not her. It doesn't help that you are so gorgeous and so out of my league.

"Anyway, I asked you a question before she interrupted us,"

He regarded me impassively and took a sip of his red wine.

"Well, now that I legally own the company you work for, I can get access to all employee records," he said nonchalantly, as if it was a ridiculous thing to have asked.

"Right. Surely there is something there like gross misuse of personal information?"

Matthew grinned at me, obviously finding my

question utterly amusing.

“Are you going to sue me?” he smiled, cocking his head to one side revealing his playful side.

I felt my cheeks instantly turn red with embarrassment. I picked up my glass of lemonade and took a welcomed sip, feeling it cool my burning skin.

“I like that I can make you blush, even with just a look,” he said, his voice low. Somehow it made me ache with desperation for the man who sat in front of me.

I choked as I swallowed my lemonade. It caught me completely off guard. He taped his long fingers on the side of the wine glass thoughtfully as if he was plotting his next ambush of words. Thankfully Little Miss. Flirty reappeared with bread and oils and placed them in the middle of the table.

“Enjoy” she said, painting on her sweetest smile, all the while only looking at Matthew before disappearing off.

Feeling as though I needed to do something to distract myself from his piercing eyes, I took some bread and dipped it into the balsamic vinegar. Matthew, still looking at me, reached for the bread and did the same. He popped a piece of bread into his mouth and chewed.

Why is he so mesmerising? I thought as I delicately took a bite of bread.

I was fixated on his mouth and lips, watching as he chewed the bread. I licked my dry lips with the tip of my tongue, still watching as he ate another bite. He finally broke his intense gaze and picked up his glass again. My heart rate increased as I watched him take another sip of wine.

"Would you like to try some?" he asked as he slid the glass across the table to me.

I nodded and picked up his glass, slowly tipping it into my mouth feeling the red liquid flow down my neck.

I slid the glass back to him. Maybe I should have ordered an alcoholic beverage for some Dutch courage.

"Good isn't it? It's one of my personal favourites," he said, his voice was now deep and throaty. And as sexy as hell.

I was just about comfortable enough to hold his gaze. As we sat in silence I noticed that it was no longer awkward. It felt nice. But it could have been the wine.

"I need -" Matthew started to speak but was halted in his tracks by the waitress who brought over our lunch. She placed the meals in front of us and left. Matthew had ordered the fillet of sea bass and it looked amazing.

We both tucked into our food and Matthew resumed our conversation.

“I need you to understand that I am finding it extremely difficult not to think about you, Felicity,”

Oh. My heart skipped a beat.

“And because of that, I wanted to see you again as I have a proposition for you,”

He must have sensed my confusion as he put down his knife and fork, causing me to do the same. He looked serious and he took a deep breath and I braced myself for what it was that he was going to say next.

“I want one week with you and your body. Seven days to worship you and please you, sexually. No feelings, no commitment, ” he said slowly, he looked at me with caution in his eyes.

What?! Was he mad? Seven days with him and what, that's it, we both walk away and never speak again? My eyes and mouth were wide open in surprise. I didn’t know what to say next.

“Why, why would I want to do that?” I said, stuttering, bemused at what he was asking of me. A week? Was he seriously asking me this!

“Because I know you want me, I can see your

reaction every time you catch me staring at you. You flush when I go near you or comment on your appearance," he smiled a slow, guileful smile at me, "and your breathing, it changes, it becomes quicker, almost like a pant,"

Shit! Was I that easy to read?

My lips became dry again and I tried my hardest not to lick them. Not wanting to give him any more ammunition than he had already. He was staring at me, analysing me with his powerful gaze.

"I'm right, aren't I?" he asked, smirking at me.

I refused to answer and we remained staring at each other. I could feel the sexual tension between us. So, that was why he followed me into the kitchen and sent me the flowers. He wanted to ask me that question. Romance had nothing to do with it. He was just after a sordid week of sex.

"So, you want me for sex for a week and nothing else?" I clarified, hardly believing what was coming out of my mouth.

"Yes, one week. One week of nothing but pleasure," he affirmed. "I'm hoping that you will give it to me,"

"But why just a week?" Why not date me? I don't understand," I whispered.

"It's so that you don't get used to me because I'm emotionally unavailable, Felicity. I don't date women,"

Huh?! My mind went into overdrive trying to understand what we meant.

I shook my head and picked up my fork, and started picking at my food hoping that it would distract me from the situation I had found myself in, or hoping that he would say something else - something better. Because to be quite honest, I felt like I'd been cheated, which made no sense as I didn't know him. But the thought of only being permitted one week with this ridiculously handsome man was depressing.

Why would I give myself to him for just a week? Who in their right mind would do that? I glanced over at the waitress, no doubt she would.

I looked down at my plate once more and took a bite of braised potato which my stomach rejected instantly.

Matthew was still watching me as I placed my cutlery back down on the table.

"I can't, I'm sorry but no. I don't even know you!" Why was I apologising for my decline of his damn right unreasonable request. Yes, I would have loved to be worshipped by him, he was handsome beyond belief. I would have loved to feel the touch of a man, Lord knew it had been a while but I couldn't, not like this, not in that way, it was just wrong.

"But if you knew me more, would you reconsider?"

Yes.

"No, definitely not," I said through gritted

teeth, "It's the most ridiculous thing I have ever heard. And anyway, how do you know that I don't have a boyfriend?"

"You wouldn't be here if you did," he replied dryly.

I felt my face turn seven shades of red.

"Please, Felicity. It will be amazing, you know it will,"

He was right, I had no doubt that it would be amazing, it would probably be mind blowing. But what good would come out of sleeping with him for a week?

Feeling intimacy without getting hurt. I frowned at my subconscious.

Was she right though? Maybe it would have been a good way to feel the touch of a man without getting myself hurt. I just didn't know if I could bear another heartache again.

I looked up at him and he was still watching me. His eyes were pleading with me and I knew I needed to say something to him and get the hell out of there. I couldn't be in such a close proximity with that man, the power he had over me was too overbearing.

"I, I need to think about it," I said suddenly feeling like I couldn't breathe, I rose to my feet and he did the same, watching me tentatively.

I was so pissed off that he'd put me in that position. I rubbed my forehead with exasperation and realised that he was walking over to me.

"Don't, please don't" I warned, pointing my finger at him causing him to visibly sag. I turned on my heels and walked away through the restaurant and out into the fresh air.

I stopped just outside on the busy pavement and took a deep breath letting my heart rate slow down. When I had just managed to calm myself down, I stepped off the curb and into the road but I missed my footing and fell.

As I was falling, I was suddenly pulled back and into someone's arms. I gazed up and Matthew was staring down at me. It all happened so fast - one minute I was falling into the road and the next I was in his arms. As I looked deep into his eyes, I was captivated even more so. His pupils suddenly became dilated and I took a deep breath inhaling his clean, fresh and intoxicating scent.

"Are you ok?" His voice was soft and genuine. He slowly lifted his hand and reached for my face, caressing my cheek.

I nodded and continued to stare into his blues. Eventually my attention turned to his mouth, I was all of a sudden drawn to his lips, his perfect plump lips. I was drawn to them like a moth to a flame. They were so perfect, everything about him was perfect.

Would a week of being worshipped by this man be so bad? As I stared at him more, I wanted to kiss him. I hadn't kissed anyone since Luke, I hadn't *wanted* to kiss anyone since Luke and suddenly I wanted to kiss this man who was clearly unattainable.

What was I doing to myself?

I caught him looking down at my lips too. He wanted to kiss me, too. I froze, I couldn't move. I was frozen to the spot. I was completely and utterly captivated by him.

Kiss me, please! I silently begged, willing him with my mind to kiss me.

Matthew closed his eyes hard and let out a sigh. When he opened them, they looked cold, they looked darker.

"I'm sorry, I can't do this, I can't kiss you. Not until you say yes," he whispered as he shook his head.

I looked up at him and furrowed my brow, I was feeling so rejected. I didn't understand, he wanted to sleep with me but he couldn't kiss me? Not unless I said yes? It didn't make any sense.

He gently pushed me away and I stood up straight, legs shaking. He had his hand on my shoulders steadying me, watching my reactions closely. I gathered my muddled thoughts and I composed myself. I was left feeling bereft and confused. All I wanted was to be kissed by him.

"I'm ok," I breathed, "thank you," I felt even more humiliated and insulted. I just wanted to get away from him and pretend the whole afternoon ever happened.

I noticed that his hands were still on my shoulders. I started to shrug them off, suddenly he realised and let go, placing his hands in his suit trouser pockets.

I wrapped my arms around my body as if to protect myself and looked anywhere but at him. I was too embarrassed and ashamed of myself for wanting him. I braved one last glance at him and turned suddenly and crossed the road, leaving Matthew standing on the pavement.

I could feel him watching me as I walked away. I just kept on walking just to get out of the area and away from him. As I walked, I felt a sudden rush of tears release and trickle down my face. My breathing was laboured, my legs still shaking.

What the hell happened? One minute I was on a date with this man who sends me flowers and won't leave me alone and the next minute, he's asked me to be some sort of sex slave.

So after all that, why the hell was I getting so upset that he didn't kiss me and why was I so tempted to say yes?

I OPENED THE FRONT door and breathed a sigh of relief to find the flat empty. I was certainly not in the mood for conversation with anyone. I was still reeling from what happened. Even after that ridiculous proposition, I was still thinking about him. Still thinking about his perfect face, his perfect lips. His perfect rock hard body naked on top of mine. I shook my head and walked into my room to get changed out of my dress.

As I finished putting my tracksuit bottoms on, I heard the front door open.

"Hey, honey, I'm home!" Heather shouted her usual greeting as she walked through the door.

"Hi Hev,"

Heather looked at me and beamed. "So how did the date go?!" She squealed.

Shit, what was I going to tell her?

"It was ok, but I won't be seeing him again," I shrugged.

"What, why?"

He only wanted me for sex.

"Erm, different points of view and opinions on things. We would clash a lot so it would never work," I said, waving my hand as if to dismiss the conversation.

Heather looked at me, narrowing her eyes.

"Oh damn, you two would have made a *hot* couple! You should just date him for the sex though, he just looks like he would know what he's doing, and besides, its been a while hasn't it?" she said to me with a wink.

Now Heather is the sort of person who would have said yes.

"Heather, not everything's about sex you know,"

"Well forget about him then! You know what you need? A night out!" Heather shouted with glee as her eyes danced with excitement.

"What? No!" I squeaked, I hated clubs and with the way I felt right at that moment, that was the last place I wanted to go.

Heather rolled her eyes and me, “pleaseeee,” She begged like a child asking their parents for a puppy. Her hands interlocked as she batted her eyelids at me and stuck out her bottom lip.

How could I say no to that face? “Fine, ok, we’ll go,” Now it was my turn to roll my eyes. I couldn’t help but wonder what I had just agreed to, “I’ll warn you now though, I don't have anything to wear,”

“Well, lucky for you, I know just the thing for you! Come with me,”

I followed Heather into her room and she rummaged through her packed wardrobe, finally pulling out a dress, a beautiful emerald green dress.

“No way, that's way too short for me! It's short enough on you and bear in mind I have an extra two inches on you! And I don’t want to flush my tits off to total strangers,”

“Oh come on, let the girls out to play for once, they get fed up being cooped up!” she said, waving her hand at my breasts. “You have a great rack!”

I rolled my eyes and snatched the dress from her hands, stomping into my room to try it on.

“I have some killer heels that go with that dress,” Heather called before I closed my door.

THE CLUB WAS LOUD, TOO hot and too busy.

It had only opened within the last month and Heather had been keen to go ever since. I was wearing the really tight emerald green dress which I definitely regretted as I had to pull it down every two minutes, worried about exposing my scars, let alone the plunging neckline that barely contained my 'rack'.

My hair was down and has been curled and styled by Ethan. I opted for the smokey eye look with a neutral colour lipstick. Heather, as always looked phenomenal, she was wearing a red dress which was even more low cut than mine, and made her breasts look amazing, even Ethan and I kept looking so no doubt the other men in the club would.

Ethan kept it simple with a pair of chinos and a shirt. Ethan Whiteman was a very attractive man and easily drew the eyes from both the women and men in the room.

"What do you ladies want from the bar?" Ethan shouted over the sound of Calvin Harris singing about Summer.

"Cosmo please Eth," Heather shouted back.

"Erm," I recalled Matthew's choice of drink earlier in the day, "I'll have Merlot Please!"

Both of them teased me about my choice of beverage as I never usually drank wine, only on special occasions. Once they eventually got the very idea of me being sophisticated out of the systems, Ethan ventured off to the bar.

Heather and I managed to get the last booth. I

looked around at the sea of bodies that occupied the dancefloor and inwardly cringed. I had some serious drinking to do if I was ever going to get up there. The music was so loud I could hardly hear Heather who was sitting directly in front of me.

"So, have you heard anything from Matt since your date?" Heather asked, trying to compete with the noise volume.

"No, I haven't, and it's *Matthew* not Matt," I said, smirking at her. Why did I feel so disappointed that he hadn't texted or called me?

"You're disappointed aren't you?" Heather said as if she'd read my mind. "Your face says it all,"

I dismissed it by shaking my head.

"Maybe you should call him. Maybe you need to go out again just to see, you might have been nervous?" she shrugged.

Oh, if only Heather knew. And in that moment I realised I needed to tell her. I needed to tell *someone.*

"He doesn't want a relationship, Hev," I said, frowning, deciding I needed a second opinion on the matter.

Heather mirrored my frown.

"Then why did he send you the flowers and ask you on a date?"

"Because Hev, it turns out that he only wanted me for sex. A week of sex to be exact."

The flashing lights of the club illuminated her face, exposing the look of shock and confusion.

Join the club. I thought.

"Did he tell you this after he wined and dined you?"

"No," I paused trying to work out how to say it without making me seem insane. Hell, I was insane. "He was in the process of wining and dining me and then he propositioned me for a week of sex."

I stopped to gauge her reaction. And, as I expected, her mouth was wide open like a guppy. "He wanted to, and I quote, 'worship and please me'," I decided to leave out the bit when I said I'll think about it, because quite frankly I was embarrassed that I was even contemplating it.

"I walked out in disgust and he followed me. Then I tripped and he caught me and then for some reason I wanted to kiss him".

Heather just stared at me, her mouth still wide open. I carried on with the story.

"And did you?" she asked, "did you kiss him?"

"No, he didn't want to kiss me, apparently he just wanted to sleep with me."

Heather blinked in dismay. "Wow."

"Yep, but I don't know what it is about him Hev, I can't stop thinking about him. It's like a force bigger than me, a force bigger than I have ever known, you know?"

"No, not really. But, I'm glad you walked out on him. You deserve better than a week in his sheets," She leant forward and took me by the hand and smiled lovingly at me.

I know she was right, but why did I feel like this? I knew I wasn't ready to move on but why was I longing for his touch again? To just be near him, to smell his amazing scent again?

Ethan thankfully distracted my thoughts when he appeared with a tray of drinks. Maybe I did need this night out, I needed to get drunk and try to forget the afternoon and the last painful eighteen months, even if it was just for a night.

We ordered drink after drink and I felt myself becoming tipsier and tipsier. I decided now that I was just about drunk enough to get on the dance floor. I grabbed Heather and Ethan by the hand and dragged them up there with me. I managed to lose myself in the music and dancing, slowly forgetting that the last few hours ever happened. Heather was right, I did need this.

We consumed multiple drinks and shots and I was now completely drunk, I was slurring my words, feeling dizzy and was sticky from the sweat. All I could smell was the alcohol that had been spilt over me by the other dancers. As we danced, our group of three suddenly became two as Ethan occupied himself with a fellow dancer.

Heather and I continued to dance together, both throwing our hands in the air as we moved our hips to the rhythm of the music. As we danced, I noticed most of the men were looking over at Heather, she was so petite and beautiful, how could you have not looked at her. One man slowly danced his way over to us, heading straight for Heather. He was tall and average looking, she was so far out of his league, it was a different game completely.

Somehow, Mr. Average managed to intercept a drunk Heather from me and they started to dance, he was grinding up against her with his hands on her hips. I was sure that Isaac wouldn't have been very happy to see another man dancing like that with his girlfriend but, I'd known Heather for twenty-one years and there was no stopping her.

After being dumped by both Ethan and Heather, I headed to the toilets, needing to splash water over my very sweaty, red face. I carefully walked towards the steps which were of course on the other side of the room. I pushed my way through crowds of people and finally reached them. I looked up and in my drunken haze, they seemed very steep. I grabbed hold of the hand rail and made my way up, slowly and carefully, trying my hardest not to trip or fall backwards.

When I reached the top of the steps and onto the landing, I stopped for a minute or two to take in the crowds below me. There were so many people in the club beneath me, there were groups of friends, a few Hen Parties and lots of couples. I stood and smiled, watching as everyone had a good time.

I felt my smile begin to fade as I thought about how long it had been since I'd actually had a good time and genuinely smiled. It felt like a lifetime ago. Of course I smiled but it was always a smile that never truly reached my eyes. It was more of a mask. I missed that feeling of waking up in the morning, and not having that moment of realisation that you were in fact, unhappy.

God, I hadn't realised how sad I am.

I was so fed up with being sad, I wanted to start looking forward, not back. I needed something to change in my life.

I opened the door to the ladies toilets and stumbled over to the sinks. I reached for the tap and cooled my face with cold water. There were a few women standing next to me touching up their lipstick and what sounded to me like moaning about their boyfriends. As I listened to them moan, I thought to myself how lucky they were that they had people to love and moan about. I couldn't listen to it anymore.

"Will you just stop," I said, slurring my words and instantly regretting it but I just carried on as I was already committed, "you are *so* lucky to have someone in your lives that you clearly care about, so shhhhh, please," I said as I pushed my index finger against my lips.

They stared at me for a minute with bemused expressions on their make-up covered faces. I was answered by their eye rolls while they muttered 'whatevers' and 'shut ups' under their breaths. They walked out teetering on their ridiculously high heels. I knew it was a lost cause, but I just had to say something.

After they left, I leant over the sink and stared into my eyes in the mirror. My eyes were looking tired and heavy from the alcohol and the dancing. They also looked sad. As I looked deeper into my eyes I realised I'd seen that look somewhere before. And then it hit me.

It was him. It was Matthew who shared the same look.

I'd seen that look in his eyes. I'd seen it in the pictures of him online. He was sad, too. He felt pain everyday and masked it, just as I did.

Is that why he was emotionally unavailable?

I fumbled as I tried to get my iPhone out of my clutch bag, I pulled up his number and I hovered my thumb over the call button.

Shit, what the hell was I going to say to him?

I looked at the time and saw that it was 00:38 a.m.

He's probably asleep now. I thought. *Fuck it.* Before I realised what I was doing, I called him. I stepped out of the toilets and onto the landing and to my surprise he answered after a couple of rings.

"Harper," His greeting was curt but his voice was gruff and sexy, which made me tingle everywhere.

"Hi *Matthew*," I had no idea what to say to him, "how dare -"

Matthew cut me off before I got the chance to embarrass myself, "Felicity is that you? I can barely hear you,"

"Yes, it's me," My voice suddenly became very high pitched and squeaky.

"Have you been drinking?" He replied, his voice was now softer and he sounded genuinely concerned.

"Yes I have Mr. Har . . . per," I hiccupped.

"What? The line is terrible, the music's too loud. What club are you in?"

"Nowhere, it's not any of your business where I am. You don't *own* me, I'm not your plaything," I looked up and saw that I was standing directly under a speaker. Just as I went to move, a group of women out on a Hen Night ushed past me and were let into the VIP lounge by a bouncer.

"I'm out and I might find a man to sleep with cos I won't be sleeping with *you*," I snarled.

"Felicity," He sounded very stern and serious.

"I'm out, I'm drunk. But, I can't stop thinking of you," I swayed and steadied myself using the banister at the top of the staircase, "I need to be happy, I deserve to be happy," I said.

I pulled the phone away from my ear and I heard Matthew saying my name again. I killed the call but I didn't feel any better.

You have just made a complete and utter fool of yourself Felicity.

A few moments later my phone vibrated in my hand, I looked down at it and saw it was Matthew. Oh why did I do that? It continued to buzz over and over again and I was about to turn it off when I noticed that he had sent me a text.

Stay there. Do not move a muscle.

Wait, what? Can he see me? My stomach dropped. I looked around to see if I could see him but I couldn't.

Ignoring his command, I made my way down the stairs. I was in need of another drink, and desperately. I looked around for either Heather or Ethan but couldn't see either of them. I headed to the bar and ordered myself a mojito.

After I was served, I took my drink and headed over to the dance floor. I let the music and the atmosphere take over my body. I danced on my own, throwing my cares and worries to one side and just let myself go. As I continued to dance, I felt someone's hands around my waist. They felt rough and hairy, I stilled in a moment of panic, but then the alcohol took the lead over my mind and body and I relaxed, sinking into the feeling of the man's hands touching me.

Suddenly, he spun me around so that I was facing him. He was in his late thirties, bald and had an eyebrow piercing. It hit me as to how drunk I was and how vulnerable I felt. I didn't want this, I didn't want to be touched, and definitely not by him. He placed his hands on the small of my back. I was straight away very aware how much my dress had ridden up, you could now see the beginnings of my scars. He moved his hand further down and cups and caresses my bottom and I panicked, freezing on the spot. I remained frozen and unable to move. I was like a rabbit caught in the headlights, rooted, accepting my fate. All the hairs on my neck stood up.

"Please stop" I mouthed but he didn't notice, instead he leant in closer to me, trying to kiss me. I leant back in an effort to avoid his dry, flaking lips from touching me.

"Come on darlin', kiss me, you know you want to," he leant in again, further this time so I could smell his alcohol infused breath.

"Please. Stop." I shouted above the music, "No. I don't want to," I pushed at him, trying to fight my way free. All of a sudden I felt the air shift in that familiar way.

He's here.

"Take your hands off her," Matthew appeared as if from nowhere, like my real life knight in shining armour. His teeth gritted in anger as his powerful glare pierced the man I was so desperately trying to get away from. The bald man looks at him.

"What are you, her boyfriend?" he smirked and I couldn't see Matthew's reaction but I could feel the anger radiating off him. He carried on regardless and pinched my behind.

Suddenly, out of the corner of my eye, I saw Matthew's fist in a tight ball come flying past me and watched as it struck the man's jaw, knocking him to the floor and freeing me from his grip.

I immediately turned and ran into Matthew's arms, nearly sending him flying onto the floor. His arms came round my body and they shielded me, I felt safe in his arms. I was overwhelmed with the security that I felt as I was pressed up against his rock hard body.

The bald man looked up from the floor, while he rubbed his face. "Man, she's not worth it anyway," He shouted while clambering to his feet. He glared at Matthew and then scurried away into the crowd.

I looked up at Matthew. "Thank you, you saved me," I said while looking into his amazing eyes.

He smiled down at me, his eyes warm. "You're most welcome," he said above the noise of the sound system. He then leant down to my ear, "and don't listen to him, you are *more* than worth it, *believe* me," The feeling of his breath on my ear as he said the words sent tingles *down there*.

I smiled shyly at him, knowing that he was fully aware of the effect he had on me. Being in such close proximity was dangerous, his scent surrounded me, *arousing me*.

"Come," he said to me as he held out his hand, "let's get you some water and talk,"

I placed my hand in his and he led me off the crowded dance floor, then up the stairs, past the toilets, past the VIP lounge and to a door with a keypad. I watched as he punched in the numbers and then opened the door.

Behind the door was a huge office. The sound from the club below instantly stopped as the door closed behind us. The floor was dark wood and the walls were painted black. There was a huge beautiful mahogany desk towards the back of the room. The space was very dark with only a desk lamp for light and a floor lamp in the corner of the room which was off.

This must be his office, I thought. *He must own the club.*

With my hand still in his, he led me over to his desk and he motioned me to sit in one of the leather chairs that were in front of his desk. As I sat down, he walked over to a mini fridge on the left of the room and pulled out a bottle of water. He poured it in a glass and handed it to me.

“Drink” he said in a way that I knew was a command that I *had* to obey.

“Yes sir,” I teased bravely. I took the glass and he walked round to his large desk chair and sat, “so, this is your club then?” I asked, feeling as though the room was swaying now I’d sat down.

“Yes, it is," He replied coolly, while staring intently at me.

I looked down at my glass, feeling like I was in the headmasters office getting told off. I looked up at him again, he was still staring at me. I felt like I needed to say something to him.

“I’m sorry I called you so late,” I muttered as I looked down again, unable to hold his gaze.

He sighed and got up out of the chair. He

rounded the desk to me, and crouched so that he was level with me. He placed his fingers under my chin and lifted my face up so that I was looking him in the eye, "forget the time, that's irrelevant," he stopped and gave me a serious look. "Are you ok though Felicity? Did that man hurt you?"

I shook my head, "I'm fine, just a bit drunk. And no he didn't hurt me," I frowned, I'd just realised that he came and rescued me moments after our call.

"How did you know I was in your club?"

He paused for a moment before grinning at me and pointing to a tv screen that was mounted to the wall, it was CCTV footage of the landing outside the toilets.

Oh.

"I just about made out the voice of Raul the security guard in the background when you called me. I looked up and saw you. After you hung up and ignored my calls, I watched you on camera as you walked down the stairs, ignoring what I just asked of you. You were only there, just behind that door. We were only a few feet away from me."

Matthew brought his hand up to my face and gently stroked my cheek with the backs of his knuckles. "As soon as that idiot came near you, I couldn't watch. I couldn't bear to watch him touch you when I couldn't. So I came down to stop it and my timing was impeccable." He said smiling like the cat that got the cream as he rose back to his feet.

I was left speechless. I felt my cheeks turning red, although I wasn't sure if that was from the alcohol or from the embarrassment of the whole evening.

"Well thank you for saving me."

"You're most welcome, Felicity." He smiled.

I sipped the water and sighed. "I'm still thinking about lunch and what you asked of me."

His eyebrows shot up in surprise, "Ok. Do you have any questions?"

"Loads! I don't even know where to start," I said as I waved a hand in the air.

Matthew regarded me for a second before he rose back up to his feet. "Which question do you think of first?"

"Erm, ok. Why me?"

He looked bemused, and then smiled at me as he shook his head. "Oh Felicity, I have been asking myself that for the last twenty four hours. I don't know what it is that you do to me but I am unable to get you out of my head. I can't focus on anything, I was unable to concentrate at work Friday afternoon. You do things to me Felicity, I *need* you. I have never needed anyone the way I need you."

Suddenly, I started feeling very woozy and faint. I didn't know if it was his words or not, but I tried to fight the drunk fuzzy feeling but it was too late, the alcohol had got to me. I closed my eyes and I felt myself pass out and into Matthew's arms.

* * *

"What's the ETA?"

"About even minutes,"

"Shit, that's too long. Her BP is going through the roof. We need to get to the hospital ASAP!"

I have my eyes shut tightly but somehow I can still hear voices. I can't be asleep if I can hear, can I? The panic in their voice is making me panic. I think I'm dying. Is this what it feels like to die? I don't want to die. Please God, don't let me leave him, I love him too much to leave him.

3

I FELT MYSELF STIR from a deep sleep, it was quiet but I was awakened by the light that streamed in from outside. I gently opened my eyes, blinking to clear the haze away. For a moment I felt serene. As my eyes opened fully, I realised that this wasn't my room.

Where am I? What happened? It suddenly hit me like a freight train.

Matthew.

The last thing I could remember was passing out in his arms. He must have brought me there and put me to bed.

Is this his bed? I thought as I looked around at my surroundings.

The room was crisp white from carpet to ceiling. Even the bedding was white. In front of me was a huge sliding door which covered the whole side of the room. The curtains were shut but not stopping the early morning September sun from flooding in.

I sat up in the King Sized bed and looked

down and realised that I was wearing red silk pyjamas, they looked expensive. Did he undress me? Where did he get them from? Does he just have women's pjs in stock in case he rescues a woman from a nightclub? The man was indeed a mystery to me, a mystery that my head was way too delicate to even try and fathom out.

I climbed out of bed and opened the curtains. The view from the room was phenomenal. There was a small balcony area and beyond that was what appeared to be Chelsea Harbour. I looked down and marvelled at all the yachts below. Some larger than others but all as equally stunning and majestic bobbing in the harbour.

As I gazed out onto the world below, I felt Matthew enter the room. I looked over my shoulder and saw that he was propped up against the door frame watching me. He was holding a glass of water in one hand and what looked like a packet of tablets in the other. I blushed, suddenly feeling embarrassed for what happened the night before.

He looked like he had just been working out. He was wearing black shorts that showed off his hairy muscular legs and a white T-shirt that had a perfectly formed 'V' shaped patch of sweat on it, why did that make him look even sexier? My thoughts turned to his sweaty chiselled body that I could see was under the T-shirt. I was so lost in thought, I was unaware that he had sauntered over to me.

"Good morning. How are you feeling?"

"Better than I should be feeling considering how much I drank," I muttered as I looked down while I pulled at the hem of my pyjama top.

Why did I feel so nervous around him? I could feel him watching me closely.

"Good. Now drink this and take these," he hands me the glass of water and a box of paracetamol.

"How did I get here? Where am I? Did you undress me?" I asked as I swallowed the tablets.

"Well after you passed out in my club, I didn't think it was a good idea for you to go home alone, so I brought you here, to my penthouse. I helped you undress but you told me to leave the room, although you were pretty much out of your dress by the time I left. Then I put you to bed in my guest room," he replied matter-of-factly answering all three of my questions.

Oh, at least I had some sense to tell him to leave while I undressed.

"Did anything happen, you know, sexually? I stuttered, as I felt the oh so familiar blush upon my cheeks.

"No, Felicity, it didn't. I would never touch you without you saying yes or without you being compos mentis," His eyes were hot and they were burning into me.

Thank God nothing happened! If I was going to sleep with him, I would at least like to have remembered it.

"Ok, thank you. I wouldn't have been alone though, I live with two flatmates you know," My eyes widened in panic, I hadn't heard from Heather and Ethan.

"They are both home and are fine," he said as if he had just read my mind. "I had my driver pick them up and escort them home," he waved it off as if it was nothing.

A Driver and penthouse?! Wow, maybe he is a billionaire.

"Thank you, I don't usually abandon them, they are like family to me,"

Shit, mum!

I suddenly panicked. I was supposed to be seeing mum for our spa day.

I rushed over to my iPhone which had been left on the bedside table to check the time. I read that it was 09:12am, I needed to go home and get ready! I started looking around the room to see if I could see my dress.

"What are you looking for?" he asked as he tilted his head to one side, looking amused. For a minute, I think he was enjoying watching me rush around.

"My clothes, I need to leave, I'm meeting my mum for a spa day," I said as I looked under the bed. I got up and placed my hands on my hips, "now where are they Harper?" I narrowed my eyes at him jokingly.

He threw his head back and chuckled at me, "Look over there in that plastic bag," he motioned over to a bag that was sitting on top of a chair in the corner of the room. I walked over to the bag and removed a pair of jeans and a top from it, clocking that my dress and heels were also in there.

"Where did you get these from?" I asked, looking at the new clothes, it was a Sunday and the shops were still closed.

"I have my ways," he grinned.

"Well, thank you, Matthew," I said, staring at him while I bit my bottom lip.

I could feel that familiar pull I had to him, the energy in the room had shifted once again and it was crackling. I'm not sure what possessed me to what I did next but I deliberately started unbuttoning my pyjama top. I felt powerful and elated as I watched his facial expression turn serious.

He was watching my fingers closely as I undid each button, one at a time, teasing him, driving him crazy. I stopped at the third button as the tops of my breasts were just starting to show. "Well if you don't mind, I'm going to get showered and head off."

I could hear his breathing quicken.

Ha! Now you know how I felt when you didn't kiss me! I thought as I toyed with the last button.

He didn't move, he just stood there, looking at me. Suddenly, he realised what he was doing and composed himself, clearing his throat.

"Sorry, I was just thinking about me undoing

the rest of those buttons. I'm picturing what is underneath and what I would do to your breasts with my teeth and tongue," He winked at me, turned and left the room. My plan well and truly backfired.

He left me standing in his guest room bereft and wanting him again, badly. What had just happened to me? How did a stranger make me feel things that hadn't for, well ever.

I MANAGED TO NAVIGATE my way to the bathroom through that labyrinth that was his penthouse. I stripped off the pyjamas and quickly clambered into the shower, desperate to wash the smell of alcohol off me. The water cascaded over my body, I held my face up to the shower head and tried to recall the previous night's events. I vaguely remembered him saying that he was unable to concentrate. And that I did things to him, and that he needed me. I replayed the words in my head over and over again. He needed me just as much as I needed him. But I couldn't have him - unless I said yes. Where did we go from here? Do we just go our separate ways? I couldn't just leave and forget about him, I felt like there was more to it than just this.

Say yes to him, my subconscious shouted at me.

But I couldn't say yes, or could I?

The water continued to wash over my body,

I was hoping it would wash away my wayward thoughts too but it didn't seem to work. The water was soothing though, I could have stayed under it forever. I looked around for some soap and found his body wash. Hmm, it smelt like him, it was that body wash mixed with his natural scent that created that intoxicating smell.

I squeezed some into my hand and rubbed it over my body, imagining it was Matthew who was rubbing his hands over my breasts, stomach, thighs and legs. My heartbeat quickened in my chest, I needed this feeling to be a reality.

I need to say yes. I'm going to say yes. I told myself.

I got out of the shower, suddenly feeling extremely hot and turned on. I grabbed two towels from the towel rail. I wrapped one around my body and used the other to put on my head to keep my hair from soaking the floor. I opened the bathroom door and scurried back to the bedroom.

I vigorously towel dried my hair but stopped when I caught sight of Matthew in the mirror. Again, he was leaning against the doorframe watching me intently. He had showered and was dressed in a casual shirt and jeans. Damn he was breath-taking.

"Can I help you?" I asked, feeling flirty while still looking at him in the mirror.

He smiled his show stopping smile and began

to walk over to me, keeping his eyes fixed on me in the reflection.

“Just admiring the view," he replied, his eyes warm and gleaming.

I smiled back at him. Even his words managed to get me in the same way as his touch did. This man was a formidable force that I was trying my hardest to resist. But I couldn’t, it was impossible. I wanted his touch. I *need*ed his touch. Even being there, being in his house with him was unbearable, he was like a drug to me and I couldn’t get enough.

“Also I came in here to let you know that breakfast is served," he said, his voice was velvety soft.

“Ok, I won’t be long," I said as he turned and left the room, leaving me watching him.

I held up the top admiring the cobalt blue colour and I put it on. The top and jeans fitted me perfectly. Luckily, I managed to find the emergency lip gloss and mascara that I had hidden in my clutch bag. I applied them and then ran my fingers through my unruly hair, as usual it refused to cooperate. My wavy hair had dried naturally and had fallen over my shoulders and down to my breasts. I took a deep breath, as I was now feeling slightly worse for wear and left in search of Matthew.

As I walked down the hall, I stopped and looked at the artwork on the walls. There were paintings and art of all shapes and sizes everywhere. *Heather would love these* I thought to myself. I continued to walk down the long hall and passed many doors. Matthew's penthouse definitely had a style, white walls, white carpet and lots of dark furniture. I eventually got to the end of the hall and directly opposite me a palatial room opened up. It appeared to be the main living area and the white theme had continued in here.

The room was huge, even the word huge didn't quite cover the giganticness of it. It must have been the size of my whole flat if not bigger. I stood in awe admiring the decor of the room and the glass wall on the left that led onto a balcony that overlooked the harbour. The view was simply stunning.

To my right there was a beautiful white leather settee, it looked as though it could comfortably have sat five people with ease. Either side of the settee were armchairs, one light grey and the other was slightly bigger and a darker grey. In the middle of the seating area sitting on a fluffy rug, there was an amazing glass coffee table with black legs.

Beyond the coffee table, tucked in the corner of the room, I spied a shiny grand piano.

Wow.

My fingers twitched with the urge to play. I loved the piano and I hadn't played for years. I played from the age of seven right up until I was fifteen, but then lost interest after I met Luke. I smiled warmly at the memories I had of me and my parents gathered around the piano. I must ask Matthew if I can have a go on his, I thought l as I continued to take in the soft furnishings around me, the room was simply breath-taking, almost as breath-taking as the man who owned it.

As I stood there gaping at the room, I was suddenly hit with the smell of freshly brewed coffee and toast. I turned slightly to my right and saw the open planned kitchen diner, and there he was, pouring the coffee into the mugs. I sauntered over to him. The kitchen was of course all white with dark worktops and had a large breakfast bar that sat four. I sat down on one of the stalls and watched as he stirred the coffee. He looked up and slid a mug over to me.

“Breakfast smells good," I said as I looked at the toast and the choices of jams and marmalades he laid out.

“To be honest with you, it's the only thing I can do, apart from cereal," he shrugged and offered me an apologetic smile. For a minute I thought I saw a hint of embarrassment flash across his face.

Matthew rounded the breakfast bar and took a seat next to me and started to butter a slice of toast. It was now or never, I needed to ask him some questions before I let him know what I had decided.

“So, I’ve been thinking about yesterday and

what you asked me," I began.

He paused for a moment then he put down the knife and he slowly turned his head to look at me. I undoubtedly had his undivided attention.

“Yes?” he said slowly.

“Before I agree, I need to ask a few questions."

He grinned and let out a slight laugh, “you attempted to ask me questions earlier this morning if you remember?”

“Yes, I do remember. And I remember what I asked too," I pouted.

"Good, and I recall answering your question,"

I sighed and shook my head in exasperation, “are you going to let me ask you questions or not?”

“Yes Miss. Walker, by all means please go ahead,” His look turned dark and heated and it made me shift in my seat. He knew exactly what he was doing and it spurred him on, so much so he continued to move closer towards me.

I gulped as he ran an index finger down my face and caressed my chin tilting my face up to his.

“Now, what was it you wanted to ask me, Felicity?”

I was unable to talk, totally at a loss for words. I was reeling from his touch and wondered why it made me feel so damn hot. His face moved forward so that it was just inches from mine, causing that stubborn lock of hair to fall onto his forehead. I had to use all the strength I had not to brush it back into place. He looked at my lips and then back to my eyes.

What was he thinking?

“Are you going to kiss me now?” I asked, my voice was barely a whisper.

“I can’t unless you say yes to my proposition,”

“Why?” I was breathless. I could feel the heaviness settling between my thighs.

“Because . . . I just do,” He placed his forehead so that it was resting against mine. He gazed into my eyes, as if trying to read my mind. He wanted me to say yes hell, he was *urging* me to say yes. And I wanted to say yes. I just needed to know what I’d be saying yes too.

“Hypothetically, if I were to say yes, what would actually happen?” I asked, looking at him cautiously in the eyes.

He removed his forehead from mine and sat up straight. “If you said yes today, then the seven days would start. We would be at each other's beck and call. For instance, if you wanted sex at the spa right there and then, I would come,” he smirked, “and so would you,"

I stifled a grin, “Does that rule apply for you too? Anytime or anywhere you fancy getting laid, do I have to come running?”

“Yes. But I promise it will be worth it,"

Oh I didn’t doubt that. I could see how amazing his frame and build was, so I could only imagine that he had the pecks to match. He was clearly very sexual, and very experienced. Would

I be able to keep up with his demands and that kind of physical activity? Lord knew it had been a while! There was only one way to find out if I could.

I took a deep breath in and released it, mentally preparing myself for what I was about to say next, "I have decided to agree to your proposition," I said nervously.

He smiled a million dollar smile at me. That alone was worth saying yes to. "I'm so glad you have agreed. You've made me very happy, Felicity. You have no idea,"

I smiled back at him, suddenly feeling overwhelmed with an emotion I couldn't quite put my finger on. This was the right decision, I knew I wouldn't get hurt this way, I knew my emotions wouldn't hinder me.

"Let's start the seven days from today. After your spa day, I will pick you up from your flat, and we can come back here,"

"Come straight here? Not out for dinner?"

"No, Felicity. I don't date women. You need to understand that it's seven days of you and I, and our bodies. It's seven days of me worshiping you and looking after your every need, *sexually*."

"Ok," I breathed as I took a sip of my coffee feeling his eyes still on me. He wanted a 'no strings attached' relationship and I needed a 'no strings attached' relationship.

"This will be good, this will be amazing in fact. You've got to trust me,"

Trust. The word was left hanging in the air between us. Did I trust him? I didn't even know the man. But, it was only for seven days. Seven days of someone *wanting* me, someone *appreciating* me. I hadn't felt that way in a long time. I deserved to enjoy it.

"Now come on, eat up, we don't want you to be late for your spa day," Matthew's voice brought me back to the room.

I nodded and I bit into my toast, as Matthew watched me intently as I chewed.

"What spa are you going to anyway?" he asked.

"Pure Spa," I replied while wiping away crumbs from the corner of my mouth.

A smirk crept across his handsome face. A smirk that told me something.

"You own that spa don't you?"

"I do happen to own that chain of spas, yes," he said, still smirking.

I rolled my eyes and took another bite of toast. Was there anything he *didn't* own in the city?

"Well, I'll be sure to give you a good review on TripAdvisor," I said dryly. "Oh, and I owe you money for these clothes you bought me," I said looking down at my top.

He frowned at me as if I had offended him somehow.

I continued on, "I can't accept them for nothing, I saw the label, I know they aren't your average brand,"

"Felicity, keep them. Trust me, I can afford it,"

he said, his voice was stern.

"But that's not the point! You bought me those beautiful roses which I know aren't cheap either. Please let me give you the money, you shouldn't have to buy them for me,"

"I bought them because I can, Felicity," he replied, his eyes lit up with a wicked glint.

"I'm not going to win this one am I?" I sighed.

"Nope," and with that he got up and took the remainder of the toast out of my hand using his teeth. I gaped at him with my mouth wide open and he winked at me.

"Come on, let's go, before I keep you here," he said, reaching for my hand.

I placed my hand in his and stood up.

Crap, I haven't brushed my teeth. I thought.

"Can I use your bathroom before we go?" I asked, smiling the sweetest smile I could muster.

"By all means as you asked so sweetly".

Letting go of his hand, I turned and headed down the hall in search of his bedroom. Surely he had an ensuite where he brushed his teeth. I opened a number of doors, finding a home office, games room and a gym.

Finally I stumbled across his bedroom. There was a large bed made perfectly like one you would find in a hotel with lots of pillow shams and cushions. The room was painted light grey with a white carpet. The whole side of the wall was made up of floor to ceiling windows with a glass door like the ones in the living area and guest bedroom. The decor in the room was contemporary and simply amazing. He either had a good eye or employed an interior designer.

The bathroom was as expected, large and excessive with a walk-in shower that you could throw a party in and a rather big oval bath. I walked over to the double basin and found his all-singing, all-dancing electric toothbrush. I felt the bristles with my finger, they were damp, he must have already used it. I was sure he wouldn't have minded if I used it too. I squirted the toothpaste onto the brush head and brushed my teeth quickly.

Why does this feel so naughty? My subconscious asked.

Once I had finished, I quickly sent Heather a text to tell her I was still alive and then headed back to the living area.

As I returned back to the living area, I found Matthew pacing the room while on his phone. His expression was stern and unreadable.

"Ok, when can we get that over to them?. . . Right, ok, and then that's everything they need?. . . Brilliant, keep me in the loop of the progress," He hung up the call and placed the phone in his jeans pocket.

"Working on a Sunday are we?" I said, making him jump.

"No rest for the wicked, Felicity. Ready?" He asked.

I nodded and followed him over to some

double doors that were on the other side of the living area. He pushed through them and on the other side was a foyer.

Wow, this foyer is bigger than the whole kitchen living area in my flat. I thought to myself as I was led over to what looked to be a lift.

Yet again the walls were filled with more artwork and in the middle of the foyer, there was a table with a magnificent bouquet of flowers on top in a vase. Matthew pressed the call button and we waited in silence for the lift. We may have both been silent but the atmosphere that surrounded us was electric. I peeked up at him and he caught me looking out of the corner of his eye. He flashed me a smile that made him look younger than his years, causing me to blush as always. The lift arrived all too quickly and the door opened.

“After you Miss. Walker,” he said to me as he stepped to one side, allowing me to enter first.

“That's very formal Mr. Harper," I said as I stepped in, “and I quite like it," I looked at him with the best sultry expression I could do.

“Oh do you know, *Miss. Walker*,” The way he said my last name sent tingles over my body. How did this man have the ability to turn me on with just the way he said my name? As the doors closed, he leant down and for a second I thought he was going to kiss me but he didn't. Instead, he tucked a strand of hair behind my ear.

Please kiss me, don’t do this to me again. I

pleaded in my head.

“You have such beautiful hair, Felicity. Such a distinctive colour,”

I took a breath in. I ached for his touch, his lips, his body and he knew it. Being in such close proximity made it exhilarating, my heart raced with excitement. That feeling was something that I'd never felt before. Not even with Luke. If that was what a high felt like, I could see why my birth mother enjoyed it so much.

He stared at me with fire and hunger in his eyes. “Jesus, I need you," he said after what felt like an eternity.

Before I knew it, he kissed me and as he did he pushed me up against the wall. His hands placed either side of my face. I lost myself in the kiss and I was surprised by how soft his lips were and the tenderness of the pressure.

I opened my mouth wider and invited his tongue to dip inside. Tasting me in gentle, long licks. His kiss was confident and skilled, and left me wanting more. As he deepened the kiss, I let a hum of approval escape out of my mouth. My tongue gently stroked his as we engaged in an erotic dance with our tongues. Oh how I'd missed being kissed.

“God, I want to fuck you right here and now," he said as the lift came to a stop and the doors opened. He released me, leaving me panting and breathless for more.

I looked up at him through my lashes, my lips

felt satisfyingly bruised. I bit down on my lower lip, relishing the taste of him that lingered on my mouth.

"There's plenty more where that came from, baby," he said as he pulled down my chin so I released my lip. He then rubbed the pad of his thumb over my lower lip. "Have you brushed your teeth?" he asked with a bemused look on his face.

"I used your toothbrush, I figured you wouldn't mind," I said with a shrug.

He chuckled as the lift dinged, informing us we had reached our floor. As the door opened, I caught sight of myself in the mirror in the lift before we stepped out. I looked flustered and my cheeks were yet again flushed. I glanced up at Matthew and he looked calm and unaffected. *Damn, he is always so perfect.* I thought.

I BREATHED IN THE fresh London air as Matthew opened the door of his black sports car, I think it was some sort of Mercedes-Benz. I'm not au fait with car makes but I recognised the badge. I climbed into the car and he closed the door behind me. I was instantly hit with the smell of leather mixed with what I could only imagine was the new car smell. The car was beautiful, and looked expensive - very expensive. Matthew got into the car and started the engine. The car came to life and the engine purred. He put the car into reverse and smoothly backed out of the space with ease.

“What car is this?” I asked him.

He glanced at me and smiled, “it's a Mercedes-AMG GT.”

I got the Mercedes part right!

“It's nice,"

“Yes, it is." he said as he fiddled with something on the dash.

“It looks like it's worth a lot of money,"

He grinned at me and the radio switched on, it then automatically connected to his phone. He pressed some of the buttons on the touch screen and the sound system sprung into life, playing a song from an artist I think recognised. The male singer crooned softly, his voice smooth yet distinctive.

“This song is lovely. What is it called and who sings it?” I asked.

“Frank Sinatra, *I’ve Got You Under My Skin*," He replied, keeping his eyes on the road ahead.

“How apt," I said, giggling to myself.

Matthew smiled, glancing at me, looking so young and carefree. He looked truly gorgeous. His smile sent that familiar tingle directly down to my groin, making me shift in the ridiculously comfortable seat. Honestly, what did he do to me? I was struggling to see how I was going to make it through the week at that rate.

“That's a lovely noise."

I looked at him confused, “what, me

laughing?”

“Yes," he replied.

I felt myself blushing, again. “You need to learn how to take a compliment too," Matthew told me as he shook his head, smiling.

He was right, I never really had many compliments from people unless they were from Heather, Ethan or my mum. I turned my attention back to the music and listened to the words Sinatra was singing.

“I guess you aren’t a fan of swing or jazz then?” he asked, his voice bringing me back to the car.

“I don't mind it, I like most music to be honest. I take it that you are?”

“Yes, big fan. My grandfather was actually a crooner back in the day, he used to sing in bars and clubs in the Fifties. So I grew up listening to the greats like Sammy Davis Jr, Dean Martin and of course Old Blue Eyes himself.” His face visibly lit up while he talked about his grandfather.

“Oh really? That's nice, I take it you were close to your grandfather then?” I turned to look at him, his expression was guarded and unreadable, much like him. After a moment he smiled warmly, still watching the road.

“Yes, I was very close to my grandfather, I still am. He’s eighty-nine now but still as sharp as a tack,”

I smiled at the thought of a younger Matthew singing along with his grandfather. Sitting on his knee while gathered around a stereo or maybe a piano singing happy, love filled songs.

"My parents like jazz, they actually met in a jazz bar in Soho. They made sure that I learnt one musical instrument growing up,"

"Oh yeah? What did you learn?"

"Piano, I loved it,"

"Piano eh? I suppose you saw my piano?" He said, looking at me out of the corner of his eye while he drove through the early morning streets.

"I did, yes," I smiled.

"That was my grandfather's piano, it's from 1976. He downsized a few years ago and didn't have the room for it anymore so I took it in. Feel free to play for me tonight," He says as he turns to look at me. I get the impression that it is more of a command than an ask.

"Ok, I would love to," I beamed, looking back at him, "do you play?"

"I've learnt on and off over the years, I can play bits and pieces but nothing to write home about,"

"Well, I can teach you," I suggested, smiling at him. He looked at me and smiled back and it was a shy type of smile, shy or maybe pity because he and I both knew it would only be a week and I was stupid for saying it. I immediately regretted it. We both turned and watched the road ahead of us, leaving Sinatra to sing about strangers in the night.

The journey back to my flat only took around

ten minutes. Matthew pulled the car up to the curb just outside the flat.

“Here we are," he said.

“Thank you," I undid my seatbelt and reached to open the door but before I could, Matthew climbed out, came round to my side and opened the passenger door for me.

“I’m looking forward to seeing you later, Felicity,” he said as I brushed my arm up against his as I clambered out of the car. I turned and faced him, he was gazing at me with hunger in his eyes.

“I’ll let you know when I am ready,"

“Ok, until then," Matthew cupped my face in his hands and placed a kiss on my lips. A soft, gentle kiss. He released me and I headed up the stairs.

Don’t be one of those girls and look back. I told myself, and before I could stop myself, I turned and gave him a small smile.

Damn, it would have been so cool if I didn’t.

The flat was silent, there was no sign of life anywhere. I walked into the kitchen and put the kettle on. It was only 10:30am so I had time for a cup of tea before I met my mum. As I waited for the kettle to boil, Heather’s bedroom door opened and she emerged. She stopped when she saw me, her face riddled with guilt.

"So, who have you got in there?" I asked her, looking over her shoulder and lifting an eyebrow.

"Shhh," She replied, gesturing to me to lower my voice as she closed the door behind her.

She tiptoed over to me. She was in only her underwear and I knew for a fact that it was not Isaac in her bed.

“Don’t look at me like that, I know I’ve messed up," she said as leant her elbows on the breakfast bar and placed her head in her hands.

“I’m not looking at you in any way," I replied, trying to make her feel better. Anyway, who was I to judge? I had just agreed to sleep with a man who I barely knew for a week. “You’re a big girl now and can make your own decisions, it doesn't matter what other people think,” Who was I trying to reassure, her or me?

“Thanks, I don’t know why I did it, I really like Isaac! I think I just got so drunk last night-” she paused and looked up. “Anyway, what happened to you last night? Where have you been?”

Shit, how was I going to answer this?

“With Matthew," I opted for the truth.

She regarded me coolly. “Please tell me you didn’t sleep with him?”

“No, no I didn’t. He was the perfect gentleman and he put me to bed in his guest room,"

As soon as the words left my mouth, I knew she was going to comment.

“A gentleman? Fliss, he asked you to sleep with him for a week. I don’t think that constitutes a perfect gentleman somehow," Now it was her turn to raise her eyebrow at me.

I felt my cheeks heat. She was right, of course she was right. But she didn't understand it. She didn't understand the connection we had or the pure desire I had to be consumed by him.

"Oh Fliss, please don't tell me you agreed to it?" Her eyes were full of disappointment and pity, which pissed me off.

"Yes, you know what I did. And it doesn't feel wrong or sordid. He was so attentive to me last night and this morning, he's not sleazy like I know you think he is. He's sweet and caring," I caught myself smiling while I spoke about him and how he was.

"So you think if you sleep with him, you'll change his mind and that he'll want to be with you?"

Is that what I wanted? Is that what I was subconsciously doing? No, no I wasn't. I didn't want a relationship. I wasn't ready for a relationship, I'd told myself that already.

"No, that's not why I'm doing it. Heather, I haven't been intimate with a man for eighteen months. And yes, I know that is by choice but I'm longing to be held, I'm aching to be touched. He kissed me this morning and it felt so good,"

She just stared at me with a blank expression. I couldn't even begin to explain how I was feeling, I didn't even know myself.

"I just want you to be careful, you've been through so much, I don't know if you would be able to handle anymore heartbreak,"

I rolled my eyes in response to her comment. “Heather, I’m not a china doll, I’m not going to break. I know I came close before, but I am stronger now, I’m ok, I made it through the other side.” I fought back the tears I felt brewing while I recalled what happened in the past. Heather had tears in her eyes too.

“I just don’t want you to get hurt, I love you so much. You are my sister, you know what right?”

I smiled and hugged her. “I know, I love you too. I’m doing this because I know it's only for a week. I won’t get hurt, its just about sex. I feel like I need it in order to try and move on or something, like a rite of passage,”

“If it's what you feel like you need to do, then fine. But please know that I don’t think it's a good idea, but who am I to tell you what to do, you are very headstrong, you always have been” Heather hugged me back and then her guest appeared at her bedroom door looking for her. He was the man from the previous night.

“I better go tell him to leave," She said looking embarrassed.

She briskly walked off leaving me alone in the kitchen. I made a cup of tea and sat on the barstool. I grabbed my phone from out of my clutch bag and unlocked it. I glanced at the date - Sunday 9th September. I paused when I realised that it was three years ago to the day that Luke proposed to me. I couldn’t believe I didn’t notice the date this morning when I was on my phone but then again, I was somewhat distracted with Matthew.

I smiled as I recalled that day. We had a walk in Regents Park after going to the Zoo. The sun was just starting to set and there was a chill in the air. Luke gave me his jacket as I was cold. We walked up to the Triton Fountain to drop money in it to make a wish like we always did, and as I threw a penny in, Luke got down on one knee and asked me to spend the rest of my life with him. I had never felt so happy. I was so grateful that we got to spend eleven years of my life with him. One of which was being engaged. I scrolled through the photos and videos on my phone, looking back at the memories we made together - the good ones anyway.

I sighed and placed my phone face down on the worktop. I shouldn't have done that, I now felt emotional. I missed him so much and I knew that wouldn't ever change. But, I needed to move on.

Come on Felicity Jayne, you can do this. I told myself.

* * *

"Ok, we've got her back, although her stats are dropping again,"

"We are approaching A&E now,"

"Thank God! I don't know how long she can hold on for like this, she's extremely tachycardic,"

I can feel my eyes closing once again, I can feel a wave of unconsciousness absorbing me, drowning me.

Suddenly, my eyes fly open and I am aware of the buzz of movement that's going on around me.

"This is Felicity Walker, she's been involved in a serious RTC. Had to be cut from the car. Suffered multiple lacerations and contusions to her body, head and her face. She's extremely tachycardic. Also, a possible head trauma as she was drifting in and out of consciousness at the scene and en route. When she's awake and coherent, she complains about numbness, particularly her left side,"

"Ok. Felicity, I'm Doctor Theobald. My team and I will be looking after you,"

She starts shining a bright light in my eyes. Why is she trying to blind me?

"Both pupils are responsive. Page Plastics and get me Doctor Watkins here now. We need an urgent CT scan,"

I ARRIVED AT THE spa and saw my mum waiting outside for me. My mum was truly beautiful, at fifty-seven and didn't look a day over thirty-five. She was so young looking, we had sometimes got mistaken for sisters or friends.

My mum's hair was silky brunette and was cut into a long bob. She had beautiful big brown eyes that sparkled whenever she was with my dad. Their love was amazing, it was what I wanted Luke and I to be, and we were until *her*. But I wanted that again. I wanted the intimacy and the security of being in a committed relationship again.

Then what the hell was I doing agreeing to this week of no strings attached?

I dismissed the thought as I knew that I was still way too fragile to get into anything serious right now. I still needed time and this was a great way to have fun without getting hurt - right?

I approached my mum and my heart swelled with the love I had for her. She held out her arms to me, exposing her manicured fingers and hugged me tightly.

“Oh, darling, I’ve missed you,” she held me at arms-length and ran her eyes over me, examining every inch of me, “you look tired, are you ok?” she asked, I could hear the concern in her voice.

“I’m fine mum, I went out with Heather and Ethan last night and it was a late one. I just need some R&R,” I told her, trying to explain the bags I had under my eyes. I had tried to cover them up but it was hopeless.

“Well it's a good job we are here then! Come on, let’s go gossip and relax," Mum linked my arm and dragged me inside and into the reception area.

As we were greeted and checked in, the receptionist informed us that we had a complimentary massage each courtesy of *'M'*. I felt a grin creep across my face knowing that Matthew had been thinking about me. The thought pleased me immensely. I caught mum out of the corner of my eye beaming with joy, she then turned to face me and I braced myself for the question I knew she was going to ask.

"Oh how lovely! Who is *'M'*?"

Think Felicity, think.

"Oh, just a friend from work, and it turns out she's a very good friend," I said, laughing awkwardly. I knew she wouldn't buy it, but I could only hope that was going to throw her off the scent for now. It seemed to work as she accepted the robe and slippers from the receptionist and trotted off.

We headed into the spa and I couldn't shake the feeling that Matthew was with me. I glanced up at the CCTV cameras and wondered if he was watching me like he did in his club.

No of course not, he has better things to do with his day, Felicity.

We entered the changing rooms and changed into our robes. The subject soon changed from which book my mum was currently reading for her book club to the topic which I most dread - men.

"So did you meet a nice young man while you

were out last night?"

Here we go.

I cringed inwardly and shook my head, "Mum, it's pretty much impossible to meet a 'nice young man' on a night out in a club these days," I shuddered as I recalled the bald man from the club, I swear I could still feel his hands on me.

"Oh, really? Maybe you need to go to a cocktail lounge or somewhere more up market?" She suggested as she popped her Kate Spade bag into her locker.

I could do nothing but smile and shake my head at her. Her naivety was endearing. My mum was a classy woman, she always wore designer clothes and somehow managed to match the colour of her bags perfectly with her shoes. She was never anything less than perfect.

My grandmother was the same, apparently they used to call her 'The Duchess', she would never have been seen dead without lipstick on. I'd always get a sinking feeling in my stomach when I thought about them both and how alike they were, it made me realise that I was not like that. That I was not actually related. They were my family of course, but not by blood.

"What?" my mum asked when she saw me shaking my head, grinning at her.

"Nothing, and anyway, I don't need a man in my life - I have you!" I told her, trying to make light of the situation.

She frowned and a sad look appeared on her

face. “I know you find the very idea of being with someone new after Luke impossible to fathom, darling. But, you will one day be ready, I promise. You deserve to be happy, Pumpkin," Mum grabbed hold of my hand and squeezed it, hard. “And besides, I want Grandchildren too,"

Babies!

The very idea of having children always terrified me. I was pregnant once, only very early when I was eighteen. Luke and I weren't ready to become parents, especially at that age. My mum never knew. The only people that knew were Luke and Heather. I’d never been sure if I wanted children anyway. I’d worry that my genes were tainted. My birth mother was a junkie and a drunk after all, and I never knew my birth father, I was never convinced that my mum knew him either. So I was hardly a candidate for genes of the year.

You are like her, you are going to sleep with a man you don’t even know.

I was halted in my tracks at the thought that was in my head. No, I was not like her. I refused to be like her. This was different, this is ‘apples and oranges’ different. I composed myself and carried on not wanting to draw any attention to myself.

My mum and I started our spa trip by swimming and occasionally mixing it up with a stint in the sauna and jacuzzi. As we sat in the jacuzzi, surrounded by bubbles and the glow of the underwater lights, I could see my mum eyeing me carefully like how a lioness would when she is stalking her prey, I could tell that she was poised to say something.

“Are you ok, Felicity? You don’t quite seem like yourself today?”

I sighed, she could always read me so well, it was so hard to hide anything from her. “It's the anniversary of our engagement today. I just keep thinking about him and how happy I was,"

I looked at my engagement ring that I now wore on my right hand, just a simple platinum gold band with a single diamond. Exactly what I wanted. I remembered the day I managed to bring myself to remove it from my finger on my left hand, and the realisation of what it meant. That he was dead. That no matter how long I kept that ring on that finger, it wouldn’t change anything.

My mum didn’t say anything, she didn't need to. She was there that night, she could see the pain I was in when they told me he died. She held me up as my legs literally gave way from underneath me from the grief. Instead of saying anymore, we sat in silence and let the bubbles around us try to melt my troubles and thoughts away.

After we had grabbed a bite to eat in the spa’s cafe, we headed to get our facials and complimentary massages done. As we walked through the corridors to get to the rooms, I looked up at the CCTV cameras again. I knew it was a silly thought, but he did say he couldn't stop thinking about me. The truth is, I couldn't stop thinking about him either.

As we got into the massage room, the masseuses came in and greeted us. Mum's masseuse was a young girl, I would have said she was younger than me, maybe twenty-three or twenty-four and mine was a young man, he was fairly attractive, although not as attractive as Matthew, but then again, who was? Mum looked at me and nudged me with her elbow. "He is nice, I wonder if he has a girlfriend?"

I rolled my eyes, "mum, no. I've already told you I don't want a boyfriend," She was just so incessant.

She looked at me and shrugged, "just pointing out he looks nice,"

Yeah, right.

THE DAY SOON CAME to an end and I said goodbye to mum and I started to head home. As I turned into my street the anxiety hit me. This is it, a week of sex, hot sex at that.

I can do this. I kept telling myself that but I needed to believe it. I entered the flat and started getting ready. What the hell was I going to wear? I know we were going to sleep together so I needed to wear something sexy underneath - or did I need to even bother wearing underwear?

You're overthinking it woman!

I was instantly hit with nerves and regret. I sat on the edge of my bed and took a deep breath. I was not widely experienced when it came to sex. Sex was not something that someone with my history - with my scars - rushed into. The more that I thought about it, the less sure I was that I was doing the right thing. I thought that maybe I should give it a chance and see how it goes. Or maybe I should explain to him that I didn't think I could do this. I was certain that he would understand, I'd seen the pain in his eyes from whatever it was that happened to him. It was only brief but it was there, I definitely caught a glimpse.

I decided that I needed to tell him. I couldn't do it, who was I trying to fool? I grabbed my iPhone and texted Matthew to tell him that I was running behind and that I'd grab a cab to his place. He replied almost instantly.

No. I will come and get you.

I wasn't surprised by his response. It seemed as though Matthew's way was the only way. This was going to make my change of mind even harder for him to take. I debated telling him over text but it wouldn't have been fair on him.

It's ok, I don't mind!

I pressed send and carried on getting ready, trying to decide what dress I could get away with wearing. My phone pinged alerting me to his reply.

No. I don't want you taking a taxi on your own. End of.

End of! Who did he think he was talking to?! I picked up my phone and typed a reply.

Honestly, I get cabs everywhere, it is London after all they are sort of common.

I knew he probably wouldn't like it as I'm sure he would have found it sarcastic, but I sent it anyway. I sat and waited for a minute but he didn't reply straight away. I changed into a red top and black jeans whilst checking my phone to see if I'd missed a text but I hadn't. There were only texts from Heather and a few social media notifications but nothing from Matthew. I felt my heart sink, how does he do this to me? I'd decided not to go through with his proposition and still he had me hanging on a string. Finally after about fifteen minutes of waiting he replied. I opened his text and it caused my sinking heart to leap right out of my chest.

I want to spend every minute that I can, with you this week.

His response really surprised me. It wasn't what I expected him to say at all. Just a few simple words and he had me rethinking my plan. As I stared at the screen he sent another text.

I'm outside.

I ran over to the window and peered through the blinds and there he was. He was leaning against his Mercedes with his arms folded. He looked around, taking in his surroundings. I smiled as I gazed down at him, and as I did, I caught myself licking my lips. He looked so yummy. I took a deep breath and grabbed my bag and my phone. I sent Heather a quick text to let her know where I'll be and headed downstairs.

After I composed myself, I opened the door of the building and stepped out. He slowly lifted his head from his phone and locked eyes with me. After a beat, he straightened up. He was dressed in a white T-shirt and jeans, simple but effective. He also donned a leather jacket that made him look unbelievably sexy. I stood there and took in the sight of him. It was just starting to turn to dusk and the dimmed light made him look even more dreamy than he already was. He smiled warmly and started to walk towards me. I felt butterflies in my stomach fly around as he approached me.

"Hello, Felicity. You look beautiful as always," he gave me his brightest smile as he ran his eyes over my dress and I of course blushed.

"Thank you,"

He leant in towards me and placed his lips on my cheek. The feeling of his lips on my skin caused the butterflies that were in my chest to flutter even more as they multiplied.

Matthew took me by the hand and walked me to his car. He gripped my hand tightly as he opened the passenger door for me, I smiled shyly at him as I got in. I looked around at all the buttons and at the dashboard, I was amazed how anyone knew what each of them did. Matthew walked round to the other side of the car and elegantly slid onto the seat. He pressed a button and the car came to life, the buttons illuminated and the music began to play. This time I knew who the artist was - Michael Bublé. He started to sing about how it's a new day and a new life. The lyrics made me think about how I had a new life. It was so different to how it used to be.

"How was the spa?" Matthew asked me as he eased out onto the main road.

I turned and looked at him, realising I was preoccupied, deep in thought. "Yes it was good thank you. And thank *'M'* for the complimentary massage please," I said, smiling sweetly.

"Oh you can thank *'M'* later," He winked and his eyes darkened.

His wink caused me to go weak at the knees and I mentally thanked God for the fact I was sitting down, if I wasn't, I would have fallen down! I still had no idea what I was going to do. I thought I did but just seeing him again he caused me to change my mind. In one moment I felt like I *couldn't* do it and that I couldn't *just* sleep with him. There was no way I would be able to detach myself from any physical emotions that came from having sex. But, I had already agreed to be his for the week. I'd made him a promise. Also, would I risk my career at LuxeLife if I said no? The thoughts kept going round and round in my head. But, at the end of the day I had made my bed and that I had to lay in it, so to speak.

"Are you ok?" Matthew asked.

"Yes, I'm fine. Just nervous I think," My voice was quiet.

He glanced back at me and frowned. He was quiet for a long minute as if he was deep in thought.

“Please don’t be nervous," he eventually murmured .

His words failed to reassure me as I looked out of the window. I really needed to make a choice before I got in too deep.

You’re already in too deep, you said yes! The familiar sound of my subconscious rings in my ears.

Matthew entered an underground car park and drove the car into a space. I took in a breath as Matthew walked round to my side of the car. He opened the door and took me by the hand again and helped me out. We walked silently, hand in hand through the car park and up the stairs that led to a lobby. I could feel my heart pounding in my chest, my hands were suddenly hot and clammy, he must have been aware of it too. We approached a lift and waited for it to arrive. Once we were in, Matthew typed a code into the control panel. The lift gently ascended up to the penthouse.

We were alone and that oh-so familiar crackle of energy instantly hit. I shifted on my feet suddenly feeling uncomfortable. The last time we were in that lift together we kissed, we more than kissed. And, if the lift hadn't stopped so quickly, we would have probably ripped each other's clothes off. I swallowed at the thought and tried to control my rapid breathing. I looked down at my hand that was still being held tightly by Matthew’s. I then looked up at him through my lashes and his head turned fractionally towards me, his eyes were as dark as coal. I bit my lip in an attempt to stifle a groan of anticipation that I could feel brewing.

"I feel it too," he murmured as if he'd read my mind. His voice was low and throaty and damn right sexy.

He continued to stare at me, eyes burning deep into me, into my soul. I smiled at him in reply to his words. I knew he could feel it, how could he not? It was a force so powerful, it made me lose my head. The lift doors opened and we exited the lift into his foyer. He opened the double doors that lead into the main living area. I'd been there before but it still felt like I was seeing it for the first time. Everything was so clean and white. And so big.

"Can I take your jacket?" Matthew asked.

Unbeknownst to me I was hugging it tight around my body. I released my grip and started shrugging myself out of it.

"Here, let me," he said, as he started to remove the jacket from my body. As he did, his hand skimmed over my bare shoulder causing goosebumps to form down my arms. Once my jacket was off, he draped it over the arm of the chair.

"Thank you," I replied. Why was I feeling so shy?

"Would you like a drink?" he said, his body inches away from mine.

I nodded back at him.

"I'm going to open a bottle of white, would you like to join me?"

"Yes, please," Suddenly, I felt suffocated from the close proximity of him.

As Matthew headed into the kitchen, I walked over to the large glass wall. It was almost dark and the city beneath us had become an array of twinkling lights, it was so mesmerising. This view wasn't something you saw everyday, well, not unless you were Matthew. The view must have been worth a fortune, hell the whole penthouse was worth a fortune! I couldn't help but fear I was in over my head. I wanted to run. Matthew was seriously rich, like over-the-top rich. What the hell was I doing there?

You know very well what you're doing here. My mind went into overdrive.

Oh yes, I want to be in the man's bed.

As I thought about being in between his sheets, I saw Matthew's reflection in the glass as he approached me.

"Here," He passed me a glass of wine, the wine glass was heavy and clearly expensive. I took a sip of it, and of course it was delicious.

"Are you ok? You are very quiet, more quiet than usual," He asked, eyeing me cautiously.

I nodded my head.

"Yep, very quiet indeed," he chuckled.

I gripped onto the glass and took another welcome sip, I could feel my heart rate slowly coming down.

"Are you hungry?" he asked.

"Yes, I am actually."

Hungry for you. I felt my cheeks redden from my carnal thoughts.

"And there's the blush I was hoping for," He put his wine glass down onto the coffee table, not taking his blue eyes off me. I could do nothing but stare back at him. He turned on his heels and walked over to the kitchen, he opened the fridge and peered in.

"Ok, well I have nothing in there," he shut the fridge, "takeaway it is,"

"That's fine with me," I smiled, how could he not have any food in when he asked me round?

"I was expecting a meal or two to be left in there for us," He said as if reading my thoughts. He stopped walking over to me and frowned, "looks like I'll be having a word with my housekeeper,"

Housekeeper?!

"What food would you like? Chinese, Curry, Italian?"

"Any of the above," I replied.

"Choose one, please. This is about you, remember?" he said as he flashed me a wicked grin.

My pulse quickened in response and my lips suddenly felt very dry. "Yes, I remember," I whispered.

How could I forget this week is for me to be

worshipped?

Matthew cocked his head to one size, regarding me closely. His gaze is always so intense.

“Felicity, you are very distracting. It drives me fucking crazy when you lick your lips like that,"

I hadn’t realised that my tongue was skimming over my dry lips. I immediately stopped and closed my mouth.

“You were doing it when we were out for lunch. It took all my strength not to jump across the table and fuck you,"

Oh my.

“Sorry," I said, my voice had suddenly become husky.

“Don’t apologise for being you. Ever” he said, his voice low, “luckily I have some self-control when it comes to you, although it is diminishing by the second standing here with you,"

I averted my gaze down at my glass, not able to look at him. I needed to talk to him about our arrangement.

“I need to talk to you about the proposition and why I am here," I began, still looking down at the glass.

Matthew leant forwards and tipped my chin up with his finger so I was looking up at him. He then removed the wine glass from my hand and placed it on the table with his.

“Shh, less talking," he whispered as he leant in closer and pressed his lips gently to mine. He then dipped his tongue deep into my mouth, I sank into the kiss, allowing his tongue to invade my mouth. Then, he cupped my face in his hands, keeping my head in place. I let out a groan into his mouth. All self-control and sanity had left me. I wanted him. I needed him right there and then.

Matthew broke away from me, leaving both of us breathless. He placed one hand on my cheek and the other on my back. My heart was racing like it had never raced before, this was it. I was really going to do this. I was by no means a virgin but this was definitely virgin territory.

“Kiss me again,"

Matthew’s heated eyes looked down at me and he stilled, his eyes moved over my face, reading me.

“Kiss me, please," I breathed. I watched as he parted his lips and inhaled sharply. He then leant down and his mouth was on mine once more. He moved his hand into my hair, holding me in place. The lust and adrenaline of being there surged through my body and I welcomed it. Matthew groaned low and deep in his throat which caused my stomach to tighten in response with desire.

“You have no idea how much I want you, Felicity Walker," he murmured in between kisses. His words caused my breath to hitch.

“I want you too," I whispered, my voice barely audible. The muscles inside the deepest, darkest part of me clenched in anticipation of what was going to happen next

"The things I'm going to do to you. . .," his words trailed off as he kissed my jaw.

He reached down to the hem of my top while he placed feather-like kisses across my jaw, chin and down my neck. Slowly, he lifted it over my head and let it fall to the floor. He stood back and gazed at me.

"You are so beautiful, Felicity," he said as he looked greedily over my body, his eyes drinking me in.

Being called beautiful wasn't something I'd experienced for a while. It made me feel good. Matthew then focused on my jeans, undoing the button and pulling down the zip of my fly. I hesitated for a second, feeling panicked. I knew he was about to see the scars that were there on my inner thigh, they were an everyday reminder of how close I came to ending my own life. He was going to see the real me, the me I hid from people, too ashamed of what I did to myself when I was at my lowest.

I was about to tell him to stop when suddenly he dropped to his knees, taking me by surprise. I watched him cautiously as he pulled my jeans down over my hips and legs. He stilled when he saw the scars, but he didn't flinch, nor did he look up. I couldn't quite make out the expression on his face, I didn't know if it was pity or perhaps something else, but my scars didn't appear to bother him as he carried on.

He steadied me at the waist as he helped me step out of my jeans. I was now standing in only my bra and knickers in the middle of his living area, feeling exposed and embarrassed. I wrapped my arms around myself as Matthew placed kisses above my hip bone and over my stomach.

He then forced my thighs open with his hand and kissed up and down the inside of both thighs and my scars. As he kissed the scars, I relaxed into it. He wasn't repulsed by them, he accepted them. I could feel the heat down there rising, I physically shook from the anticipation as he continued kissing my thighs, teasing me with his sweet torment.

With his teeth, he pulled on the waistband of my underwear and with one swift, careful motion, he removed them. I stepped out of them leaving them piled on top of my jeans. He got back up from his knees and stood tall, taking a step back.

"Oh, Felicity," he breathed, his voice low and sexy. "You have the most beautiful skin. I want to kiss every inch of it,"

I flushed and ran my eyes up and down the man who was standing before me. *God he is gorgeous*, I thought to myself. *Too gorgeous*. It was then that I realised he was still wearing his shirt. All of a sudden, feeling brave either from the adrenalin or from pure desire, I walked over to him and started to unbutton his shirt. Suddenly, he grabbed my hands, stopping me in my tracks. The look on his face was hard and stern. But very quickly, his expression softened and he finished what I started and let his shirt drop to the floor.

Wow, his body, his abs, just wow.

His body was a sight to behold, I could almost imagine the feeling of running my tongue over each chiselled muscle, I could picture my fingers pulling and playing with the dusting of hair that was splayed on his chest. I just about managed to avert my eyes away from his beautiful abdomen and chest to reach down and undo his fly.

Next, I unbuttoned him and pulled down his trousers. I could see that his erection was hard and constricted under his boxers. Licking my lips like I was about to devour a sweet treat, I slipped my finger inside the waistband of his Ralph Lauren boxers, teasing him. I watched as he grew thicker and harder underneath. His breathing hitched as I pulled down on his waistband and released him, freeing him.

Wow. My eyes widened in disbelief.

He really was the definition of man. He was long, thick, throbbing and ready. It had suddenly become very overwhelming.

Matthew looked at me and his mouth curved in a slow, sexy smile, "It will fit inside you, don't worry. But first, I want to work on getting you relaxed,"

Matthew eased me down so that I was laying

on the settee. He kissed my navel, then gently nipped his way down to my right hip bone, then across to my left hip bone.

I groaned as the pleasure coursed through me, teasing me. He looked up through his long lashes as I hummed my approval.

He made his way down to my pubic bone. "Do you like that, baby?" he purred against my skin.

"Yes," I breathed. I was lost for words, unable to speak.

He then leant forward, running his nose up the apex between my thighs. I was barely able to keep still from the feeling of his touch and mouth. As I wriggled, Matthew looked up at me and revealed a look I'd not seen before, a dark look. He removed his lips from my body and leant forward so that he was leaning over me. Grabbing both ankles, he quickly jerked my legs apart so that I was spread eagled beneath him.

"Keep still, baby," he said, his words almost a warning. Matthew's hand came round to my back and in one swift, fluid motion he unhooked my bra and discarded it on the floor. He stepped back and stared at my now completely naked body running his eyes greedily over every inch over it.

"Your breasts are amazing, Felicity," He reached down and cupped my heavy breast in his hand, "they are the perfect size,"

Matthew leant down and placed a kiss on my lips. As he deepened the kiss, I reached up and in an attempt to put my hands on his back, but he grabbed my wrists and pinned them down over my head so I was unable to move or hold him, I was totally at his mercy now.

"Can I trust you to keep your hands here or do I need to tie them up?" he murmured against my lips.

Tie me up?!

"Yes, you can trust me" I whispered. I was desperate for him now, I would have said yes to anything.

Matthew continued to kiss me and then he slowly made his way back down to my jaw, then my neck before trailing kisses down to my breasts. He gently took my nipple in his mouth, sucking and teasing it with his tongue, my nipples hardened instantly in response.

His hand moved to my other breast. He cupped and pulled at my nipple with his thumb and forefinger, while his tongue and teeth worked the other. His right hand then moved from my breast down to my vagina, slowly he began circling my opening.

"Ah," I groaned as he inserted his finger deep inside of me. Instinctively, I lifted a little to give him better access, and to force him further inside. He carried on his slow torture and just as I got used to the idea of having him inside me, he slid another finger in, sending me towards the edge.

He closed his eyes briefly, and his breathing

hitched. "You are so wet and ready," He breathed, looking up at me from my breasts. Unexpectedly, he withdrew his finger and then thrusted it back inside me with force, causing me to cry out in pleasure. He palmed my clitoris, causing me to cry out once more. As I was panting, he pushed inside me harder and deeper than I thought was possible. I let out a moan as he removed his fingers, leaving me breathless and hungry for more.

"Are you on the pill?" he asked me, taking me by surprise.

I shook my head. I hadn't needed to be on the pill since my sex life was non-existent.

Matthew didn't respond, instead he leant over me to pick his jeans up from the floor. He grabbed a foil packet out of the pocket and opened it with his teeth. I watched as he rolled the condom onto his considerable length.

Once it was on, he moved his hand to the small of my back, urging my hips up to him and with one easy move, he slid himself inside me, filling me. *Claiming me.*

I let out a moan, the feeling was sensational, excruciatingly good. I had forgotten what it felt like to have my body taken over by a man.

Matthew closed his eyes and groaned as he thrusted into me, hard. I cried out again as the heat rushed through my veins.

"Oh God, Felicity, you are so tight." His voice was a hoarse whisper.

He continued to move, thrusting in and out of me, both of us panting and groaning like wild animals. My hips found his rhythm, meeting his every thrust. He kissed my neck while he claimed my body. Matthew increased his pace, pounding into me, picking up speed. My heart pumped faster. He kissed my mouth again, and I felt his teeth pulling at my lower lip.

"Ah, God. Don't stop," I begged as I felt myself stiffening beneath him. I was going to explode with pleasure.

"Come for me, Felicity," he demanded through gritted teeth.

And his words are my undoing. I let out a cry as I let go around him, coming hard. My body was pulsing from the pleasure and when he followed, he exploded inside of me, emptying everything he had while calling out my name. I closed my eyes as I savoured the feeling. I was left bereft, trying hard to slow my erratic breathing.

Wow.

When I opened my eyes, I saw his beautiful face up close. His forehead was pressed against mine, his eyes closed. He was out of breath too. Matthew's eyes opened and he gazed at me. Leaning down, he gently pressed a kiss on my mouth then slowly pulled out of me, causing me to wince.

"Are you ok, did I hurt you?" Matthew asked as he shifted so that he was just about laying on the edge of the settee with me.

I shook my head, my mouth so dry I was unable to speak.

We laid there together for I don't know how long, both of us trying to catch our breath. As I did, my mind raced.

What did I just do?

I just had sex.

I just had good sex.

I had sex for the first time since Luke died. I'd only ever had sex with Luke and nobody else. And now, I'd slept with a man who only wanted me for my body for his pleasure. I thought I was strong enough to separate my feelings and just have sex - but I wasn't. I needed the emotional side of it too, the emotional attachment that every woman craved. I couldn't just sleep with him and walk away after a week, especially as he now owned the company I worked for.

What the hell was I thinking! Realising I had just made a huge mistake, I sat up and climbed over him, reaching for my clothes.

"Are you ok?" Matthew asked, sitting up as I put on my bra.

I looked over at him, his naked body was all I saw in my clouded haze. I shook my head rigorously. I needed to leave. I couldn't do it. I wasn't ready, I wasn't ready for intimacy with a man who is emotionally unavailable. I felt dirty. What was I thinking? Had I not been through enough already without doing that to myself?

"I need to leave, sorry, I can't do this,"

He rose to his feet, his perfect body shimmering from his sweat. “Did I hurt you?” I could hear the concern in his voice.

“No,” I sighed, “I just need to leave, I’m sorry,”

He stared at me for a beat and then walked over to where I was standing. I stepped back when he reached me. He brought his hand up to touch my face.

“Felicity,” he was almost pleading with me. He ran his fingers down my cheek again. That very motion sent tingles through my body. I felt like I was going to melt from his touch.

“I just - I’m sorry, this was a mistake. We shouldn't have done that. I can’t do this - I’m not ready,” I looked at him and moved my head away from his touch, his eyes wide and wary.

“Ok. I’ll take you home,” he started putting on his boxers.

“No, please, I need to be alone,” I pleaded.

And not with you.

His mouth was set in a grim line and then he let out a sigh.

“Ok, but this isn't over Felicity. I will get you to change your mind back. I always get my way,"

His words sent a chill down my spine. I stood, routed to the spot, unable to move my feet.

Leave, Felicity, damn it! I told myself.

I finally managed to get the courage to move and I turned and walked over to the double doors that led to the foyer. I could feel him following behind me. I got to the lift and pressed the call button, waiting for my escape. Matthew walked up to me in just his jeans. I was unable to move, I had nowhere to go, I felt like a trapped animal. He leant down and planted a kiss on my lips. I stopped breathing as he kissed me, I didn't react or kiss him back either, I couldn’t.

The lift doors opened, and I hurriedly got in. I really needed to get out of there. I turned to look at him, the anguish in his expression was palpable, his blue eyes burning into me.

“I’ll see you around, Miss. Walker," he said as a farewell.

“Mr. Harper,” I said, nodding my goodbye.

And after the doors closed. I sank to the floor, sobbing.

4

I FINALLY DECIDED TO finally decided to get out of bed after laying there wide awake for most of the night. It was Monday morning, and for the first time in a long while, I was dreading going to work.

I'll see you around, Miss. Walker.

Matthew's words echoed around in my head, filled with promise, taunting me. I really couldn't see him today. I don't think I could take it. There was no way that I would survive the embarrassment of seeing him again after what we did, and after I ran. I headed to the bathroom to get ready before the others. Heather got in late after some gallery event and I was asleep before she got home, so I hadn't had the chance to see or talk to her. I already knew what she would say, she would tell me 'I told you so'. Why didn't I listen to her? She made questionable life choices of her own, but when it came down to me, she was always right and she and I both knew it.

I jumped in the shower and as I washed

myself, I tried to block out the thoughts of the previous day's shower - at *his* house, and the intoxicating smell of his shower gel. I pictured his face the moment I left. The anguish and darkness in his eyes. I dismissed the thoughts and let the water fall over me.

As I walked into the kitchen, Ethan was sitting at the breakfast bar eating cornflakes. He looked up when he saw me.

“Hey, Fliss," he said with his mouth full.

I smiled at him and grabbed some orange juice out of the fridge and poured it onto a glass.

“I haven’t seen you since Saturday night, what happened?” he asked.

I sighed and turned to face him. How was I going to explain it to him? How I went home with a man who wanted me for just sex, for a week? And that I actually agreed to it. Oh and then I slept with him and changed my mind because apparently, I was either not ready to have sex with anyone that wasn’t Luke or that maybe I might actually have liked him and wanted more than a week.

“I ended up getting really drunk, went home with Matthew who now happens to be my boss and then decided to sleep with him last night." I said, as I threw back the orange juice as if it were a shot of something.

“Oh, ok...," he replied in disbelief as I slammed the glass down onto the worktop.

“And then I freaked out,"

"Ok," he repeated.

"It's such a long story, Eth, a really long story," I rubbed my forehead in exasperation.

Ethan got up and rounded the breakfast bar, enclosing me in his arms when he reached me. I let out another big sigh and hugged him back, tightly.

"I'm here for if and when you want to talk about it," He kissed the top of my head and released me.

"Thank you," I smiled. It then occurred to me that it was 07:30 and Ethan was up, eating breakfast, "what are you doing up at this hour anyway? Shouldn't you be asleep."

"I've got a doctor's appointment," he shrugged, not giving much away.

"Ok, well I'm going to run to work now. I'm praying that I don't run into Matthew," I rolled my eyes and grabbed a banana as I left. "Good luck at the doctors."

I JUST GOT TO MY DESK as Amber approached me. She was dressed very smartly in a black retro inspired bodycon dress. She stood over me, her eyes wide as I popped my bag into the bottom drawer of my desk.

"Have you read the email yet?" she asked.

"Good morning to you too," I said as I fired up my Mac.

"Oh, yeah, morning. Have you seen the email?" she said frantically.

"No. What email?" Suddenly, I was feeling concerned.

"Just read it,"

I logged in and opened up my emails. And there it was. An email from our new Chairman, Matthew Harper of MWH Group Holdings. I swallowed the lump in my throat as I started to read it.

All,

Hope you all had an enjoyable weekend.

As you may be aware, my company, MWH Group Holdings, finalised the takeover of LuxeLife Magazine Friday morning.

The objectives of this email are to introduce myself and to update you on how the integration of the two businesses is going to progress and to start by thanking you for your cooperation and patience. Integrating two companies is tough, and I recognise that some individuals have put in significant additional effort to help the two companies begin to operate as one.

We still have more to do however, I am determined to keep the disruption to a minimum. MWH Group owns a variety of different companies, so myself and my team are no stranger to the challenges it faces and we want to assure you all that we are working with the senior management team of LuxeLife to make sure it runs as smoothly as possible.

You'll be hearing more about this in the weeks to come and will be seeing me and my team in and around the office. I will personally greet all of you Monday, and talk to you all individually about your roles within the business, and how you think we can make any changes going forwards.

I hope this email is a demonstration of my commitment to the company and to you as individuals. We are putting together a detailed communication plan to ensure that all employees will be informed about our progress on a regular and timely basis.

I look forward to meeting you all.

Kind regards

Matthew Harper
Chairman, MWH Group Holdings.

Holy shit. He was coming here! I looked up at Amber and she was primed, awaiting my response, and all I could do was gape at the screen.

"See you were right, he is our new boss!" she said, waving her arms in the direction of my monitor.

"Yeah," I sighed.

"So, are you going to tell me what was happening with you and him in the kitchen Friday morning?"

Shit.

"Nothing, why?" I squeaked.

"Well, there was a helluva vibe going on between you two when I walked in. And the way he was staring at you, damn he wants you, girl! You must have noticed it, how could you not?"

I felt my cheeks begin to turn red. She was

right, the 'vibes' were sure as hell there. Even an outsider could see it.

"Ok, he sent me roses and we went out for lunch Saturday but that's it," I lied.

"Oh my God!" Her mouth hit the floor. "And. . .," she said, urging me to continue.

"And, that's it," I opted for another lie, "he never called me back,"

Amber narrowed her eyes at me, debating whether or not to believe me.

"Well, that blows, he was hot!"

"Yeah, well sometimes things don't work out the way you expect them to," I shrugged.

Which was true.

After discussing what antics Amber got up to at the weekend, and the news that she had a hot date that night, she trotted off back to her desk. I re-read Matthew's email and sat back in my chair with a sigh. I couldn't have a one-to-one meeting with him, there was no way that I could be alone in the same room with him. Not after yesterday. I filed the email away and started proofreading recently typed articles to try and take my mind off the situation.

I glanced up at the time and saw it was 10:03am. I looked over at the bank of offices where Ron and the other managers sat and could see that they were empty. I grabbed my mug from my desk and headed to the kitchen, glancing into the meeting rooms as I passed. And sure enough, Ron, Evelyn and the other senior managers were in there.

When I got back to my desk, I took my bag out of my bottom drawer and pulled out my iPhone. I sent Heather a quick text as I hadn't seen or really spoken to her since she had warned me to be careful.

Hey,

So I saw Matthew last night and freaked out after I slept with him.

As soon as I pressed send, she read it and replied.

Oh U didn't! Are U okay?

I felt my heart pounding in my chest as I typed my reply.

I'm ok, now.
You were right,
I can't just have a fling with him.
Because I think I like him.

There, I said the words. I. Like. Him. It liberated me to finally admit it to myself. It had been a while since I had felt like that, it felt nice.

I wondered if he maybe felt the same way about me, there was an undeniable chemistry between us. And I knew he could feel it too. My phone pinged with a response.

Aw hun, did you speak to him about it??

Yeah, that would have been the sensible thing to do, instead I bolted like a racehorse! He probably wondered what the hell he did wrong!

Oh, so now you feel guilty. My subconscious snarled at me. I dismissed the thought as I replied to Heather's text.

Nope. I got dressed and left him.

Seeing the words written down *did* make me feel bad. Maybe I should have explained. That would have been the more adult thing to do instead of running. But, I was thinking about my feelings. I didn't want to get sucked into something I knew was only going to last seven days. I would have gotten attached to him. It felt like I was already attached in some way with the raw sexual connection we had. All I could do was pray that he equally didn't want to talk to me, alone.

There was a buzz of activity behind me, and I looked round to see the managers and Ron emerge from the meeting room and start to head to reception.

He's here.

Panicking, I picked up my full mug of tea and brusquely headed to the kitchen again. I stood there for a while with my heartbeat echoing in my ears.

What are you doing? I thought to myself. This was pathetic, *I* was pathetic. Why was I hiding out in the kitchen for God's sake? If anything, he should have been the one who was ashamed of himself, not me.

I peered out of the door and scampered back to my desk, this was déjà vu. I looked over at Amber and she read my mind. She got up from her desk and headed over to me.

"What's happening? Is he here?" I asked.

"Yeah, he walked through the office and I swear to God he was looking for you,"

Looking for me!

For some reason I jumped for joy on the inside.

"He's gone into the smaller meeting room with Evelyn," she said, using her chin to point over to the room, "oh, and he's looking rather yummy in his suit today," she winked. I rolled my eyes at her as she walked back to her desk, chuckling.

I watched as one by one my colleagues went in to talk to him. Some of them were with him longer than others. I silently thanked God when it got to lunchtime and I still hadn't been called in.

Amber and I headed to the deli down the road. The weather was typically British and as soon as we stepped out the door, it started to rain. We both ran to the deli, using our jackets as a shelter from the rain, and when we finally got in, we went up to the counter and placed our orders. I opted for a grilled chicken and cheese panini with a strawberry and banana smoothie. Amber ordered a tuna sandwich and luckily, we managed to find a table in the crowded deli.

We talked about work while we ate, laughing at the recent celebrities who had thrown strops and of those Amber got the pleasure of writing about. The time passed all too quickly, and when we headed back to work.

Just as we entered the office, Matthew came out of the meeting room. He stopped dead when he saw me, causing me to do the same. Even from across the other side of the room, I could feel the sexual tension and the electricity. His blue eyes shrewd and assessing.

"Good luck, I think you're going to need it with that look, girl," Amber said as she meandered away to her desk.

I didn't move, instead I stood there staring back, holding my ground. He cracked first and broke eye contact with me as he looked away. He called Gabriel - who sat next to me, in with him. I let out a breath I was holding. Feeling triumphant, I headed to my desk. I got stuck into work, aware that everyone around me had gone in, apart from me.

Maybe he is avoiding me? I thought to myself as I finished fact checking an article.

It was nearly 4pm when Matthew finally emerged from the meeting room. I watched as he wandered over to the restrooms. Surely he hadn't left me until last. Or maybe he wasn't going to speak to me? I was hit with a sudden wave of disappointment. Gah! How did he manage to make me feel like that?! He needed to be seen talking to me, he was my new boss after all, he needed to be professional and not single me out.

"Miss. Walker?" His smooth, silky voice distracted me from my thoughts.

I froze for a moment and then turned in my chair, locking eyes with him once again. He moved his head in the direction of the meeting room, signalling for me to go in. I got up and smoothed down my tapered trousers, wiping my now sweaty palms on them.

As I walked over towards him, I could feel Amber's eyes on me. I entered the room and he closed the door behind me. We were now alone, and right on cue the atmosphere crackled and fizzed with the familiar energy.

"Hello, again," he purred, the vibration of his voice made me ache all over, "please, take a seat."

He pulled out the chair that was opposite where he had been sitting. I wobbled on my patent black stilettos as I walked over to the chair, my knees feeling weak from the very sight of him. He was dressed in a charcoal grey suit, white shirt and a red tie. As always, he looked devastatingly handsome. I took a seat and pressed my thighs together, trying to curb the ache I felt down there.

"So-" he began, unbuttoning his suit jacket as he sat.

"-I want this to be a purely professional relationship," I said, cutting him off before he could get a chance to say anything.

He looked dumbstruck for a beat and then frowned at me. "Oh, believe me I would love for this to be strictly professional too, Miss. Walker. But as I've said, I find it very hard to control myself when it comes to you,"

"Actually, *Mr. Harper*, you told me yesterday that you *do* have some self-control when it comes to me. So don't play that card with me," I pointed out, feeling overjoyed that I'd corrected him.

Matthew regarded me carefully, his right arm was resting on the smooth wooden surface of the table, his long elegant fingers tapping the surface. I could imagine the feeling of those same fingers inside me, pleasuring and stroking me again.

Matthew opened his mouth to say something and then closed it again. I think I managed to render him speechless. He continued to tap, obviously trying to work out how to answer me. I tried hard to ignore the tapping, instead I focused my attention on my breathing.

I glimpsed his wrist at the end of his cuff on his left arm. I could see his olive skin and his dark brown arm hair. He was just so manly.

“And now, after that comment, I have just lost all the self control I had,"

I swallowed and gripped the ends of my chair’s armrests, feeling the heat rising. His beautiful face was impassive as he spoke, not giving anything away. His mask was firmly in place.

“Look, I’m sorry but - "

Matthew's left hand came up to silence me. This time it was his turn to speak.

“Please Felicity, can you give it another chance?” he pleaded, taking me by complete surprise. “I *need* you, I need what we had last night, it was something I’d never felt before. Fuck! It was amazing!”

He continued to stare at me, his face pensive,“but, as I’m a businessman, I will be willing to make a deal with you if that's what it takes to be inside you again," his voice shifted and it became sterner.

A deal? My ears pricked up.

“What kind of deal?” I asked, scowling at him.

“I’ll extend the offer to two weeks, three, or even a month if I have too. I just need to fuck you, again, you are like my drug. You have taken over my body and my mind,"

I inhaled sharply at his words as I felt exactly the same. Well, if he's a businessman I could make him a counter offer.

"Date me," I said.

He recoiled as if I'd verbally abused him, furrowing his brow. The look on his face was one of disgust and confusion.

He then shook his head, "I can't. I've told you, I'm emotionally unavailable, Felicity,"

"Bullshit," I fired back, causing his eyebrows to shoot up.

We sat in silence for what felt like eternity, staring at each other across the table. He leant back in his seat, his hands clasped together and his elbows on the armrest. Finally, he opened his mouth to speak, breaking the unbearable silence that stretched between us. "Do you want a relationship, Felicity?"

I paused, not knowing how best to answer the question as I still didn't know myself. "In all honesty, I don't know. I don't know what this is," I waved my hand from me to him, "all I know is that I can't stop thinking about you, it's driving me crazy, you are constantly on my mind. And the sex last night, God, the sex was amazing. I *need* to find out what there is between us, it's too powerful not to."

Matthew nodded in agreement.

"I need you to know that I can't promise you a relationship, Felicity. It's not in my blood, it's not what I do. You can't get used to me. I don't do all of that romance shit. I won't buy you flowers or chocolates, I'm just not that way. I don't know how to be, I need you to understand that," he said, clearly exasperated.

My mind boggled at the information he gave me. "Ok," I replied. I looked down at the table, not wanting to look at him as I suddenly felt embarrassed and a little disappointed by his response. I knew he would say no but still, it was worth a shot.

After another painful silence, I glanced back up at him and he was staring, his eyes fixed on me. I could almost see the thoughts flying around in his head as he worked out some sort of calculation. Finally, he nodded as if he was replying to an unspoken question.

"But," he began, "I would be willing to make an exception. For *you*. If dating is the only way I get to fuck you again, and regularly, I would be willing to give it a go. But, like I said, don't expect too much. Maybe we can start by taking it one step at a time and go out for dinner, say once a week and try the 'dating thing' that couples do,"

I beamed at him, I was practically giddy with joy. I even did a little celebratory dance in my head. "Thank you," I said.

It's just dating, Felicity, not a relationship, don't get too carried away, girl. My subconscious reminds me.

"You should know that you are the only woman that has made me do this. The only woman who has made me *want* to do this" he got up from his seat and walked round the table until he was standing next to me.

I turned in my chair and looked up at him, my hazel eyes meeting his ultramarine blues. As he looked down at me, I remembered what I saw the first time we'd met - the tremendous power and steely control. But, now I was the one with the power and control. He bent down and placed a tender kiss against my lips which made me melt into the seat.

“I certainly saved the best employee until last," he murmured against my lips.

“Hmm, you did," I said, kissing him again. “I promise you that I will make your change of heart with it,"

“I'm sure you will, Miss. Walker. Can I see you tonight? We can talk more about this then,"

“Yes, you can," I breathed against his lips.

A smile touched his lips and it made him look impossibly more handsome. My God. Never had I been so ridiculously attracted to another human being.

“Now, if you'll excuse me, Mr. Harper," I said, getting up from the chair, “I have some work I have to attend to. If you want to talk to me about the recent merger or any other event, please feel free to discuss it with me over dinner tonight, say 8pm, The Olive Tree in Mayfair," I purposely brushed past him, feeling his erection as I do. I turned to look at him before I got to the door, and he was standing there, gawking at me. God, I felt so good.

I SAT BACK AT my desk and in an attempt to try to curb my excitement, I started working on the department's expenditure. I felt Matthew walking behind me and I tried to ignore him as he walked past. I was aware that his eyes were fixed on me as I could feel them piercing into me.

Once he had his back to me, I glanced around the office, and I could see my female colleagues watching him like vultures, whispering and nudging each other as he passed them. He really was a stop-what-you-were-doing-all together good looking man.

I peered over the top of my screen and watched as he walked through the doors and into the reception area. Feeling excited, I opened the website for the restaurant and reserved a table. I was just about to shut my computer down when my email pinged and I saw an email flash up in the corner.

Felicity,

As always, it was a pleasure to see you.

I will arrange for my driver to pick you up as I will unfortunately be in the office until late, so I will meet you there.

I very much look forward to discussing the recent events over dinner, and maybe dessert . . .

Kind regards

Matthew Harper
Chairman, MWH Group Holdings.

My face split in two from my grin. I quickly type my reply before heading home to get ready.

Dear Mr. Harper,

Thank you very much for your kind words.

I look forward to meeting your driver, and meeting you there.

I can't promise that I will have room for dessert . . .

Kind regards

Felicity Walker

Junior Writer/Editorial assistant
LuxeLife Magazine

I pressed send and shut down. I said my goodbyes to Amber who was chomping at the bit to find out what happened in the meeting room. I promised her that I will fill her in at lunchtime and wished her luck with her date. I smiled to myself as I exited the building, she wasn't the only one with a hot date.

AS I LEFT MY bedroom, Heather appeared, startling me. Her eyes gave me the once over and then she raised her eyebrow giving me a quizzical look.

"And where are you off to, looking like that?" she asked as she waved her hands at my dress.

I was in a scarlet red halter neck dress, it was just above the knee and had an A-line skirt. I paired it with nude heels and a matching clutch. Both of which I'd borrowed from Heather without her knowing.

"Erm, I have a date," I replied, trying to act aloof.

"Ok, so let me get this straight, since seeing you last, you've slept with a man, admitted to me and to yourself that you like him and now you are going on a date? Presumably it's a date with Matthew or is it with someone else?" she asked, scratching her head.

"Matthew, of course!" I said in defence.

"But I thought he didn't want a relationship?"

"He doesn't, but he agreed to date me."

She frowned at me. "Huh? How does that work? If you date someone for long enough then eventually it becomes a relationship?" she paused and then both of her eyebrows shot up, "that's totally what you are hoping for isn't it! Oh my God, that *is* what you are doing!"

My face turned crimson. Yes, I suppose subconsciously I was hoping that if we dated, he would realise we are good together. And he would start liking me for me and not for my body or looks.

“Felicity Jane Walker," Heather said, shaking her head, “you sly fox,"

“Well, it might not become a thing, it might turn out that we have nothing in common," I shrugged.

“You slept together for God’s sake!” she squeaked, “and you told me Saturday night that he was a force bigger than you, so you must have *some* chemistry! And that was even before you slept with him,”

If my face could have turned any more red, I would look like a tomato. We certainly had chemistry and a whole lot of sexual attraction to each other but things in common, I wasn’t so sure. He was clearly insanely bright and very successful and as for me? Well, I was just plain Felicity Jayne.

“Yeah, well we’ll just have to see what happens. I need to go, his driver is outside waiting,” I walked past her and started to head towards the door.

“Driver? He isn’t picking you up then?” she asked, confused.

I turned and offered her a shrug. “He’s had to work late,”

“Well, please be careful, sexually and with

your feelings!" she shouted as I closed the door behind me, trying not to roll my eyes at her too much.

I WAS GREETED BY Stanley, Matthew's driver. Stanley was tall and had a large build. He had pale skin and greying hair. He greeted me with a nod and opened the rear passenger door for me to get in. It wasn't the usual Mercedes that Matthew picked me up in, instead it was a 4x4 car. I climbed up into the car and clocked the badge on the steering wheel, it had four rings, I think it was an Audi. The drive to the restaurant took just over half an hour which wasn't bad for London traffic. We arrived just after 8pm. Stanley got out of the car and came round to open the door for me.

"Here we are, Miss. Walker,"

"Thank you," I said, smiling warmly at him.

"Mr. Harper is inside,"

I thanked him again and walked unsteadily on Heather's heels, highly aware that I was exceptionally clumsy. I opened the door and spotted Matthew straight away. He was standing at the bar, drinking a glass of red wine. He was dressed in a different suit from what he was wearing earlier, this one was dark navy and he was wearing a pale blue shirt underneath and sporting with it, a silver-grey tie. I sighed at the sight of him.

Of course he looked gorgeous, when did he look anything but?

I stood for a moment before walking over to him, admiring the view, drinking him in. He began to lift the glass up to his lips but stopped halfway. He glanced over his shoulder, and stilled when he saw me. Blinking a couple of times, he then shot me a billion dollar smile that quite frankly rendered me speechless. After a beat, I managed to compose myself and I started walking towards him. He placed his wine glass on top of the bar and walked gracefully over to me, meeting me halfway.

“You look stunning, Felicity," he said as he leant down to kiss my cheek.

Taking my arm, he led me to a table where the waiter stood with menus. He pulled out a chair for me to sit and then took a seat opposite.

The waiter handed us the menus and asked us for our drink orders. Matthew ordered a bottle of Don Melchor and the waiter vacated.

“Are you nervous?” he asked, his voice calm and soft.

It was not until he asked that I realised I am.

Why was I so nervous?

“Yes, I am,"

He leant forward.

“Me too," he whispered.

My eyebrows shot up in surprise, he didn't strike me as the nervous type. He smiled an adorable shy smile at me. The waiter arrived with a bottle of wine, a small dish of mixed nuts, and another of olives. The waiter removed the cork from the bottle and poured a little wine into Matthew's glass. He reached out and took a sip.

"That's fine, thank you," he said, not looking anywhere else but at me.

The waiter then proceeded to fill both of our glasses, "can I take your order sir?" he asked as he set the bottle down on the table.

"Please can you give us a couple more minutes to look? Matthew asked.

"Very well," the waiter nodded and made a bisque exit.

"So," I said, picking up the menu, "is there an agenda for this meal or is it a date-date?"

Matthew's eyes lit up with amusement. "Well, I can't say I have been on many dates, in fact, I haven't been on any, so I'll let you take the lead with this one, Miss. Walker,"

"You haven't been on any dates? Like none at all?" I said, my eyes wide with shock.

He shakes his head, "nope,"

Wow

"Ok, well I'm a bit rusty myself so we will just see how it goes. But, I do remember that we have to ask questions, so that we can get to know each other,"

He regarded me coolly, not giving anything away with his look. He finally opened his mouth to speak, "Questions huh?" He paused, "Well I just hope the answers don't make you want to runaway from me again,"

I was mid-gulp when he spoke and it caused me to choke on my wine. His words were completely unexpected and took me by surprise.

"Are you ok?" he asked, his concern genuine.

"Yes, fine," I dabbed my chin with the crisp white napkin. "I'm sorry that I left,"

"Which time?" he smirked.

I fought the urge to roll my eyes, "the second time. I think the first time was justified, don't you?" I replied, mirroring his smirk.

Matthew opened his mouth to speak but then the waiter returned over to us. I ordered the steak au poivre, choosing to ignore the price and Matthew ordered the grilled skate wing.

"So, what sort of questions does one ask you on a date?" Matthew asked, seriously.

I took another sip of wine, this time not choking on it.

"Erm, questions like, 'where did you grow up?', 'what are your aspirations in life?', 'what do you like to do in your spare time?'" I put the glass down on the table and continued, "I would suggest, 'what do you do for work?', but I think we have that one covered already," I said, offering him a warm smile.

"Yes, I think we do. I've heard a lot of good things about you," he paused and looked at me tentatively while fiddling with the stem of his wine glass, " I have a confession to make,"

Oh shit, what? My heart dropped into my

stomach.

"I knew of you before I finalised the deal,"

"What do you mean?" I asked.

"Well, before I buy a company, I like to do a little bit of research and your name popped up. I searched for you on LinkedIn and the social media platforms and knew then that I wanted you,"

"You wanted me? What, like a possession?"

He stopped, eyeing me cautiously, contemplating how to answer my question. "Well, I knew that I wanted to meet you, and ask you my proposition,"

I frowned. Reality hit me again like a ton of bricks. Reminding me that he only wanted me for my body. He only wanted me for sex. Was I wasting my time? Did I think I could honestly change his way of thinking?

"But," he continued as if he was reading my thoughts, "that's changed since I've met you. Yes, I want to sleep with you, again. But like I said earlier, you are the only woman that I have agreed to date. There's something different about you and I can't deny the chemistry we have,"

I smiled a shy, bashful smile at him, suddenly feeling like a schoolgirl who had been noticed by the good looking popular boy.

"I'm glad you feel it too. It's like something I've never experienced before," I said to him, suddenly I frowned, I never once felt like that with Luke. Sure we had chemistry, but not in the same way.

The waiter appeared at my side with our food. He placed it down in front of us and scurried away. We tucked into our meals, both sitting in silence for a while as we chewed. I could feel the unspoken question bubbling up inside of me, fighting to come out.

"How many women have you, ah, propositioned?" I asked, not knowing how best to word it.

He put down his knife and fork and picked up his glass, he eyed me over the rim before taking a sip. He then placed the glass back down on the table.

"Do you really want to know how many women I've been intimate with, Felicity? I'm no expert, but I'm pretty sure that's not a question you should ask on a date?"

He was right, did I really want to know? Judging by his raw sexual magnetism and his expert fingers, I probably didn't. I shook my head and carried on cutting my steak. We sat in silence for a while, although it was a comfortable silence.

"What other questions do we ask each other on a date?" Matthew asked, catching me off guard as I put a piece of steak in my mouth. I chewed quickly so that I could answer him.

"Let me think," I paused and wracked my brain for inspiration, "Oh - what about, 'what is your favourite film?'" I said, excitedly.

He paused mid chew. He was really thinking about his answer.

"I would have to say my favourites are probably the James Bond's films," he said, nodding, clearly certain of his answer.

I let out a small giggle from his reply, "that's not fair, you have to pick one, not the millions they have made," I said, still giggling.

"Are you laughing at me Miss. Walker?"

"Maybe,"

"I thought as much. I'll have you know, they haven't made millions, they've made twenty-five to be exact," He said as he flashed me a know-it-all smile. "What's your favourite film then?" he asked as he topped up both our glasses with wine.

"*Pride and Prejudice*," I said without hesitation, "it also happens to be my favourite book too, I must have read it like two hundred times," I clasped my hands together, recalling the epic love story of Mr. Darcy and Elizabeth Bennet.

I looked back at Matthew and he was looking at me, his expression impassive, I couldn't make out what he was thinking. He then looked down at his plate and pushed some mashed potato onto his fork.

What did I do or say that was so wrong? I thought.

We sat in silence, once again this time it felt more uncomfortable. I needed to say something,

I needed it to go back to how it was before I opened my mouth about my favourite film. That's why he became quiet. It had to be. Maybe he really didn't do romance.

"I like Jaws too, that's not romantic," I said, looking at him through my lashes.

A slight smile appeared to brush his lips, and I think I saw a hint of relief flit across his perfect face. "No, its not," he put his knife and fork down on his empty plate, "now hurry up and finish your dinner, I want to take you home and fuck you into oblivion," he said, calmly but deadly serious.

I gulped, his words were like an aphrodisiac to me. "You're very presumptuous Mr. Harper. Not everyone has sex after a date you know,"

"I just cut to the chase, no point denying the inevitable, you want it, I want it," his eyes were alive with a dark kind of glee.

"Am I that much of a sure thing?" I asked. He was right, I was dying to sleep with him again. To feel his body inside of mine.

"You know I don't need to answer that, Felicity,"

"Yes, that's true." I muttered quietly, feeling somewhat embarrassed about my pure desire for the man sitting in front of me. "But, we haven't discussed our situation," I pointed out.

"No, I suppose we haven't,"

I took a deep breath. "So, we go out for dinner occasionally and have sex, and that's it?" I asked, not knowing if I wanted to know the answer. “And how long do we do that before we call it a day?” I added, feeling as though I needed to prepare myself for the beginning of the end.

Matthew leant back, his eyes dark and hooded.

“Yes, we have sex and occasionally go out for dinner, bowling or whatever people do when they date,"

“Ok, but what’s the time frame? When do we stop?”

“I don’t know,” he said honestly.

“Is it whenever you get bored of me and move onto the next conquest? One who might only give you a week, no strings attached?”

He grinned at me and shook his head. “Felicity, I don’t think I will ever get bored of you. You go from shy and timid and then to ballsy in under ten seconds, it's quite entertaining, it will keep me on my toes, that's for sure,”

Gah! The man was so frustrating, he never gave me a straight answer. I was still none the wiser about what was happening.

“Look,” he said, leaning forwards and grasping my hands in his, “I couldn’t possibly put a time frame on this with you. All I know is that with you, it is different,"

My face turned warm, and I could picture the red appearing on my cheeks.

He smiled warmly at me and continued, “so, let's just enjoy the moment and each other. Lets enjoy the connection and chemistry that we have because, for once I don't want to put a deadline on it, I know I did before, but once I felt what it was like to be inside you and to touch you, I couldn't care less about the fucking time frame,"

I looked nervously around at the other diners that were near us, hoping they couldn't hear our conversation. No one had reacted or were looking over, so I think we were safe.

"Ok," I agreed, "I'm happy to take this as it comes,"

What did I have to lose? I'd already slept with him, I was already in too deep at this point, I might as well drown.

Matthew nodded and then reached up and cupped my face in his hand. I leant into it as he used his thumb to caress my cheek. God, this man was something else.

"Turns out I do have room for dessert after all," I said, my voice low.

Matthew groaned and waved over to the waiter.

WE ENTERED THE LIVING area and Matthew took my jacket and clutch bag from me. I drank in the huge expanse of the room again and glanced over to the settee on which we had slept together for the first time.

My gaze then headed over to the grand piano in the corner of the room. I walked over to it and ran my fingers over the ivory keys. I pushed down middle C with my thumb. My fingers itching to play. The piano was so beautiful, so sleek and timeless.

"You can play something if you want to," Matthew said from over in the kitchen area. I turned to look at him and he was pouring what I assumed was whisky from a decanter into a tumbler. I grinned and turned my gaze back to the keys.

Taking a seat on the cushioned stool, I positioned my hands. I hadn't played for a few years and I felt strangely nervous as I had an audience. I closed my eyes and began to play Franz Schubert's *Ave Maria*. With each note I played, I fell deeper in love with the piano again. My nervousness floated away with the gentle sound. I felt Matthew walking over to me, he stood by the piano, not moving a muscle as he watched me. Once I had finished playing the piece, I let out a contented sigh. Relieved that I remembered the song after all those years of not playing.

"That was beautiful," Matthew said, "you said you were good but I underestimated that you'd be that good,"

I got up from the stool and sauntered over to where Matthew was standing. I leant up onto my tiptoes and kissed his cheek. Catching him completely off guard. Matthew closed his eyes as if to savour the feel of my lips on his skin.

"I am good, I'm a grade 7 I'll have you know," I gazed up at him, drinking in his beautiful features.

He kissed me on the top of my head and then let go of me to pass me a glass of water.

"Drink," he commanded.

I eyed him, and took the glass sceptically.

"We know what happens when you drink too much wine," he winked.

I smirked sarcastically at him, his face instantly turning serious.

Shit.

"Smirking and laughing at me. I'm going to have to do something about that,"

I gulped, "and what would that entail exactly?"

Matthew edged closer to me so that we were almost touching, "well, I might put you over my knee or over the table and spank you senseless,"

The heat rose instantly causing my breathing to hitch up a notch.

He was into spanking?

The air around us was fizzing, it felt so intense. This feeling was something I wasn't used to, I'd never felt this pull to another human before. It was like he was my drug, he was my high and I had to have it no matter what it cost me. Matthew leant in closer to me, so close the end of his nose touched mine.

"God, you are so beautiful, Felicity," he murmured.

"You're not too bad yourself," I replied, barely

able to speak.

"It's just a face, baby," He smiled a shy, sweet smile at me. He then closed his eyes briefly, inhaling as he did. When he opened them, they were full of pain. The pain that I had seen in his eyes before.

My heart constricted in my chest at the sight of his eyes. I slowly lifted my hand up and went to place it on the side of his face. As I did, he visibly flinched and stilled. And in that moment, I saw the anguish in his face. His mask was ever so slightly slipping away. I eyed him wearily and he pulled away from me, grabbing my wrist.

"How do you feel about being restrained in bed?" he asked.

Wow, someone's into BDSM.

"Erm, I don't know. I've never done that sort of thing before," I replied honestly. Luke and I didn't do anything like that. We were never adventurous when it came to sex.

Maybe that's why he slept with another woman? I mentally kicked my subconscious. I had spent so long blaming myself for him cheating on me.

Matthew frowned at me.

"You've never tried any form of bondage or restraints when you've had sex before?"

I shook my head and Matthew paused before nodding.

"Ok, well would you like to try it?" he asked.

I squirmed uncomfortably. I remembered he had threatened me with that when we had sex the first time.

Matthew tilted my chin up so that I was looking at him. There was nowhere to hide now.

“It's for your pleasure, I promise. Everything that we’ll do will be,” he must have seen the worry in my eyes as he tried to reassure me.

I nodded at him, I couldn’t use my mouth to speak, it was too dry from the nerves or maybe the anticipation. Matthew smiled down at me, causing a rush of pleasure down to my groin.

“Come, let's go,” He held his hand out to me and I put my hand in his. His eyes were bright and intense.

I walked on shaky legs as he led me through the living area and down the hall, we walked past his bedroom, which surprised me, and straight to the spare bedroom where I had slept Saturday night. The bedroom was bigger than what I remembered it to be and the view out onto a lit up London was simply amazing.

“Why are we in here and not your bedroom?” I asked as he closed the curtains on the view.

“Because I prefer it that way,” he said matter-of-factly, “please don’t dwell on the finer details, just be in the moment. The moment being that I am going to worship you until you lose your mind,"

Oh my.

I was standing just by the door when he walked slowly towards me, confidence was prominent in every step he took, his eyes blazing.

My heart began to pound. Why was I so nervous all of a sudden? I'd already slept with him. Desire pooled in my belly as I recalled the feel of him inside me. He stood in front of me, staring down into my eyes, pinning me to the spot.

"You will enjoy it, I promise," he said as he ran his fingers round the nape of my neck, he then leant down and gently kissed me. I kissed him back, pushing my body flush against his. He let out a low groan in his throat. I parted my mouth slightly, allowing his tongue to dip in and explore my mouth. Matthew then hoisted me up into his arms, taking me by surprise. He walked me over to the bed and gently lowered me down so that I was on my back on the bed. He bent down and kissed me once more.

"I'm going to fuck you whilst you are in this beautiful red dress," Matthew hummed against lips.

I could feel his hand travel down from my face, down my side and down to my thighs. He then lifted the skirt of my dress up so it was bunched round my waist and using his index finger, he hooked my thong and moved it to one side, allowing easier access as his finger on his other hand slipped leisurely inside me.

I parted my mouth in pleasure as his finger slipped in and out of me. I was slick from desire and I let out a small whimper.

"You're wet and ready," Matthew said as he continued his slow rhythm with his finger.

Abruptly he withdrew his finger and sat up. He then removed his tie from around his neck.

"I'm going to tie you up with this," he said, indicating his tie, "are you still sure?"

I nodded.

"Good, I want you to think of a control word,"

"Control word?" I asked, already feeling breathless from wantonness.

"Yes, a word that you can remember and shout out if it becomes too overwhelming. I will stop what I'm doing immediately and cease all physical contact with you. Though, I hope you never have to use it, that isn't my aim,"

I blinked my eyes at him, "erm, I don't know,"

"I can be anything, anything memorable,"

"Ok, what about, 'rainbow'?" for some reason that was the first thing that came to mind.

Matthew stifled a grin, clearly amused by my choice.

"Very well, Miss. Walker, if that's what you so wish it to be," He bought the tie up so I could see it, "hold out your wrists, keeping them together," he commanded.

I did what I was told and he wrapped the tie tightly around my wrists so that I was unable to part them.

Why is this so hot? I thought to myself.

After he was done, he bent down and planted a chaste kiss on my lips.

"You look remarkable, baby," he smiled, his eyes burning with need. Matthew then took my wrists in one of his hands and placed them so that my arms were over my head.

"Keep them here, ok?"

It was then that I realised he had done that to me so I couldn't touch him. I remembered how he froze and grabbed my wrist when I went to unbutton his shirt. What happened to him for him to be like that?

"Felicity, do you understand?"

I was halted from my thoughts by his soft, velvet voice.

"Yes, I understand,"

"Good,"

Matthew then removed his shirt and trousers and tossed them to one side. I could see his erection under his boxers. It was large and the anticipation I felt heightened. Looking down at me and he caught me looking at him and he smiled a salacious grin. Then, not taking his eyes off me, he pulled his boxers down so that he sprung free. I took a sharp breath in, and my lips parted. I wanted him. In one swift motion, Matthew leant over and took the foil packet out of the drawer of the bedside table.

He keeps condoms in here?

I tried to ignore the disheartening thought and focused on the man that was before me. He expertly rolled it on and gazed down at me.

"I hope you are ready," he breathed. And before I knew it, he was filling me, holding my bound wrists tightly over my head, whilst thrusting into me deeply. A groan escaped my mouth. God, it in fact felt so good.

Matthew twisted his hips from side to side, the feeling was magnificent, it was simply mind-blowing. I wrapped my legs around his waist, in order to hold him the only way I could. As soon as my legs were around him, he really started to move, he pounded into me like it would have killed him if he didn't. He was not making love to me, no - this was fucking, this was the definition of fucking my brains out. I groaned. It was just so raw, so carnal.

I closed my eyes, feeling the pleasure building up inside me. Matthew moved in and out of me with ease, his eyes were closed tightly as he enjoyed the moment, he parted his lips slightly as his breathing increased.

Watching Matthew enjoying me only intensified the pleasure, pushing me higher and higher to the brink. I moaned loudly, enjoying every thrust that filled me. He opened his eyes briefly to look at me and he picked up the pace, thrusting faster and harder. My body moved to his rhythm, my insides quivered and my legs stiffened around him.

"Come for me, baby. Come," he commanded and my body obeyed his request, the need in his voice sent me over the edge and I cried out. The intensely erotic spasm rocked my core as I came.

He slammed into me one last time and stopped suddenly as he reached his climax. He pulled out slowly and collapsed down next to me, as breathless as I was.

"Jesus," he breathed.

"Hmm," I was unable to say anything else, words had escaped me.

"That was, wow," He turned to look at me, his chest rapidly moving up and down as he tried to catch his breath. He propped himself up onto his elbow and with one hand, he untied my wrists, freeing me.

"Did you enjoy being restrained?" he asked as he discarded the tie onto the floor.

As soon as the words left his mouth, I realised I did enjoy it, in fact, I more than enjoyed it. It was the best sex of my life. And just like that, I felt the oh-so familiar blush creep across my face and I smiled, shyly.

He let out a chuckle and kissed my red hot cheek, "there's that blush I wanted to see," he then smoothed my dishevelled hair away from my forehead, "now that I've got you dirty, lets go and get you clean,"

Matthew eased up from the bed with such grace. It was at that moment that I realised that he kept his boxers on round his knees the whole time. He removed them and dropped them onto the floor with his other clothes.

"Come," he said as he offered me his hand to help me up off the bed. I placed my hand in his and he pulled me up. My skirt fell back around my hips and legs and I walked with him to the bathroom. As we walked hand in hand, I noticed my legs were like jelly. He literally made me weak at the knees. The thought made me smile.

Matthew glanced down at me, "has something amused you, Miss. Walker?" he asked, mirroring my smile.

"You, Mr. Harper. You have literally made me go weak at the knees, well done,"

"All in a good day's work," he replied, clearly proud of himself.

We entered a bathroom that was further down the landing. Letting go of my hand, Matthew walked over to the bath and turned the taps on. He poured oil into the tub and the room was instantly filled with the divine smell of jasmine. The walls were covered in large black tiles floor to ceiling. The bath was white, deep and egg-shaped. It would fit two people in with ease.

Behind the bath was a large window and the familiar view of the London skyline. Matthew pressed a button next to the bath and blinds started to come down over the window. I was standing in the doorway as I watched, my arms wrapped around myself. Matthew turned his body so that he was facing me, he gazed at me, his eyes dark as he held out his hand to me.

I stepped further into the bathroom and took his hand again. Raising his other hand, he ran his fingers gently down my cheek. He coaxed me into the tub and I gently lowered myself down into the enticingly hot water, I was suddenly aware just how sore I was. I winched slightly as I sat down.

"Are you sore?" Matthew asked as he slipped in behind me, causing water to slosh over the edge of the bath.

"Yes, a bit,"

"Good, I want you to think of me every time you sit down."

I gulped. *Oh. My. God.*

Matthew pulled me against his chest and placed his legs over the top of mine, encasing me. He buried his nose in my hair and inhaled deeply, letting out a contented sigh.

"This is nice," he murmured against my head.

"It is," I closed my eyes and leant my head against his chest. I was relaxed, I was content.

"If this is what couples do after they go out for dinner, then we are doing this seven days a week rather than one," he said.

I giggled, "I don't think all couples do this," I said as I opened one eye watching Matthew reach for a bottle of body wash.

I watched as he squirted some of the liquid into his hand. Then, he rubbed his hands gently together, creating a soft, foaming lather.

Matthew moved me forward slightly and started to rub the soap into my neck and shoulders, massaging me. I groaned, the feel of his hands on me was something else.

"Do you like that?" I could hear his smile as he spoke.

"Hmm, I do,"

His hands slowly glided across to my breasts. I inhaled sharply as his fingers started kneading and pulling at my nipples. My body gave into him and I pushed my breasts into his hands, my nipples were tender and oh-so sensitive.

"Hmm," he repeated my hum of pleasure from earlier deep in his throat, but he didn't stay at my breasts long before his hands travelled down to my stomach. My breathing increased and I could feel his growing erection as it pressed against me.

How could he be ready to go again so soon after? Was it normal? Luke was never like that, I was lucky if I got sex twice in a week, let alone twice in one evening.

"Are you always so ready for sex, Mr. Harper?"

He stopped mid way down and kissed the top of my head.

"Sex with you, yes," he said as moved his hands again, this time travelling to my thighs and he began to wash between my legs.

I held my breath when I realised what he was doing. *He was washing my scars.* My heart lurched into my mouth with wonder. My hands rested on his firm, muscular thighs as his fingers skilfully aroused me.

The feeling was so intense, the sensations took over my body and my hips started moving on their own, pushing against his hand. I tilted my head back, my eyes rolling in my head, and I groaned.

"That's it, baby," Matthew whispered in my ear then, very gently he nibbled my earlobe with his teeth. Abruptly he stopped and withdrew his hand from my inner thigh, leaving me wanton.

What? No!

"Why did you stop?" I asked, panting.

"Because, Felicity, I need washing too. But I want you to wash me in the shower,"

He very elegantly clambered out of the bath and sauntered over to the walk-in shower which was the size of my whole kitchen. He twisted a knob and suddenly water started to cascade over his beautifully sculpted body that was shimmering from the bath water. I was watching him as I leant my chin on the edge of the bath.

"Are you going to join me or not?" He asked, with a wicked grin.

I scrambled out of the bath, trying not to slip and pad my way over to him. I joined him under the flow of the water.

Before I knew it, in one swift move, Matthew had me pushed up against the tiled wall. It was cold against my back, but quite frankly I didn't care. His hands cupped my face as he kissed me with such raw passion while his tongue invaded my mouth.

I lifted my hands up and placed them on his back, aching to touch him. He immediately removed his hands from my face and grabbed mine, pinning them up over my head. He leant his body to me, I was now completely trapped, unable to move. I was under his control.

Matthew then stopped kissing me and bent down, but he soon rose back up and handed me the body wash, his sweet-smelling body wash. I kept my eyes fixated on his as I squirted some into my palm and held my hand up in front of his chest. I gently placed my hand on his sternum and started to rub the soap into his skin. His lips parted and his breathing increased as I ever so slowly made my way down to his stomach, barely taking my eyes off him.

He leant forward and placed his palm flat against the tiled wall, panting with anticipation as I tauntingly made my way down to his thick, pulsing erection. I glanced down and looked at it, knowing what I wanted to do.

I ran my tongue along my bottom lip then and, leaning forwards, I placed one of my hands around him. He closed his eyes briefly and he let out a hiss of pleasure through his teeth. I moved my hand up and down with a firm but gentle grip, my fingers tightening around him. He closed his eyes again, and I could hear his breath hitch in his throat.

"Oh God, baby," he said looking down at me with scorching eyes, "that feels so good,"

Matthew flexed his hips into my hand, clearly enjoying the feeling. Spurring me on, I grasped him tighter and picked up pace.

I heard a low groan deep within his throat as

I pumped him with my hand. It turned me on knowing that it was me making him feel that way. I had control this time. I was in charge.

"I'm going to come," Matthew said through gritted teeth.

And in one swift movement, I crouched down and placed his hard, long length in my mouth and tentatively sucked, running my tongue over his tip. I peered up at him and saw his eyes fly open in surprise.

"Ah, God, yes!" he hissed.

He started thrusting into my mouth, pushing himself deeper into my mouth until he reached the back of my throat. He grabbed my hair as I twirled my tongue around the tip again, tasting the beads of his pleasure.

He flexed his hips and I bared my teeth, sending him over the edge. He cried out and I felt the warm, salty liquid enter my mouth. I swallowed quickly trying to get rid of the taste.

"Wow," he breathed.

I beamed up at him with a triumphant smile on my lips.

"That was unexpected. I'm speechless, literally speechless," he said, his breathing ragged.

We stepped out of the shower and he wrapped a large white fluffy towel around me. They were as soft as the ones you'd get in a hotel. Once he'd wrapped a towel around himself, he pulled me into his arms and kissed me hard, pushing his tongue into my mouth.

"I can taste myself," he said grimly, clearly not liking it.

I laughed at his reaction.

Ha! Now you know what it's like.

"Come, let's go to bed,"

"I'm not that tired,"

"Who said anything about sleeping? And besides, I owe you another orgasm,"

Another one! This man was incessant.

As we walked hand in hand, I realised just how much I could get used to this.

* * *

"Right, CT results are back, she needs to go up to theatre now. She has a subdural haematoma."

"Felicity, you have a bleed on the brain, we are going to take you into surgery now, ok?"

I look up at the doctor, I am unable to move my head to nod but the doctor knows I am trying to tell her yes.

Surgery? Oh God. They are going to open my skull. I want my dad. He would know what to do.

"Ok, let's take her down. Has her next of kin been informed? Any partner that needs informing?"

5

I COULD SMELL THE burning of the tyres from the vehicle having to do an emergency stop, but failing. The smell was so strong. Suddenly I saw him, I could see him standing there, watching.

"Hello?" I shouted.

He didn't say anything, instead Luke just stood there. He was still.

"Felicity?" I heard someone that wasn't Luke call my name.

Luke turned and began to walk away from me. He walked towards a woman, a woman who I'd seen before. It was *her*, the one who destroyed what we once were.

"No! Please, Luke. I need you!" I screamed.

"Felicity? I'm here, it's ok, I'm here,"

A dark figure has appeared, standing above me, looking down at me. Suddenly, I was awake, Matthew was shaking me awake.

"It's ok, baby. I'm here, it was a bad dream," he said as he sat on the bed and pulled me against his chest.

It was then that I realised I had tears running down my cheeks. It was just a nightmare, I was ok. I wasn't being cheated on. But I was left breathless, my heart pounding hard in my chest. I was covered in sweat. The T-shirt that Matthew gave me to wear was now drenched.

Matthew pushed me away from his chest so that he could examine my face. He wiped away the tears using his thumb.

“Are you ok?” he asked, his voice laced with concern.

I nodded my head at him in reply, unable to speak. I hadn't had a nightmare in so long. Matthew kissed my forehead and held me tightly to his chest again. We sat like that for I don’t know how long, both in silence.

He rocked me while gently stroking the back of my head, comforting me. I finally managed to find my voice again, “I’m going to take a quick shower, I’m all wet and clammy," I mumbled against his hard body.

“Ok, want me to come in there with you?”

“No, I’m fine. Thank you though," I replied as I scrambled out of his arms and out of the bed. We were still in the guest room and not in his room. I decided against bringing that up again before we went to sleep. I was so tired after the orgasms, I couldn't care less where we slept at that point.

I made my way to the bathroom that I used Sunday morning. I stripped off and got into the shower. I cooled my skin under the lukewarm water, washing the remnants of my nightmare away. I stood under the water, my body lax. I could still feel my heart racing in my chest.

What had triggered the nightmare? I'd been doing so well. Was it because of Matthew, was I feeling like I was somehow betraying Luke? I knew that I hadn't thought about Luke as much since Sunday, but that didn't mean I had forgotten him. I could never forget him. He was my first love.

I turned the shower off and quickly dried myself, wanting to try and get back to sleep. I made my way back to the guest room and Matthew was nowhere to be seen. My heart sank at the sight of the empty bed. Where was he? I *needed* him.

I decided to look for him so I headed down the hall. His penthouse was so big, with lots of doors it was so easy to get lost. I reached a door that I hadn't been to before, I pushed open the door and behind it was a huge library.

The room was dark, the only light was a glow that was coming from a lamp. The lamp sat on a mahogany pedestal desk. I couldn't help but feel drawn to the room. I started to walk in and I looked up, admiring the books on the shelves. There were rows and rows of books. I loved reading but I could never seem to find the time anymore. I made a mental note to make an effort to read.

I walked over to the desk and ran my finger

along the smooth green leather that was on the top. Next to the desk was a large oxblood red leather wingback chair. I could almost picture Matthew sitting in the chair with his long legs crossed while reading something like *To Kill a Mockingbird.*

As usual, I felt his presence before I saw him. I didn't have to turn around to know he was walking over to me. He took my damp hair in his hand and wrapped it around his fist, pulling at it to allow my head to tilt. His lips found my neck, he planted featherlight kisses from my earlobe to the base of my neck.

"Hmmm," I groaned.

"Do you like that, baby?" he whispered against my skin as he continued up and down my neck, sending shivers of pure desire down my body. He then gently tugged at my earlobe with his teeth, pleasure began to build down in my groin. He spun me around so that I was facing him, my back to the desk. He carried on kissing my neck, trailing sweet kisses up and down.

"I would love nothing more than to fuck you on this desk," he said as he kisses me, "but I won't, least not now. You need your sleep," he removed his lips from my neck leaving me hot and needy, again.

"Let's go back to bed," Matthew took me by the hand and led me through the halls, this time to his bedroom.

I climbed into his bed, naked, and he slid in

next to me. I placed my head upon his chest while he gently stroked the tops of my arm.

"Do you want to talk about your dream?" he asked, breaking the silence.

"No," it was the last thing I wanted to talk about.

"Ok, but I'm told it helps to talk," he murmured, placing a kiss on top of my head.

"I'm a 'solve your own problems' type of girl,"

I could feel myself slowly drifting off. I glanced at the alarm clock on the bedside table that read 03:48.

"Ok, go to sleep, beautiful,"

And, before I knew it, I was sound asleep.

IT WAS VERY QUIET, I was comfortable and very warm. I was tranquil and at peace. I turned over and reached for Matthew. But he wasn't there. I sat up and listened to see if I could hear him. Where did he disappear too? I turned my head and looked at the clock. *Shit!* It was 07:41, I should have been up ages ago!

I threw the duvet off and practically jumped out of bed. What was I going to wear? I only had my red dress from the night before and that was way too fancy for work. It was then that I noticed there was a monochrome check skirt and black ribbed roll neck top laid out on the armchair by the window. Feeling very grateful, I took the outfit and hurriedly made my way to one of the many bathrooms.

I showered and dressed quickly. The clothes were a perfect fit. I noticed the skirt was made by DKNY so I knew it was expensive. I looked at myself in the mirror and noticed that I had a glow about me that I had never seen before. My eyes were sparkling and my cheeks had more colour. My lips felt more plump too. I looked different. *I felt different.*

I wandered into the living area, looking for my bag, hoping to find some lipstick and found Matthew sitting at the table reading a newspaper, of course it was the *Financial Times.* There was a selection of fruits and pastries laid out on the table and orange and apple juice. How did he have time to do all this?

Matthew suddenly peered over his newspaper at me and smiled.

"Good morning, beautiful," he said, folding up the newspaper and putting it on the table.

"Hello," I said, beaming at him.

"Please, sit. You must be famished. I know I am after last night," he said with a wink.

How could him winking at me be so hot?

I took a seat opposite him and helped myself to a Danish pastry. He poured me an orange juice as I ate.

"We'll leave for work in fifteen minutes if you are ready?"

"Yes, I'm ready. Do you know where my handbag is?" I asked.

He nodded his head over in the direction of the living area, “yes, it's over there by the console table,"

“Thank you. Did you get all this food in for me?” I asked as I put another piece of pastry in my mouth.

“I didn’t personally, but my housekeeper did," he smiled.

Oh yes, the housekeeper.

“Where did you go last night? After I had a nightmare?”

He looked up at me, his expression unreadable. “I went to get a drink," he replied, his voice serious, too serious. He was a terrible liar, but I chose not to probe him anymore.

“Can I see you again tonight? Maybe dinner and a movie here?” Matthew asked, changing the subject.

I smiled a shy smile at him, feeling all gooey that he wanted to see me again, so soon after, “yes, of course you can,”

He nodded and popped a chunk of melon in his mouth. I couldn’t help but smile at him, he was just so handsome.

“What?” he said, cocking his head to one side like a puppy would when curious.

“Just you, “I cocked my head, mirroring him.

He smiled briefly but the smile didn't quite reach his eyes, “we’d better head off," he said, checking his watch. He rose to his feet and I did the same, brushing the crumbs off my top.

THE DRIVE TO THE office in the 4x4 Audi was quiet. Matthew had suddenly become withdrawn from me. I didn't know why. We sat in silence most of the way. I didn't think he'd even looked at me even once. I could almost feel the connection between us slipping further and further away. Had I said something wrong?

Stanley, Matthew's driver pulled up outside my office building.

"Stan, can you give us a minute please?" Matthew asked, his tone serious.

"Yes, sir," Stanley got out of the car and stood on the pavement.

Matthew shifted in his seat so that he was facing me. He leant forward and took both my hands in one of his and cupped my cheek in the other. I stared into his blue eyes, they looked lost and it made my heart ache.

"Why are you being so distant?" I asked.

He shut his eyes and when he opened them again they were no longer lost but instead filled with warmth. He tugged my hand, pulling me onto his lap. He had his arms around me, and his nose was in my hair. He breathed in and exhaled.

"I don't know what it is that you are doing to me, it's - strange. So unexpected. It's like your body calls to mine, I'm breaking all my rules with you. " The seriousness of his tone sent a surge of warmth through me.

“Rules are there to be broken," I whispered into his chest.

Matthew released his grip on me and held me at arms-length, looking at me with sincerity in his eyes.

“Seriously, how have you done this to me? It’s different with you, you -” he smiled again, this time it reached his blue eyes, “you amaze me, you’ve captivated me,"

I beamed at him, my smile reaching ear to ear. I held up my hand and placed it on his beautiful face. Hazel eyes meeting blue.

“You’ve captivated *me*," I told him, because it was true. Before him, I was stuck in a pit of doom that I couldn’t pull myself out of, I was just about getting by day to day. I didn’t realise how miserable I was.

Maybe Matthew was hurt in the past, maybe that's why he didn’t date women. He was willing to give it a chance with me, he wanted to give me more, like I wanted to with him.

I caught sight of his perfect white teeth from his grin as he pulled me in for a kiss, a kiss that made me melt deeper into the seat. Matthew then pulled me into him again, I rested my head against his chest while he kissed my hair repeatedly. I inhaled his scent as I pressed my nose against his suit jacket, he smelt of fabric softener and body wash.

He smells so good. My subconscious crooned.

“I better let you go to work now, otherwise I will never let you go,"

“Don’t let me go," I said, looking at him through my lashes, a look that told him I was talking about us full stop and not the here and now.

“Ok,” he breathed as he held me tightly again. And in that moment, I think you would call that a breakthrough.

I SAT AT MY desk with a fresh cup of tea. I scanned the office to see if I could see Amber but she was nowhere to be seen. Maybe she's running late but, *She’s never late* I thought. I decided to give it until 10am and if she still hadn’t turned up, I’d send her a message. I fired up my Mac and loaded up my emails. As I scanned through them, I noticed that Matthew had sent me one at 08:51, around the time I got out of the car. I smiled to myself as I read it.

Felicity,

Think of me today, I will be thinking of you - last night, in the bed, bath and shower.

Kind regards

Matthew Harper
Turned on Chairman, MWH Group Holdings.

Thoughts of the previous night flooded my mind. Thoughts of the hot, steamy and utterly mind blowing sex. How could something that is so perfectly human and natural feel so different with another man?

"Felicity, are you ok?" Evelyn asked as she walked past me.

I cleared my throat and shook my head, hoping that would clear the sensual thoughts that are in my head.

"Yes, fine, thank you. You?" I tried to act nonchalant as I attempted to close the email with shaky hands. I did not want my manager to know that I was sleeping with her boss's boss. Or the fact that I was feeling extremely turned on. How did he manage to turn me on just by an email?

"Yes, thank you. It's just that you looked away with the fairies,"

"Sorry, late night," I shrugged, hoping she would drop it and walk away. She gave me the once over and offered me a fake smile and walked over to her desk.

Once she was out of view, I opened the email and typed out a quick reply, hoping that no one else walked by.

Mr. Harper,

I find your emails exceptionally inappropriate. Especially when I am nearly caught out by my manager.

I am of course thinking about you too, and last night.

Somehow already, you have me missing you.

Now get back to ruling the world or whatever it is that you do.

Kind regards

Felicity Walker
Wet as hell Junior Writer/Editorial assistant
LuxeLife Magazine

His response was almost immediate and made me giggle.

Miss. Walker,

Would you like me to refrain from emailing you at work? Although, I am technically your boss so I deem it appropriate.

I don't rule the world, it's an empire actually, The world is next on my list.

Kind regards

Matthew Harper
Emperor, MWH Group Holdings.

Matthew and technicality! I needed to end the conversation before I got carried away.

LET ME GET ON WITH SOME WORK!

Kind regards

Felicity Walker
Distracted Junior Writer/Editorial assistant
LuxeLife Magazine

He was so distracting, and witty. It was annoying but I couldn't help but smile.

Miss. Walker,

I am simply emailing one of my employees, it's totally innocent . . .

Now get on with some work, you need to help me work on conquering the world.

Kind regards

Matthew Harper
Chairman, MWH Group Holdings.

I closed the email and tried to focus. I was aware that Amber still isn't in and it was starting to worry me. I asked around to see if anyone in her department had heard from her. Only her manager had. Apparently she wasn't feeling well. I pulled out my phone from my handbag and sent her a text.

Hey,
Are you ok? Apparently you are feeling unwell? x

The morning went by slowly but I managed to get a lot of work done in between worrying about Amber. I hadn't heard back from her yet, and I hadn't heard from Matthew since his earlier emails either. As I was typing, my mind wandered to him and what he was doing. I decided to send him an email as I was missing him.

Boss,

How is your morning going?

Kind regards

Felicity Walker
Junior Writer/Editorial assistant
LuxeLife Magazine

The time approached noon and I locked my Mac. Feeling hungry, I popped out to get some lunch. I walked to the local cafe and ordered a cheese toastie. I checked my emails on my iPhone to see if Matthew had replied. I was disappointed to find that there weren't any emails.

As I walked back to the office, I stopped dead

when I noticed a familiar looking car parked up outside of the office. I was certain it was an Audi. I was even more certain that it was the same one I was in that morning but then again, how many other Audis are out there. Just then, I spotted Matthew out of the corner of my eye leaving the lobby of the building I worked in.

And, he isn't alone. My scalp prickled with a strange feeling of jealousy. He was with a tall, leggy blonde - a beautiful blonde.

Who is she? What was she doing with him?

I stepped to one side so that I was out of view. I watched as he walked her over to the Audi with his hand at the small of her back. They were both smiling from ear to ear, looking like they were enjoying each other's company. They stopped and she kissed his cheek, grinning up at him.

She then placed her hands on his upper arm and he visibly flinched like he did when I went to touch him. He soon composed himself and relaxed. She was overly friendly with him, *too friendly* and I didn't like it.

Matthew opened the door for her and with such elegance, she climbed in. Matthew stood on the pavement and watched as the car, presumably driven by Stanley, drove off into the London Traffic. Matthew then turned on his heels with his hands in his pockets and walked back into the lobby.

And just like that, he disappeared from view. I held back for a beat before walking into the lobby, waving back at Bob at the security desk as I passed.

I just caught sight of Matthew in the lift as the doors closed, he looked up but somehow didn't spot me. The lift ascended up to the top floor. I'd worked in the building for three years and I had no idea what was up there. What was Matthew doing going up there?

I stood and waited for the next lift, racking my brain. There must be a logical explanation as to why he was so friendly with that woman. Was she one of the many women I was sure he had propositioned like he did with me?

The lift finally arrived and I got in and pressed the button for my floor. As the door closed, I leant up against the mirrored wall and closed my eyes. Why did I have a feeling in my stomach that something was wrong? Or was it just pure jealousy that he was with another woman? God knows that I knew that feeling all too well.

I walked through reception and entered the bustling office. Once I'd sat down, I checked my emails and saw that Matthew had finally responded. Three minutes ago.

Very busy. Yours?

Kind regards

Matthew Harper
Chairman, MWH Group Holdings.

I frowned at the screen, his reply was curt, cold even. His tone had changed. He didn't seem as playful as he was in his emails earlier.

Of course he's not, he's just been fucking Miss. Blonde-hair-long-legs, you're the last thing on his mind, my subconscious snarled at me.

I didn't know for sure if anything happened between those two but they did look rather cosy and she was beaming at him. I knew that look all too well. Hell, that was me the previous night after our sex-athon. Why would he be involved with another woman after what he said to me only hours before in the car? Or maybe he was still pursuing other women while dating me? But wasn't I enough? The thought made me feel sick.

I took a deep breath in, determined not to let it cloud my concentration at work. I couldn't let it happen to me again, not like before. I couldn't let a man who I had only just started seeing make me feel this way. I decided to ignore the email and try to do some work. I needed the distraction.

The last few hours dragged, I struggled to concentrate on anything but the thought of Matthew. I *needed* to know what was up on the top floor. I needed to know what they were doing up there. I got up from my seat and scurried off out of reception and through the doors that led to the bank of lifts. I pressed the call button and waited for the lift to arrive.

My heart thumped frantically in my chest as I approached the top floor. The doors opened and I stepped out. There was plastic sheeting hanging from the ceiling sectioning off different construction areas. There were no workmen on the floor so I assumed they had finished for the day. W*hy was Matthew up here?* I kept thinking.

I moved the plastic sheet to one side and over on the far side of the room, I spotted an office, there didn't appear to be anyone in it, just a lone desk and chair. I pushed the door open and stepped in.

I could smell the remnants of a sweet smelling perfume lingering in the air, and I knew it was hers. The blonde woman had been in here.

Did they fuck on the desk? My stomach was in knots. *I can't be here.*

I ran out of the office and through the construction site towards the lifts. As soon as I reached my floor I ran into the ladies and threw up. Emptying everything that I had inside me. I couldn't do this. Not again. It hurt too much.

Once my stomach had emptied, I did my best to compose myself and then headed back to my desk. I sat down and unlock my Mac, hoping that no one had noticed that I'd disappeared. I opened my emails back up and saw that Matthew had emailed me again.

Felicity,

You must be very busy as I haven't heard back from you?
Kind regards

Matthew Harper
Chairman, MWH Group Holdings.

My cursor hovered over 'reply'. For once I didn't have anything to say to him, so I closed my emails and carried on with the task I was working on. It approached 5pm and my desk phone rang, it was a number I didn't recognise.

"LuxeLife, Felicity speaking," I said, by way of a greeting.

"Good, you are still alive then,"

It was Matthew.

"Yes, I've been busy, sorry,"

Why am I sorry?! I thought.

"I find ignoring someone exceptionally rude," he said, his tone clipped.

I frowned down at the phone cradle.

"Right, ok. Duly noted," my voice dripped with sarcasm.

Matthew sighed down the phone. "I'm sorry, I didn't mean to be abrupt with you. I was worried because I hadn't heard from you, that's all,"

He was worried about me? I was the one worrying that he had a lunchtime quickie. We were as bad as each other.

"Why were you worried? Are you afraid I'm going to change my mind about our arrangement?"

There was a long silence before he took a breath in. “Yes, you’ve walked out on me twice before,"

“That’s not fair, that was different," I said in defence. “It was before I -” I stopped what I was saying.

No *Felicity. Don’t say it. It's too early to admit to him that I liked him.* My subconscious willed me to stop.

“Before what?” he asked.

I shook my head, not wanting to say the words out loud to him “No, forget it,"

“Tell me,”

I couldn’t, I was terrified of getting hurt again because I wasn’t sure he felt the same way, or if he did, not to the extent anyway. I felt like I had to be with him all the time, If I held the words in then it wasn’t happening.

“Ok, don’t tell me then,"

“I’m not going to leave you. Just know that," I breathed.

I could sense his smile down the phone.

“Ok, and just to let you know, we don’t have an arrangement, we are *dating*, remember?"

Suddenly I could hear a woman’s voice in the background.

“I’m going to have to go, Miss. Walker. See you around 7pm?”

“Yes, it’s a *date*,"

“You bet it is," he said and the line went dead.

* * *

I RODE UP TO his penthouse in the lift and made my way through the double doors of the foyer and into the living area. There he was, pacing around the room on his phone.

"Yes. . . I know. . . That's what we need to get the plans finalised with them," He must have sensed me as he turned and faced me. "Good, send it over," He cut the call and started to walk over to me. His jaw set in a tight line and his gaze focused on me. I was in his arms moments later and he kissed me, hard.

"Hello, you," I said once he had realised my lips from his. I was left breathless from his kiss.

"Hello," He replied, his eyes warm as he smiled down at me.

I was itching to ask him who that woman was and why he was on the top floor with her but I resisted the temptation telling myself that it was nothing to worry about.

I found out that Luke had been sleeping with another woman when I confronted him about always going out with his friends. It just so happened that I saw his 'alibi' in the local supermarket one of the nights he was supposed to be with him. When he got in late that night I called him out on it and I finally learnt the truth. Rightly or wrongly I stayed with him after he apologised and said he would stop - which he did - but I feared it made me paranoid. I didn't want to be that woman.

"How was your day?" I asked, trying to keep the question as innocent as I could.

Matthew walked over to the kitchen and poured two glasses of red wine. "Quite busy actually," he walked back towards me and handed me the glass, "how was yours, darling?"

Darling? He'd never called me that before.

"It was pretty mediocre," I gazed up at him over the rim of the wine glass as I took a welcomed sip.

He mirrored me, taking a sip from his glass. I looked up at him, willing him to volunteer the information about him and the blonde.

"I saw you earlier, outside of work,"

"I know, I saw you too," he replied, taking another sip.

Wait, he saw me?

"Oh,"

"She's an old friend and colleague, Felicity," he looked at me as he answered my unasked question. He put his glass onto the coffee table and continued. "And she is working on my current project. She's an architect, well a commercial architect,"

"Oh," I said again, feeling stupid.

He looked down at me, his expression unreadable.

"I'm moving my head office into the building

you work in,"

I gaped at him, my mouth wide open in shock as Matthew regarded me coolly.

"Why?" I asked.

"Well, it's a good location within the City, it's bigger than my current HQ and there's a few empty offices which I can fill with some of my other companies. It makes sense to have the majority of them under one roof,"

Why did I feel so disappointed that he did say, *'because you are there Felicity'?*

"And of course, it means I can be closer to you" he smirked as his voice lowered. It was as if he had read my mind again.

His smirk made the preverbal blush creep across my cheeks. How did he do that to me? My blush soon disappeared when a thought suddenly occurred to me.

"Why didn't you say you saw me earlier when you called? Or when you emailed me?"

"You obviously didn't want me to see you, judging by the way you ducked out of view. So I was waiting for you to bring it up,"

"Right," I said, trying so desperately to hide the fact that I was even questioning it.

"Why did you hide?"

How was I going to tell him that I had trust issues and that the love of my life cheated on me and ripped my heart right out of my chest, leaving me broken beyond repair. And then even more broken after he died? He would think I'm crazy. Like I was some sort of bunny boiler!

"I - I don't know," I replied as I lowered my head, looking down at the floor to hide my embarrassment.

He dipped down so that his head was level with mine. "I don't know what has happened in your past to make you act this way - although I could probably guess. But, please know I will never hurt you, I'm a one woman man, Felicity, I always have been. I won't ever hurt you like that, I won't hurt you in anyway,"

"I know, and it's way too early for me to go psycho bitch on you" I joked, trying to make the conversation easier.

"Oh, God. Please don't go psycho, I can't deal with psycho women," He threw his head back with laughter.

And with Matthew's laugh, I was put at ease again. The afternoon and my own insecurities had been pushed to one side. At least for the time being.

"WELL THAT WAS INTERESTING," Matthew said as he switched the television off. I was disturbed from sleep as he shifted on the settee so that he was facing me. "Were you asleep, Miss. Walker?" He asked, his eyes danced with amusement.

"Yes, I must have dozed off," I sat up and rubbed my eyes. Not surprisingly a documentary about the financial crash wasn't enough to keep me awake.

Matthew kissed my forehead and rose up off the settee. As he stood up and straightened on his long legs, he offered me his hand to help me up.

"Bed time, I think,"

"Yes please, I'm exhausted,"

"I hope you aren't too exhausted," He said with a glimmer in his eye.

I inwardly groaned, I loved having sex with this man, I really did. But, I was exhausted after our session just before our pizza arrived. He'd fucked me into oblivion, literally!

"I have never known a man with such an unattainable appetite, Mr. Harper" I said as I placed my hand in his and he pulled me up.

"What can I say, I get hungry,"

We made our way to his bedroom and I collapsed onto his bed, huffing loudly as I do.

"Can we skip sex for tonight? I don't think I can physically have any more orgasms. I think it may kill me," I joked as I stared up at the ceiling.

"Ok. If that's really what you want" Matthew said, his voice full of disappointment.

I sat up and looked over at him, he was pouting at me. "Really? Are you actually going to try and make me feel bad about not having sex with you? We had sex two hours ago, it's not like it was two weeks ago,"

He smiled and shook his head as he lifted his

T-shirt over his head. I was left staring at his perfect chiselled torso. I ran my eyes down his snail train that led down to his pubic hair and I licked my lips in appreciation.

Matthew walked over to the bed, pinning down me with his intense gaze. I swallowed as he stood, shirtless, in front of me at the foot of the bed.

“Like what you see?” His voice was deep and throaty, sending chills down my body.

“Yes," I breathed.

“Too bad you are tired," he said as he kissed the top of my head and sauntered off into the ensuite.

Bastard!

Matthew emerged from the bathroom a few minutes later and gracefully slid into bed. He picked up his iPad from the bedside table without so much as a glance in my direction. Clearly on purpose.

I sighed and walked to the bathroom to brush my teeth. After I‘d finished, I looked at myself in the mirror. I looked different. I looked, despite our sex-athons, well rested. I realised that after a long time, I finally felt at ease with myself, even after what happened today, I still felt good.

My mind then switched to Amber and how I never heard back from her. Something definitely wasn’t right. I decided to give it a couple more days and if she still hadn’t made contact, I’d pop round to see her.

I headed back into the bedroom and got into bed. Matthew was typing out an email as I laid down and closed my tired eyes. I was just drifting off to sleep when Matthew snapped the cover of his iPad shut, startling me, my eyes flying open in shock.

"Oh, sorry. Did I wake you?" The sarcasm in his voice was undeniable.

"Yes, I was just drifting off," I sat up and adjusted my pillow when it occurred to me just how natural it felt to be in the bed next to him again.

This man, who I knew nothing about made me feel so at ease, a stark contrast to how he made me feel just a few days previous. This was now the second night I had spent away from home.

Once I had finished adjusting my pillow into the perfect position, I looked up at Matthew who just happened to be gazing down at me, his expression soft and warm.

"What's that look for Harper?"

"What? Oh, nothing," he shook his head.

"You know what?"

"What?"

"I was just thinking, I know next to nothing about you. Besides the fact that you own a whole empire,"

Matthew looked at me with a questioning look. "Where are you going with this?"

"As we are *officially dating*," I said emphasising the 'officially dating' part, "I want to get to know you better. You know, things like where did you grow up, if you have any brothers or sisters, what your parents are like -" I stopped talking immediately when I noticed how tense Matthew had suddenly become.

What did I say to make him feel so uncomfortable?

"Why do you need to know that? It's the past. Shouldn't we focus on the here and now and just enjoy each other?" He replied, kissing the corner of my mouth.

"But I *want* to know those things about you, especially if this is ever going to turn into a relationship,"

I caught sight of the trepidation in his eyes, as if my words were hurting him. "Felicity, please -"

"I was once engaged. Not that long ago actually," I said, interrupting his plea. I was hoping that if I shared some information about myself, he would do the same.

But, Matthew just stared at me and said nothing. His eyes were wide with what? Panic? Surprise? After a moment he composed himself and cleared his throat.

"Please, Felicity. Don't tell me these things because I don't *need* to know. I don't *want* to know. I want to know about your past and your past lovers about as much as you want to know about mine - and that's not at all. "

"Lover not lovers, I'm not like you, I don't just sleep with people for fun," I said ignoring him. “His name was Luke, we were childhood sweethearts. We met when we were fifteen -”

“Please, stop," he said looking down at his knotted hands.

But I ignore him and carry on, “He died,”

He looked up from his hands and his blue eyes were on me again, burning into me. His eyes were dark and he had a guarded, hooded expression on his face.

“He was bleeding internally from the debris that was inside him,” I could feel the bile gather in my throat as I relived the moment my life was ripped out from beneath me.

“There was nothing they could have done. They tried but he was already dying,” I felt a tear that I was trying my best to hold back, break free and roll down my cheek and down to my jaw.

Matthew didn’t say anything. Instead, he just listened to me as I talked and watched me intently. His expression was hard to read, but I could see the angst and I could sense the uneasiness radiating off him.

“Baby, you don’t have to do this,"

“I know I don’t. But, if we are seeing where this goes, we should know these things about each other. I want you to know me, to know the things that not many people do. Because,” I stopped myself and took a deep breath in, “because, I like you, I *really* like you, Matthew. And I haven’t liked anyone for a while," I looked up at him as the words left my lips.

He looked uncomfortable, I could see him processing the words I had just said. Suddenly, closed his eyes tightly.

“How can you like me? You don’t even know me, Felicity. Not really," he whispered, his voice wobbling as he spoke.

“Exactly! That's what I’m trying to say to you. I want to know you. I don’t understand why you won’t let me. Just give me something, please,"

“Felicity, I can assure you that if you knew the real me you would run a mile,"

What? Why?

“I doubt that very much, Matthew. I like you. I can’t imagine much would want to make me run. I know I ran before, but it's different now, we’re different. You need to get that into your thick skull! You need to talk to me, you have to give me more. I want more.”

He shook his head and closed his eyes.Leaning forward, I clasped his hand, and placed a chaste kiss on his lips. He stopped breathing for a moment and when he reopened his eyes, they were hot. They were heated and full of lust. And just then, I realised that he used sex as a weapon. When the going gets tough, he wanted sex.

“Please talk to me. Please don’t use sex as a distraction, because its not fair to me,"

“I never said I would play fair, Felicity,” His voice low. It was deep, dark and dangerous.

“Is this just a game to you? Am I just a play thing?”

"No, of course not,"

We sat in silence. Neither of us breathing a word. And I knew that no matter how hard I tried, he was not going to budge. He wasn't going to tell me anything, it was a lost cause.

There was something he wasn't willing to share with me, something about his past that he was running from or just simply afraid to tell me. *He* was deep, dark and dangerous. With the thoughts in my head, I turned away from him and reached for the bedside light, plunging the room into total darkness.

* * *

"Right, Felicity, count back from ten with me, ten, nine, eight-,"

I feel lightheaded as my eyes close, I am at the mercy of unconsciousness. I feel myself slipping away from the pain, from the world.

I am now in total darkness.

Suddenly, a figure appears in front of me.

"Felicity?"

"Hello?" I shout, squinting my eyes hoping to see

better.

"Felicity?" the voice repeats. It is a voice that I recognise. "It's me,"

All of a sudden there is a flash of light and the figure emerges.

What the?!

"Oh my God." I say in disbelief, "It can't be, is that really you?"

"Hello, Felicity,"

"What? How can you be here?"

"I am here to help you,"

"Help me?"

Suddenly, he starts walking towards me, "Yes, I'm here to take you back with me,"

"Take me back? I don't understand,"

"You need to come with me. We need to be together again,"

"I- I can't,"

"Yes, you need to. Take my hand, Felicity,"

6

I WATCHED AS THE torrent of water flowed down from the shower head. The steam quickly filled the room as I stepped into the shower and closed my eyes. My thoughts turned to Matthew. It was nigh on impossible to have a shower without thinking about him. Without picturing how the water travelled over his rock hard abs and down to his large penis. Showering would forever be a reminder of Matthew.

He wasn't in bed when I woke up. I wasn't certain he was there at all during the night. His side of the bed didn't look like it had been slept in. Goodness knows where he was as I hadn't seen him since I woke up.

I reached for the shampoo and lathered up. Matthew's words from last night floated around my mind. I didn't know where we would go from here. How could I date a man who point blank refused to open up and talk to me? All I wanted to know was a little more about the man I was sleeping with and supposedly dating. It would never develop into a relationship if it stayed like that.

But, he said he doesn't want a relationship. He told me that at the beginning, he told me that it would be just for sex, no feelings, no getting attached. But I ignored all of that and suggested dating. What was I expecting? Did I honestly think he would suddenly change and become 'emotionally available' over night? I was clearly deluded if I thought that was the case.

I grabbed the towel and dried myself off then wrapped it around my body. I couldn't believe I was back here again. Why did I keep doing this to myself? It's like I was addicted to the pain. I needed more, I couldn't just have a 'wait and see' type of relationship, I needed stability now more than ever.

I hurriedly headed for the guest bedroom and found the clothes I packed yesterday and quickly put them on. I opted for a pinafore dress with a black turtle neck top and paired it with a pair of high black court shoes. I dried my hair and did my make up, I didn't do too much, just some mascara, a touch of foundation so you could still see the dusting of freckles across my nose and some lipstick. I was aiming to look good for Matthew but it seemed wasted now somehow. I glanced at myself once more in the mirror and grabbed my bag.

I hastily made my way down the hall and into the living area. I kept my eyes firmly fixed onto the double doors in front of me, aware I was walking in very high heels and I was very accident prone. I caught sight of Matthew at the breakfast bar as I walked past.

"Felicity?" He called after me as I pushed through the doors. I could hear his footsteps quicken behind me as he chased after me.

"Where are you going?" His voice became louder as he got nearer to me.

Suddenly, he grabbed my arm, pulling me to a grinding halt. I turned around so that I was face to face with him.

I looked up at him and all of a sudden he pulled me in closer to his body. The proximity of him and his intoxicating smell sent my mind into overdrive. Where was I going? I was running again.

I placed my hands on his forearms and gazed up at him, my breath hitched and my pulse quickened.

"Felicity?" He was as breathless as I was.

"I don't want to keep running,"

"Then don't,"

"But, I-I can't do this anymore, I need *more*,"

Matthew lowered his head so that his lips were hovering over mine. For a moment I thought that he was going to give me a chaste kiss just to stop me from talking, but as his lips enclosed over mine, he leant into me and his hands fist and pulled at my hair. He was kissing me with such passion.

I gave in and opened my mouth for him, allowing his tongue to explore. I tightened my grip on his arms and deepened the kiss. Matthew stopped his tongue and pulled away from me, his breathing laboured.

"I don't think I can give you the type of relationship you want, or need. I don't think I'm capable of giving you more, I want to try, trust me I do, but I can't,"

He wanted to try, with me.

"Yes, you can, you just need to talk to me, we need to be open and honest with each other, that's how you build a relationship or at the very least an understanding of each other," I said.

"But I can't,"

"Oh, but you can. You are stronger than you think - believe me,"

Matthew's eyes became clouded from emotions.

"Oh sweetheart, you try and see the best in me and that's what kills me. I am a monster. I am beyond help. I tried to warn you. I did." His voice was full of pain and that's what got to me. He did try to warn me. And now I was in too deep. His words from the night before echo in my ears. He told me he was emotionally unavailable but a *Monster?* Surely not?

"A monster? How can someone like you be a monster?" I reached up to cup his face, he flinched as I raised my hand to his cheek. Then it hit me, *he doesn't like to be touched.* He flinched and recoiled every time I went to touch him, I remembered noticing he did it when his architect friend touched him.

I looked into his dark blue eyes and I could see the pain and the look of panic in his eyes, the same look I'd seen in his eyes before. What has caused it?

Suddenly, I pieced it together. I could see why.

He'd been abused.

That's why he thought he was a monster, that he was beyond help.

Oh poor Matthew.

"Who has done this to you?" I said, trying to keep my voice from wavering. "Who has hurt you like this? Who has taken your ability to open up and trust?" I could feel the tears building. I tried my best not to let them out but they flowed from my eyes, who'd hurt this poor man?

Matthew suddenly let out a whimper. "Oh, Felicity. No. Please don't," and he pulled me into him, encasing me in his arms, gripping me tight as if to protect me. "I don't want your tears. Anyone's but yours," He gripped me so tightly, I struggled to breathe.

I pulled away and looked up at him. His face and eyes were full of sorrow and hurt. "This is why you are the way you are, you can't trust that people aren't going to hurt you?"

He shook his head and closed his eyes tightly. "I want to trust you. I want to trust you so badly that it hurts. You are different, you make me want to open up and *try,* but I am too afraid that you won't see me in the same way. I'm worried you won't want me and that you will leave me, this time for good,"

My heart constricted in my chest. Every time I walked away from this man, he broke a little bit more. I couldn't do that to him. But, could I be the one to put him back together again? Did I have that kind of strength in me? Even if I did, I couldn't fix what I didn't know.

"Listen to me, I am not going to go anywhere, ok? I'm not going to leave. I told you that last night. But, I need to understand you a little bit more. You will push me away unintentionally otherwise,"

He nodded his head as he wiped away my tears with his thumb. "Ok, I just need time. I have never done anything like this before, or even wanted to do anything like this, I don't know how to,"

"Ok, believe me, I understand. And when you are ready to share more with me, I will be here and waiting. I promise,"

Matthew smiled at me, it was a shy, vulnerable smile that I hadn't seen before. My heart tightened in my chest as he took me by the hand, "Come, lets go have some breakfast,"

AMBER STILL WASN'T AT work when I arrived, nor had I heard anything from her. It was so unlike her, she hadn't taken a day off in the years she'd worked there. I pulled out my iPhone from my bag and sent her another text.

Hey you.
Please let me know that you are ok,
I'm really worried about you.
x

I couldn't have another person to worry about, it was too much already worrying about Matthew! But, I did feel like I had made some headway with Matthew, although he was quiet and subdued on the way into work but he was somehow different too. A good different. He needed to know that his past couldn't define him, that it shouldn't sculpt his future. That was what I'd been told anyway.

The morning reached 10:30am and I checked my phone again. There was still no word from Amber. I put it back in my bag and turned my attention back to image proofing when I heard my computer ping, alerting me to an email.

Felicity,

I hope you know how much you have enchanted me, you have truly beguiled me, Miss. Walker.

Enjoy your day.

Kind regards

Matthew Harper
Chairman, MWH Group Holdings.

Oh, Matthew, if only you knew how much you have affected me. I gazed at the screen, re-reading the words he had typed out. I beguiled him? Me?! The thought made me practically giddy with joy. I quickly wiped the child-like grin off my face and decided to type out a reply that would hopefully make him feel as good as I did.

Dear Mr. Harper,

Many thanks for your kind words, they are much appreciated and make a somewhat dull day, a whole lot better.

You should know that you are a force so powerful that I can't keep away from you - no matter how hard I try, you keep pulling me back for more, and more, and more.

Now, go and take on the world - I know you are more than capable ;)

Kind regards

Felicity Walker
Junior Writer/Editorial assistant
LuxeLife Magazine

I smiled to myself, hoping he would understand the meaning behind the last line. He could do anything, he could get past the shame and fear he may have about his past. He would one day be able to take the bull by the horns and open up and tell me what happened, and then we would be able to get through it together. And maybe then, just maybe, he would be open to a relationship. Because Lord knows, I definitely wasn't going to give up and walk out on him, not this time.

I minimised my emails and carried on with the proofing when my desk phone began to ring.

"Good morning LuxeLife, Felicity speaking,"

I instantly knew who the caller was by the silence that was at the other end. I could almost feel him smiling down the phone at me.

"I want you," his voice was breathy.

His unexpected words took me by surprise. "I want you, too,"

"The things I want to do to you right now. Just thinking about them gets me hard,"

I was silent, unable to think of what to say, completely caught unawares.

"I want you to go up to the top floor at 12pm and wait for me there. Naked,"

Why was his bossiness such a turn on?

"Then, when I arrive, I will show you just how capable I am. I'll show you how capable I am of making your body quiver at my every command, baby,"

As he spoke, I became very aware that my breathing had become more rapid. I squeezed my legs tightly together, trying to suppress the feeling of wanting that was flooding my body.

“I’m going to bend your sweet little body over the desk and take you from behind. I will pound into you so hard and so fast that you will lose all control and you will come, hard, around me,"

“I have already lost all control, when it comes to you,"

He groaned my name down the phone. “God, you have no idea just what it is that you do to me, do you?”

“Believe you me, I do. You’ve done it to me too,"

I was now hot and flustered, he wasn't even there but he did things to me. We were both silent for a few seconds, as I tried to bring my breathing under control.

“So, 12pm, yes?”

“Oh yes, definitely. And by the way, I’m going to be the one who is going to make *you* lose your mind," I said, quickly hanging up.

How was I going to make it until 12pm, it was going to be a long hour and a half.

I STEPPED OUT OF the lift onto the top floor. It was deserted again with nothing up there besides tools and step ladders. I made my way over to the office I was in yesterday. The first thing I noticed was how cold it was in this room, and if he thinks I was going to take my clothes off in here, he must have been mad.

All of a sudden I felt his presence and I knew he was standing behind me. All my hairs stood to attention. Before I got the chance to turn around, I could hear him walking towards me. He stopped just before he reached me, but he didn't touch me. Instead, I could feel him lower his head down and he breathed onto my neck, instantly sending goosebumps up my arms.

"You're still fully clothed, Miss. Walker,"

"It's too cold in here, Mr. Harper,"

"Well let me warm you up then,"

He moved my hair to one side and started kissing my jawline in a slow sensual torture. I stopped breathing for a split second as he continued to torment me. He then moved up to my earlobe and took it in his mouth. He sucked, pulled and nibbled at it causing a surge of pleasure down to my groin, I groaned in response to his touch.

"I can't get to your neck when you wear this top," He pulled at my turtleneck, trying to expose more of my neck. "You leave me no choice but to strip you of this,"

"Do it," I panted as he ran his hands over my breasts, making his way to the buttons. Still standing behind me, he carefully and skilfully undid the buttons and removed my pinafore from me. Then, he slowly lifted my top up over my head exposing my neck, leaving me in nothing but a bra, tights, knickers and heels.

Matthew walked round so that he was now standing in front of me. He stared at me in appreciation, drinking the sight of me in, standing there before him.

“Do you have any idea just how sexy you are, Felicity?” his eyes were firmly fixed to my body And right on cue, I felt myself blushing.

I was suddenly overwhelmed with the intensity of his gaze. I felt so exposed and suddenly sheepish, I pulled at my fingers and then crossed my arms across my body.

“Please, let me look at you. You don’t need to be embarrassed or feel awkward. Not in front of me,"

He was right, I shouldn’t have felt embarrassed. I’d slept with this man for goodness sake. Why did I feel this way all of a sudden? I took a deep breath and unravelled my arms, once again revealing my pale body to him.

Matthew looked me in the eyes and very slowly stepped closer. He was inches from my body now. I could feel the heat radiating from him, he was as intoxicated by me as I was him.

“You do things to me, Felicity. Things that no one else ever has," he whispered in my ear.

I inhaled sharply while gazing at him. I was unable to find the words to speak. I was too focused on trying to maintain some composure.

“How would you like me to take you? Do you want to be bent over the desk or, would you like me to lift you onto it and I fuck you with your legs wrapped around my waist?"

"The latter, please,"

Before I could say another word, he lifted me up and placed me onto the desk, lowering me gently down so that my bare back presses against the cold surface of the desk. He then began to plant a trail of kisses down my neck and made his way down to my breasts.

He pulled the cup of my bra to one side and he took my now hardened nipple in his mouth, sucking and biting it, sending waves of pleasure down *there*. His other hand found its way down to my tights and my knickers and in one easy manoeuvre, he ripped them both off.

"We haven't got long, so I will make you come very quickly," he murmured against my skin before straightening up so he was now standing.

"Ok," I breathed, propping myself up on my elbows so I could see him.

Matthew removed a condom from his back pocket and then undid his fly. He lowered his suit trousers along with his underwear, allowing his impressive erection to spring to life. My breathing faltered from the sight of him. I then watched as he rolled the condom onto his sizable length.

Matthew placed one hand under my back, lifting me up to him for better access and, before I realised it, he impaled me in one swift move.

"Ah!" I cried out as I curled my legs tightly around him, securing me in place.

Matthew grabbed hold of my arms and kept them pinned down by my side, obviously in an attempt to stop me reaching out to touch him. He thrust himself into me - in and out - in and out. The sensation was unbelievable, it was almost unbearable.

“Be quick, Felicity. I want you to come first, I want your pleasure," He said to me through gritted teeth.

I groaned as I felt the familiar build of pleasure deep inside me.

“Come, baby. Come for me. I want to hear you,"

And with his words, I came. I shouted his name as my body took me over.

“Yes! That's It! Ah God!” Matthew hissed as he came violently inside me.

I laid there on the desk, breathless and sated. Once Matthew had regained his breath, he withdrew from me and stood up straight. He removed the condom and leant down, rubbing the end of my nose with his.

“I wish you would spend the night with me again, baby,"

“Hmm” I replied. That was all the sound I could muster in my post-coital haze.

“Please. Stay with me again,"

I lifted my head up slightly, “I can’t. I’m going to have to go home and face the Spanish Inquisition from my friends sooner rather than later,"

He visibly sagged and let out a slight sigh.

"Fine. But there's nothing I can say or do to change your mind?" He said as he helped me up off the desk and onto my feet.

"There are definitely lots of things you can do, but I need to go home. I'm sorry. And besides, aren't we supposed to be taking it slowly?" I asked as I pulled my turtleneck over my head.

"Well remembered, Miss. Walker," Matthew said as he handed me my pinafore.

"I think a bit of space for the evening will do us both good,"

Matthew stepped closer to me and caressed my cheek. "I don't think I want space from you though,"

I flashed him a wicked grin. "Mr. Harper, are you starting to become attached to me?"

An unnerving look flitted across his perfect face. "I - it's possible Miss. Walker," he then placed his hands on my face and kissed me, passionately. "I've told you, you've enchanted me,"

"Right back at you, Harper," I replied as I kissed him back.

I SHUT DOWN MY MAC and headed out through the lobby. I walked out with a smile on my face recalling our lunchtime activity. However, my smile was soon wiped off my face when I saw the weather outside. I groaned inwardly as I knew I was about to get soaked head to toe.

I used my coat as shelter over my head as I ran to the tube station, trying to avoid puddles at all cost. My legs were now bare and I was wearing nothing underneath thanks to Mr. delicate fingers.

I managed to get some reprieve from the rain as I entered the station. As expected, it was busier than usual with people doing all they could to avoid the typical British weather. Thankfully, the tube arrived and I stepped in the carriage. The heat from being underground allowed me to dry off for a bit before I stepped back outside again.

Once I'd emerged from the underground, my phone pinged in my bag. I scrambled around the bottom of my handbag with my coat still over my head, in the vain hope that it was Amber. Instead, Matthew's name was on the screen.

I do hope you have a good night,
but not too good without me.
Missing you already,
M

His text made me grin from ear to ear. *He misses me!* I sent him a quick reply and hurriedly made my way home.

Miss you too ;)
x

All was quiet in the flat as I headed into my bedroom to get changed out of my wet clothes. As I changed into my jogging bottoms and a camisole top, I heard the front door open. It was Heather.

"Hi Hev" I shouted.

About ten seconds later she appeared in my room. "Hello, stranger!" she beamed. "And where the hell have you been hiding?" She walked over to me and gave me a tight squeeze.

"I know, I'm sorry," I said, offering her an apologetic smile.

"God, you look so different, you are literally glowing. What's happened to you!"

I let out a laugh. I knew I could tell that I'm different but, I hadn't realised my new found sex life had made that much of an impact on my appearance that other people could notice.

"Ah, well that would be sex,"

"We are going to go and open a bottle of wine and talk about this!" Heather dragged me out of my room and into the kitchen.

"Unless it's a bottle of Don Melchor, I'm not interested," I joked.

Heather looked at me with a confused expression and got a bottle of white out of the fridge. "Sorry, it's only a cheap bottle," she shrugged and grabbed two glasses out of the cupboard. As she poured the Pinot Grigio into the glasses, the Spanish Inquisition began. "So, what's it like?"

"What?" I asked as I took the glass from her.

"The sex!"

"Oh! Well, it's amazing, mind blowing even," I grinned from over the rim of the glass.

"Better than Luke?" She asked.

I hesitated, suddenly feeling overwhelmed with guilt from the fact it was true.

I nodded.

"Really? I could tell just by looking at his pictures that he'd be a good lay, he's just so damn sexy!"

"Heather!" I said, laughing. I could only imagine the amount of women who thought the same thing

"What? He is!" She laughed, "Has he said anymore about not wanting a relationship?"

"Yes, he has. He says I'm different to anyone he's been with before and that he wants to try to give me more. Oh and he texted me on my way home to tell me he is missing me" God, I sounded like a schoolgirl!

"Sounds like he's falling for you babe, he would be stupid not to, I mean look at you! You're gorgeous," Heather said, waving her hand at me.

I blushed, Matthew's words about not being able to take a compliment came to mind. "Thank you, Hev,"

"How's Ethan?" I asked, trying to change the subject away from me. "I haven't seen or heard from him since he went to the doctors a couple of days ago,"

Heather finished her wine and placed the glass down on the breakfast bar. “Oh yeah, he's ok. He had to have some tests or something. He hasn't really said much to be honest,"

“Tests? What kind of tests?”

“I don’t know, I didn’t ask. He’s seemed ok though, so it can't be anything too serious, can it?”

“I hope not. Where is he, is he at work?”

Heather refilled her glass and topped up mine. I’d been drinking it slowly as it wasn’t not very nice. I had well and truly been spoilt when it came to wine in recent days.

“I think so. He was here last night with Sam. It was nice having them both here, I had Isaac over too, just need you and Matthew round as well!” Her eyes suddenly widened, I’d seen that look before, she had an idea. “Why don’t we arrange a couples night? That would be so much fun!” she said as she jumped up and down on the stop, clapping her hands.

I froze mid sip, I couldn't picture Matthew sitting chatting to my friends somehow, “I don’t think we are quite ready for that just yet,"

“Are we not good enough for the billionaire? Is it because we don't eat caviar or drink expensive wine,” she winked. I didn't want to tell her she was probably right.

“Well, maybe one day we will actually see this mega rich mogul in the flesh,”

"I hope so," I said as I finished the glass of wine.

THE NIGHT WENT BY far too quickly as usual and before we knew it was gone 11pm. I asked Heather what she would do if one of her friends from work suddenly disappeared without any warning. She told me to stop by her house, the thought had crossed my mind. Maybe I would. As I said goodnight to Heather and entered my bedroom, I heard my phone ping.

Felicity, I do hope you had an enjoyable evening without me. I've been working but I've been thinking about you the entire time.
M

I sent a reply straight away.

It has been nice, thank you.
We braided each other's hair and had a pillow fight in our underwear ;)
x

I giggled at my reply and placed my phone on my bedside table. As I was changing into my pyjamas, my phone pinged again.

**Oh, you are torturing me here,
Miss Walker. If you were here,
you wouldn't be wearing any underwear . . .
Now go to sleep. It's late.
M**

Oh, Matthew, as bossy as ever! I texted him good night and headed to the bathroom to brush my teeth.

**Sir, you are extremely bossy.
I wouldn't be having a pillow
fight with you anyway. . .
Dream of me.
x**

By the time I got back to my room and got into bed, he'd replied.

**I was thinking more on the
lines of another physical activity.
I always dream of you.
Go to sleep.
M**

I smiled and I couldn't resist sending him one last message.

Oh, were you now.
I'm always up for physical activities with you..
x

I put my phone face down and it vibrated almost immediately.

GO TO SLEEP, FELICITY.

I rolled my eyes at the screen at his shouty capital letters, and turned the bedside light off.

I snuggled into bed and realised how strange it felt to be going to bed alone once again.

7

THE MORNING HAS BEEN pretty uneventful, I'd been in the weekly team meeting and also proofread a few articles before they went to print. I realised that I was missing Matthew. He'd only sent me a couple of emails in the morning, saying he would be in meetings most of the day so won't be able to talk much. But, we had arranged to see each other later, after I went to see Amber. As I was busy typing out some minutes from this morning's meeting, I saw Evelyn approaching my desk.

"Felicity?"

I looked up at her.

"Could I talk to you for a minute?"

"Sure," I grabbed my notepad from my desk and followed her into her office. The feeling in my stomach told me this wasn't going to be good.

As Evelyn closed the door behind me, my apprehension increased. "Is everything all right?"

"Yes," She said as I took a seat. "I don't really

know how to say this," Evelyn suddenly looked very awkward.

"Ok." I replied, feeling very uneasy.

She looked at me with a hint of embarrassment. "Listen, it's not my place to interfere with your personal life. I'm your manager and there's a line that comes with that. However, I'm going to cross that line,"

My stomach tightened. "Ok," I said blinking, I was startled by the direction of the conversation.

"It's just that it's been brought to management's attention that you are courting Mr. Harper. He's handsome and rich so I understand the appeal, trust me, I do. I just want you to be careful. I don't want it going around the office and then people accusing you of sleeping with the boss to 'get ahead.'" She talked fast with obvious embarrassment, causing me to shift in my seat.

"Thanks," I said quietly, hoping I didn't look as sick or as pale as I felt.

"And, I like you, Felicity. You do some really good work and I want you to work here for a long time. I just don't want you to get hurt,"

This was the sort of warning you'd expect from a friend, not your boss. I knew that my colleagues would think of me as just another one of his many conquests because I would have thought the same, judging by what I Googled.

"Evelyn, it means a lot to me that you care about me that much and also that I'm valuable to you. But, you don't have to worry about me. I'm big enough and ugly enough to look out for myself. Besides, nothing is going to get me to quit this job - I love it too much,"

She let out a breath, clearly relieved. “All right. Let’s leave it at that and get back to work, eh?”

I nodded and smiled at her. As I rose to my feet a thought occurred to me. “You said it’s been brought to management's attention, well who told you all?”

Evelyn stilled, looking awkward once more. “Erm, we - well I saw your name on the guest list for the MWH Group annual fundraiser tomorrow night, and as it’s only the management from the different companies who get invited, I put two and two together. Because, why else would you be invited?” She said, looking at me cautiously.

I froze for a moment, *what fundraiser?!* “Well, your maths is excellent because yes, we are ‘courting’ but it’s only happened in the past few days. It’s still early days and I don’t even know what it is between us yet,” Why was I telling *my boss* this?!

“Oh. Ok then. But I do mean it when I say be careful, please. Because from what I’ve heard, he’s got a bit of a reputation for being a ladies man. He’s always being pictured with a different ‘bimbo’ at these types of events. I don’t want you to be a name on his long list. You are too respectable for that,"

I nodded again and offered her a grateful smile. I headed back to my desk and got back to work. Trying to avoid all temptation of Googling Matthew's name again.

My mind kept replaying the conversation, especially when Evelyn mentioned the fundraiser. I needed to ask Matthew about it, as it was tomorrow evening. And what the hell was I supposed to wear? Did he want me there considering the fact he hadn't actually told me about it? Did I even want to go? I definitely didn't want to be labelled as a 'bimbo'.

I decided to email him, I knew he might not reply for a while but at least I would have started the ball rolling.

Matthew,

I have been made aware about the forthcoming annual fundraiser.

Do you want me there? When were you going to tell me about it?

Kind regards

Felicity Walker
Junior Writer/Editorial assistant
LuxeLife Magazine

I locked my computer and went out to lunch

with a few members of my team. I was hoping that the company would distract me, at least for an hour.

When I got back to the office, I made myself a cup of tea and sat back down at my desk. Sure enough, there was a reply from Matthew.

Felicity,

Yes, there is an annual fundraiser tomorrow night.

We can either go or we can stay in. The choice is yours . . .

Kind regards

Matthew Harper
Chairman, MWH Group Holdings.

Gah! The man was so frustrating, he skirted around questions like a politician! Were we going or are we not going? Surely he *had* to go!

Mr. Harper,

If you would like me to go, please say so.

I'm pretty certain you *have* to go.

Kind regards

Felicity Walker
Junior Writer/Editorial assistant

LuxeLife Magazine

I rubbed my temple while I re-read his reply. Maybe email wasn't the best way to communicate with this man about this. I decided to leave it for now and as we could pick this up later, in person.

The afternoon went by in a flash once I got my head stuck into work. Before I knew it, it was half past five. I closed my computer down and threw my bag over my shoulder and headed out the door.

I flagged down a cab and soon arrived outside Amber's flat. I pressed the buzzer on the intercom and waited for her to answer. Nothing. I tried again and again. I stepped back and glanced up at the windows of her first floor flat and I briefly caught sight of the blinds moving.

She's in.

"Amber? I know you're in, I saw you," I shouted.

I stood and waited a few seconds. "Please, I'm worried about you, we all are! Please talk to me. I'm not going to leave until you at least tell me that you're ok, Passers-by stare at me as I shout up.

Suddenly, the intercom buzzed and the door released. *Finally*!

I made my way up to the first floor and walked up to her front door. Before I got the chance to knock, she opened it. Amber stood before me, although it wasn't the Amber I knew. She looked forlorn and exhausted. Her usual big brown eyes were dull and lifeless with dark circles under them and she was wearing dirty clothes.

Shit, she's in a bad way.

“Amber," I said, my voice quiet and sympathetic.

Tears began to build in her eyes and her lip quivered. She stepped aside, allowing me to come in. As I entered, I noticed her usually neat and tidy flat was anything but. There were discarded crisp packets on the floor and wine glasses and bottles strewn over the coffee table. It was as if she had given up on everything, I knew that feeling all too well.

Once I'd absorbed the scene. I turned to face Amber, she had her arms wrapped tightly around her body as if to shield herself and she was looking down at the floor. She glanced up at me momentarily but then looked down at the ground again. She was unable to look at me.

“Amber, are you ok? What happened?” I asked.

“I - I," She tried to talk but she couldn't.

“Right, sit down. I'm going to make us a cup of tea and we are going to talk, ok?”

she nodded her head and sat on the settee.

As I boiled the kettle, I looked round and managed to find some clean mugs. I put the tea bags in and sent Matthew a text.

Might be longer than I thought.
Have dinner without me.
x

He knew I'd come round to check on Amber but I never envisaged that that would be this bad, what on earth had caused her to plummet into this kind of darkness? As I poured the boiling water into the mugs my phone vibrated.

Take your time, I'm going to the gym anyway.
Anything I can do to help?
M

The image of Matthew all wet and sweaty and the gym did things to me but, I shook off the image and typed back a reply. I shouldn't have been thinking of things like that, not when my friend clearly needed me.

I don't even know what I can do to help.
Enjoy your workout.
X

I made my way over to where Amber was sitting and set down the two mugs on the coffee table. Amber managed to muster a brief smile that didn't quite reach her eyes.

"So," I began.

"I'm sorry I haven't been replying to your messages," she said as she played with the hem of her sweatshirt.

"Don't worry about it, I was just worried about you," I paused for a moment, "I'm still worried about you," I said honestly.

Amber stopped playing with the hem and slowly looked up at me. "I, I, erm," she hesitated and closed her mouth again. It was as if she didn't know what to say.

I shook my head, "it's ok, you don't have to tell me if you don't want to. I just want to make sure that you are eating properly, otherwise you are going to make yourself ill-"

"I was raped,"

I gaped at her. My mouth wide open in shock, in horror at what she had just admitted to me.

What should I say? I was rendered speechless. All I wanted to do was to wrap this woman up and take her away from the pain she must have been feeling right now.

"Oh my God," were the only words I managed to get out of my mouth. "I-I don't know what to say. I'm so sorry,"

Amber didn't respond, instead she just sat there staring down at her hands that were clasped firmly together. I then realised it was to try and stop them from shaking like a leaf.

"Have you spoken to the police,"

A single tear flowed down her cheek. She shook her head.

"Ok, well that's the first thing we are going to do," I said as I leant over and cupped my hands over hers.

She looked at me with wide eyes. She was scared.

"Please don't be scared. I'm going to be with you every step of the way, you know that right?" I tried my best to reassure her.

"Thank you," she whispered.

"No need to thank me. Do you want me to make the call?"

She nodded her head.

ONCE THE POLICE HAD left, I made a start by washing up. It was past 10pm by the time I left. I stepped out in the fresh September evening and hailed a cab. I felt bad for leaving Amber alone. I did offer to stay but she was so exhausted from talking to the police, that I think she was happy for the peace and quiet.

I paid the cabbie and rode up in the lift to Matthew's penthouse. I made my way through the foyer and opened the double doors where Matthew was waiting for me in the living area. I took one look at him and for some reason I was hit with a wave of emotions.

"Hey, come here, darling," his voice was warm and welcoming as he encased me in his arms.

This was my safe place, in this man's arms. I wished that Amber had a safe place that she was able to run to, to seek comfort.

"Thank you,"

"For what?" He asked as his nose nestled in my hair.

"For being you, for making me feel safe,"

I buried my face into his shirt, inhaling his scent that was body wash and Matthew.

He held me at arms length and studied me, frowning. "Of course I will make you feel safe. It's my job too. I look after the things I care about, you know," His frown deepened, "what's all this about? What happened?"

I took his hand and led him over the white leather settee and told him about tonight's revelation. He listened as I explained that Amber went on a blind date with this monster she met online, what the police said and what the next steps were.

"Right, that's it. You aren't to go anywhere on your own. My driver will drive you around," he said as he rose to his feet.

I mirrored him by standing too. "What? Why?" I squeaked. "She went on a date with him, he isn't going to do the same to me!" I said, exasperated. I couldn't stand the thought of losing my freedom and control.

"Oh really! And you can say with absolute certainty that he or any other excuse for a human being won't - God forbid - do that to you?"

He rolled up his sleeves and placed his hands on his hips. He meant business.

I opened my mouth and closed it again.

Damn he is right, I can't. I thought.

"Exactly!" he said. "So that settles it then, Stanley will be your chauffeur anywhere in and around the City,"

"Oh this is just ridiculous!" I said as I flumped back onto the settee like a sulky teenager. How long was this going to last?

Matthew looked down at me and sighed. "Yes, I know. You should be able to go round the city freely and not worry but, the truth is you can't," He sat back down beside me and took my hands in his. "It's a fucked up world out there and I wouldn't be able to forgive myself if anything were to happen to you," he looked at me with warm eyes and brought my hands up to his mouth and kissed my hand sweetly.

And, in that moment I realised that he was doing it for all the right reasons. Because he cared about me. I grinned at him and he tilted his head to one side, clearly confused by my smile.

"What's that for?" he asked as he mirrored my smile, it was clearly contagious.

"Nothing. Just you,"

"Oh, Miss. Walker, what am I going to do with you?" He pulled me onto his lap and kissed the top of my head.

"I may have some ideas," I said, grinning once more.

I MADE MYSELF A sandwich before climbing into Matthew's bed as I didn't have any dinner. I had asked Matthew about the fundraiser although my worries and concerns seemed pretty irrelevant in the scheme of things. Matthew said his company had a fundraiser for a charity each year. It comprised the managers from each of the companies within the group. Even though I wasn't a manager, he wanted me there as his date or he said he would miss it this year if I didn't feel comfortable going. So the ball was well and truly in my court!

"You can't not go to a charity event that *your* company hosts,"

"Believe me, I can. I've been hosting and doing the speech for the last nine years, so I can have the year off. I'm sure I won't get reprimanded too much,"

Nine years!

"So this will be the tenth year? You *have* to go! It's a big year!"

"Like I said, I will go if you go with me," Matthew unbuttoned his dark blue shirt and threw it in the laundry basket, distracting me with his perfect body.

"But what would I wear? I haven't got any nice dresses, not the type for a fundraiser anyway," I was sure that a dress I would wear to a nightclub didn't really scream 'charity event' somehow.

“Don’t worry about the dress. I can deal with that for you,"

Ah yes, his magical power to source clothes at short notice.

I stared at him for a minute, trying to work him out. But he was beyond readable. Could I go to a charity event where *all* my managers would be? I knew I wouldn't feel comfortable and I knew what people would think but, I think he wanted me there and he was willing to not go to spend time with me.

“Fine, I’ll go," I said.

His face lit up. “Excellent. I’ll have a dress ready for you. It starts at 7pm with dinner at 7:30pm followed by the speeches and the auction. I’ll have you finish work at 4pm so you can come here and get ready," I watched as he talked. He was genuinely excited about it.

“Ok, thank you. What do I say to the others when I leave early?” It would seem odd for me to just up and leave an hour and a half early.

Matthew unbuttoned his suit trousers and started pulling them down. “Say what you want, tell them where you are going in fact," he seemed bewildered as to why I had asked the question.

I stopped for a minute, thinking. I couldn’t tell my colleagues, not yet, not until I knew if this thing between us was serious or not. Especially after what Evelyn said to me in the morning.

I opened my mouth and said what I was thinking, “I don’t want people - especially my colleagues - to think of me as just another one of your 'bimbos'."

He paused for a minute, one let out of his trousers and the other still on. "Bimbo? Why on earth would people think that about you?"

"Because of the pictures online with you and lots of women," I replied quietly. "I don't want to be added to the long list of your conquests,"

"Felicity, where has this come from?" His mouth was set in a grim line.

Shit he's mad!

I looked over at him and sigh, I was suddenly hit with an overwhelming need to lay down and close my eyes, I felt so exhausted. "No one, forget it, it doesn't matter," I lied.

"Felicity?" His voice was stern, It was the sort of tone that sent a shiver down your spine. If he was your boss, you'd know shit was about to hit the fan if he used that voice.

"Ok. Evelyn pulled me into her office today, and she politely advised me that me being with you might be perceived as me wanting to 'get ahead' within the company. You know, like sleeping my way to the top,"

Matthew's expression changed from mad to livid at the speed of light. "She had no right to say that," he said through gritted teeth. "Besides, what we do doesn't concern her or anyone else for that matter,"

He looked deep into my eyes and his expression softened immediately. God, this man had so many emotions that I couldn't possibly keep up. “Who cares what people think? I wouldn't have gotten half as far as I have now if I took notice of what other people said or thought,” He laid down in the bed and pulled me down with him. “Anyway, we know what there is between us,”

Do we? I would like to know what it is! I thought as I snuggled into him.

“Now, go to sleep. It’s late and we have a long day ahead of us tomorrow," he leant down and placed a tender kiss on my lips. I closed my eyes and very quickly drifted off to sleep.

I WOKE UP WITH a jolt. Matthew was sitting over me saying my name over and over again. I could feel my heart pounding in my chest. *I had another nightmare.*

“Felicity?” he said softly but concern was etched all over his beautiful face. I tried to control my breathing and sat up.

“I’m awake," I said.

“You were having a nightmare, are you ok?”

“Yes, I’m fine," My voice is barely a whisper.

“You were talking, too,"

Talking? What the hell did I say? I hadn’t talked in my sleep for a while, well at least that was what I’d been told. Heather used to have to come in my room and shake me awake some nights.

"What was I saying?"

"You were shouting his name,"

Oh shit. I couldn't remember doing it.

"Luke?"

He nodded his head, his mouth was in a grim line.

"I'm sorry," I whispered.

He pulled me into his arms and I think in that moment, I was forgiven. "It's ok,"

"I don't even know what I was dreaming about!"

"Well it can't have been nice, I ran into the room when I heard you shouting. You were thrashing around, the duvet was caught round your legs,"

I could feel Matthew's eyes on me but I couldn't look at him, I was too embarrassed. I was shouting out my dead fiance's name in my sleep for goodness sake!

"Sorry,"

"Stop apologising to me,"

As he held me a thought occurred to me. "You said you ran into the room. Where were you?" He stopped stroking my back momentarily but then carried on.

"I was in the spareroom, I -I struggle to sleep with you here,"

"What do you mean?" I asked, my stomach quivered.

"I'm not used to sleeping in a bed with anyone, and if truth be told, you are the only woman I've had in my bed. For any reason,"

He gave me a knowing look and I knew what he was referring to and strangely the thought pleased me. I was the only woman that he had sex with in *his* bed.

He tried to change the subject, "I also have nightmares, well my therapist calls them 'night terrors',"

"Do you see a therapist for what happened to you?" I asked carefully, not wanting to pry too much as he'd already volunteered more information than I expected.

"Yes," he replied. "I have a shit load of issues, Felicity. It's why I tend not to get involved with dating woman,"

"Then, why me? Why date me?"

"As I've told you before, you are different. I don't know why but with you I really *do* want to try, and I am,"

And in therapy, that moment is called 'a breakthrough'.

"I know you are," I said with warmth in my voice.

"Us. You and I, I want to try. I want to try a relationship with you. I want to give you more,"

I beamed at him and my happiness was reflected back to me from the smile on his perfect face.

"Thank you," And before I realised what I'm doing, I jumped at him so I was laying on top of him, and I kissed him passionately.

WE LAID POST-COITAL for I don't know how long. My head was on his chest and his finger was stroking gently up and down my arm. I glanced over at the alarm clock that read 05:47. I probably should have tried to get some sleep. But to be honest, I was too nervous. I didn't want to fall asleep just in case I had a nightmare - night terror - again. It wasn't good for your new boyfriend to hear your dead fiance's name being called out while you slept.

"Does therapy help you?" I asked, breaking the silence.

I felt his head turn slightly so that he was facing me. "Sometimes,"

"But not all the time?" I questioned.

"It depends on the situation, Felicity. Sometimes even therapy can't help me,"

What did that even mean?

"Did you have therapy? You know, after the accident?"

My eyebrows shot up in surprise from his question.

"No,"

"Maybe you should think about it. It would help you with your night terrors. Or, maybe we could go couples therapy together," He suggested.

The very idea of sitting in a room on a settee revealing the deepest darkest secrets about myself was definitely something I swore I wouldn't do. "As I told you before, I solve my own problems, it's the way I was brought up,"

Matthew sighed and shifted so that I moved off his chest. "Maybe you should try it. After all, I'm trying for you,"

"Touché, Mr. Harper," Damn he could certainly drive a hard bargain! He was right, maybe I should see a therapist, I thought. But then again, it's just not me.

"Can we talk about this another time? You have once again killed me with your body?" I asked, trying to inject some humour into the conversation and change the subject completely.

"Nicely done, Miss. Walker," He kissed the top of my head and turned off the bedside light. "Go to sleep,"

8

IT WAS FRIDAY AND the night of the Fundraiser. I told my colleagues that I had a dentist appointment so would be leaving early. I knew Matthew wanted me to tell them where I was actually going, but I still had reservations. It was still very early days with Matthew and I, and I wanted to be sure before I went shouting it around that I was in a relationship with the chairman of the company.

I kept my head down and worked through lunch so that I felt that I wasn't taking advantage.

Your boyfriend owns the company, woman! The advantage is there to be taken! The words of my subconscious filled my ears and I tried to ignore them.

Since my talk with Evelyn, she'd been overly polite with me. She clearly knew that her name might be brought up during 'pillow talk' with her boss's boss.

I'd also received texts from Amber saying

she would be back in the office from Monday, which made me smile. Being back at work would probably do her some good and help take her mind off it while the police did their investigation.

It approached 3pm and I received an email in my inbox from Matthew.

Felicity,

Your chariot will be outside waiting from 3pm.

See you later, baby.

Kind regards

Matthew Harper
Excited Chairman, MWH Group Holdings.

I couldn't help my childish grin as I read his email. I replied immediately.

Mr. Harper,

Thank you - your attentiveness is gratefully received.

I look forward to seeing you all suited and booted ;)

Kind regards

Felicity Walker
Junior Writer/Editorial assistant
LuxeLife Magazine

It soon turned 3pm and I shut down and said my goodbyes. As expected, Stanley was standing by the 4x4 Audi. He greeted me and opened the door for me and I climbed in.

The drive to Matthew's penthouse didn't take too long considering it was a Friday afternoon in the City. Stanley pulled up outside the building and once I was out of the car, he pulled away and down into the underground car park.

"Miss. Walker?" a gentleman at the security desk called as I made my way into the lobby.

"Yes?"

"Mr. Harper is still at the office but he asked me to let you straight up,"

"Oh, ok, thank you," I said as he punched in the security code for the penthouse. He stepped aside and I got in the lift. I didn't know why I expected Matthew to be there. He owned God knows how many companies and they didn't run by themselves.

I stepped out of the lift once it reached the top floor. The penthouse was quiet, eerily quiet and suddenly I had this overwhelming feeling of missing Matthew.

Get a grip, woman. You'll be seeing him soon. I thought to myself.

I walked over to the unnecessarily large dining

table and saw a note.

Felicity,

Please make yourself at home. I will be with you as soon as I can. I have arranged for the hairdresser and make-up artist to arrive at 4pm.

Can't wait to see you,

M

His note made me grin. But a hair and make-up artist? Was that really necessary? A sudden thought occurred to me - there were going to be photographers there. I don't know why I didn't think of that before. Everyone was going to see me pictured with Matthew.

Evelyn said he was always pictured with women at those sort of events. It didn't click that I would be photographed! I heard the double doors open and a man and a lady step in.

"Oh, hi," The man said as he waved. "You must be Felicity?"

I nodded and he walked over and shook my hand. He was mid-thirties and had kind eyes. I liked him instantly.

His colleague also shook my hand. I would have said that she was younger than him but older than me. "I'm Shona, I'll be doing your make-up," she said in her Essex accent.

I greeted them both and they sat me down and began their magic.

IT WAS JUST AFTER five by the time they had finished with me, and I hardly recognised the woman that was looking back at me in the mirror. Just then - right on cue - Matthew walked in.

"Wow," he said as our eyes locked in the reflection of the mirror. He walked over to me and I turned to face him.

"You look incredible. You are breathtakingly beautiful," He lifted his hand up to my face and one of his long fingers toyed with a strand of my hair.

Martyn, the hairstylist, had put my long, naturally wavy hair into a low ponytail and backcombed my hair at the roots to create volume. He had also cut in a long parted fringe to apparently 'frame my face'. I have to say, he did a good job, and Matthew seemed to think so.

Shona had applied a plum coloured lipstick to my lips and opted for a subtle smokey eye look. Both of which complimented my natural auburn hair and fair complexion.

I was still, however, yet to see the dress that Matthew had chosen for me but, I was assured by both Martyn and Shona that the hair and make-up would go perfectly.

Matthew took me by the hand and led me to his bedroom and into an adjacent dressing room that I never knew existed. There, hanging up, was possibly *the most* beautifully perfect dress I had ever seen. It was a bardot pleated floor length dress in emerald green with a plunging neckline. It was simply gorgeous. Next to it, I spied a pair of black, open toed heels.

"Thank you," I said as I ran my fingers over the material of the dress. It was silk and felt delicate to the touch.

I felt Matthew walk up closer behind me. He leant down slightly and kissed the side of my neck. "You are most welcome, baby,"

He spun me around so that I was now facing him. He gazed at me and his eyes were heated and full of lust. I knew that look, I knew it very well indeed. He slowly and slyly moved his hands down to my waist and loosened the tie of my dressing gown. The dressing gown parted, exposing my naked body.

His eyes traced every contour of my body. "You are fucking perfection,"

I felt my cheeks heat with pure desire. "Stop looking at me like that, I've just had my hair and make-up done,

"Am I that readable, Miss. Walker?" A salacious grin creeped across his face.

"You aren't usually, it's only when you want sex that I can read you,"

He let out a slight chuckle and tore his eyes

away from me for a second. “Here,” he slid open the mirrored wardrobe door and bent down. He picked up a black box tied with a light pink bow and handed it to me, “I got these for you,"

I stared down at the box and carefully removed the lid. The inside of the box was padded out with pink tissue paper. I unwrapped the tissue paper and inside was a bra and a thong. A beaded thong. I removed the bra from the box and then held up the thong as if it had already been worn.

“It’s called a pearl thong," he said nonchalantly.

“I do hope you aren’t expecting me to wear this,” I examined it, still holding it at arm's length.

“Yes, you are. Trust me, it's for your pleasure. And mine,”“How on earth is this for my pleasure? It looks grossly uncomfortable!”

Matthew smiled and shook his head. “You have to trust me,”

I was still not convinced. How was a pair of thongs, made scarcely from lace with the majority of it being beaded pearls, ever going to be comfortable, or pleasurable!

I looked from the thong to Matthew and then back to the thong again and sighed. “Fine,”

Matthew shot me one of his show stopping smiles and walked out of the dressing room, leaving me with the thong.

I got dressed into the underwear and dress and

I stood looking at myself in the mirror of the wardrobe doors. I didn't look like Felicity Walker at all. I looked like I should have been on a red carpet. My mum would have been proud. She was always secretly a bit disappointed that I wasn't as 'girly' as she would have liked me to be. I wore make-up and the occasional dress but I didn't prune myself to an inch of my life like her and other women did. Smiling at the thought of my mum's face, I took a selfie and sent it to her along with a message.

Do you like my dress?
I'm off to a fundraiser.
I'll tell you more this weekend . . .
Love you mama,
Fliss xxx

She wasn't aware that I was dating an extremely wealthy man, or that I was dating anyone at all, so I was sure she would have lots of questions about where I was or who I was with. I popped my phone into my black suede clutch bag and made my way out of the room to find Matthew.

As I walked down the hall, I discovered what Matthew was talking about, the underwear *was* for my pleasure. As I walked, the pearls glided across my intimate area. Making me feel stimulated and so ready.

I found Matthew in the living area. The sight of him made me stop in my tracks. He was looking out the window with a tumbler of what looked like whisky while a singer crooned softly over the surround sound speakers.

Matthew must have felt me staring at him as he turned around. He was dressed in a black tuxedo, matching trousers and a crisp white shirt with a silk satin bow tie.

Wow. He looked so yummy.

Matthew smiled as I entered the room. He looked at me expectantly, obviously knowing that I had felt the full effect of the thong.

“Hi," I said softly, my shy smile meeting his.

“Hi,” he said. “I have no words right now. I am speechless looking at you in that dress,” His eyes were alight with lust as he made his way over to me.

“You look pretty damn fine yourself, Mr. Harper”

My God, he did!

“It's all smoke and mirrors, baby,” he replied, his voice husky.

"Trust me, it's not,” My attention turned to the song that was playing. “Who is this?” I asked, looking up at the speaker in the corner of the room.

“Oh, Felicity, you need educating on the world's greatest singers” He said smiling and shaking his head at me in disbelief. “This is Nat King Cole, *Unforgettable*,”

"It's nice," I admitted.

Matthew traced his knuckles down my cheek, and I felt it all the way down *there*. The ever so familiar purr of pleasure began to erupt inside me.

"Dance with me," he asked, and I knew it was not a question, but a request.

He held out his hand for me. I was completely tranced by his beauty, he was truly mesmerising, even more so in the tux. I placed my hand in his and his smile widened, he pulled me into his embrace and he started to sway to the music.

I put my right hand on his shoulder and grinned up at him, as he looked down at me he looked so carefree, and so young. We glided round the living area and all the way over to the kitchen, twirling and spinning me in time to the music. All the while the pearl thong worked overtime. I couldn't help but giggle to try and hide my arousal. He smiled warmly at me as the song came to an end.

"I've said it before, but I'll say it again, I love it when you laugh," We were still in hold, unable to take our hands off each other. "Come, we have a fundraiser to get to. But, I don't want to be there too long, I want to peel you out of that dress later,"

He grabbed my hand, and picked up a green shawl that matched my dress from one of the barstools. He led me through the double doors and to the lift. Matthew pressed the ground floor button and as the lift descended, he draped the shawl over my shoulders and I felt his fingers brush over my skin. I was so turned on, I could have combusted.

The lift door opened and Matthew took me by the hand once again and led me through the lobby. I snuck a peek up at him and he had his eyes fixed firmly on the door in front of us. I did however see a hint of a smile brush his lips. He was enjoying a private joke. A private joke that I happened to be part of.

"Something amusing you, Mr. Harper?" I asked, sweetly.

"Not at all, Miss. Walker. How are you feeling?"

"Fine, thank you,"

"Are you sure?"

I nodded my head as casually as possible under his intense gaze. His eyes danced with amusement as he grinned and shook his head.

"Ok. Two can play that game, Miss. Walker,"

AS WE SAT IN the back of the Audi, Matthew took my hand and brought it up to his lips and placed a soft, chaste kiss. I tried not to squirm as I felt the sensation building in my groin. I stifled a groan as Stanley was sitting in the front. Matthew knew exactly what he was doing and he smiled at me, his eyes gleaming wickedly.

"Try to relax," he whispered as he leant closer into me.

“Easier said than done,” I tried to focus on the road ahead.

“If it is too much for you to handle, let me know and I will gladly remove them from you. with my teeth," he purred.

Oh. My. God.

I swallowed. “No, I’m fine," I closed my eyes and shook the image of Matthew tearing them off me.

When I opened my eyes again, Matthew was watching me closely. As I looked at him, I noticed his beautiful, chiselled mouth and strong jaw. He looked so handsome, and so sophisticated. He simply took my breath away.

“So, what happens at this event?” I tried to focus my mind away from the delectable feeling deep down inside of me.

“As I said, there will be dinner, speeches, an auction where hopefully people will flash their cash around and then followed by dancing," He smiled widened as he spoke.

“Will you be making your tenth speech?”

He nodded. “Yes, I will be,"

And for the first time, I started to feel a little excited about the event. I couldn't wait to see him up there.

As we pulled up closer towards the venue, I saw a line of taxis waiting to drop people off.

Matthew took me by the hand again. “Ready?” he asked as we edged closer to the drop off zone.

I nodded at him. *Here we go.* I thought as I felt

the butterflies flapping around my stomach.

"You look sensational, Felicity. All eyes will be on you once we get in there but, remember you are mine," He kissed my hand and got out of the car.

Matthew rounded the car and opened the door for me. He offered me his hand to help me out. Taking it, I gathered my dress and slowly swung my legs out of the car and placed my feet on the ground.

A dark red carpet started at the bottom of the limestone steps and ran up into the magnificent building's entrance hall. As we made our way up the steps, Matthew placed a protective arm around my waist and I think it was in an attempt to reassure me.

My eyes were fixed to the ground, I was trying my best not to trip and make a fool of myself. Once we made it up to the doors of the entrance hall, photographers gathered the guests to pose for pictures.

"Mr. Harper, Mr. Harper!" one of the photographers called while waving him over. Matthew nodded at the photographer and we walked over to him.

"Is this your date?" he said, shouting over the buzz of excitement that surrounded us.

"Yes, it's the magnificent Felicity Walker,"

My face instantly reddened with embarrassment. I was not used to the attention. Matthew then pulled me closer to him and the next thing I knew was that we were posing for a photo.

"Where will that photo be? Will it be online?" I asked as we stepped into the entrance hall.

"It will be, if I agree for them to release it. Why? Don't you want it to be?"

How was I going to explain to this man that my crazy, junkie birth mother might see it and come crawling out of the woodwork again, and not to mention the fact that there would be no denying our 'courting' then.

"I'm just not sure I want the world to know about us just yet."

"Why? Are you embarrassed to be seen with me?" He asked, concern etched over his handsome face.

"Oh, God no! Definitely not!" I shook my head vigorously, "it's just that we are still trying to get to know each other, we don't want or *need* any added pressure,"

Matthew remained silent for a long minute before finally saying something, "ok, I'll tell them not to release the photo to the press. But, we will be able to purchase a copy later as a souvenir. "

"Well, I will definitely be buying one of those," I smiled as I stepped up on tiptoes and placed a kiss on his cheek.

We waited in a line that moved slowly past the cloakroom, Matthew exchanged pleasantries with the couple that were in front of us and when we finally reached the end of the line, waiters held silver trays full of glasses filled with champagne. Matthew handed me one and I tentatively took a sip. I wasn't usually a fan of champagne but that one did taste nice.

It's probably because it's so expensive!

Once we made our way past the waiters, we walked through two giant open doors and into a beautiful room. The room was huge and spanned as far as the eye could see. The ceiling was amazing, it had beautifully carved wooden mouldings that had been intricately painted. I stopped and took in the huge expanse of the room while MWH Group's management, dressed in their finery, walked past me.

As we made our way further into the room, the noise of the guest's voices got louder. I noticed a stage at the end of the room but couldn't see any sign of a band or DJ yet. I figured it must be for later. Gripping my hand tighter, Matthew led me over towards the bar area where the other guests were congregating.

"Matthew!"

We both turned and a woman appeared from out of the crowd.

"Sophia," Matthew greeted her cooly as he briskly placed a kiss on her cheek. "Sophia, this is my girlfriend, Felicity Walker, Felicity, this is my cousin, Sophia Atwood,"

Girlfriend! He'd never called me that before.

"Felicity, Darling," she air-kissed me on each cheek. "You look divine!"

I would have guessed that Sophia was around Matthew's age, maybe thirty. She had the same dark chocolate brown hair that Matthew had and was as equally well spoken as him. She was dressed in an ink blue, full-length chiffon gown. She looked stunning. And in that moment, I had never felt so grateful to be dressed to the nines, courtesy of Matthew, *my boyfriend.*

"You must come and meet my parents later. They won't believe me when I tell them that Matthew *finally* has a girlfriend!"

I shot a quick look at Matthew, who drilled his eyes into Sophia. He was clearly not amused. Realising she had annoyed her cousin, she spotted another guest and excused herself rather swiftly.

"So you do have family!" I said sarcastically.

Matthew rolled his eyes at me and placed his hand at the small of my back in an attempt to usher me away from the building crowd. "Yes, her mother and my mother were twins,"

Were?

"That's the first time you've called me your girlfriend," I said as I smiled up at him as we tried to navigate our way through the crowds.

"I've referred to you as that before, just not to your face." he said nonchalantly.

"Oh, really. Are you saying that we are now exclusive?"

"If you want to put a label on it, then yes, we are. You and your body belong to me and only me," he leant down and whispered the words in my ear, sending a delicious surge down to my groin. "And I intend to take full advantage of it tonight."

I didn't know if it was him, the champagne or the thong, but I was just about ready to leave the party and take him up on the offer right then.

I spent the next fifteen minutes being introduced to Matthew's colleagues and associates who work at MWH Group Holdings HQ. I had yet to see any of the managers from LuxeLife. As Matthew talked to the guests, he kept me close to his side, not letting me out of his sight. To which I was grateful for.

The waiters glided through the growing crowd of guests and continued to replenish our glasses. As I popped my empty champagne flute onto the silver tray and collected a new glass, I realised that I'd drunk far too much already. I was beginning to feel light-headed.

"How are you feeling?" Matthew whispered in my ear.

I knew he was referring to the lace thong that I was donning underneath my dress. "I'm ok," I replied. I was trying not to think about it too much, otherwise I think I might have exploded.

"Albert, this is Felicity," The lady we were talking to said to a balding gentlemen as he passed.

Albert shook my hand. "Nice to meet you, Felicity," He looked to Matthew and then back to me. “You must be his date?” He looked back to Matthew before I got a chance to say anything, “I haven't seen this one before!” he chuckled.

My scalp prickled.

What does Matthew do, rent dates for these sorts of things?! My mind raced.

Matthew inhaled, clearly feeling irritated. “No, she's my *girlfriend*, Albert,"

“Oh, you finally managed to get one to stay, eh!”

“You’d be wise to stop talking, Albert,” Mathew said firmly through gritted teeth.

The lady who introduced Albert to me looked at me and offered me an apologetic smile.

“Albert, there's someone we need to talk to over here," She pulled him away and disappeared into the crowd.

“Well, he was an arse," I murmured.

“Indeed," Matthew narrowed his eyes in the direction they walked over too. “He’s just got himself fired too,"

I whipped my head up at him “Wow, I wouldn't want to be on the wrong side of you!”

“No, you wouldn’t” he winked.

Ladies and gentlemen!” The master of ceremonies said over the speakers. “Please make your way to the dining room, dinner will be served shortly,"

We walked into yet another stunning room where the tables were set up for dinner. There were at least twenty tables if not more and each table must have been able to seat about ten easily. The tables were dressed in white linen table cloths, and in the centre were tall clear vases with lilies and other foliage in.

Matthew looked at the seating plan and led me over to a table, which happened to be at the front by yet another stage where a lectern stood.

Ah, this must be where the speeches happen.

As we were walking to our table, Evelyn appeared and I hardly recognised her in her dress. “Felicity!”

“Oh, hi, Evelyn," I said, smiling warmly at her, it was nice to see at least one face I knew.

“Mr. Harper," she said, greeting Matthew coolly.

“Evelyn," Matthew nodded back at her.

Evelyn turned her attention back to me, “I haven’t seen you all evening! Ron, Phil and Krishna are all here,"

“Sorry, I’ve been with Matthew - Mr. Harper,"

She looked up at Matthew again with a hint of a frown. “Well, come and say hello later, we are on table twenty three,"

“Sure,” I smiled, feeling uncomfortable with the look she gave Matthew.

The MC asked everyone to take their seats and Evelyn made her way to her table. Matthew held out my chair and I sat down. I looked over to where my colleagues were and suddenly I felt out of place and that I should have been over there with them.

Matthew greeted everyone who was already at our table and introduced me. On our table was Sophia, her parents - Harriet and John who were yet to take a seat, Gwen - who was Matthew’s right hand woman and a few more of Matthew’s senior staff. There was however another seat empty. I was unable to read the place card as the empty seat was directly in front of me. Out of the corner of my eye, I caught sight of an older couple approaching the table.

“Harriet, John. This is Felicity," Matthew said as he got up to greet them.

I was struck by how much Harriet looked like Matthew. You could definitely see the family resemblance. Like her daughter and nephew, she had dark chocolate brown hair and the same olive skin that Matthew had. But, she and her daughter had dark brown eyes that almost match their hair colour, Matthew had obviously inherited his piercing blues from another family member.

“Oh, how very nice to meet you dear," Harriet beamed as she shook my hand. We exchanged pleasantries and took our seats.

There was a sudden boom over the microphone and a gentleman appeared by the lectern, causing the sound of voices to die down.

“Welcome, ladies and gentleman, to our annual charity fundraiser. I hope that you enjoy what we have in store for you tonight and that you'll put your hands deep into your pockets despite the current economic climate and support the fantastic work of this year's chosen charity - Lifeline. It is a charity for victims of child abuse and neglect. It also happens to be one of the charities that is close to Mr. Harper's heart,"

I glanced up at Matthew who sat looking impassively at the stage.

Oh my poor, poor Matthew. My heart swelled in my chest at the thought of someone hurting him.

“So, without further ado, let's eat, donate and be merry!”

The room suddenly filled with an excitable applause, then the babble in the room started again. The waiters started to serve us our starters. They placed the plates in front of us in complete synchronisation. The starter was smoked salmon with prawns, and what looks like horseradish cream and a lime vinaigrette. It smelt delicious!

“Hungry?" Matthew asked so only I could hear. He was not referring to the food but I decided to plead ignorance.

“Very," I smiled sweetly, meeting his heated gaze and playing along with our inside joke. I heard a low groan come from his throat as he picked up his knife and fork.

John, Matthew’s Uncle, engaged me in conversation immediately. He was a lovely man and so easy to talk to. As we talked, Matthew placed his hand on my thigh trying to put me at ease and I relaxed a little. We all finished our starters and the waiters appeared again and swiftly removed our plates and cutlery.

Matthew hastily stood and did up the button on his tux. I watched as his face lit up in a way I'd not seen before. I turned to see what or who was the cause of it.

It was her.

"Lydia!" Matthew called. He was clearly very pleased to see her.

Lydia, the 'commercial architect' greeted Matthew and kissed him on both cheeks. I surveyed the rest of the table, gauging their reactions. They all looked uneasy, awkward almost. And I knew for a fact that they were more than 'old friends.'

"Lydia, this is Felicity Walker. Felicity, this is Lydia Rodrigo,"

"Hello, Felicity. It's a pleasure to meet you, I've heard so much about you, I feel like I already know you," She laughed, throwing her head back so her perfect blonde hair fell perfectly down her back. I immediately hated her. Not only was Miss. Blonde-hair-long-legs, breathtakingly beautiful, but she had Matthew hanging off her every word and laughing along with her. It was sickening.

"Oh, no, the pleasure is all mine I'm sure," I insisted, shaking her perfectly manicured hand.

She was wearing a cream cowl neck dress

which happened to be backless and had a long split up the side. *Tart.* She might as well have been naked! I smiled sweetly at her as I thought my catty thoughts.

The conversation at the table ebbed and flowed while we ate our dinner. Lydia, being as impossibly beautiful as she was, was of course at the centre of attention with all the men. I watched as Matthew, Gwen and a few other of their colleagues talked about the various projects the company was undertaking. I noticed that as Matthew listened to the others, his eyes kept drawing towards the direction of Miss. Architect.

Right, this needs to be stopped. I thought as my brow furrowed.

Slowly, I reached my hand down under the table and taking full advantage, I slowly caressed him, letting my fingers explore his thigh. Reminding him that I was there. He momentarily paused for a second mid sentence, but composed himself and carried on as I made my way up to his groin area.

Matthew's hand swifty reached below the table and stopped me in my tracks. He looked at me out of the corner of his eye, his stern glare was a silent warning to stop.

Shit. he's mad. I instantly regretted doing it.

He moved my hand back onto my lap and then draped his arm around my shoulders, and kissed my temple. I was sure it was an attempt to soften the blow of his rejection. His thumb then rhythmically stroked my back, sending tingles down my spine.

Throughout dinner, a steady stream of men in dinner jackets came up to our table, keen to speak to Matthew, they all shook his hand and started conversation.

By the time we'd finished dessert, it was 8:30pm and I was extremely uncomfortable. Not just from the food but also from the thong. It had really turned me on.

I have to take the thong off, I thought to myself as I grabbed my clutch bag and started to get up.

"If you'll excuse me," I said to Matthew.

He looked at me quizzically. "Do you need the ladies room?"

I nodded.

"Do you know where you are going?" he asked.

I shook my head. Unable to speak due to the surge of pleasure that was building with every move I made.

Matthew rose to his feet, putting his napkin that was on his lap, over his chair. "I'll show you where they are,"

"Matthew, darling, I'll show her, I need to use the ladies myself,"

I inwardly rolled my eyes at the sound of Lydia's overly sweet voice.

"No, no. It's fine. I can find them," I insisted.

Please don't come with me.

"Well, I need to go too so it would be silly if I don't come with you,"

Bollocks.

Matthew took his seat again and Lydia walked with me to the toilets. As we walked through past the other tables, Lydia was merrily chatting away as if butter wouldn't melt. We finally reached the ladies and I darted into one of the cubicles. I stepped out of the thong and let out a sigh of relief. As I placed the thong in my clutch, I realised just how aroused I was.

I flushed the chain and headed to the sink. Lydia appeared from the cubicle next to the one I was in.

"You know, you won't ever have his full heart,"

I frowned and looked at her reflection in the next mirror. "Excuse me?"

"You think you are finally getting somewhere with him. He starts to open up to you and you are on the same page. And 'bam' the book suddenly slams shut again." Lydia scanned her eyes over my face, "And besides, you're not even his usual type,"

What is she talking about?

"I'm sorry but I have no idea what you are referring to,"

She smiled at me after she turned the tap off. "Of course you don't. You are too infatuated with him to see," She took a paper towel from the basket next to the sinks and dried her hands. "Trust me, I know. I was you, once,"

She is really pissing me off now.

I turned to face her, "look, if you have

something to say, just bloody well say it,"

"I'm only trying to warn you. I don't want you to end up like me. I will never be off his hook. I will never be free of him. I physically can't, he still owns a piece of my heart. Do you think I want to be here, with you?"

"You're crazy. You're nothing more than a pathetic bunny boiler who is jealous that the man she still loves has moved on," I shook my head at her and turned swiftly on my heels and headed back to the table, but not before I heard her shout something like 'apparently I would see'.

I passed the table where my LuxeLife colleagues were and ignored their calls for me to come over. I was too pissed off.

"There you are," Matthew said as I took my seat. He frowned when he saw my expression. "What's wrong?"

"Oh nothing, just Lydia, sticking her nose in where it doesn't belong,"

He stiffened. "Why, what did she say?"

"Oh, so there's something to be said?"

"No,"

I scowled at him, but he wasn't going to volunteer anymore information "We'll discuss this later. I don't want to let her ruin my evening anymore than she has done already."

He regarded me carefully.

I was feeling frustrated - irritable even. Matthew took my hand and gave it a squeeze but

I refused to make any effort to squeeze it back. I didn't even want him to touch me. I was that angry.

Thankfully, the MC stepped up to the lectern again. "Right, ladies and gents. It is finally that time!" the buzz of the room multiplied. "Please can one member of the table open the brown envelopes that are currently being handed out by our fabulous staff.

Matthew nominated Gwen to do the honours with the envelope that had just been handed out to our table.

"Inside, you will find the list of the things that are up for auction. And paddles that I hope you will be raising a lot when you are making bids."

Gwen distributed the paddles around the table along with the list of the auction prizes.

Jesus, there are some very expensive prizes!

As I scanned through the list, I spotted that there was a three night stay in an apartment overlooking Central Park in New York with travel included using the private jet owned by MWH Group Holdings.

I blinked up at Matthew.

"What?" he asked.

"You own a private jet?"

"Yes, the company does," he replied, all matter-of-factly. "The apartment is mine too,"

I gaped at him. That man was seriously rich. Mega rich.

"Do you own property anywhere else?" I asked.

He nodded and brought his index finger up to his lips, effectively telling me to be quiet. The auction was underway, and I had to keep my voice down. I didn't want to make a bid without realising!

Suddenly, the whole room erupted with applause and people whistling with their fingers. It seemed one of the prizes had gone for five hundred pounds.

"I'll tell you where the rest of them are. We can go to one someday,"

Oh, he wanted to take me away. What happened to the man who claimed he didn't do romance.

The bidding continued for what seemed like forever. I kept quiet, only applauding when necessary, as each prize was sold for a staggering amount of money. Finally, we reached the last prize, Matthew's New York apartment and jet. Bidding was in full swing when a high bid came out of nowhere.

"Going once, going twice," The MC called. "Sold! To the smartly dressed gentleman at the back."

We all turned in unison to the impeccably dressed man who had just paid sixteen thousand pounds for a trip to the Big Apple. *Wow.* How did people have so much money?! I came from a well-off family but I doubt my parents would have paid that much!

Matthew lifted his hand up to his head and

saluted him.

"Who is that?" I asked.

"You can meet him later," Matthew said over the applause, clearly not giving anything away.

"Well that concludes the auction for this year. After all that excitement, I will hand you over to the man who makes all this possible, Mr. Matthew William Harper."

I wasn't really aware of what was happening until Matthew stood up to a round of applause and took to the stage. I watched him as he confidently walked to the lectern, I couldn't help but admire his grace and how attractive it was. I knew for a fact that every woman apart from his cousin and Harriet were doing the same. Every step he took commanded attention and respect, you couldn't help but look at him

He reached the lectern and looked straight at me. He took a deep breath before looking down at his piece of paper he took out of his breast pocket. "In the Untied Kingdom," he began, "it is estimated that one in five adults aged eighteen to seventy four years of age have experience at least one form of child abuse,"

My stomach dropped at the statistics, and from the passion that was so clear in his voice. It was a topic that was so close to home for him. It was still so raw and clearly still affected him today, it was the reason I couldn't touch him.

"Take a look around you. Someone at your table is either a survivor or knows someone who is. Abuse comes in many forms, whether it is emotional, physical, sexual or witnessing domestic abuse from a young age. This simply isn't on," Matthew's voice was strong but I could tell that it was hard for him. But that's what made it so moving, you could sense how passionate he was. I glanced over my shoulder and everyone else was just as fixated on him as I was.

When he had finished, I leapt up from my chair and applauded him, taking both him and myself by surprise. The others in the room joined me in the standing ovation. I could hear the buzz of conversations from the tables around me, people quietly voicing compliments that were well and truly deserved. Sophia and her parents beamed with joy as Matthew made his way down the steps and towards the table. His eyes never left mine.

Harriet intercepted him as he walked over me. "Oh, darling boy, that was fantastic. Your Mother would be so proud," she pulled him into a tight and clearly awkward embrace. After she released him, he offered her a warm smile and walked over to me.

"That was a wonderful speech, Matthew!" I said as I beamed up at him. My earlier anger, a mer memory.

Matthew's eyes were alight with passion, and from nowhere both of his hands were on the side of my face and he kissed me, he kissed me with everything he had. He kissed me like it was the last time he would ever kiss me.

"Get a room!" Sophia called.

Matthew reluctantly released me and stared deep into my eyes. I was left breathless. I didn't think we were aware of everyone else in the room. It was like we were the only two people in the world at that moment.

"I can't wait to take you home." he breathed in my ear.

Suddenly, Matthew received a tap on the shoulder from the gentleman who made the extortionate bid for the apartment. "Harper,"

"Roberts," Matthew greeted.

As I stood there watching the two men talk, I noticed Lydia got up from her seat and watched as she skulked away from the table. She exited the dining room, presumably heading for the exit.

Matthew turned to me. "Edwin, this is Felicity."

"Ah, *the* Felicity. Nice to meet you." he shook my hand. "I've heard so much about you, I feel like I already know you." Matthew had obviously spoken about me.

"Felicity, this is Dr. Edwin Roberts,"

"Hello," I greeted him.

"He's my therapist,"

I looked from Matthew to Dr. Roberts and then back to Matthew again.

Oh, so this is the shrink he spoke about.

"Will you excuse me for a moment?" Matthew said as put his hands on my shoulders and gave them a reassuring squeeze. He then turned and headed over to Sophia.

As Dr. Roberts talked, I watched over his shoulder as Matthew talked to Sophia. They looked like they were having a heated discussion. Matthew then looked over to the direction of the exit, clearly he was more concerned about where his beloved Lydia had gone. After a beat, he briskly stormed out of the dining room, presumably after her. The master of ceremonies announced that we were all to make our way into the other room as the band was about to begin playing.

"Would you like to accompany me to the dance floor, Felicity?" Dr. Roberts held out his arm for me to take hold.

As Matthew wasn't coming back anytime soon, I thought I might as well have some fun. "Yes, please,"

The band began to play a song, and Dr. Roberts pulled me into his arms. He was much younger than I imagined him to be. He was tall, but not as tall as Matthew, I would have said he was about five foot eleven inches.

"So, are you enjoying yourself?" he asked.

"Well, I was,"

"Was? Well I hope it's not me that has caused that?" He replied and gave me a brief, warm smile.

"Oh, no, it isn't you." I felt a frown creep across my face as I looked over at the door where we'd just come from, hoping that Matthew would reappear. I shook my head and tried to focus on dancing.

Dr. Roberts studied me for a minute, I think he was trying to read me. "What is it?"

My eyebrows shot up in surprise at his question. "Oh nothing and anyway, shouldn't you be able to work that out?" I asked.

He chuckled. "I may be a therapist, but I'm no mind reader. Believe me, it would make my job a lot easier if I were."

I giggled at his reply. "I'm sure it would! Especially when dealing with Matthew."

"He certainly is an interesting young man. He has achieved so much in his short life." The Doctor's eyes were full of admiration as he spoke about his patient.

It was then I realised that he wasn't going to give anything away. I suppose he was doing his job and keeping his word about confidentiality.

The music finished and Dr. Roberts thanked me for the dance. "It was a pleasure meeting you, Felicity,"

"You too, Dr. Roberts,"

I walked back into the dining room to get my clutch bag and check my phone. Matthew was still nowhere to be seen.

"Felicity!" Sophia said as she waved at me.

"Hey, where's Matthew?" I asked.

Her smiley face suddenly turned serious. “Erm, he had to pop out for a bit,”

“You mean he went after Lydia,”

She remained silent and my fears were confirmed. *Of course he has.*

“What is the deal with those two? Like, were they together?”

Sophia put down her glass, and shifted uncomfortably in her seat from my questions.

“Were they serious?” I asked.

“She was, he wasn’t. She was in it more than he was,”

“Oh, really?”

“Don’t worry, he is totally different with you,”

That still didn't reassure me much as I thought it would have. He didn’t do relationships, full stop. That's what he said. *He lied.*

My stomach was churning. I needed more answers. “How long were they together?”

“It doesn't matter, it’s over, Felicity. It’s ancient history.” Her voice was deadly serious. I think she was warning me not to ask or say anything else, whatever it was, it was clearly something I didn’t want to know.

“Well it's obviously not history, they’ve both been hanging off each other’s every word!”

I looked down at the ground and closed my eyes and sighed. “Please, Sophia, I need to know. For my own sanity,” I begged.

She shook her head and I already knew that I didn't want to hear the answer.

"They were together for about a year-," She abruptly stopped herself.

"And. . .?"

"And they were engaged," she said as if the words pained her.

My heart stopped beating. All the air left my lungs. No, how could he have been. He didn't do relationships. He told me that. He told me himself. I had to fight hard just to get him to agree to date me.

"I'm not that type of man. I don't do all of that romance shit." his words rang in my ears.

I couldn't believe this was happening. I needed to get out of there. How could I be with a man who kept such a big secret from me, especially when I had told him about Luke? I know we still had so much to share with each other but an ex-fiancee? That was definitely something that I deserved to know.

"Felicity?" Sophia said, "Are you ok? You look grey,"

I turned to look at her, my mouth wide open in shock. I shook my head and got up from the table.

"Felicity? Shit, wait!" Sophia got up and followed me out of the dining room.

I walked away and didn't look back. I kept on walking and as I did, I passed Matthew who was heading back into the entrance hall.

"Baby?" he said as I bolted past him, nearly sending him over as I did.

I heard Sophia close behind me.

"What the hell did you do?" Matthew shouted at her.

I didn't hear her response as I pushed through the doors and hailed a cab. I needed to get away. *Away from him.*

9

I LET THE TEARS flow down my cheeks as the cab pulled away. I was free. I had escaped. I sobbed in the back of the cab the whole journey back to my flat. I wasn’t sure what I am more hurt from, I didn't know if it was Matthew running after Lydia, Lydia ambushing me in the ladies or Sophia telling me the man who portrayed himself as cold and non committal was in fact engaged once before. I just knew that I felt so messed around by him.

I got my keys out of my clutch bag and with shaky hands, unlocked the door. It was past 10pm and Heather was watching a film with Isaac. She turned around when I entered the living area, her face dropped the moment she saw me.

“Oh my God, what’s happened?” she asked, immediately getting up.

I took one look at her kind face and that was it, the tears really began to flow and they didn't stop.

"Oh, Fliss." she took me in her arms.

"I'll go, babe," Isaac said as he got up and grabbed his shoes. "I'll call you tomorrow,"

Heather nodded and I heard the door close. I felt my phone continually vibrate in my clutch bag, just like it had been on the cad ride home.

"Right, come and sit down,"

Heather led me over to the settee her and Isaac were just lounging on. "What happened? What did that bastard do?" she asked. She heard my phone vibrate again and without hesitation, she opened my clutch bag and got it out.

"Fuck off, you prick," she hung up and switched it off. "There, that's one problem dealt with. So, what happened?" she asked again.

I told her the story from the start, from how he said he couldn't commit to a relationship, seeing Lydia with him at lunchtime and then about what happened tonight.

"Don't ever see or speak to him again, Felicity. You deserve better, he's not worth it,"

Oh how I wish that were true! In the world of Heather Ross, everything was easy. If anyone screwed her over, she moved onto the next one. She was very black and white.

"But," I paused, stopping myself from saying what I wanted to say out loud. "I think I'm falling for him, Heather,"

Heather inhaled sharply. "Well, he's not good enough for you,"

Her words made me weep more.

"Oh, honey. Please stop. You are so beautiful and he's an idiot, you deserve someone who will worship the ground you walk on and never make you doubt him - or yourself,"

She was right. I shouldn't have felt like that. I'd already been through that feeling of doubt once before, but somehow, it now felt much worse. "I know. I just hate that he is so closed off to the idea of commitment with me but, turns out he was all for it with her."

Heather pulled me into a bear hug and slowly rubbed my back in an effort to try and soothe me. "Well, I'm not trying to defend the bastard, but maybe she's the reason he is so closed off? Maybe she put him off. You don't know what happened between them,"

I thought about what she'd said for a moment, maybe she was right. Sophia did say that Lydia was in it more than he was. And that it was different with me. But what did she mean by that? And why did they call off the engagement? There were so many questions that I wanted answers to but I couldn't bring myself to ask them.

If I were to see him again, I would cave and go back to him. I'd already done what I swore I wouldn't do again - I'd got hurt. And I wasn't sure how much more my heart could withstand.

I pulled away from Heather and rubbed my nose with the back of my hand. "I don't know, I don't know what to think anymore. All I know is that surely it shouldn't be this hard so early on. It was hard before it even bloody started!"

Heather offered me an apologetic smile. "No, I don't think it should be this hard." She moved a loose tendril from my newly cut fringe and tucked it behind my ear. "Look at you and Luke, I remember you saying to me all those years ago when he'd just started at our school, 'Heather, when I'm with him, it's so easy, it's like I've known him my whole life.' Remember saying that? It was when we got drunk off that cheap vodka when my parents were out."

I nodded and smiled fondly at the memory. I did say that, I remembered it like it was yesterday. But, did that really mean anything? Luke still cheated on me after all. If we were really soulmates, would he have done that?

I glanced over at the clock on the oven and realised it had past 10:30pm. I was exhausted and in need of a good night's rest. I got up and grabbed my clutch, purposely leaving my phone on the coffee table where Heather had put it.

"I'm going to get some sleep now,"

"Ok, sleep well. Fancy a girls day tomorrow?"

"Yeah, sounds nice." I said as I headed into my bedroom.

✻ ✻ ✻

"You have to choose, Fliss. Me, or him?"

I frown at the ridiculous question. Why was he asking me this? And how can he be? He is dead. How can he be here with me now?

"Luke, you aren't real, you are a figure of my imagination. A dream. I am asleep. I am asleep on an operating table while surgeons operate on my brain,"

"Oh but I'm not your imagination. I'm very much here with you. Yes, I am dead. And you are very close,"

"Please stop,"

"No, you need to hear this. I am here for you. I am here to look after you,"

"Oh, because you did such a good job in life" I say as I roll my eyes. I still couldn't understand what was happening.

"Felicity, just choose,"

"No, I can't,"

Luke let out a sigh in frustration, he ran his hand through his hair in the way he did when we argued.

"What even happened to me?"

"You don't remember?"

I shake my head. My mind is so foggy.

"You were in a car accident. Felicity, make a choice, me or him?"

"Please, don't make me do this,"

I THINK MATTHEW GOT the message to leave

me alone as he made no effort to contact me over the weekend whatsoever. The silence was excruciating and I didn't know why I was so disappointed. But, at least I could get on with my life and start to move on and get over him. I just hoped I wouldn't see him at work.

Monday morning arrived and I dragged myself out of bed after a weekend of drinking and generally feeling sorry for myself. I hadn't hardly spoken to anyone. Heather and Ethan had tried their hardest to cheer me up but it was a lost cause. I never even answered the phone when my mum called. I just wasn't in the mood for people.

I was feeling irritable and tired and the weather was reflecting my mood, dark and miserable. I had been trying to keep my mind as blank and as numb as possible, never allowing myself even a second to think about him. And, despite how much alcohol I consumed over the weekend, it didn't help in the long run as I still felt like shit.

As I meandered through the lobby, smiled and waved hello to Bob, I realised that I was nervous about going up to my floor and seeing Evelyn and the others. Also, I was dreading turning my Mac on. What if he had emailed me? But why would he when he could have texted or called me. I dismissed the thought and rode up to the first floor.

I exited the lift and walked into the office, and I was relieved to see Amber at her desk. She looked better than what she did just a few days ago. She had colour in her cheeks and her eyes weren't so hollow. She looked as though she managed to get some rest.

“Hey, you,” I greeted as I walked up to her desk.

She looked up at me and smiled. “Hey,”

“It’s good to see you back, you look better.”

“Thank you, I feel it!” She frowned and studied me. “Are you ok?”

“I’m ok, just tired, I was out late Saturday night,”

“Oh, with Matthew? What happened with that by the way? I never got to hear the story!” she grinned.

“No, with Heather. Whatever it was with him is over now, it was very short lived,”

“Oh that's a shame! He couldn't take his eyes off you in the kitchen,”

“Yeah, well. Sometimes things don’t work out the way you expected them to,” It was then that I realised that Amber knew this better than most. “Sorry, I just realised how insensitive I’m being!”

“No, it’s fine, honestly. It’s nice to have a distraction from it all.”

We headed into the kitchen and continued to talk while we made ourselves a cup of tea. I was overjoyed and relieved to learn that the police had arrested the man who raped Amber and that he was currently in custody. I headed to my desk and fired up my Mac ready to begin the working day. And, as I feared, I had an email.

I miss you.

Kind regards

Matthew Harper
Chairman, MWH Group Holdings.

There, on my screen, were three words that I didn't want to see. Three simple words. Three words that made me want to cry. Again. Why did he email me, why not call or text me? At least then I would have had some chance of ignoring it. Why did he have to do this to me at work? At a job I loved. It wasn't fair on me.

Mr. Harper,

Going forwards, I would appreciate it if we can keep our relationship strictly professional.

Please only email me if you need something work related.

Kind regards

Felicity Walker
Junior Writer/Editorial assistant
LuxeLife Magazine

I don't know what to say or do.

Kind regards

Matthew Harper
Chairman, MWH Group Holdings.

I laid my head on my desk. *Please, just leave me alone. I can't do this, not today*. Do I ignore it? I asked myself. I knew I should. But I knew I wouldn't. And sure enough, I was soon typing a reply.

PLEASE DON'T SAY OR DO ANYTHING.

Kind regards

Felicity Walker
Junior Writer/Editorial assistant
LuxeLife Magazine

I closed my emails down, needing a reprieve from them. I was thankful that it was time for our Monday morning team meeting. And to make things better, Evelyn was on holiday today.

IT APPROACHED LUNCHTIME when the receptionist, Claire approached my desk behind a huge bouquet of flowers.

“Someone's a lucky lady,” she said as she placed them down onto my desk.

I took one look at them and I already knew who they were from.

“Thank you,” I said as Claire walked away.

“Woah, they look expensive,” Amber said as she appeared over my shoulder.

In the bouquet were an array of flowers such as pink roses and what looked like carnations. I think there were some eucalyptus in there too. Nestled inside the bouquet was an envelope. I unclipped it from the stem and took out the card. As I stared at the typed card, my heart constricted in my chest.

Felicity,

I am truly at a loss of what to say.
I have never had to do anything like this before.
I’ve never wanted to try.
Please give me the chance to explain.

Please talk to me.
M

I examined the flowers - they were beautiful, and I couldn't bring myself to throw them in the rubbish. It wasn’t their fault.

"Amber, please can you take them for me?" I asked.

"Are you sure?"

"Yes, please. I can't deal with him or them right now,"

Amber nodded and took them away from my desk as I breathed a sigh of relief. The gesture was lovely, it was just too little, too late.

The day dragged and finally it reached home time. Amber and I grabbed our bags and headed to the gym. We hadn't been since our first time so I knew it would be hard. But, I figured it would be a good way to let out some of my pent up anger and fury.

We worked out on the treadmills and tried out some weights. As I lifted a 10 kilo weight, I got the overwhelming feeling that I was being watched. I took a cautious glance around the gym. No one was staring. There was hardly anyone in the room. But for whatever reason, I couldn't shake the feeling.

Once we had completed the full hour, we grabbed our towels and I wiped my brow. After a quick swig of water, we made our way out and into the corridor.

We headed towards the changing rooms, chatting away and I actually felt a little better, it was like I'd relieved the stress and woes I was carrying around. I was determined to continue doing so, and I even had to fight the urge to go back in for another round.

We passed door after door, all with glass windows so that you could just about peek into each class that was in session - Pilates, spinning and kickboxing. I thought I might even try one or two. As we passed the final door before the women's changing rooms, something caught my eye. It was a punching bag swinging. That looks like fun, I thought. Tomorrow morning before work, I was going to kick the shit out of that bag until there were no more traces of Matthew Harper left or the pain he'd caused me.

I DECIDED TO GET a taxi back home, after all I'd worked my legs hard enough for one day. As the cab approached my road, I got the feeling again that I was being watched. I glanced round and then over my shoulder. Was I being watched, or was I going crazy? All I could see behind me through the window was a car's headlights. It was distorted through the beads of rain that were running down the rear window, so I couldn't see or make out what car it was.

The cabbie pulled up right outside my house, I paid the driver and got out. As I stepped onto the pavement, the car that was behind pulled over too. My heart immediately leapt into my mouth as I realised what car it was. It was a Mercedes. It was *his* Mercedes. My steps quickened as I raced forward and started to climb the steps that lead up to the front door.

"Felicity, please!"

I felt my body physically shake as I tried to escape from sight. Just before I reached the last step before the door, I tripped and fell, banging my head on the brow of the concrete step. *Shit*, I thought. I heard Matthew call my name again as he ran over to me. And then I blacked out.

I stirred from my clouded haze, and could feel that my head was pounding. I was laying on the settee in my living area. I touched my forehead and could feel a bump. Ouch. Feeling a little woozy and disorientated, I started to ease myself up onto my elbows when Matthew appeared over me.

"Felicity, are you ok?" he asked, his voice firm but caring at the same time.

I nodded, unable to talk from my dry mouth.

"Would you like a drink."

I nodded again.

Matthew walked over to the kitchen and filled a glass from the tap. He returned and handed it to me. "How are you feeling?"

I looked up at him and glared. "Really?"

"Felicity, you have taken a nasty fall, I'm still debating whether or not to take you to the hospital."

"I'm fine. And anyway, what are you even doing here?"

"I was concerned about you, I haven't heard from you since the fundraiser,"

"Why? I'm not your concern anymore. Go run

back to Lydia," I snapped back at him.

Matthew took a breath in and closed his eyes, clearly feeling exasperated. "Please. I want to explain, or at least try to."

I shook my head and folded my arms. "I get it, you only wanted me for sex, you even told me that. You saw me and thought I looked desperate and vulnerable enough to say yes to you and when I said no, you didn't like it so you forced me into a corner -"

"What? No!"

"Don't interrupt me!" I shouted. Matthew visibly flinched, clearly shocked by my raised voice.

"You forced me into a corner and attempted to make a deal with me just because you wanted sex with me again. You saw that I still wouldn't budge, so you agreed to what I asked anyway just to keep me sweet so you could get your dick wet. You took advantage of me, Matthew,"

Matthew stared at me, his eyes wide open and weary.

I continued on, "I realise now how stupid I was getting involved with you," I placed my head in my hands, feeling utterly embarrassed at the whole situation.

"And then you bring me to the fundraiser Friday night where your ex-fiancé was! What did you expect to happen?" I looked at him in disgust.

"That's why I never said anything about it to

you!" He shouted, taking me aback by the anger in his voice. "I put you on the list as I wanted you there but then my Aunt opened her big mouth and invited Lydia." he ran his hand through his chocolate brown hair in frustration.

"Look, I have never wanted anyone the way I want you. I want to *try*, with you. I want to try *more*. I don't know how many times I have to say it to you before you believe it!" he said.

Matthew's words were my undoing and I felt the tears streaming down my face. I wanted him so much. It was the first time since Luke that I could finally picture myself being happy again. But, he had sent me so many mixed signals, I just didn't know what to think anymore.

"Please, please don't cry," he pleaded.

I didn't want to cry. It angered me that I was crying in front of him. I'd cried so much lately, I didn't know how I had any tears left.

Matthew perched on the settee and lifted me into his lap. I sobbed into his shoulder as he caressed my back.

"Shh," he whispered in my ear.

"You are so complicated. I don't know if I'm cut out for it. You go from being cold and closed off to being so lovely and even slow dancing with me, and it's only a matter of time before you close up again. I'm just so tired. I'm so tired of getting my heart broken," I said in between sobs. " I don't think I can survive it anymore. It's too hard."

"Oh, but you can. You are stronger than you think - believe me," Matthew said, mirroring the words that I'd once said to him when he began to open up to me, like I was so desperate for him to do.

"You know my shit is caused by the past, and I know that's no excuse because we've both been hurt but, we can get through this - together." He stated.

I leant away from him so that I could look at him. I'd missed his beautiful face. His beautiful face that was now filled with so much anguish from my words and the pain he had remembered.

"I'm sorry," I whispered.

"Shhh, don't say sorry. I should be the one to say that. I can see why you are so angry, I understand it now." he clapped my face in his hands and looked intently into my red, puffy bloodshot eyes.

"No, I mean it," I sighed. "I get so paranoid and self conscious. The one man who I thought would never hurt me, did. He ripped my heart out and trampled all over it with a blonde woman."

"Oh, I see. Like Lydia?"

I nodded. "So, seeing her and the way you were with her made me feel like shit and brought back all these emotions. And then I have to hear from your cousin that you two were engaged! I felt like you hid it from me considering all that I shared with you. It just took me back to that dark place."

Matthew was silent for a moment, trying to digest what I had just said.

"Is that why you have those scars? Because of how much he'd hurt you?" he asked.

I shook my head, surprised at his question. "No, I did that to myself after he died because I blamed myself for his death."

"You blamed yourself? Why? How did he die, what happened?"

I felt my voice falter as I spoke. "We had an argument one night about where he had been. I was worried that he was playing away again, and -" I stopped talking, unable to say anymore.

"Shhh, its ok, you don't have to tell me anymore,"

"But I do. It sounds crazy that I was still with him after he cheated on me. But, I loved him. And I truly believed that love conquered all and that we could find our way out of the mess he caused. And then, he walked out during our fight and got mowed down by a drunk driver," I closed my eyes, trying to curb the pain of reliving it, "I gave up. I stopped believing in everything."

When I opened my eyes again, Matthew was looking at me with a chilling gaze.

"I need you to understand me. Like I want to understand you." I said looking at my hands, but feeling his eyes still on me. "Heather, my best friend, stopped me from cutting anymore. She saved me from myself. And to her, I owe my life.

I am damaged too. Maybe not in the same way as you, but I am. I am my abuser," I closed my eyes and took a deep breath, feeling a little lighter for telling him.

"When I was nine years old, my mother died from breast cancer," he said quietly, causing my eyes to fly open as he spoke. "I was very close to my mother. It broke me, and my father. My father unfortunately turned to alcohol, which then led him to violence. There were days when he never returned home," he looked me in the eyes as he bravely talked. "I would have to get myself ready for school and attempt to cook my own dinners."

My heart sank in my chest as I pictured him as a little brown haired boy, alone and scared. *Oh poor Matthew.*

I knew he was trying to be brave, but I could hear his voice starting to crack as he talked.

"One evening when I was eleven, my father came home drunk from wherever he had been and was aggressive towards me, even more so than usual. I just remember him looking at me with pure disgust and saying 'why are you here? You are no good to me. I can't even look at you.' and then, he struck me. And he didn't stop until I was on the ground, unable to get back up. He left me black and blue but somehow never left any scars, just emotional ones."

Jesus Christ.

My tears began to flow again, this time for him. For the poor innocent little boy who suffered at the hands of his evil father. Matthew's expression suddenly turned from anger to warmth as he wiped my tears away with his thumb.

"It's ok, I got away in the end," He said as he kissed my nose. His eyes were full of unshed tears. "I left him and moved in with Harriet and John. They looked after me for a bit until I was able to leave and go it alone."

"Did they know what happened to you?" I asked. I'm sure they would have.

"They didn't at first but they did find out in the end when my father came looking for me." he said as he recalled a memory.

"Where is your father now?"

"I don't know," he replied, shaking his head. "I don't know if he is alive or dead - nor do I care."

"Thank you for telling me that. And I'm sorry you had to go through that.

"I'm sorry it's made me the way I am. Roberts says I push people away and never commit as the one person who I loved the most in this world left me when she died. And then the person who was supposed to get me through it and take care of me, hurt me." he shrugged.

"You didn't need an expensive shrink to tell you that." I joked.

Matthew let out a chuckle, "If only I'd met you sooner, I would have saved myself a fortune!"

I smiled at him but I still had one question to ask. "Why didn't you contact me over the weekend?"

"Because, I wanted to give you space, you looked so angry as you were walking out Friday night, I knew that you wouldn't speak to me." Matthew looked down at his watch. "It's eight O'clock, you must be hungry?"

I shake my head. "Not for food."

"Miss. Walker, are you flirting with me? Does that mean all is forgiven?"

"Possibly,"

He smirked, "well, I'm famished."

WE WERE IN MY BEDROOM watching *Friends* while we ate pizza. And it felt nice, comfortable. Like it was before. Heather was staying round Isaac's but had checked in with me a couple of times to make sure I was ok. I'd not told her Matthew was round. I thought it was best if we had that discussion face to face, once I worked out what to tell her.

"This is nice," Matthew said as he finished the last slice of pepperoni pizza.

"I think so, too." It was nice just being with him and doing what normal couples do.

I was laying on my front at the foot of the bed with my feet in the air. Matthew was sitting propped up against my headboard. When the episode we were watching finished, I turned and glanced over at him. Matthew's eyes went from the television to me and he smiled.

"What?"

"Nothing, it's just that you look cute. Sitting there in your shirt and suit trousers eating pizza on my bed."

"Cute?" he repeated.

I nodded and bit my lip. Oh, I wanted him badly.

"I know that look,"

"Oh yeah?" I said as I got up onto my knees and started crawling over to him, mindful not to kneel on the empty pizza box.

"Yes, I do."

When I reached Matthew, we were face to face, inches away from each other. I could hear as Matthew's breathing hitched.

"Now who's using sex as a distraction?" he breathed, echoing the same words I'd said to him.

"It's not a distraction," I murmured against his soft lips.

"Felicity . . ."

I placed a chaste kiss on his mouth, Oh how I'd missed his lips those past two days.

"Please,"

"Please, what?" I said as I took his bottom lip carefully between my teeth.

"Please stop,"

Abruptly I pulled away and sat up.

He wanted me to stop? Why?

"Stop?"

"Yes. After tonight and recent events, I think we need time, and besides, I think you might still have a bit of concussion."

Time? What? How much time?

"Time?"

He nodded.

"Well how much time?" I was not sure if I wanted to know the answer.

"For however long it takes for you to actually trust me, and to see that I'm not just in this to, how did you so elegantly put it, oh yes, 'to get my dick wet.'"

I rolled my eyes and collapsed next to him. "Fine, but I feel like I'm being punished,"

"Oh believe me, Felicity, I'm the one who is getting punished." he said as he fervently kissed me.

10

I WOKE UP WITH a jolt as the alarm on my phone went off. I scrambled around trying to silence it. As I moved around I noticed that my head hurt.

Why does it hurt? I thought as I cancelled my alarm. As I became more awake I noticed Matthew's suit jacket was hanging on the back of my dressing table chair.

Oh yes, I tripped and he was here last night, it wasn't a dream.

I got out of bed and noticed the smell of toast coming from the kitchen. I opened my bedroom door and there in the kitchen pouring a glass of orange juice, was Matthew.

"Good morning," He said, looking up at me.

"Yes, it is indeed," I replied, rubbing my eyes. I was still half asleep so not completely trusting what I was seeing in my kitchen.

"How long have you been up?"

"About half hour or so, come sit, the toast is ready,"

I complied and took a seat on one of the bar stools. Matthew placed a plate consisting of two slices of toast in front of me. “There you go.”

“Thank you,” I said as I reached for the marmalade “I guess you didn’t sleep in my bed?”

“No, I slept on the settee. I’ll work on sleeping in the same bed as you. I’ll speak to Roberts about it. Anyway, how was the gym yesterday?” he asked, suddenly changing the subject as he took a sip of orange juice.

Smooth one, Harper.

“How did you know I went?”

“I have my ways,”

I put down the knife I’d used to spread the marmalade on my toast with, “you own it don’t you?”

He didn't say anything, he didn't need to as the huge smirk that crept across his face told me I was right.

“You were watching me weren’t you?” I asked, suddenly remembering the feeling I had like that time at the spa with my mum.

“Yes, I can view all my business’s CCTV footage on my phone.” he said as he waved his phone up at me.

I narrowed my eyes at him. He thought he was being cute, but really he was just being creepy and stalker-like.

“Did you wait for me at the gym and then follow me home?”

“Maybe,”

"That's a little creepy you know,"

"Hey, last night you said I was cute, now I'm creepy? Sorry if I care about you and wanted to make sure you got home safety" he said jokingly as if wounded by my words.

"Oh shhh, you," I said as I took a bite of toast. "I'm going to get ready for work, shame you won't be able to shower with me, you know, because you want to give it 'time'," I dramatically sighed.

And with that, I took my toast and walked into the bathroom, but not before Matthew let out a groan.

* * *

Matthew pulled up outside the office. "Are you seeing Lydia today? You know, regarding your new office?" I asked him. I wondered if he caught up with her Friday night.

"No. I have decided to work alongside her colleague until she works out her notice period,"

Notice period!

"She's leaving?"

"Yes, we both agreed that it's for the best, given the history,"

Inside I was leaping for joy. *I win!*

"Speaking of," I said feeling brave but needing to broach the subject, "can we talk about that, tonight?"

"Talk about Lydia?" He seemed confused at the question.

"Yes,"

"There's not much to talk about, Felicity."

"You were engaged!" I squeaked.

"So were you,"

"That was different. I actually loved him,"

"Fine. Tonight," he said as he edged closer to me.

"Tonight." I repeated.

He kissed me and I climbed out of the Mercedes and walked into the lobby. When I walked through the lobby, I smiled at Bob, this time I actually meant it. I felt so much better. It was amazing how twenty four hours could change everything.

"Well, you look good!" Amber said as I made a cup of tea.

"You know what, I feel good,"

"Does this glow have anything to do with the gym?" she asked.

"No, I'm afraid not. It's Matthew. We spoke last night and sorted things out, I think we might be ok,"

"Good! I'm glad. You deserve someone who treats you well, or someone who will send you flowers at work and grovel when they mess up, because let's face it, he's a man, and he will, a lot," she winks.

We both laughed and I headed to my desk and sent my mum a quick text, apologising for not calling or texting her back this weekend. It reached 10am and my email pinged. It was Matthew and this time, the email had an attachment.

Felicity,

I thought you would like to see this photo taken the other night.

P.S I hope your morning is going well.

Kind regards

Matthew Harper
Chairman, MWH Group Holdings.

I clicked on the attachment and a photo of us filled my screen. I looked at Matthew, he looked good, as always. And I noticed that he looks different in this photo from the others I'd seen of him on the internet. He appeared to be more relaxed, almost less stiff and awkward. As I stared into Matthew's yes on my screen a grim thought crossed my mind. What if *she* sees this? What if she *sees* who I'm dating and comes crawling out of her hole, wanting to talk to me.

"Where did you disappear to on Friday?" Evelyn asked over my shoulder, distracting me from my train of thought.

I scrambled to close the photo. "I didn't feel well." I said.

She eyed me carefully. "Ok. As long as you are ok now?"

"Yes, fine, thank you. Did you enjoy Friday night?" I tried to keep my voice as quiet as possible as my colleagues didn't know.

"Yes, I did," Evelyn turned to leave, "nice photo of you both by the way," she said as she walked away.

Mr. Harper,

It is a very nice photo, thank you for sending it to me.

Until later,

Kind regards

Felicity Walker
Junior Writer/Editorial assistant
LuxeLife Magazine

What would you like to do this evening?

Kind regards

Matthew Harper
Chairman, MWH Group Holdings.

Oh I know what I want to do.

Kind regards

Felicity Walker
Junior Writer/Editorial assistant
LuxeLife Magazine

Let's do something more conventional. What about Bowling? I've heard it's fun.

Kind regards

Matthew Harper
Chairman, MWH Group Holdings.

He'd never been bowling? And more to the point, why did he want to?! Surely he hadn't come up with this idea himself.

Sir,

Are you seriously telling me you have never been bowling?

And more to the point, how did you stumble upon the idea?

Kind regards

Felicity Walker
Junior Writer/Editorial assistant
LuxeLife Magazine

Madam,

You would be correct. I have never been. I look forward to losing my bowling virginity to you.

I may have had a little help with the idea . . .

Kind regards

Matthew Harper
Bowling Virgin, MWH Group Holdings.

His change of signature made me giggle. At least he really was trying, I couldn't exactly picture him at the bowling lanes, wearing the two toned shoes.

I got called into a meeting just before I got the chance to reply and when I finally got out, it was a little past 12pm and I had an unread email from Matthew.

Would you like to invite your friend, Heather?

I know how much she means to you.

That's if she doesn't want to murder me.

Kind regards

Matthew Harper
Chairman, MWH Group Holdings.

He wanted to invite Heather? Had he had a sudden change of personality? I headed to lunch with Amber before I replied. I needed to think about what to say. Really, I wanted it to be just us two, so we could talk. But his idea of bowling and inviting Heather made it impossible to talk to him about Lydia and what happened Friday night. I realised that was probably why he suggested it.

After we grabbed lunch in the local deli that was quickly becoming our favourite place to go, Amber and I went back into the office. At least we were going to the gym so we didn't have to feel guilty about eating there all the time. I made myself yet another cup of tea and settled down at my desk to start the afternoon's tasks. My email pinged again.

Felicity?

You have not answered my question.

Kind regards

Matthew Harper
Chairman, MWH Group Holdings.

When I saw Matthew's email, I immediately knew what to respond with.

Yes, I'm here.

I've been busy. You see, some of us have to actually work to keep your empire running.

Kind regards

Felicity Walker
Junior Writer/Editorial assistant
LuxeLife Magazine

I smiled to myself and carried on with the task in hand. A few minutes later my office phone rang.

"LuxeLife -"

"Hello."

And now he was calling me.

"Hello, Mr. Harper. How can I be of help?"

"I have many, *many* answers for that, Miss. Walker but, I won't get into them now. Have you invited Heather?"

"No, I think she might be working,"

"Really?"

"Yes,"

Where was he going with this?

"You are a terrible liar, Felicity,"

"I know. I always have been. It's just that I don't know if I'm ready to involve other people in our relationship just quite yet,"

"Ok,"

"As you said in your email, she might want to murder you, and I don't think I can deal with the blood," I said in an attempt to try and lighten the conversation.

"You want to talk about Lydia don't you?"

Damn, was I that easy to read?

"Yes, and if Heather is there, no way that is going to happen,"

"It will, we have the whole night. I want your friends to like me,"

How could I say no to that? Matthew and Heather were more alike than I realised, they both knew how to play me.

"Fine, I'll text her,"

"Excellent, until later, Miss. Walker," And with that, he ended the call.

Great, now I needed to somehow persuade Heather to come bowling. She was going to think that I'd gone mad. I wasn't sure she would even want to go if she knew Matthew was going to be there. How would I even begin to explain to her that we'd kissed and made up? It's not like I could even tell her the circumstances as he told me something so deeply personal about his past. Dreading what I was about to do, I got out my phone and texted Heather.

Hey,

**So this may sound weird but,
do you wanna go bowling tonight?**

X

As soon as I put my phone back in my bag it started ringing, as I expected it would.

"Hey," I said.

"Bowling?" Heather questioned.

"Yes,"

"Why?"

"Because it will be fun!" I answered, trying to convince myself too.

"Will it?"

"Ok, the truth is I'm back with Matthew - and before you say anything we have talked through things and we are ok, better than ever in fact. But it was his idea to invite you, he wants to get to know my friends."

"Ok, I can't promise to be nice though, I'll invite Isaac too!"

"Ok, I kinda expected that anyway,"

"What time?"

"Erm 7pm, I'll come home first anyway,"

"Ok, cool, see you later,"

"Bye,"

We ended the call and I emailed Matthew to let him know that Heather and Isaac will be coming tonight so we have a double date. It would be a very interesting evening indeed.

MATTHEW PICKED HEATHER AND I up in the 4x4 Audi. It was a frosty journey to the bowling alley, with Heather quizzing Matthew on all manner of topics. I caught him glancing at me as Heather chatted away in the back.

As we pulled into the car park, Isaac was already waiting for us. Heather jumped out and nearly knocked him off his feet. It was so nice to see her all loved-up with someone. And from what I'd seen and heard about Isaac, he seemed nice. I prayed it would work out for them, but knowing what Heather was like and the fact she had brought home another man recently, who knew.

Heather and I did the introductions and both men shook hands. They were complete polar opposites, Isaac had tattoos covering both arms and had long sandy brown hair which he tied into a bun. He was good looking but in his own way and I could see why Heather liked him. And Matthew, well he was Matthew, he was in a whole league of his own. He had changed into a grey zip neck jumper with a white t-shirt underneath and a pair of jeans.

We walked over to the reception desk and

booked our lane. Isaac was nominated by Heather to type our names in.

"Ohhh, do silly names!" Heather giggled as she jumped up and down on the spot like how a child would.

"Ok, babe, you choose the names?"

Heather relayed the names she'd chosen to Isaac.

"I guess I'm 'douche bag' then?" Matthew looked up at the screen above our lane and smirked.

"I guess so," I replied with a sympathetic look, "She'll come round,"

As we began to play, we all started getting more comfortable around one another and I think Matthew started to enjoy himself. Heather was still a little cold towards him but I think she was mainly doing it on purpose.

Matthew, never having been bowling before, was of course a natural. As he was with everything, was there anything this man couldn't do? And before long, he was way ahead of us all on the leaderboard.

Matthew soon became warm in his jumper and he took it off. As he did, his white T-shirt lifted slightly, revealing his toned stomach and his trail of hair that led down *there.* I watched as Heather and others in the room stopped what they were doing to appreciate the man who was mine.

"Is anyone hungry?" Isaac asked, trying to get

Heather's attention away from my boyfriend.

“I'm starved!” Heather said, coming back to the here and now.

“I could eat,”

Matthew, who had just scored a strike, turned with elegant grace and walked towards us.

“Want to order some food?” I asked him.

He looked around. “What, order food from here?” He wrinkled his nose at the thought.

"Ok, Mr. Megabucks, is this sort of food not good enough for you?” Heather said in a way that was a little too serious for my liking.

“No, I'm sure it is fine,” Matthew responded, politely not biting.

I glared at Heather and glanced over at the table at the end of the aisle and noticed that she'd had a couple of drinks, but that wasn't an excuse by any means. Isaac grabbed some menus and once we had decided what to have, he took down our food orders and went to the bar to order.

Matthew then excused himself to use the toilet.

“Hev, please cut him so slack, this is a big deal for me,” I said to her, trying to hide my frustration.

“Sorry I just don't trust him!”

“Well, I don't need you to trust him, I need you to be at least pleasant towards him,” She looked at me and rolled her eyes. “Please Hev, do it for me,” I couldn't believe I was actually having to ask her to be pleasant to Matthew.

"I will, for you. But I just think you could do better, you've been different since you've met him. You've cried a lot more, and you never cry,"

Before I got a chance to reply, Isaac returned with another round of drinks.

"Here you go, girls," he placed the tray down and Heather grabbed her rum and coke. She seemed to be drinking a lot lately. I shrugged it off.

I grabbed the ball and took my turn. Once I had bowled, I saw Matthew walking over to our lane. He looked stressed.

"Darling, there's a situation that I have to attend to at work, I'm sorry but I need to go,"

Oh. my heart sank.

"Is everything ok?" I asked, trying to disguise my disappointment.

"Yes, just needs my attention. Come back to mine when you are done, I'll let security know to buzz you up,"

I nodded my head and he kissed me on the cheek. "Thank you for understanding, I'll get Stanley to collect you all when you've finished," He turned and left me standing there.

"Where's he off to?" Heather asked, looking smug.

Shit. This will give her even more ammo.

"There's a situation at work he needs to deal with,"

"A situation? At 8pm?" she questioned.

"Yes,"

"Ok," Heather said, nodding and raising her eyebrows

I tried to ignore the look she gave me and the horrible feeling I had deep down in my stomach. I knew he had to work, and being the owner of a fair few companies came at a price. But, I couldn't help feeling abandoned.

Shortly after we had finished the last game, the barman brought over our burger and chips and we sat down to eat them, although my appetite had completely vanished. Isaac and Heather split Matthew's burger and I picked at my food.

As promised Stanley was waiting outside for us when we left. He pulled up outside our flat to drop off Heather and Isaac.

"Are you going to his?" Heather asked as Stanley brought the Audi to a complete stop.

"Yes,"

"Ok," she said, but her tone reeked of judgement.

"What?"

"Nothing, just be careful, yeah?" She said with a seriousness in her tone.

"Babe, come on, leave it now," Isaac piped up.

Leave what? What is he talking about, have I missed something? I thought as I frowned in confusion.

"Why does everyone keep saying that to me? Do you know something I don't?" My voice was slightly more raised than I intended it to be.

"Just - I," she stopped. "It doesn't matter," she held up her hands in defence.

"No, come on, you can't leave it like that, tell me," my frown was becoming deeper by the second.

"It's just that, well he's just not Luke, you aren't behaving the same way you did when you were with him, you're different and I don't like the person you turn into when you are with him. He treats you like shit, and one minute you are ok and the next he has you in tears. And then you are more than happy to keep running back for more. I'm sorry but he's not the guy for you, he will never compare to Luke,"

I recoiled from her harsh words. Why did everyone think that Luke was such a saint? He was far from it. Maybe it was time that people learnt the truth about him.

"Oh Heather, if only you knew," I said, shaking my head in anger. I was dangerously close to losing it.

"Knew what?" She asked, her frown was now mirroring mine.

"Luke wasn't as squeaky clean as you thought he was, he hurt me in a way that I will never get over," I could feel the tears begin to build.

Don't cry, Felicity. Don't cry, Felicity. I kept repeating the words in my head like a mantra.

"What are you talking about?"

And before I could realise what I was doing, I screamed the truth. "He cheated on me!".

"Oh my God, what? When? Why didn't you tell me?"

"Can you get out now please?" I asked her, feeling mortified that the evening had led to this.

"Fliss, no. Talk to me,"

"Oh so now you want to be my friend? I thought you didn't like me," I snarled at her.

"No, that's not what I said at all. I don't like how you are when you are *with* and when you talk about him. You act so needy and insecure and that's not you. That's not normal. That's not the Felicity I know,"

"Yeah well, your perfect Luke made me like this. You seem to love him so much, I'm surprised you didn't sleep with him too!" I screamed again, unable to keep my feelings inside any longer.

"Oh, that is uncalled for!" she said, clearly stung from my words.

"Just get out, now," I said, my voice was left feeling husky from screaming at her.

"Heather, let's leave now," Isaac looked at me with kind eyes, he could read the situation that his hot headed girlfriend couldn't.

"This discussion isn't over," She said to me as she climbed out of the car.

She slammed the door closed and the tears I was holding back began to flow And they continued to flow until we reached Matthew's penthouse.

Stanley walked round to the rear passenger

door and opened it for me. I climbed out and offered him a smile as a thank you.

I made my way up to the penthouse after being buzzed up by security as Matthew said I would. I entered the living area and curled up on Matthew's leather settee and cried. I released tears for the pain I still felt from being cheated on all those years ago and for the new pain of having an argument with my best friend, who clearly did not like my boyfriend. I wasn't sure how long I was laying there weeping but I eventually fell asleep.

"Felicity?"

I was awoken from my doze by Matthew. He was standing over me, the glow from the floor lamp emphasised his handsome face.

"Hey,"

"Why are you laying here?" he asked, cocking his head to one side.

"I just sat down and fell asleep," I shrugged.

"You could have come and found me, I've been in my office down the hall,"

"Oh, sorry, I didn't know, I thought you were at the office,"

"Turns out it was an issue that I could deal with in my home office, I did text you to let you know I was here,"

I pulled out my phone to check for any unread messages. "Oh, my phone ran out of juice," I said as I held it up to show him.

Matthew bent down so he was level with me.

"You've been crying," he reached his hand out and caressed my cheek with the backs of his knuckles.

"I had my first ever argument with Heather,"

"Over what?"

"What do you think?" I said, offering him a slight smile.

His face fell when he realised it was over him. "Oh, I see," he looked away from me, "I could tell that she's not my biggest fan,"

"Yeah well she loved Luke, no one will ever be able to hold a candle to him," I rolled my eyes in irritation.

"Didn't you say he cheated on you?" he asked, looking very confused.

"Yes, but she didn't know that, until I told her tonight,"

"Oh,"

"And the look on her face when I told her! Anyone would have thought that he'd cheated on her!" I said, throwing my arms up in the air.

"We'll I won't ever do that to you, I promise, you have my word,"

"Thank you. So you did sort the 'situation' in the end?"

A look of unease flitted across Matthew's face. "Almost. It's late, do you want to go to bed?"

"I do but, I want to talk about Lydia,"

Matthew let out a dramatic sigh, clearly hoping I had forgotten.

"Fine, let's get into bed and talk,"

"SO, WHAT DO YOU want to know?" Matthew asked as he got into bed next to me. He was shirtless wearing only his boxers. He looked amazing.

"Ok, why did you break off the engagement?" I asked.

He laid down on his side and propped himself up with his elbow so he was facing me. "You don't hang around do you?"

"No. Spill, Harper,"

"Because, we were young, naive and stupid and I realised it was a mistake,"

"That is *the* worst answer." I said, rolling my eyes at him.

"Well it's true. I was only twenty three, she was twenty six and besides Harriet and my mother, she was the only woman ever to show any affection towards me. It felt - nice. Familiar even -" A look that I couldn't quite put my finger on spread across his beautiful face. "-but, as time went on, Lydia grew more and more impatient for us to set a date for the wedding. And In the end I couldn't deal with her and her pressure. As you've probably noticed, I like to do things at my own pace."

"No, I've never noticed," I sarcastically replied.

"She wanted to settle down and have kids and I'll be the first to admit that I panicked. I guess I knew she wasn't right for me."

"But, Dr. Roberts says you can't commit as a result of your mother's death. But at the moment you decided to propose, you obviously wanted to commit?" I asked.

It just seemed an odd thing for a man who claimed to be 'emotionally unavailable' to do!

"Ah, that's the thing - I never proposed. She did."

She what!?

"She proposed? To you?" I said, my voice insanely high.

"Yes,"

"How long were you together when she asked you?"

"Five months."

"Woah!"

"Exactly,"

"No wonder you said you didn't ever want a relationship, you must worry every Tom, Dick and Harry will propose to you!"

"More like every Tilly, Dawn and Heidi," he smirked.

"Ha ha, that's hilarious, Harper," I stopped and frowned, "but, why am I different?"

"What do you mean?"

"Well, Lydia is stunning and I should know because she quite literally stunned me!"

"I'm not following you," he said as he set an alarm on his phone.

"Well, you need to be with someone a little more in your league, I mean look at you!" I waved my hand at him lying next to me. "If Lydia of all people can't get you to settle down, why on earth would I be able to?"

"What are you talking about? Look at *you!* You are easily the most beautiful woman in any room you enter. All the men stop and look at you, which drives me mad by the way. But, you have something that Lydia will *never* have,"

I felt my cheeks heat with embarrassment and pure desire for the man beside me.

"There, see the way your cheeks redden, you have a personality, and feelings for one! You are beautiful, kind and you see me in a way *no one* ever has. You *understand* me."

His words, his amazing, reassuring words were exactly what I needed to hear. He was right, I could see him in a way others couldn't. People were wary of what they couldn't see. They couldn't see or read him and that's why people didn't trust him. But I did. I trusted him. I would trust him with my life. With my heart.

"I trust you,"

"What?"

"I see you, Matthew. I *trust* you," My words finally broke through his confusion. I said the words that he so desperately needed to hear from me.

"Oh thank God,"

And with that, Matthew was on top of me, kissing me as if his life depended on it. His tongue deep in my mouth as we engaged in an erotic dance. He continued to kiss me, his breathing harsh against my mouth. I had been craving for his touch having starved myself over the weekend. I was finally going to get my fix.

"I need you," he breathed, his voice low and husky.

"Take me, please" I begged.

Matthew moved his hands down to my underwear and suddenly, his fingers were inside me. He stroked my clitoris, the sensation was unbearable. I moaned against his lips and abruptly he withdrew his fingers, leaving me panting for more.

Matthew thrusted his fingers into my mouth and I instinctively sucked. I tasted salty, wet and ready. He then removed his fingers but left his index finger in my mouth. I gently bit down on the pad and he groaned.

"Oh, Miss Walker," he said, his gaze never leaving mine.

"I need you, please,"

"Not yet," he bit down on my bottom lip, "I want to try something with you,"

"Ok,"

Matthew momentarily got off the bed and disappeared into the dressing room. I heard him open a drawer and then close it again. Moments later, he returned to the bedroom holding a tie, a sky blue tie. The tie he was wearing the day we met.

"I am going to use this as a blindfold, it's for

your pleasure. It will heighten your senses and your orgasm will become more intense."

More intense? Is that even possible?! I thought as I tried to wet my now dry lips . . .

"Ok,"

"Are you ready?"

"Yes," I lied.

"Lift your head," he commanded and I did what I was told.

Matthew placed the tie over my eyes making everything dark. "Now, I want you to get on all fours," without hesitation, I sat up and compiled.

"Good girl." Leaning down, he planted a kiss on my naked behind. "You are a fine sight. Now, I'm going to take you from behind, ok?"

"Yes," Everything south of my waist clenched from the anticipation.

I heard the tell-tale sound of the condom wrapper and before I knew it, in one quick move, Matthew was inside me.

"Argh" I cried out. He was right, the feeling was indescribable. It was so intense.

"Christ," Matthew hissed through his teeth as he pounded into me, his rhythm frantic, primal full of need. Listening to his harsh, erratic breathing was enough to send me to the brink. Knowing that h wa's lost in me, knowing his need for me.

"Matthew, I'm going to come," I panted, as I tried to keep my body from collapsing onto the bed.

"Let go, baby. For me."

And I came, and it kept going. I called out his name and he followed suit, holding onto my hips, he exploded inside me.

He was breathless and his body was limp as he pulled out of me. I gave in to my body and collapsed in a heap onto the bed, trying to catch my breath. "Welcome back to the room," he said as he untied and removed the blue tie from my face.

"Wow,"

"Yes, wow," he said gruffly as he placed a kiss on the tip of my nose. "I told you I'd worship you,"

"You did,"

Matthew shot me a told-you-so grin that I couldn't help but giggle at. He then removed the condom he was wearing, tied it and then discarded it in the bin near the bedside table. "We need to get you on the pill,"

"Ok," I yawned. I was suddenly overwhelmed with exhaustion.

"We'll you look thoroughly fucked and bone tired, I think it's time for you to sleep,"

"Ok," I wasn't going to argue with that.

I closed my eyes and snuggled under the duvet while Matthew held me close to him. It felt so nice. I was feeling so content, despite what had happened with Heather.

* * *

"Shit, she's gone into cardiac arrest," an echoey voice says.

"What? What's happening?" I say to Luke.

"Your hearts stopped pumping blood. Your body is answering my question, Felicity, its choosing for you,"

"No, no it hasn't, I pick him, not you! Him!" I scream, and I don't stop screaming until my voice is sore.

I have a strange feeling in my chest, I look down and see that it's moving.

"They are doing CPR, I had the same happen to me when I was laying at the roadside,"

"I'm-I'm dying. No, please, God no! I can't, it's not my time,"

"Charging one twenty," the voice shouts.

"And now they are using the defibrillator," Luke says.

I use everything I have to try and fight the overpowering urge to take Luke's outstretched hand.

"No you can't take me, I'm not ready to leave him. You left me, but I'll be damned if I'm leaving him. He doesn't deserve to feel the way I did. He's a good man, not like you,"

No, no, no!

I fight and I fight, determined not to let go, determined not to leave him. He can't have another woman he loves leave him. . .

11

I WAS DISTURBED FROM sleep by the sound of Matthew's voice. He was moaning and shifting restlessly in the bed next to me. He stayed in bed with me. The sounds he was making were full of pain and torment.

"Don't touch me," he cried, "please,"

I froze, I didn't know what to do. Should I wake him or let him ride it out? I thought.

My heart raced in my chest. His words rang out in my ears, it hurt me to listen to the fear and anguish.

"No!" He shouted as his back arched.

"Matthew," I said, gently trying to wake him. I touched his hand and he writhed, his legs kicking at the covers. I flinched and tried to swallow past the lump that had formed in my throat.

"Don't. No . . . It hurts. I want mummy!" I couldn't bear it any longer, I couldn't watch him as he called for his dead mother, it was too awful.

"Matthew, wake up!" I shouted as I grabbed

both of his upper arms and tried to shake him awake, but barely able to move his heavy dead weight. Suddenly, he snarled, his hands were fisting at his sides and his legs were kicking restlessly. I moved back slightly but it was too late. Matthew struck me with the back of his hand, across my face. I gasped and my hand immediately went to my cheek.

"Matthew!"" I screamed at the top of my lungs as I reached for the bedside lamp, my throat burning. I turned it on. He was in agony. His whole body was dripping with sweat, the sheets were drenched.

Now that I had been hit, I feared even more for my own safety, and his. I shoved his shoulder with all the strength I had with both hands, "Matthew, damn it, Wake up! Please!" My scream finally managed to break through his nightmare. His eyes flew open and he jerked upright, his eyes darting frantically. I jumped out of bed and retreated to a safe distance away from him. My face was still throbbing but I endured the pain.

"What?" he gasped, his chest heaving. "What is it?" He took one look at my face and where I was standing and realised what he had done. "Jesus. No, Felicity. What have I done,"

"I'm ok, I'm fine,"

His eyes immediately darkened with shame and he looked down, unable to look at me.

"You were having a nightmare. You scared the shit out of me!"

"I'm so sorry, I - "

"Was it about your father?"

He nodded his head, still not able to look at me. I stared at him from across the bed, trying to work out what to say to him. What the hell do I say to a man who had assaulted me in his sleep. I knew he didn't mean to but it scared me. I'd never had so much as a slap from my father, I was never spanked or punished physically as a child.

Matthew's chest expanded on a deep breath and then he released it in a rush. "I'm so sorry I've done that to you."

I pinched the bridge of my nose and I closed my eyes tightly. My eyes were stinging with the need to cry for him, to cry for the torment he'd once lived through caused by the one person who should have loved him, especially after all they had both been through together. I also wanted to cry for me, and for us.

"I shouldn't have fallen asleep next to you. I told myself as I watched you drift off to sleep, that I would get up and sleep in the spare room, like always do," he stopped and ran a hand through his hair, "I can't believe I have been so *fucking* stupid." he gritted his teeth as spoke. He was angry, very angry.

"I'm ok, honestly,"

He still hadn't looked at me, not properly anyway. I didn't think he could.

"Matthew, look at me," he raised his eyes up to meet mine from the opposite side of the bed. But soon looked away again.

"Matthew!" I shouted, raising my voice a little louder than I intended to. He needed to look at me. We needed to get past this. And being shouted at seemed to work as Matthew forced himself to look at me. I held his gaze and watched as his eyes moved to the hand print I now had on my face.

"I. Am. Fine." I alliterated each word slowly to emphasise the point that I *was* ok.

"I just can't believe that I've hurt you." He looked away again in disgust.

"Will you stop, please," I started walking round the bed but Matthew moved back, walking into the chest of drawers that was behind him.

"Please don't come near me," he said, begging me.

What?

"Why? You aren't going to do it again, Matthew,"

He shook his in shame, "I can't look at you, your face, its-" he stopped as if he physically couldn't say another word. "You can't be near me and I can't be near you right now, I'm going to have a shower. And when I have finished you won't be here, I'll get Stanley to take you home."

My eyes widened in fear. "What?! No!" I cried, "Don't give up on us, not because of this!"

"I can't, Felicity. This is why I said I didn't date. I can't trust myself. I always stay awake when you fall asleep, just so this wouldn't happen! I can't believe I've allowed myself to be so stupid!"

My world felt like it crumbled at my feet from his words. "Is this not worth saving?" I said in between sobs.

"I told you not to get used to me, Felicity. I did warn you but you wouldn't listen to me, you got in too deep, and now look."

His words were like a knife to my heart, cutting and stabbing at it until he had it in his hands, ready to destroy it completely. But, my sadness then quickly turned to anger.

"I'll leave now, save you the bother of calling Stanley." I grabbed my clothes and threw them on. Matthew didn't move from the spot, he didn't even look at me as I left the room.

I grabbed my bag from the coffee table where I'd left it when I got back from bowling and I rushed out the door, into the foyer and to the lift. The doors began to close with me inside just as I caught sight of him.

His nearly naked body guaranteed that he wouldn't come after me and I was thankful for that. I was too wounded, physically and mentally. I caught sight of him long enough to notice that his mask was firmly in place again, the same mask that he wore when I first met him, and when I met him at the restaurant where we propositioned me. That strikingly unreadable face that kept the world at a safe distance, was now keeping me at a safe distance.

I was shaking as I leant against the brass

handrail for support. I was taken back to the time I ran away after we first slept together, I ran into this lift. We had come so far since then, learnt so much about each other. I was torn between hating him right now and my concern for him. I looked up and caught sight of myself in the reflection in the lift doors. My face was red from where he had hit me, it felt warm, red hot like it was on fire.

He didn't mean to. He was dreaming.

"I also have nightmares, well my therapist calls them 'night terrors'," He even warned me. He did, he might not have even known but the warning was there. I wiped my wet cheek and took a deep breath in an attempt to collect myself before the doors opened.

I stepped out into the lobby and stopped. What was I doing? It couldn't end like this. We'd both put so much blood, sweat and tears into it. We could get through this. We had both been through so much in our lives, we needed something good to come out of it all.

I quickly stepped back into the lift, making it just before the doors closed on me. I punched in the code the security guard gave me earlier and rode back up to the penthouse, *to Matthew.*

I dashed through the foyer, through the living area and down the hall and I reached his bedroom. I slowly stepped in and he wasn't there. I could hear the shower in the ensuite running. I walked up to the door and froze. I could hear a whimpering noise coming from the other side of the door. *Shit, he's crying.* I burst through the door and there he was.

There, under the torrent of water, Matthew was sitting on his knees - sobbing. My heart broke the sight of a usually powerful, strong man, who was now broken, kneeling on the floor. He was a shadow of his usual self, it was as if he'd reverted back to that little boy, abused and neglected.

"Matthew," I breathed.

And, before I knew what I was doing, I walked into the shower and sank to my knees in front of him. Water began to soak my clothes but I didn't care. It was too much to see him like this and tears began to ooze down my cheeks at the sight of him, crying, sobbing uncontrollably.

Please don't cry, please.

"Matthew, look at me," I tilted his chin up so he had no choice but to look at me.

"Y-you came back?" he wept.

"Yes, I did. Look at me,"

He shook his head. "I'm no good for you. I don't deserve you."

No, no, don't say that!

"Yes, you are!" I shouted over the noise of the cascading water. "And don't you ever think you aren't worthy of my love."

We both stilled. Love. I'd just said *love*.

"Love? You love me?"

I smiled, "Yes, Matthew I. Love. you." *Holy shit,*

I love him! "You are everything I need," as I said the words I gazed into his beautiful blue eyes.

"You are worthy of my love. More than worthy, even if you don't realise it. You're sexy and successful. Kind and caring - all those things. I'm not worthy of *your* love." I sniffed as I wiped my nose with the back of my hand, gazing at his impassive expression. "I don't understand what you see in me."

I was sure his expression softened but it was hard to tell. "You are everything *I* need. *You* make me stronger," he said.

His words made me cry, but this time with relief. "Then please don't push me away anymore."

"I was so ashamed," he looked down again but then he lifted his head back up, "I can't believe I hurt you like that," He raised his hand slowly to my face and rubbed my throbbing cheek. "And after I hurt you, I just wanted you gone, I didn't want you to see me in this way, like the monster I am," he murmured.

"Matthew, you are not a monster! Please don't ever say that! You are a man who has suffered terrible things. Things that were totally out of your control. Because you were a *child*. You are not a monster."

"But, I did that to you and you still came back for me,"

"I promised you I wouldn't leave, didn't I? And besides, I didn't really hurt that much," I smiled,

I was trying so desperately to make him feel better.

"So, you weren't actually running?" he asked, almost to clarify what I'd just said.

"I was, but then I realised I need you too much."

Matthew closed his eyes again and his whole body visibly relaxed. He then reached out and took my hand.

"You are the only one who is able to fix me when I'm broken." he breathed, as he kissed my knuckles. Then, he gently tugged at my hand in a silent command to come closer. I abided and he lifted me onto his lap. He moved my hands so that they were over his shoulders and around his neck. I was usually never allowed to hold him this way while he was naked, but this time, he was letting me hold him, letting me touch him. His eyes were wide with worry and fear but I placed my forehead to his and he closed them. He composed himself slightly, as if he was getting used to my touch.

"I'll go with you," I said.

"What? Go where?" he asked, opening his eyes.

"To couples therapy, I'll try it. It might help me with my issues too," I had to at least give it a go.

He peeled his forehead from mine and gazed into my eyes with affection and admiration. "Oh my sweet girl, you never stop amazing me, you are so forgiving." He placed a kiss on my lips. "Thank you."

We remained on the shower floor for I don't know how long, it could have been minutes, hours, I don't know. But I didn't move from his lap. I was soaked through to the bone and exhausted. But I didn't care. I was in the arms of the man I loved. I loved him. I never expected to love anyone again. I didn't expect to fall for Matthew quite this hard, but I had.

Matthew eventually shifted so that he could reach up to turn the shower off. He scooped me up in his arms and placed a towel round my wet body without saying anything. And we continued not to say anything as he placed me onto his bed and removed my sodden clothes from my body. He threw them onto the floor and then used the towel to dry my hair. A simple act, yet it felt so intimate. Once he had finished, I shuffled my way under the sheets.

"You've made me believe again," I said, closing my eyes.

He paused and then bent down. "Sleep, darling girl," he said, placing a kiss on my head and tucking me in.

He turned the light off and closed the door behind him. I glanced at the analog clock on the bedside table and it read 03:54. I closed my tired eyes and slipped into a deep sleep.

I AWOKE TO THE sight of Matthew sitting next to me on the bed, awake and dressed. I sat upright in a panic. *Shit, what time is it?*

“It’s 8am, but it’s ok, I’ve already told Evelyn that you won't be in today. Good morning by the way.” Matthew said, replying to my unspoken question.

“What? why?” I asked.

“I think we need a day to ourselves, we had a late night.”

“Yeah, we did.”

“I’ve got my PA to reschedule my meetings for today and told her not to contact me, not even if it's urgent.”

“Not even if the HQ is on fire?”

“Not even then,” he grinned. “What do you want for breakfast?” he asked as he got off the bed with elegant ease. He was dressed in a navy blue jumper and jeans. He looked so yummy.

“Erm, I don't know.”

“Well, Audrey, my housekeeper, is here so she can rustle up anything you want.”

Oh yes, he has a housekeeper. I remembered.

“Why don't we go out for breakfast?”

“Ok, if that's what you want to do,”

I nodded my head, “I think it will be nice, but only if you are up for it though,”

“For you, I will do anything,” he placed a kiss on my nose, “get showered and I will be waiting for you,”

I watched as Matthew meandered out of the bedroom leaving me alone. I checked my phone for any unread messages and notifications and headed to the bathroom.

Once I got back to the room, I noticed that Matthew had laid yet more clothes out on the bed. This time there was a black and white striped jumper and a pair of jeans. Where did he get these from? I quickly pushed the thought aside, and put them on.

Matthew was waiting for me in the living area when I emerged from the bedroom. He seemed to be engrossed in watching a program on the television, it looked like it was about the stock market. I started to walk up to him and he caught sight of me out of the corner of his eye.

"There she is," he smiled as he walked up to meet me. He bent slightly and planted a kiss on my lips.

"Thank you for the clothes, again,"

Matthew let out a laugh, "Don't thank me, thank Stanley. He is the one who I send to get your clothes. His wife works at a department store."

Oh!

"Well, can you thank Stanley, and his wife for me?"

"I sure will," he kissed me again. "Come, let's get some breakfast, I know just the place."

I took Matthew's outstretched hand and we made our way to the lift and straight down into the car park. For the first time, I noticed how many nice cars there were in the car park.

"Are these cars the other residents of the

building? Or do you own them all?" I asked in jest.

"I don't own them all. Just the really nice ones," he winked.

He threw me as I expected him to unlock the Mercedes, but this time when he pressed the car key the indicators of a little blue BMW flash.

That is a nice car!

Matthew, ever the gentleman, opened the passenger door for me , "there we go, my lady,"

"Why, thank you, Sir," I replied back in a posh voice as I tried not to giggle.

"What BMW is this?" I asked as Matthew got in the driver's seat.

"It's the new BMW M8 Competition Coupé," he said as he pressed a button and the engine roared to life. "And it's top of the range," he beamed.

"Of course it is," I replied, sardonically.

"I only drive German cars, in case you didn't notice,"

"Matthew, I have no idea about cars, I can't even drive," I admitted.

He whipped his head round to look at me. "Really? You don't know how to drive?"

"I've always lived in London and been close to the Tube so never really needed to." I shrugged, why did I feel so silly all of a sudden?

"Would you like to drive?"

"Maybe, if I were to ever live outside of London."

"Would you like to live outside of London?" he

asked as we pulled out onto the main road.

"What's with all the questions?"

"I'm trying to be a good boyfriend, I want to know these things."

I smiled at him, you had to give him marks for trying! At that moment he looked so young and so happy and I wasn't sure if it was from driving the insanely nice car or just being with me but, I hoped it's the latter, however, I had a feeling it's the car.

"Yes, maybe one day. I would like a garden that I can sit out in and maybe a nice woodland nearby where I can walk my dog."

"So, you want a dog and a garden. See, I'm learning something,"

I smiled at him. "What about you? We'll you've probably got several houses dotted around the UK,"

"Yes, I have a few. I have houses in Cornwall, Norfolk, and one in Yorkshire."

"Wow, I haven't been to Cornwall, and I don't think I've been to Norfolk either. We only went on holiday abroad."

"We'll, you have been missing out. This country is beautiful, I'll take you to Norfolk soon if you would like?"

Was he asking me if I wanted to spend the whole weekend away with him? *Hell yeah!*

"I would love to!"

"Ok, we'll drive up on a Friday night after work. How about next weekend?"

This was definitely progress for our relationship! And despite what happened last night, we were getting somewhere, finally. A whole weekend together would really put our relationship to the test.

“Sounds perfect,” I said, beaming from ear to ear.

Matthew smiled at me, looking genuinely excited as he drove the car through the busy London traffic, weaving past buses and other cars as we approached the Wellington Arch.

“Where are we eating?” I asked as we joined Piccadilly and passed the Hard Rock Cafe.

“I thought I’d take you to The Ritz,” he said as if it was something that happened everyday.

“The Ritz? Oh wow, thank you!” I was elated, I had never been there before.

We pulled up outside The Ritz and Matthew handed the keys to the awaiting Valet.

“Mr. Harper,” he nodded in a way of a greeting as we breezed past him.

Matthew and I walked into the lobby and I was immediately struck by the sheer grandness of the building and the beautiful decor. There was a richly patterned carpet and a grand staircase. It was simply stunning. And in pride of place in the lobby was a beautiful gold clock. There were flowers in grand vases dotted about too, it was like an extravagant wedding venue.

We were shown through to a dining room which was laid out for breakfast. The waiter pulled out a chair for me and I took a seat. He unfolded the napkin that was on the table and handed it to me. Once Matthew and I were settled he handed us a menu each.

"Thank you," Matthew said to him as he walked away.

I glanced down at the menu and my eyes nearly fell out of my head at the prices! *Jesus*, no wonder I'd never been here before!

"Are we dressed up enough to be here?" I asked, looking around at other diners and the fancy decor.

Matthew smiled a sweet smile at me. "Yes, they have a less formal dress code in the mornings, so don't worry,"

"Oh, good." I said as I looked back down at my menu, feeling a little better.

The waiter brought over a pot of tea containing Twinings English Breakfast Tea and a Cappuccino for Matthew. "Are you ready to order?" he asked.

Matthew looked up at me, "I am if you are?"

"Yes," I said, "I'll have the classic English breakfast with scrambled eggs with bacon and sausages please."

The waiter nodded, "Very good Ma'am and what would you like, Sir?"

"I'll have the Eggs Benedict please. Oh, and can we have some of the pancakes too?"

"Certainly, Sir." he took our menus and scurried off.

I tilted my head to one side, “hungry are we?”

“Ravenous, Miss Walker.”

I giggled at his playful reply.

“Are you laughing at me again?”

“I wouldn’t dare, Sir,” I teased.

“That’s a shame, because if you were, I would have taken you up to one of the very nice rooms and shown you just what I thought of it.”

I swallowed, I could feel my throat and mouth becoming dry from his threat. “I *was* laughing,” I said as I bit down on my lower lip in an attempt to curb my desire that I felt building deep inside of me.

Matthew didn't take his eyes off mine. “Excuse me, please can you send the order up to the Trafalgar Suite?” he asked a waitress who happened to walk past.

“Yes, certainly, Mr Harper,” she said.

“Come,” he grabbed my hand and pulled me up off my seat.

“The Trafalgar suite? How did you know it's even available?” I asked as we headed to the front desk.

“I pre booked it,” he said to me before facing the young blonde at the reception desk, “Can I have my key?”

“Yes, Mr. Harper,” The receptionist blushed as she handed him a room key card. I was then pulled to the direct of the stairs. It was good to know I wasn't the one who blushed in his presence.

Matthew practically dragged me up the stairs and we finally reached the door. He then opened it and stepped aside, allowing me to step into the suite before him.

Wow.

I was taken aback by the grandeur of the room. As I walked closer into the room, I couldn't help the feeling that I'd been here before. Of course, I knew that I hadn't but it was strangely familiar.

"Have you ever watched the film, *Notting Hill*?" Matthew asked from close behind me.

Yes, of course it was the suite from the film! The suite where bookshop owner William Thacker interviewed the Actress Anna Scott.

I turned and smiled, "yes, I love that film! I knew I recognised the suite!" I squealed.

Matthew mirrored my smile, "and here's me thinking you liked it for the historic decadence,"

I cocked my eyebrow and stepped onto tiptoes and planted a kiss on his cheek. "It's a lovely suite," I placed my hand on his cheek, "and what do you intend to do in it?" I asked, my eyes dark with lust.

"Oh, so many things, Miss. Walker."

"Show me," I goaded.

Matthew pushed his hands through my hair and kissed me with raw passion, "get naked, now." he said huskily, commanding me rather than asking me.

With thumbling fingers, I undid the button of my jeans and unzipped the fly. I pulled my jeans down along with my knickers. Matthew eyed me carefully as I removed my feet from my jeans. I then lifted my jumper up over my head and threw it onto the floor.

"You really are beautiful, Felicity," Matthew said as he took a step closer to me. I reached round and unhooked the clasp on my bra, freeing my aching breasts from their prison. Matthew sucked in breath as they were revealed. He ran his eyes over my breasts, greedily drinking them in.

Before I knew it, Matthew placed his mouth over mine. His tongue possessed me. He wrapped his arms around me and I kissed him back, my tongue joining in with his leisurely dance.

He suddenly pulled away and I was left breathless. Ready. Wanting.

My hands gripped onto his muscular arms for balance. "You're still dressed," I breathed, looking at his blue jumper.

"It appears I am,"

I pushed my hands up beneath his jumper to feel his damp skin and the hardness of the muscles beneath it. I looked up at him, aware of how he felt about being touched unexpectedly. He gazed at me and I knew he was replying to my silent question.

I lowered my hand down to the hem of his jumper and started lifting it, unveiling his hard slabs of muscle. He lowered down so that I was able to lift the jumper over his head. I threw it to the ground and all I could do was stare. I stared at his perfect body from the top of his chest all the way down to his V-shaped muscle on his pelvis. He was the ultimate definition of pure primal male. He was what women all over the word fantasised about, and wished for. And, he was all mine.

I was routed to the spot, unable to tear my eyes from him. From his beautifully defined lines, all the way to how his pecs and abs flexed. As I was busy starting, I caught sight of him taking out a foil packet from his pocket before he removed his jeans and boxers.

"Come here, I want to feel your body against mine. Skin to skin," Matthew reached his hand out for me to take and I placed my hand in his. His large hand encased mine.

He pulled me towards him so that I was flush against his body, our chests up against one another. He held me tightly to him, not waiting to let go. And, I then realised that he was giving me what I wanted all along, he was giving me more. He was giving me intimacy.

Matthew released me and walked me over to the rather large bed. We stood naked in front of each other, totally exposed and vulnerable. All our scars and flaws were known to one another, out there for each other to see, there was nowhere to hide now, or no point in running.

I was pushed down onto the mattress by Matthew's weight as he devoured me with his mouth once more. We rolled across the mattress, our limbs tangled round one another. He touched and caressed me with his hands, leaving behind trails of hot, burning fire that I didn't want putting out. The smell of him and his body wash was like an aphrodisiac to me, intoxicating me, igniting my desire for him.

"You are all I want," He murmured against my now moist skin. He plumped a breast in his hand before taking the other in mouth, his tongue deliciously working my nipple. I let out a whimper in response to the feeling of his tongue, and the blazing heat that was quickly building in my core, caused by every slow delectable suck.

I slid my hands over his sweat-damp skin, he moaned into my breast in response. I marvelled at how amazing it felt to touch him, and how brave he was. He gave off this facade that he was so strong and unbreakable. He was an alpha male, always leading. Well, this time, I was going to lead him. I was going to be the one who was in charge.

I attempted to roll him with my legs, but he was too heavy. He lifted his head and smiled down at me, "Oh, you want to be on top do you?"

I nodded in response. The feelings I had for this man were only intensified in that moment, seeing his smile and the passion in his eyes, it was just so intense. I had fallen for this man, fallen hard and it was too deep for me to ever get out.

He kissed me deeply and then rolled over taking me with him so that I was on top of him. I looked down into his sweet, heated blues. Everything about him turned me on, from the way he felt beneath me to the way he was looking at me as I ran my hands over his sternum and played with the splattering of chest hair he had. His mouth formed an 'o' as he inhaled with pleasure, momentarily closing his eyes as if to savour the feeling.

Everything clenched tightly as I felt his penis harden in response to my touch. Our bodies were in-tune with one another's, both feeling the pleasure of one another.

"God, the sight of you on top of me, it's - it's amazing," he said as he gazed up at me, then running his tongue across his perfect, plump lips, my eyes following as he did.

I leant down and kissed him, "I'm going to fuck you," I whispered against his lips.

He let out a groan from deep in his throat, "Do me now!" he begged, "here," he handed me the condom wrapper, "put it on me,"

Taking the foil packet, I placed it in my mouth between my teeth and tore it open, being careful not to damage what was inside. With quivering hands, I took it out of the packet. I looked at it and frowned, I had never put one on a man before, I hadn't even touched one since sex education classes at high school.

"Gently hold the tip and slowly roll it

down," Matthew said, obviously realising my incompetence.

With my hands still shaking, I carefully placed my finger and thumb on the tip and gently rolled it down over his long length.

"Christ, even watching you do that was hot. I've never wanted anything as badly as wanting to feel you around my cock, now."

His words were my queue. Grabbing his wrists, I pinned his hands down to the mattress and I gently lowered myself onto him, claiming him.

"You are so tight, Felicity, I love it," he hissed through clenched teeth.

I began to move my hips, feeling him deep inside me. He brought his hips up to meet my every thrust. I rocked from side to side slowly to savour the moment. Then, I picked up the pace taking Matthew by surprise. He grasped the duvet underneath him so tightly, his knuckles turned white.

"Felicity, I'm going to come. Slow down, I want you to come first." he panted as I rode him.

"No," I breathed as I clenched around him, relishing the feeling of him inside me, filling me.

Matthew let go of the duvet and reached for my hips. "Ah, Felicity!" He clasped me so tightly I felt his fingers digging into my skin as he came long and hard. "Jesus," he said, breathless. "I'd never been so hard before." Matthew knitted his brows, "you didn't come, baby,"

"I know," I said, trying to catch my breath. I'd

never realised how much a man had to work. "That was all for you," I looked down and gave him a big grin.

Matthew shifted beneath me, and I lifted myself off him.

"Shit," Matthew said.

"What?"

"The condom split. Fuck! Fucking fuck!" he shouted.

I shuddered at the realisation of what that could mean. "It's ok, don't worry I'll sort it." I replied. I'd have to go to the chemist asap.

"No, we'll sort it together," he said as he carefully removed it and cleaned himself up. "We need to get you on the pill so this sort of thing doesn't happen again. I get so carried away when it comes to you,"

"Ok," I said sheepishly as the memory of the termination filled my mind.

"Hey, it's not your fault, you know," Matthew said as he tilted my chin up so I had to look at him. "Mistakes happen,"

"Yeah, I know," I said, the irony was definitely not lost on me.

"How about I arrange for a private Gynaecologist to meet us at mine later?"

"What?" I asked. *He can just do that?!*

"Saves you a trip to your local doctor's surgery. And the gynaecologist can give you the morning after pill and prescribe you contraception." He shrugged as if it's as simple as that.

"No!" I squeaked.

"Why?"

"Because you're my boyfriend, it's just weird."

"Felicity, I have seen every inch of your body and have done things to it that other men can only but dream of doing, now is not the time to be embarrassed or coy,"

He had a point.

I sighed, "Fine."

"Good, now that we have sorted that issue out, let me give *you* an orgasm that you won't forget in a hurry,"

AFTER WHAT COULD ONLY be described as possibly the best orgasm of my life, we enjoyed the rest of the day doing touristy things. Things that when you live in London, you wouldn't usually get to do. We went to Madame Tussauds and then went on the London Eye after lunch. It had been a brilliant day despite what happened in the morning and my impromptu trip to the chemist for the morning after pill.

We had just enjoyed an amazing three course dinner in a restaurant in Mayfair when Stanley pulled up in the Audi to pick us up. Matthew arranged for the BMW to be collected while we were in Madame Tussauds.

"Where to, Sir?" he asked as we climbed into the back of the car.

"Home please, Stan,"

Matthew clasped my hands the whole way back to his penthouse. We made our way up in the lift and the lack of sleep from last night finally hit me. I let out a large yawn and Matthew looked at me with amusement.

"Tired?"

"Very," I said.

"Bath and bed after the gynaecologist?"

"Sounds perfect,"

We arrived back at Matthew's penthouse a little after 9pm. Dr. Mackenzie was due to arrive at half past.

"How did you manage to get a Gynaecologist to do a home visit this late?" I asked, intrigued at how he managed to wangle that one.

Matthew raised an eyebrow at me and smirked as he shrugged off his jacket. "People will do anything for the right price,"

I smiled and shook my head, of course it was money.

"Wine?" Matthews asked as I sat down on the settee.

"No thank you,"

Matthew poured himself a glass of red wine and joined me. I turned the television on and flicked through the channels aimlessly until the doctor arrived.

After Dr. Mackenzie had left, Matthew ran me a bath. As I waited I made my way into his library and took in his large collection of books, he had everything from *The Great Gatsby* to *The Hunger*

Games. One book however, caught my eye, *Pride and Prejudice.* I removed it from the shelf and ran my fingers over the red cover. Suddenly, I was very aware that Matthew was standing behind me, it was like my body was attuned to him. I turned and faced him.

"You have this book," I stated.

"We'll, you said it's your favourite book, and film. I thought it was time I got acquainted with it,"

I grinned at him, touched by the gesture. "Have you actually read any of it yet?"

A hint of a blush touched his cheeks, "erm, not yet,"

"It's the thought that counts," I said jokingly.

"Come, your bath is getting cold." I placed my hand in Matthews and we made our way to the bathroom.

I undressed and stepped into the bath, noting that Matthew had been watching me the whole time. "Are you going to join me then?" I asked him.

His face lit up from my questions and before I knew it he had stripped and was getting in with me. Water lapped over the edge of the bath as he sat down in front of me but he didn't seem to care. I closed my eyes and let the bath salts do their job.

"So, what method did you choose?"

"Sorry?" I asked, opening one eye.

"Contraception,"

"Oh, I went for the implant,"

Matthew raised his eyebrows and nodded.

"Is that the one that goes in your arm?"

"Yes,"

"Saves you taking a pill every day,"

"Yes, I was on it when I was with Luke and always forgot to take it," I said.

Matthew chuckled awkwardly in response, his facial expression told me he clearly did not want to think about me having sex with another man.

"We don't really want to put ourselves in that particular situation. I'm definitely not ready to share you, I want you all to myself,"

"Me either, and I don't want to go through all that again," I said as I closed my eyes, feeling the full effect of the relaxing bath salts. As I rested my head on the fitted headrest, I suddenly realised what I had just said. *Shit.* I never told him about my termination.

I opened my eyes to find Matthew staring at me, his expectation unreadable.

Shit, shit, shit. I was going to have to explain myself to him now.

"You've been pregnant before?" he asked, his voice quiet.

I opened my mouth but closed it again. Instead of saying anything, I just nodded.

Matthew's eyes widen from my confirmation, "I see," by his expression it was clear he wanted me to elaborate.

"Yes, I was pregnant," I said finally finding

my voice, "but, we were young so we didn't go through with the pregnancy,"

"Ok,"

Matthew's face remained blank.

God, I wish I knew what he was thinking.

"What?" I asked.

He shook his head, "Nothing,"

I frowned at his frostiness towards me.

"Well somethings wrong. It's like you can't even look at me."

He didn't say anything.

"You know I had sex before you and that I wasn't a virgin, right?" I said sarcastically.

Maybe that's what it was, it was like he was seeing me in a new light or something.

"I know. I just never imagined or pictured you having sex before me. But now I know this, it's somehow confirmed that you have. I don't know how to explain it."

That's it, he sees me differently now.

"Do you think I'm a slut then? Because I can assure you, your number is a lot higher than mine,"

I suddenly felt embarrassed. It was like he now saw me as used or damaged goods.

"Oh, God no! It's just a bit of a shock as you didn't tell me before, that's all,"

"It was a long time ago, we were only eighteen!" I said, trying to reassure him.

"I'm sorry," he said, suddenly looking uncomfortable. "Anyway, how do you know what my number is?”

“I don’t but I can only imagine, have you seen you?! You are like the definition of sex!” I said waving my hand at him.

He smiled and let a slight chuckle escape from his throat, “Like I’ve said before, it's all smoke and mirrors, baby,”

“Have you ever got anyone pregnant?”

Matthew stilled for a moment, an expression I’d not seen before fitted across his face. “No, not that I’m aware of,"

“Just imagine if there are loads of little Matthew’s running around from your many, *many* conquests and you had no idea,” I mocked.

Matthew’s eyes widened in panic, “ok, that’s enough of this conversation,”

Once we’d had our bath, I finally crawled into bed just after 11pm, feeling the effects of the previous night's sleep and today's busy day. Matthew kissed me goodnight and left me to sleep. Oh how I wished he was able to sleep next to me.

12

I GOT INTO WORK earlier than usual as Matthew had Stanley take me to work as he had to travel to the other side of London to meet a client. I'd already made myself a cup of tea, and as I had time to kill before 9am, I loaded up Safari and browsed the web.

I was used to looking at our rival's websites for their take on the latest fashion and the recent shows they have reported on but, I very rarely found myself on the gossip pages and blogs. I was a little freaked out by the headline that appeared on the page from the first link I'd clicked on.

"Business Tycoon Matthew Harper spotted out bowling with friends and a mystery redhead."

"Oh, shit," I breathed as I saw a picture of Matthew bowling. I scrolled down and continued to read on.

"Matthew Harper, 33, who is better known as London's most eligible bachelor since Prince Harry, was spotted enjoying a game of bowling or two with friends at a bowling alley in London Tuesday

night. He was joined by an unidentified redhead (pictured), whom he has been seen with in London sightseeing, and also pictured with her at a charity event recently. The pair seemed to be very friendly and they even shared a passionate embrace. We have contacted the PR department at MWH Group Holdings (Mr. Harper's Company) to see if they will comment on who this mystery woman is. We imagine hearts are breaking across the country this morning as the news breaks. More to follow when we have it."

I closed the page and then Googled Matthew's name and yet again, there were other websites leading with a similar story. I clicked on images and scrolled through various pages to see if I could find the one that was taken on Friday night at the event. Thankfully, I couldn't seem to find it.

I sat back in my chair, alarmed. They knew we went sightseeing, and bowling! Someone must have followed us there, or someone recognised Matthew and tipped off the press. All I could hope was that the picture from the fundraiser had been destroyed and people at work wouldn't put two and two together yet, or worse, my birth mother would see it.

My hands were shaking as I closed the tabs before anyone saw them over my shoulder. I hadn't considered the press coverage, I should have really, considering the industry that I worked in. But, I wouldn't have dreamt that they would be interested in Matthew's relationships. I take out my phone from my bag and send Matthew a text.

We have a problem.
The press knows about us.
x

Yes, I was made aware Tuesday evening that the photo of us from Friday had been leaked. I have managed to stop it being used by the press.

The photo was obviously why he had left Tuesday evening while we were bowling. He did say he was sorting out a 'situation'.

Ok, is that what you were dealing with when you left?
P.s I hope you get to your meeting safely
x

Yes, it was. Try not to worry, it's being dealt with See you later, darling.

If he said it was being dealt with then it was, I trusted him wholeheartedly. I just had to keep my head down and remain on the down low.

Oh, don't be so stupid, there are hundreds of redheads in London, you silly woman!

My subconscious was right, how were the press ever going to know that it was me when there weren't any pictures out there? I just had to carry on as normal and hope that a celebrity has a nip slip or some bodged botox soon so that their attention was diverted elsewhere.

As I tried to get lost in work, my mind kept turning to Heather and our fight Tuesday evening after I told her that Luke had cheated on me. That was our first ever argument. And I was hating the radio silence.

I shook my head clear and carried on researching the next season's bags. As I do, I heard my phone buzz. I looked down expecting it to be Matthew but I was suddenly hit with a wave of guilt when I saw my mum's name on the screen. I'd been MIA the last few days, she must have been worrying.

Felicity, it would be nice to know if you are alive and well?? please give me the courtesy of letting me know.
X

I cringed at the message and its tone. My mum's lovely and would do anything for anyone, but if I didn't text her back within twenty four hours, all hell broke loose. I decided on replying sooner rather than later, hoping it would soothe her wound a little bit.

Sorry mum, been busy with work.
I'm ok thank you. Hope you
and dad are ok?
X
So busy you don't have a spare
minute to text your mum it seems!
Anyway, you still haven't told me
about that fundraiser you went to!
Who did you go with? Was it with a man?
X

I thought I'd better rip that plaster off and get the news about Matthew over and done with.

Yes it was with a man.

I decided the less my mum knew the better. It was probably a discussion to have in detail with her face to face.

Oh Felicity! That is wonderful news, you must bring him to dinner tomorrow night!
X

Tomorrow? I frowned and glanced over at the calendar.

Bollocks.

It was my 'adoption day'. Every year my parents celebrated the day they adopted me as well as my birthday. As a child it was brilliant - I got two parties, two cakes and two lots of presents. But, as an adult it became somewhat of an inconvenience. I mustn't be ungrateful though. Those two amazing humans adopted me and welcomed me into their lives with open arms. I never wanted for anything, and to be honest, I still didn't because if there was something I needed or wanted - they would make sure that I had it. I was well and truly spoilt and I knew it.

But I couldn't bring Matthew, it will be too awkward for him. We were still too new and I didn't know if we were ready for such a big, big step. Meeting the parents wasn't something to be taken lightly. It was nerve racking enough for me when he met Heather!

It's a kind offer but we've already made plans.
x

I put my phone face down on my desk and resumed work. I barely typed one word when my phone buzzed. I picked it up and inwardly groaned when I saw my mum's picture.

"Hello?" I said, trying to hide my exasperation at the fact she can't take no for an answer.

Oh, just like someone else I love.

"Hello, darling. So, when were you planning on telling me that you were seeing someone?"

"Mum, it's still quite new between us. I don't want to force him to come, he isn't what you'd call a conventional man,"

"What does that mean?"

I let out a sigh.

"Mum, please. I have to do things at my own pace,"

My mum paused and I knew she was itching to say something.

"Ok, but can I see you this weekend? So I can give you your gift?"

"Yes, of course," and I don't know what came over me, but I felt guilty. I felt like I was pushing away from her when all she wanted to do was love me. "Do you want to meet me for lunch?"

"Today?" Her surprise was evident.

"Yes, does 12pm work for you?"

"Yes, it does!" I heard the excitement in her sweet, posh voice, she was practically giddy with uncontrolled glee.

We ended the call and I got back to work. I knew I was going to get the third degree at lunchtime and I didn't know if I was ready for that just yet.

IT REACHED LUNCHTIME AND I made my way down to the lobby. I stepped out of the lift and immediately spotted my mum. She was waiting over by the revolving door and looked as though she was taking in her surroundings. She gazed up at the ceiling and at the artwork that hung on the tall walls.

She was dressed in jeans paired with black heels and a dark red blazer. She looked so youthful and elegant. My eyes were fixed on my mum when all of a sudden my line of sight was broken as Matthew sidestepped smoothly in front of me out of nowhere, blocking my path.

"Felicity," he said as he cupped my elbow, steering me out of the way from the next wave of people exciting the lifts behind me. As he did, I saw the two men who'd hidden him from my view.

The men smiled at me and Matthew introduced them. He then excused us and took me to one side, away from earshot.

"Are you grabbing some lunch?" He asked.

"Yes, I'm -"

"Oh excellent, I'll join you. I'm famished!" Matthew said, cutting me off.

Shit.

"Oh, erm, Matthew, I'm meeting my mum for lunch," I said, offering him an apologetic smile.

His brow furrowed for a moment but then his expression shifted.

"Your mother?" he asked.

I nodded. Where was he going with this?

"Can I join you two?"

Oh no.

"Erm, I-"

"Please," he asked.

How could I possibly say no to him when he used his boyish charm on me?

I sighed.

"Fine, come on, she's waiting over there," I grabbed his hand and led him over to where my mum was waiting. "Just to warn you, she will ask you lots of questions, it will feel like an interview,"

He chuckled, "I'm sure I can handle it,"

As we approached my mum, her mouth dropped open. She stared at Matthew taking in the sight of him from head to toe.

"Mrs. Walker," Matthew offered her his hand, "Nice to meet you, I'm-"

"Oh I know who you are, Mr. Harper," my mum interrupted him as she shook his hand.

How did she know him?! I thought.

"We've met briefly before, you are an ambassador of my husband's hospital, well not his hospital, the one he works at! Or used to work at - he's semi-retired now" my mum rambled on, giggling shyly like an idiot.

I rolled my eyes, she was affected by his sheer handsomeness too. *Like mother, like daughter.*

"Well, it's lovely to meet you, again, and I can see where Felicity gets her smile from," Matthew said, flashing her a heart stopping grin.

Oh the irony!

"Shall we?" Matthew said, gesturing towards the door. Matthew let us through first and followed closely behind.

As we stepped out into the fresh September air, my mum linked her arm in mine and leant in towards my ear, "why didn't you mention that you are dating a rich bachelor?"

"Mum, it's not all about the money you know!" I replied quietly.

My mum had come from money. My grandparents were wealthy and apparently when my mum married my dad, it was almost frowned upon. A renowned neurosurgeon still wasn't good enough for their little girl. I wondered idly what my grandparents would have made of Matthew if they were still with us today.

"So, did you ladies have some place in mind to eat?" Matthew asked.

"Erm, well I was thinking that deli down Cole

Street," I said.

Matthew looked almost disgusted with my choice. "Oh, I think we can do better than that! Come, Stan is round the corner,"

Mum was beaming ear to ear as Matthew opened the rear passenger door of the Audi for her. She gracefully got in and I clambered up into the seat next to her. We made our way out of the City of London and headed towards Covent Garden. I hoped it wasn't far as I only had an hour for lunch and it was 12:20pm already.

"Matthew, where are we going? I'm conscious I only have an hour for lunch," I said leaning over to the front passenger seat.

My mum shot me a disapproving look that told me to watch my manners. The same look I got when I was eight years old and I had my elbows on the table.

"Don't worry about the time," Matthew said and he pulled out his phone from his pocket.

"What are you doing?" I asked, my eyes wide as I knew exactly what he was doing.

"There, now you have all the time we need,"

"Matthew!"

"I've emailed Evelyn, I've told here you are taking an extended lunch break,"

"Why? Why would you do that?" I was mortified. I didn't need Matthew doing that on my behalf.

"Felicity," my mum scolded.

I crossed my arms and sat back in my seat, who

did he think he was?

He's your boss's boss's boss, stupid. I rolled my eyes at my subconscious.

Stanley dropped us off outside a restaurant and Matthew rounded the car, opening the door for me. As I climbed out, Matthew leant down so that his lips were almost touching my ears.

"I've upset you, haven't I?" he whispered.

"No, you've not upset me, you've *pissed* me off,"

I walked round him towards my mum, leaving him standing behind me. The doorman opened the doors and we stepped inside *Café Luna.* It was a large restaurant with lots of leather banquettes and a long marble dining bar. The Maître d' greeted us and we were seated on a round table at a booth. He handed us the menus and took our drink orders.

"So, Matthew, tell me about yourself," My mum said to him.

"Well, Mrs. Walker, what do you want to know?"

"Oh, please call me Meredith!" My mum blushed.

"Very well, what would you like to know, Meredith?"

The pair of them discussed Matthew's job and the charity work my mum occasionally dabbled in. I was saved from boredom by the waiter who brought over our lunch.

"Matthew, I hear you and Felicity have plans tomorrow evening?"

Oh no.

I looked over to my mum and gave her a scowl. She knew exactly what she was doing.

Matthew looked to me mid-bite of his steak, “Erm, do we?”

Brilliant.

“Well, you definitely do now!” My mum clapped her hands together, “Felicity's father and I would love to have you round for dinner tomorrow night, to celebrate Felicity's special day!”

Shit. Shit. Shit.

Matthew looked at me with a bemused expression on his face, “I would love to come to dinner for Felicity's special day.”

“No, no you really wouldn’t,” I said as I gave my mum a look that told her I wasn’t happy.

“Nonsense, he would love it!”

I leant over to Matthew, “We’ll talk about this later,”

“I look forward to it, Felicity,” he smirked.

Lunch finally came to an end and we started to make our way out of the restaurant. As we stepped out onto the pavement, we were suddenly mobbed by people with dictaphones and cameras.

Shit, it's the press. I thought, panicking as I tried to turn away from the flashes.

Matthew calmly took mine and my mum’s hand and pushed his way through the crowd. Stanley swiftly opened the door of the Audi and we all climbed in. I was dazed by all the flashing lights as we drove away.

"Shit," Matthew muttered under his breath.

"How did they know we were here?" I asked.

"Someone must have tipped them off,"

I frowned, who the hell knew where we were?

"So, the press knows about you two then?" my mum said nonchalantly, causing me to roll my eyes at her tone.

I was nowhere near prepared for the circus that seemed to follow Matthew and I.

Once we were back at the office I said goodbye to my mum and Matthew walked with me through the lobby.

"What are we going to do about the press?" I asked him.

"Don't worry, I have my lawyers on it, they are contacting the relevant people to find out where they got the information from."

I looked up at him, "you can do that?" I asked, I have to say, I was impressed.

"Felicity, I am a very powerful man," he smirked, "so," he said changing the subject, "what is this special day your mother has invited me to dinner for? I know it's not your birthday as that's in February,"

I just knew he'd been itching to ask me that the whole way back to the office.

I sighed and pressed the call button for the lift. "No, it's not my birthday."

"Then what is it? Why are you being so coy?"

The lift arrived and we stepped in. As it was past 2pm it was empty and we were alone. “It's my adoption day,” I said quietly.

Matthew looked perplexed, “you were adopted?”

“Yes,”

“Why didn’t you tell me?”

I looked down at the floor, “It’s because you are so perfect and well, I’m not. Meredith and Hugh are perfect too, but my mother, she wasn’t so perfect. She was a junkie and a drunk -”

And before I could say another word, Matthew lunged at me, pushing me up against the mirrored wall. Both hands were on my face, keeping me in place as his lips were on mine. I moaned loudly, allowing his tongue to invade my mouth. He took full advantage of the empty lift.

“You. Are. Perfect.” he said in between kisses. “Please don’t ever say you are anything but, ok?”

As his kind eyes burnt into mine, I felt a rogue tear slowly escape and roll down my cheek. I nodded my agreement.

“Good, and you know I’m far from perfect too,”

Matthew pulled me close up against his chest, his chin resting upon my head as he stroked me back in a soothing motion.

“Your mother may not have been perfect, but she made you,”

“Hmmm,” I said against his chest.

And Matthew continued to hold me until the

lift reached my floor.

I OPENED THE FRONT door and gingerly walked in. Silence. The coast was clear. I hastily ran to my room and closed the door.

Oh this is ridiculous.

Why was I the one who was tiptoeing around? She was the one who had upset *me* and slagged off my boyfriend, the man I love. I packed an overnight bag for tonight and Friday night. As I was zipping up the bag I heard the front door open. Momentarily my heart leapt into my mouth.

Shit.

I heard footsteps outside my bedroom door, they slowly started disappearing out of earshot. I fumbled with the zip and slung the duffel bag over my shoulder. I placed my hand on the door handle and paused. I took a deep breath in and opened it.

Please don't be Heather. Please don't be Heather. I repeated in my head.

I opened the door and stepped out, as I headed to the front door I heard my name behind me.

"Fliss?"

I turned, relieved at the sound of Ethan's voice.

"Hey, you,"

"I haven't seen you in, well forever," he said.

He was standing with his hands in his pockets and his shoulders were scrunched up around his ears. His usually sparkling green eyes were red and bloodshot. He'd been crying.

"Sorry I've been MIA lately. Heather and I had a fight," I said, shrugging my shoulders.

He offered me a slight smile although it didn't reach his eyes.

"Yeah, I heard. She misses you, you know?"

Ethan's words were like a kick in the stomach. I missed her too.

"Well, she should have thought about that before picking holes in my relationship,"

Ethan didn't say anything, instead he just stood there, muted. Usually he would have something to say about the situation, even if Heather and I argued about the smallest thing, he would always have an opinion on the matter.

"What's wrong?" I asked, cocking my head to one side.

"Oh, nothing," He removed his hands from his pockets and instead crossed his arms in defence.

I frowned at my friend's dismissal, "you've been crying,"

Ethan sighed and looked away from me. He squeezed his eyes shut, "come sit with me," he said.

I followed Ethan over to the settees and took a seat next to him. He turned to face me and I moved so I was looking at him.

"You know I went to the doctors last week?"

"Yeah,"

"Well, I've had some tests done and it turns

out I have cancer,"

Fuck! No!

I felt the blood drain from my face.

"What? No. Cancer? But you're so young," He couldn't have cancer. He just couldn't, there must have been some mistake.

"I know, that's what I thought. But I noticed a lump on my groin and decided to get it checked out. They did a biopsy and well, I have Hodgkin lymphoma,"

I didn't say anything. I couldn't. I didn't know what to say to him.

"I-," I tried to search for the right words to say, "Ethan, I'm so sorry,"

"Thanks, I know it sucks but they said its early stages and they should be able to treat it,"

Oh thank God!

"Will you have to have chemo?"

"Yeah, which will suck but it's what I have to do,"

"Well, thank you for telling me. Have you told Sam?"

He took in a deep breath and shook his head. "No, not yet,"

"Heather?"

"Nope, just you,"

I offered Ethan a warm comforting smile and placed my hand over his tightly grasped hands. Just as I did, the front door opened and Heather walked in.

"Oh, hi," she said, looking at me. She then

looked down at my hand. “What's happened?”

I turned to face Ethan who then looked at me. Heather flung her bag onto the floor and walked over to us. She took a seat in the arm chair and asked again.

“I have cancer,” Ethan said quietly. It was as if every time he said the words aloud it physically hurt him.

“No you don’t,” Heather laughed.

I looked over at Heather who read my expression causing her face to fall.

“Jesus, Eth,”

“Yeah, it blows,”

“Just puts things into perspective doesn’t it,” I said, looking at Heather.

Ethan looked at me and then to Heather, “come on you two, please make up. I can’t be going through chemo knowing my two best friends are at each other's throats,”

“He’s right,” I said.

“Yeah, he is,” Heather replied, fiddling with her nails. “I’m sorry for what I said to you, Fliss, I just love you so much. I just want you to be happy. And I had no idea about Luke. If I knew, I would have kicked his butt you know,”

I let out a chuckle, “I know, but don’t worry, I made him pay,”

“And I’m sorry for what I said about Matthew, and I didn’t mean to call you needy and insecure, you're not - you are just -” she stopped, “oh I don’t know,” she said shaking her head.

"Shit, you called her needy and insecure? Whoa," Ethan said, joking.

"I know, right? What a bitch!" I said giggling.

Heather rolled her eyes and got up, "I don't know about you, but does anyone fancy a drink?"

"Yeah, fuck it! My chemo hasn't started yet," Ethan said, getting up to get a beer from the fridge. "Let's order a Chinese too, I think we need a night to ourselves, what do you say?"

Ethan looked at me and then I looked at my duffel bag that was abandoned on the floor. I'm sure Matthew would understand that I needed to be with my friends right now. I sent him a text and joined them by pouring myself a glass of wine.

I GOT TO WORK the next day feeling a little worse for wear. We managed to drink and eat the night away in spectacular fashion. The Tube ride into work was horrendous and I slowly made my way to the kitchen for a large coffee.

"Felicity, can I see you for a minute, in my office?" Evelyn called from behind me just as I sit down at my desk.

Just what I need. I said as I rolled my eyes before turning round to face her.

"Yep, of course," I picked up my note pad and made my way into her office.

As I entered, I saw Ron the Managing Director sitting on the chair in the corner of Evelyn's office.

"Oh, Hi, Ron." I said.

"Felicity," He nodded brusquely, "come, take a seat,"

Feeling somewhat uneasy, I sat down in the chair opposite Evelyn's desk. Ron moved so that he was standing behind Evelyn with his arms folded leaning against the wall.

"So," Evelyn started, "we have noticed that your work and time keeping is slipping slightly,"

What?

"I'm sorry?" I asked in disbelief.

No it hasn't.

"You are somewhat distracted as of late," Ron said, piping up.

I looked from him to Evelyn, trying to read them.

"Is this about Matthew - I mean, Mr. Harper?" I asked.

It has to be. Maybe they do have a problem with me sleeping with their boss.

Ron suddenly seemed uncomfortable and shifted on his feet, unfolding his arms and placing them firmly in his pocket. Evelyn's expression remained stern, her eyes still fixed on mine.

"Yes, Felicity, it does," she stopped and then carried on, "your focus has switched and I meant what I said about not wanting to lose you. But, if you carry on, we won't have much choice,"

"What?" my voice was raised slightly. Was that

a threat?

"We need our team to be one hundred percent focused at all times. And, you are unfortunately not. Not to mention the fact that your name is splashed all over the tabloids this morning,"

Fuck.

"What we mean is," Ron said, piping up once more, "that we are going to be reviewing your performance closely over the next few weeks or so,"

"Also, we've heard mumbles from your team about the fact you're sleeping with the new owner of the company. We can't be viewed as treating you any differently,"

"I can't believe this," I said, shaking my head.

After all the time and effort I had put into the company over the last three years, and even after Luke *died*, I still made an effort to come in. All this just because I had taken a long lunch hour today, took yesterday off and left early *once* to go to a charity fundraiser. I was being penalised just in case my colleagues didn't like who my boyfriend was?

"Who I may or may not be sleeping with is no one's concern but mine. It's not yours and nor is it the guys out there," I got up from the chair, feeling enraged.

"I'm not with Matthew just to 'get ahead', we are in a relationship and I LOVE HIM. We are a couple and if you two or anybody else has a problem with it, I suggest you take it up with him, he is your boss after all,"

I turned on my heels and headed for the bathroom. I was fuming. I pushed through the doors and into a cubical. I locked the door behind me and sank to the floor, releasing the tears I was holding back in front of them. The tears flowed with voracity and I couldn't stop them. I cried for Ethan, I cried for all the anger I had for Heather from our fight, I cried for poor Amber and I cried for me. I was in an impossible situation. I felt I was being forced to choose between the man I loved and the job I loved.

I finally managed to compose myself and peeled myself up off the floor. I couldn't let this get to me. Not today. It was a happy day. It was the day I was rescued and finally loved and I would be damned if I let anyone ruin that for me.

I returned to my desk after I cleaned myself up and got to work. I needed this day to go as quickly as possible. I was quiet for the rest of the day, only speaking to people to answer them or taking phone calls. I only received a few texts from Matthew during the day as he was in meetings and I didn't let on to what had happened this morning. I heard whispers around me, my colleagues gossiping and surmising. Amber was the only one who asked me if I'm ok, given that she knew about Matthew.

It reached bang on 5:00pm and I closed my Mac thanking God that we finished early on a Friday.

I really need to get outta here.

I made my way down to the lobby feeling like shit. I hadn't felt like this when leaving work before. I actually felt relieved that I didn't have to go back for two days. As I entered the lobby, Matthew was already waiting for me.

"Hello," he said to me as I reached him.

"Hi,"

"What's wrong? You're upset," Matthew said, frowning down at me as he studied my face.

I shook my head, pretending everything was ok, "Just a rubbish day, but it's over now,"

He nodded once and took me by the hand leading me to where Stanley was waiting by the Audi. Stanley smiled and opened the door for me. Matthew walked round to the other side and got in next to me. "I'll get Stan to drop you off at home, I'll come and pick you up. What time do we have to be at your parents house?"

Oh, where is he going? I thought.

"Half seven, where are you going then?" I asked.

"I have something that needs attending to ," he replied quickly.

I frowned at his abrupt reply.

"Are you mad?" I asked.

He took a sharp inhale of breath and ran his hand through his chocolate brown hair, "No, I've got a lot on my mind, that's all,"

"Oh, ok."

"But, as you've mentioned it, we made plans,

plans that you cancelled last minute,"

Oh. He was mad at me for cancelling on him last night.

I blinked at him in disbelief, "I cancelled because I needed to be with my friends? And that's what has made you mad?"

"Yes, that among other things,"

"Oh my God," I said, shaking my head.

"When we make plans, I expect you to follow through with them or at least have the courtesy to let me know why you are cancelling on me,"

"My friend just found out that he has cancer," I spat back at him.

Matthew didn't even flinch, he just stared at me with his ocean blues.

"Are you really that insensitive?" I asked not giving a shit to the fact that Stanley could hear us.

Matthew turned his gaze away from me and instead stared at the road ahead.

"He is one of my best friends, he is like a brother to me. He told me and Heather and we decided that we all needed a night together, you know to support him,

"I'm supposed to come first," he said bluntly.

I looked at him with wide eyes, totally dumbfounded at what he was saying to me. Him of all people should know what going through cancer was like considering he lost his mum to it.

"You do come first, I love you for Christ sake!" I unbuckled my seat belt, slid across the seat and crawled onto his lap, taking him by surprise. “Sometimes in relationships you have to juggle the people you love. Me cancelling or changing plans doesn't mean I love you any less. I have to make time for the other people in my life you know, as much as my life starts and ends with you,”

Matthew relaxed and squeezed me tightly. “I’m sorry, I’ve never been in this situation. If someone says they are going to see me, they generally do,”

“What happens if someone wants to cancel a meeting?” I asked, pulling away so that I could see him.

He smirked down at me, his eyes dancing with humour, “oh baby, people never cancel on me. If they do, they don’t get another chance and they know it,”

I rolled my eyes at him, “Surely Long-Legged-Lydia ditched you sometimes?”

“Long-Legged-Lydia?” he said as he cocked an eyebrow in amusement, he then stopped to think about the question, “no, I don’t recall her doing so. She was like a puppy, always under my feet, there awaiting my every beck and call. I could never get rid of her or get a moment to myself,”

“Oh really?”

“Yes, and anyway, I like your little legs, they are more than long enough, especially when they are wrapped around my neck, ” he winked.

“Shhh,” I said, putting my finger up to my lips

and looking over at Stanley.

"Baby, don't worry about Stan, he can't hear a thing,"

I frowned, not understanding.

"Earphones," he said pointing to his own ear.

"Oh," I breathed a sigh of relief.

MATTHEW PULLED ONTO THE paved driveway of my parents Tudor-Style house. The house was breathtaking, it was picture perfect even the bushes out the front were perfect with not even a stem out of place. The traffic was surprisingly clear for a Friday evening so we made it to Richmond in good time.

"Are you ready for this?" I asked as Matthew switched off the ignition of the Mercedes.

He took my hand and gave it a reassuring squeeze, "I am indeed,"

I wish I was. I thought as I smiled at him.

Matthew climbed out of the car and opened the passenger door for me. He held my hand again as I peeled myself out of the seat.

Before I was even out of the car, my mum opened the front door, practically beaming. She looked stunning and sophisticated in a grey wrap dress. She was youthful beyond her years and was the definition of a trophy wife.

"Hello, you two," she greeted as we approached the front door.

"Hi, mum," I said as she wrapped me in a warm

hug.

"Matthew, how lovely to see you again,"

Matthew looked as though he had stopped breathing for a second when my mother leant up slightly to place a kiss upon his cheek. Then, from behind my mum, my dad appeared. My dad was a tall man, as tall as Matthew, if not slightly taller. My dad welcomed me with his kind warm eyes and bear hug.

"Hello, darling,"

"Hi, daddy." I lifted up on tiptoes and squeezed him tightly, embracing the feel of being in my dad's arms.

My dad released me and held me at arms length, examining every inch of me. "You look well, Fliss,"

I smiled back at him, "I am well," realising that Matthew was standing behind me, I introduced them, "Matthew, you've met my mum, Meredith. This is my dad, Hugh. Dad, this is Matthew Harper,"

Matthew took a step forward with his hand outstretched, "Mr. Walker, what a pleasure to meet you." he said, smiling his usual megawatt smile that always won people over.

My dad paused for a beat and then took his hand and shook it, "Please, call me Hugh and the pleasure is all mine, Matthew,"

The two men shook hands and Matthew was the first one to release his grip and look away. It was then that I realised he was uncomfortable, maybe even nervous. I'd not seen him respond like that in anyone else's company before. Normally, he would be the one in control and the one who made others feel unsettled. But, for some reason my dad was making him feel that way.

"Come in, it's chilly out here," my mum said, ushering us into the hallway.

Matthew removed my leather jacket and my dad took it from him, placing it over the banister.

"Can I get anyone a drink?" My mum asked.

"Please," Matthew and I answered in unison.

"Already in sync I see," my mum gushed, "Matthew, would you like a beer or wine?"

"Wine, please,"

"Certainly, we are having lamb so is red ok?"

"Even better," he replied with a smile.

My mum blushed slightly and turned to me once she'd composed herself, "and what would you like, darling?"

"I'll have a glass of red too,"

My mum looked at me with a quizzical expression but then nodded and headed off into the kitchen.

"Please, take a seat," My dad said to us.

We turned and headed into the living room, my dad took a seat in his arm chair and Matthew and I sat on the two seater settee.

"So," my dad began, "where did you two meet?"

I felt my face flush with embarrassment at the thought of how we met. "Erm, well it was quite embarrassing," I said.

Matthew squeezed my hand that had suddenly become sweaty, why was I suddenly so nervous?

"We met when I came in for a meeting, just before I bought out the company Felicity works for," he smiled warmly down at me as he recalled the meeting. "She was bringing in our drinks and tripped, and well, lets just say she made an impact on me,"

My dad smiled at me, he more than most knew about my clumsiness.

Just then, my mum reappeared with two glasses of wine, "here you go," she handed us a glass each.

"Thanks, mum,"

"Yes, thank you, Meredith," Matthew took the glass from my mum's hand and took a sip, "hmm, is that Châteauneuf-du-Pape?" he asked.

My mum blinked, "Why yes, yes it is!"

"One of the best bottles of Grenache in my opinion,"

Oh he was earning brownie points!

"I love him!" my mum said to my dad.

"So, do I," he replied.

My dad's subtle approval was what Matthew apparently needed to hear as he visibly relaxed and started to be himself.

I smiled as my dad and Matthew talked about all manner of things, work, cars, the economy.

"Dinner is on the table," my mum announced from the doorway.

We all stood and dad led the way first. I went to follow, but Matthew clutched my elbow, bringing me to an abrupt halt.

"Are you ok?" I asked.

"Yes, I just wanted a second alone,"

Oh.

Matthew placed his wine glass on the side table and placed his hands on either side of my face. He leant down and placed a soft, tender kiss to my lips. I sank into it, my knees weakening from his touch, although it may well have been from the wine I'd had.

"That was nice," I whispered as he removed his lips from mine.

"You are amazing, you know how I feel about you, don't you, I never want to be without you," he said, his eyes full of admiration.

I smiled at him as tears of happiness and love began to fill my eyes. It was the first time he had said anything like that to me. I reached up, touching his cheek, I watched as his expression changed to one of panic and then back to admiration.

"You look stunning in this dress," Matthew breathed as he ran his fingers underneath the strap of my little black dress. It was a bodycon dress so it hugged my curves nicely, "I can't wait to peel you out of this later. I'm going to fuck you senseless," he growled.

His voice was low and throaty which made me all the more hotter for him.

My mum appeared from behind me, causing us to break contact, "come on, it will get cold,"

I took Matthew's hand and we walked into the dining room. I was always hit with nostalgia every time I was in this room, it was home to so many memories from Christmases, Birthdays and of course adoption day dinners.

A crystal chandelier hung over the wooden table and a portrait of my great-great Grandfather hung proudly on the wall. Supposedly he was a Sir or something important back in the day.

My mum had laid the table as beautifully as always, it was covered with a crisp white linen tablecloth, and in the middle of the table was a candle centrepiece.

We took our places. My dad was opposite me next to my mum and Matthew was seated beside me.

"To you two," my mum raised her glass. I smiled as we all followed her lead and raised a glass. "Now, dig in!"

We ate our dinner while chatting and swapping various stories, mainly about my childhood. It was all very embarrassing.

"So, Matthew, tell me about your childhood," My dad said.

Matthew instantly froze and became rigid. I could feel the panic radiating off him.

Change the subject, Felicity.

"Mum, have you read the new book by - "

"Felicity Jayne, don't interrupt," my mum scolded me, cutting me off mid sentence.

Matthew cleared his throat and put down his knife and fork. "My early childhood was a very happy one," I felt Matthew's hand grab hold of mine under the table, "but, unfortunately my mother died when I was nine years old,"

"Oh, Matthew, I am so sorry," My mum gasped.

"Thank you, it was a long time ago now,"

"That must have been very hard for you, being so young," My dad said.

"Yes, it wasn't easy, but you learn to live and deal with the grief,"

"Did your mother work?" My mum asked, trying to steer the conversation away from her death.

"She did, she was a Theatre Nurse at Queen Mary's Hospital,"

"Oh my goodness, was she?!" My mum gasped with surprise and then turned to my dad, "Hugh, when did you work there?"

My dad paused, his fork midway to his mouth, "um, I can't remember, early nineties perhaps,"

Matthews eyebrows shot up, "That would have been when she worked there, she was working there until I was around six or seven years old and then she left, although, I can't remember why, she did. Her name was, Katherine Harper,"

"How old are you, Matthew?" My mum asked

"Thirty three,"

My mum looked up at the ceiling, while

appearing to do some sums, "ok, so you were born in 1989 and if you were six or seven when she worked there, that would have been 1995," she turned to my dad again, "yes, Hugh, you were definitely there that year, because we were having IVF then,"

My heart swelled in my chest at the thought of my parents going through IVF due to their fertility problems. That was another reason I never told my mum about my termination. I couldn't bear the guilt of having fallen pregnant so easily and by accident, when my parents tried for years with many miscarriages until, they decided to adopt me.

"Oh yes, of course," my dad said as he poured more gravy over his lamb chop.

"Did you know my mother then? Matthew asked, his face lighting up at the prospect.

"No, not that I can recall but, there were always nurses moving around from ward to ward after surgeries,"

Disappointment was written all over Matthew's face. I'd not seen him look that way before, he looked like a child who had just dropped his ice cream onto the floor. He obviously wanted to hear stories about the woman he so clearly adored and missed terribly.

My mum, being my mum, was completely oblivious to the situation and continued to chat away about my dad's time at the hospital.

Once we had finished, my mum got up from

the table and took our plates into the kitchen.

"Can I help mum?" I asked, feeling bad that she had cooked such a delicious meal and now had to clear up.

"No, certainly not. Stay here with Matthew and your father, I will bring dessert in shortly,"

As soon as she left the room my dad excused himself to use the bathroom.

"Are you ok?" I asked as I grasped Matthew's hand.

"Yes, thank you, are you?" He asked.

I nodded, " you seemed quite during dinner, you know after talking about your mum,"

He frowned, "I'm sorry, I didn't mean to be,"

"I know all of this is a big step for you,"

Matthew's eyes softened as he bought my hand up to his lips, "I wouldn't have done this for anyone else,"

"Not even Lydia?" I asked as his soft lips brushed over my knuckles.

"No, she was estranged from her parents who live in Portugal, so I never met them,"

"Well, I feel very honoured," I winked.

My dad returned to the dining room just as my mum brought in one of her famous sherry trifles. "I hope you have some room in those stomachs of yours!" She placed it down in the middle of the table and stepped back to let us all admire her handiwork.

As always, it looked incredible. It had a perfect amount of sponge fingers that had soaked up the layer of jam, and laced with sherry. Everything, even down to the white syllabub topping, was mouth wateringly good. Mum served us each a generous portion and we dug in.

Once the trifle had been devoured, we all moved into the living room for an after dinner coffee, and also for my parents to give me my 'Adoption Day' present.

Mum handed me a glittery pink gift bag. I ripped the piece of tape that was holding the bag shut and pulled out a rectangular shaped box. I removed the lid of the box and inside was a beautiful white gold bracelet. I carefully removed the bracelet from the box and inspected it up close. A row of sparkling white stones adorned the bracelet, and more stones dangled from it. It was simply gorgeous, and screamed expensive.

"Thank you, mum, dad. It's beautiful," I beamed.

"Anything for our little girl," My dad said.

"Happy Adoption Day, darling. We are so glad you came into our lives," Mum pulled me into a tight embrace. I could see Matthew looking at us over her shoulder. He was smiling warmly at us. And suddenly I felt guilty. I felt guilty at the fact I had loving parents that loved me and would do anything for me. He didn't, not anymore. He hadn't had that since he was nine years old. The thought broke my heart.

We had enjoyed our coffees and before we knew it, it was 11:30pm. I let out a yawn and that was our queue to leave. We said our goodbyes to my parents and Matthew drove us back to his penthouse. I was half asleep when we pulled into the carpark.

"We're home, darling," Matthew whispered to me as he caressed my face.

We walked over to the lift, hand in hand and Matthew put in the numbers for the penthouse. Once we arrived at the top floor, the doors opened and we exited the lift into the lobby and then through to the living area.

Matthew tossed the car keys into a dish on the console table and suddenly he turned towards me, with fire in his eyes. Before I could process what was about to happen, his hands were at my face and his lips on mine. He pushed his way into my mouth with his tongue, I tilted my head up and he deepened the kiss further. His lips firm, yet so soft, His tongue found mine and he was deep, licking and tasting me. The sensation caused goose bumps to spread like wildfire all over my body. I could feel him begin to thicken and lengthen against my leg.

"You are so fucking gorgeous, baby," he growled as he came up for air.

"Matthew . . ."

"Christ, you turn me on so much,"

One of his hands cradled my nape, holding me, capturing me so I was unable to move. I arched myself into him as my fingers gripped into his muscular upper arms. Everything tightened and clenched. *God, I needed him so badly.*

Suddenly, Matthew bent down and lifted me up off the ground, the whole time his mouth never left mine. I wrapped my legs around his waist while he made his way down the hall and into his bedroom.

He dropped me onto the sheets and he began to strip himself of his clothes. I licked my dry lips in pure desire for the sight of the powerful, sexy man that was standing above me, naked.

His knees sank into the bed and his lips found mine once more. "You drive me crazy," he said in a sexy, husky voice. He moved his mouth from my lips and began nipping at my jaw and chin, tiny nips that sent bursts of pleasure pulsing through me and down to my core.

I tried to stifle a cry as he continued his sweet, sweet torture, "Matthew.." I breathed.

His eyes opened and he gazed down at me, they were full of heat and desire, "You. Are. So. Beautiful," he said in between kisses.

Matthew started making his way down my body with his hands and mouth, kissing my shoulders and arms, while his hands skimmed over my dress until they were at the hem.

"Arch your back, baby,"

I complied and I lifted myself up, giving him better access to where he wanted to be. He pushed my dress up so that it was bunched up over my waist. His eyes lit up in appreciation at my lack of underwear.

"Oh, Miss. Walker, you are full of surprises,"

I shot him a wicked grin and he groaned. All of a sudden his head bobbed down and his tongue found my clit. As his tongue circled, a soft sound escaped me. Reaching down, my hands found his hair and I gently pulled at the strands. The feeling was so overwhelming, I was on the brink of an orgasm already.

"Matthew, I'm going to come,"

The pleasure builds inside me with each sensual lick until my body can't take anymore and I find my release. My orgasm ripples through me as I quiver from his touch. As I came, I felt a tear slide down my cheek. It was all too much to bear, the pleasure and the man who loved me.

"Felicity, what's wrong, did I hurt you?" Alarm was palpable in his voice as he sat up to look at me.

"No," I said, still crying as I smiled up at him, "It's just -" I sniffed, "It's you, it's everything. I love you so much,"

"Oh, baby,"

Matthew pulled me up so that I was in his lap. He gently smoothed my hair away from my face and gently wiped away the errant tears that were still flowing.

"I'm sorry," I whispered, pressing my forehead against his.

"What are you sorry for?"

"Everything, I'm sorry for what you have been through. I'm sorry for ever walking away from you. I'm sorry for crying,"

"Shhhh, it's ok, I'm ok," he placed a kiss on my lips and rocked me until I stopped crying.

This man was my safe place, my safe haven. He was all I ever wanted and more.

* * *

I can feel pain, excruciating pain. Everything hurts, my chest, my arms and my head, it's like nothing I have ever felt before. What happened? Where am I?

I try to open my eyes but nothing happens. I cannot open them. Why?

I can hear faint noises in the distance. Muted tones. They start to become clearer and clearer to me. I can hear a woman and a man.

It's Matthew.

My Matthew.

Suddenly, all the pieces begin to come together. I was in a car accident. I had brain surgery. I saw Luke, I chose Matthew.

"She's suffered what is called a Subdural haematoma, it's a bleed between the skull and the surface of the brain,"

"Christ, why is she still unconscious?" his words are anguished.

"Miss. Walker is in a medically induced coma. She suffered a cardiac arrest during her surgery so we had to resuscitate her. She will wake up when she

is ready, you just have to give her a few days and be patient. All her vitals are stable at the moment which is promising but, we will know more when she wakes up,"

I can hear Matthew exhale in a rush, "know what?"

"If there is no lasting damage to her brain,"

"Oh, Christ," I can feel my hand being squeezed. I try to squeeze it back but it's no good, I can't. I can't do anything and I can't move anything.

"She's going to need a good support system when she wakes up, she'll need a lot of help. She'll most likely need rehabilitation such as physiotherapy to help her with things like movement and muscle weakness,"

I can hear the doctor speaking about me but nothing is going in. All I want to do is tell Matthew that I'm ok and to tell him that I chose him. That I'll always choose him over Luke. I want him and nobody else.

I can hear footsteps slowly fading away from me, Matthew is still holding my hand. We are finally left alone in silence. I can feel Matthew squeezing my hand again as he plants a kiss to my cheek.

"Keep fighting baby, I need you," Matthew says, his voice cracking as he is speaking, "please come back to me, I'll love you no matter what happens, I'm here for you. We'll get through this together,"

I try to open my eyes again but it's no use, I can't.

Suddenly, unconsciousness claims me once more and I am back to a deep slumber.

SHORTLY AFTER SEVEN IN the morning, I was wide awake. I woke up from a dream about Matthew and I. We were walking hand in hand on a white sandy beach along the shoreline of a crystal blue ocean. It was perfect. The remnants of the dream still clung to me as I stirred.

I was laying on my back when I glanced to my left and saw Matthew sound asleep. Had he been there all night? He usually left me to go sleep in the spare room. He looked so peaceful. One arm was under the pillow and the other down by his side as he slept mostly on his stomach. The duvet cover was draped over his hips so his muscular, sculpted back was bare, revealing just a hint of his firm bottom.

He was so beautiful, he was relaxed and calm, he was the definition of tranquil in that moment.

I loved him so much.

I wanted to run my hands and mouth all over his bare back. I wanted to make him breathless and hot like he did me last night.

I sat up gently, trying not to wake him and I pressed my lips to his back, working my way from left to right reaching his shoulder blade.

"Hmmm," he murmured as he stretched.

"Good morning, you," I said as I nipped his skin.

I shifted so that I was sitting on top of his back.

I continued to kiss him, making my way to his neck. I planted sweet kisses from the nape all the way to his throat.

"What time is it?" He asked, his voice low and sleepy.

"Shh, don't worry about the time, it's just you and I, and no one else in the world," I brushed the tendrils of his overly long hair from his face.

Matthew flexed his muscles underneath me, telling me that he was about to move. I slid off him and watched as his powerfully big frame rolled so that he was now on his back.

"Come here," he commanded, patting his thighs.

I did as I was told and climbed back onto him, this time into his lap so that I was straddling him. I smiled at him and his sleepy demeanour. I marvelled at how sexy he looked in the morning with his five o'clock shadow gracing his chin. I took a mental picture, trying to savour the moment with this perfect man who I'd fallen in love with.

I bent down and ran the tip of my tongue over his lower lip and his strong hands gripped either side of my hips. He opened his mouth signalling for my tongue to enter.

"I love you, Matthew," I whispered into his mouth.

He then tilted his head up to me, deepening the kiss and taking control. His firm lips pressed against mine. His tongue stoked mine, my skin heating in response. I could feel his growing erection beneath me, trying to push its way free.

I leant forwards into him more so that my breasts were pushed up against his chest. My nipples tightened, aching for his touch. His hand moved from my hip and cupped the back of my head, pushing me closer into him as he sucked on my lips. My palms were flat against the mattress supporting my weight as I moaned into his mouth.

"You drive me crazy, you know that?" he moaned, breaking our kiss.

He shifted me slightly and brought up his knees for me to lean back on, forming a cradle. I leant back on him and his hands slid up under my pyjama tip and to my now heavy breasts. He cupped them, and circled my hard nipples with his thumb. They were aching for his touch.

"I love your tits, they are amazing," he said as his jaw tightened. He then removed his hands from my breast leaving me panting and wanting more. He trailed his hands down to my thighs and praised them apart with the backs of his hands. I was dressed in pyjama shorts so he had to work his way in through the leg. His fingertips gently stroked my clit.

"I love how ready you are for me," he said gruffly.

"You and only you," I said breathlessly as I fumbled around trying to lower the waistband of his boxers, wanting to free him.

Finally, he sprung free, standing to attention. I moaned and reached forward, gently gripping him in my hand as worked his shaft from the tip down to the root. Matthew hardened in response to my touch, desire rippling through his body.

Matthew's other hand reached back up to my breast and continued its slow sensual rhythm of circling my hardened nipple.

I leant my head back as I basked in the feeling of true intimacy. The moment was filled with lust, desire and *love*.

My hands continued to pump his erection with adoration as his hands did the same to me. I wanted to show him how much he meant to me and how much I needed him. His cock was hard and I could feel it throbbing in my hands, his thick head laced with pre-cum.

He clenched his jaw, trying to suppress a moan. He pushed down harder on my clit, causing me to lose my mind.

"Ah, God, Matthew. I need you," I panted, writhing on top of him.

"I love it when you beg for me, baby,"

"Oh yeah," I said in between breaths, "well get ready for some serious begging, cos I need you like crazy,"

Leaning forward, Matthew removed his finger from my pulsing clit and ripped apart my pyjama top, causing me to gasp out in pleasure.

God, this man was something else.

Using the tip of his tongue, he flicked it over

my nipple. I was so overwhelmed with pleasure I could have come from the sensation. And in that moment, I felt the heat radiating off him.

"What do you want, Felicity? Tell me?"

"I want you," I breathed, unable to find my voice.

"How do you want me?"

"Inside me, fuck me,"

"Fuck me, what?"

"Please,"

His chest expanded on a deep breath and in one swift move I was suddenly laying on my front with Matthew stripping me of my pyjama bottoms. I gasped as he forcefully entered me. The feeling was not one of pain, but one of relief. Relief to finally have him where I so desperately needed him to be.

"I'm going to fuck you hard so, I need you to remember your control word, only use it if it becomes too much or too painful. Do you remember what it is, Felicity?"

"Yes,"

"Say it,"

"Rainbow," I whispered.

"Good girl, you ready?"

"Yes,"

And that was it, he pounded into me, hard. So hard in fact that it felt unbelievably deep. I was lost as I tried to absorb the pleasure. He groaned and grunted as he continued to thrust. My body was pinned down to the mattress, I was physically unable to move. My face was pressed against the pillow and I could feel Matthew gathering my thick hair around his wrist. He pulled at it slightly, lifting my head off the pillow.

Our bodies rubbed together, skin to skin. I could feel the sweat transfer from his body to mine, and vice versa. I longed to look at Matthew's beautiful face but I couldn't. I squeezed my eyes shut, in an attempt to control my imminent orgasm that was building with every thrust. But, I couldn't suppress it. I was helpless, I was his, I was at his mercy. It was too intense but I didn't want it to stop.

"Come on, baby," he said through gritted teeth, "come for me,"

I erupted around him, again and again. I screamed loudly as the pleasure from my orgasm ripped me apart. I was breathless and sated. Matthew continued to fuck me like a man possessed, as if it was the last time he would ever be inside me. I felt the relentless drive of his cock while I still trembled from my climax.

Matthew came with a ferocious roar, coming so hard that I felt him spurting inside me. He collapsed onto me, his lungs desperate for breath.

"Oh, Jesus, Felicity," Matthew said as he panted in between breaths, "what have you done to me,"

"Mmmm," I replied, it was the only sound I could muster.

“Come, let’s go and get ourselves cleaned up,” he said as he kissed my back.

AFTER OUR SHOWER, MATTHEW left me to get dressed and headed to his home office. I put on black jeans and a khaki long sleeved tunic. I left my hair to dry naturally while I applied my make up. After I deemed myself decent enough, I made my way down the hall and in search of Matthew. As expected, he was in his office. He was on his phone looking out of the window at the London skyline, his back facing the door.

“Ok, get me the figures . . . Very good . . . Yes, that's correct,” he turned around so that he was facing me. He must have sensed me like the way I sensed him whenever he was near. Our bodies hummed with awareness in each other's company, we were so in tune with one another.

“Send it over, I’ve got to go,” he cut the call and dropped his iPhone onto the desk, his eyes never leaving mine. He strode over to me with such purpose, such grace.

“Hey, baby,” his mouth engulfed mine, leaving me breathless once again. I’d only just recovered from this morning!

“Hi,” I said, smiling from ear to ear.

Matthew sat down on his luxurious, plush looking office chair, “I am nearly finished here, what did you want to do today?”

I walked round to the side of his desk and bent

down, resting my hands on the arm rests of his chair, "you," I said.

"God, you are greedy aren't you," Matthew said.

"Well, I was starved of any physical activity before I met you," I grinned.

"Is that so? It seems like I've created a sex hungry maniac,"

"Shall I start calling you Frankenstein then?"

Matthew threw his head back with laughter, "We'll if I'm Frankenstein, you are definitely Dr. Jekyll and Mr. Hyde,"

"Huh?" I asked as I tilted my head to one side in confusion.

"Well, one minute you are this reserved, independent woman who doesn't let anything or anyone get in her way," he explained as he looked deeply into my eyes, "and then, you are like this, hot and needy, or should I say *greedy*," his eyes sparkled with a wicked gleam.

"Is that so? Well it's a good job I'm like this with just you, and not everyone else, isn't it, Frank," I winked.

"Frank?" He cocked an eyebrow at me.

"Yes, Frank,"

"Well it's a very good job because I'm not very good at sharing what's mine, come here, Doc," he patted his lap for me to sit.

I obeyed and sat on his lap, his arms coming round to hold me. I glanced down at his desk, it was pretty empty besides a laptop, paperwork, his iPhone, pens and a lamp. But, there was something else that caught my eye. A photograph in a black sleek frame. But it wasn't just a photograph - it was a photograph of us at the fundraiser.

"Since when did you have a copy of this framed?" I asked, reaching over for it.

I could feel him watching me as I lifted it up to have a closer look. I inspected it closely, looking at it like it was the first time I'd seen it.

"I purchased a copy before they cancelled the release to the press," he said as he kissed my shoulder.

"We look so happy,"

"We *are* so happy," he clarified.

"Yes, we are," I turned slightly so that I could kiss him.

"So, besides me, was there anything else you wanted to do today?"

I hesitated. What did I want to do at the weekend with a business mogul? But, I knew what I *needed* to do, "Well, I need to go home at some point, I haven't seen Heather or Ethan since he told me about his cancer-,"

"I wanted to talk to you about that," Matthew said, interrupting me, "is he having chemotherapy? If so, I want to pay for him to have it done privately,"

Whoa!

"Oh, Matthew, that's so sweet of you,"

"He's your friend, I know how much your

friends mean to you,"

"But you haven't even met him," I said, smiling through the tears that were building due to the gratitude I felt.

"If you like him, I like him,"

"You are an amazing human being, you know that right?" I said kissing him again.

"I don't know about that,"

"Trust me, you are," I cupped his cheeks in my hands as I gazed lovingly into his beautiful blue eyes.

"I suppose I need to like your friends too. Anyway, you never mention your friends, who are they? What are their names?"

Matthews mouth set into a grim line, "I erm," he stuttered, "well, I don't have any friends,"

"What?!" I gapped.

"Well, in the business world it's dog-eat-dog so you tend to make more enemies than friends," he shrugged.

"That's so sad! There's not anyone at all?"

Matthew stopped and thought about his answer for a second, "well, there's Nigel but we just play golf occasionally, but I wouldn't call him a friend, more an acquaintance if anything,"

"You could make friends with him,"

"I'm happy being acquaintances, it's easier that way,"

"Well, what about Stanley?" I asked.

"Felicity, he's an employee, not a friend,"

"Ouch, that's so cold,"

Matthew let out a careful chuckle, “see, told you I’m a monster,”

“Oh shut up you,” I scolded.

Matthew just looked at me with humour dancing around in his eyes.

I leant back, “what?”

“To think only a few weeks ago you could hardly look at me, and now you are telling me to shut up,”

“Yes, I know, we’ve both come a long way,”

“And apparently I’ve become lovable too,”

I smoothed his hair off his forehead, “You have, and I know it's happened all very quickly, but I do,”

“Thank you,” he placed a kiss on my lips.

“Any time,” I knew it was so early on in our relationship to say it but I couldn’t help it, I loved him. It was like no other feeling I’d ever felt before, my love for Luke didn’t even come close!

“I’ll get there, I promise,” he said quietly.

“I know,” I whispered.

I OPENED THE DOOR and walked into my flat. I was hit with a sudden wave of familiarity and comfort at walking into *my* home. I’d spent so much time at Matthew’s recently, I’d almost forgotten what the place looked like.

“Fliss!” Heather practically screamed when she saw me.

“Hey, you!” She hugged me tightly.

"How are you? How's it going? How did dinner at your parent's go? Did they like Matthew?" she asked, barely coming up for breath.

"Which one do you want me to answer first?"

"Sorry, I'm excited to see you," she blushed "how are you?"

"I'm very well thank you," I said grinning from ear to ear.

"Oh I bet you are, does mind blowing sex have anything to do with it?" She winked.

"Mind blowing orgasms more like,"

"Oh, Felicity, how you've changed," Heather giggled while playfully slapping my arm.

"Honestly, Hev, I feel like a new woman. He's changed me in a way I can't even begin to even explain,"

"Sex would do that to a girl,"

"Yes, but-" I stopped, "never mind," I shook my head, deciding not to share what I was about to.

Heather cocked her head to one side, looking at me, "but what?"

"Have you ever cried, you know, after you erm..," I blushed, it was very unlike me to even be talking about my sex life.

"After I came, climaxed, orgasmed?"

"Yes,"

She shook her head, not even needing to think about it, "no, I've never cried but, I think it's normal, I've read about it in magazines,"

"Oh, right,"

"Or, you were crying because it was that damn

good," she giggled.

"Yeah, probably," I said as I giggled with Heather.

HEATHER AND I DECIDED to grab some lunch, needing a proper catch up. As we left the flat and walked down the steps, I'd noticed that there was someone standing by one of the trees that lined the road. The figure was dressed in dark clothing with a hooded jacket that was covering their head. My guard was instantly up, something about the situation didn't feel right. Who were they and where were they loitering outside?

I tried to ignore the feeling of unease that I had as we grabbed a cab. We made our way into Belgravia and to a restaurant that was one of our favourite places to eat. After a good gossip over some paninis and a few too many Strawberry Daiquiris, Heather jumped on the Tube and travelled to Isaac's and I headed back to the flat to pack an overnight bag.

The taxi driver pulled the cab up to the pavement opposite my flat. I paid him and stumbled out of the back, feeling the full effects of one too many drinks. As I was thumbling round the bottom of my bag for the keys, I suddenly felt a presence behind me. I froze. Rooted to the spot.

"Felicity?"

The voice behind me was raspy and worn.

I didn't need to turn around to see who it was, I knew exactly who it belonged to. That voice would forever be burnt into my mind.

I took a breath and turned.

And, as expected, it was my birth mother.

I immediately sobered.

She was slightly shorter than me, her frame small and frail. Her once auburn hair was greying and was limp and lifeless. Just like her.

Her hollow eyes were heavy and dark but, even so, I could see the striking resemblance between us. A thought that I hated.

"What are you doing here?" I asked, my heart thumping in my chest.

"Why, what do you want?" I placed my hand on my hip.

I knew exactly what she wanted. It was either to get to know me or money.

"I want what I've always wanted, I want to know my daughter,"

Bingo!

My breathing caught in my chest at her words. I had no interest whatsoever getting to know the woman who neglected me and her body.

"No, I have a mother, I'm not your daughter anymore, we've covered this before,"

"Please, Felicity? I'm clean, I've been clean for six months now," she started rummaging round her coat pockets, "look, I have a chip," she proudly held up a round blue chip with six months prominently stamped in the centre.

I frowned at the chip that was being thrusted in my face. I couldn't understand what this proved. Sure, she hadn't had a fix for six months but that didn't mean she had *changed*. She was still the woman who was supposed to care for me and keep me from harm's way. She did neither of those things. In fact, she put me in harm's way, nearly causing me to starve to death. One time, I even attempted to cook chicken nuggets myself by standing on a chair while turning on the hob. Luckily, she woke up from yet another overdose and stopped me from setting fire to the bag they came in.

"No, I'm sorry but no," I paused, why was I apologising? "Actually, scrap that, I'm not sorry. *You* should be the one apologising to *me*. But, even then they would be just words,"

Her bottom lip quivered in response, clearly taken aback by my outburst, "Please,"

I shook my head, "nope, not happening," I turned and began to walk away from her.

"What would you say if I told you something I know about your boyfriend?"

I stopped just before I reached the first step of the staircase that led to my door.

Ah, the real reason she's here.

"He has a daughter,"

I felt the blood instantly draining from my face.

I shook my head at her again, "no, you are just saying that to hurt me, he doesn't. He would have told me such a thing,"

"I know her mum, she is a recovering addict like me,"

"Stop, just stop it!" I shouted, causing her to visibly jump at the anger in my voice. "What is your purpose for being here? For telling me this?" I looked over her painfully thin body, "do you want money? Is that what it is?"

"No, like I said I came here to get to know you. I wanted to make sure you were ok,"

"Well, you can go back to whatever hole you crawled out from because, I am fine!"

My heart was going ten to the dozen in my chest, my breathing had become erratic, I could feel the anger and panic building inside me. I was too enraged to cry but that wasn't stopping my tears threatening to spill out.

"How do you know I have a boyfriend anyway? And how do you know where I live?"

"I - I've been following you,"

Following me? What the fuck!

"And when I learnt that you were with *him,* I wanted to make sure you were being looked after. He certainly doesn't look after Ophelia,"

"Ophelia?" I asked even though I knew who she supposedly was.

"His daughter,"

"I - I need you to go now, please," I whispered, staring down at the floor.

"Felicity, please? I have changed,"

I shook my head and turned my back on her

again. I couldn't deal with her right now and the hand grenade that she had just thrown into my relationship.

13

I SENT MATTHEW a text telling him that I wasn't feeling very well. I needed not to see him until I got my head straight. Whenever I saw my birth mother, there was always a drama that followed behind her. Usually, it was money for her next fix or for her ever growing debt. But this time it was different. She had made it personal.

I moved the arm that was draped over my face and peered down to my side when I heard my phone ringing. It was Matthew calling me. It was the fourth call in a row. I knew that if I didn't answer soon that he would be round in a flash. I sat up on the sofa and picked it up, answering it.

"Hello?" I said, my voice horse from the crying that I had done.

"Sweetheart, what's wrong? Are you ok?" The concern was evident in his voice.

His voice was my undoing, causing the tears to flow down my cheeks.

"No, no I'm not," I said snivelling, "everything is messed up, it's all shit,"

"What's messed up, Felicity? You're not making sense,"

"She, she said -," I couldn't stop crying, I knew he couldn't understand me through the tears.

"Baby, try to calm down and breathe. I'm on my way, I'll be there as fast as I can,"

After he'd cut the call, I broke down again, crying into a cushion. Desperate sobs escaped my mouth as I dampened the cover with my tears. I wanted what *she* told me to be a lie so badly but I had a horrible feeling that this time she was actually telling me the truth.

The buzz of the intercom jerked me back to life. I wiped my eyes dry with my sleeve and slowly rose to my feet. I walked on shaky legs over to the door and pushed the button, before I could gather myself, Matthew burst into the room.

"Felicity," he breathed.

Milliseconds later, I was in his arms, being held tightly. Usually, it was my safe haven, whenever I was in his arms I felt as though nothing bad could ever happen. But now, well now I wanted to be anywhere but there. Suddenly, I couldn't breathe, my body began to tremble. I could feel the blood in my ears pounding in rhythm with my beating heart.

I pushed against his solid chest, trying to push my way out of his grip but it was impossible, he was too strong for me to move, "I can't breath,"

Matthew released me, "right, listen to me," he

cupped my face in his hands and bent down so he was eye level, “take a breath in and then out, Felicity.”

I followed his breaths and finally I managed to calm my erratic breathing.

“I’m ok,” I said, panting, feeling sick from my panic attack.

“Good. Come, let's get you a glass of water,”

Matthew walked over to the kitchen, “what cupboard are you glasses in?”

“The one above the dishwasher,”

Matthew took out a glass and filled it from the tap. He strode over to me on his long legs and handed me the glass.

I took a welcomed sip and sighed, putting the glass on the coffee table as I sat down in the armchair. I noticed how much my head was now throbbing with pain, I began to rub my temples as Matthew stood in front of me, hands in his trouser pockets.

“Are you going to tell me what that was about?” he asked, cocking his head to one side as he regarded me.

I stared down at the glass on the coffee table as I gripped my hands tightly together. Taking another breath, I opened my mouth but then swiftly closed it again. Not knowing quite what to say. Was I ready to confront him and detonate the hand grenade?

Suddenly, I found my voice, “My birth mother paid me a visit,” I said, still looking down at my glass.

"Oh? What did she want?"

"Who's Ophelia?" The words were out of my mouth before I could stop them.

Matthew stilled, not moving a muscle. I could see the answer written all over his face.

"Well your lack of response speaks volumes," I got up from the armchair, causing Matthew to take a step back, and walked over to the front door, "I'd like you to leave now," I said as I held the door open.

"Felicity, please let me explain,"

I slammed the door shut making him jump, "No! You don't get to explain," I shouted at the top of my voice, "You wanted me to trust you! And well, that's completely shot to shit now!"

Matthew recoiled from my repressed anger. "I'm sorry," he whispered under his breath so it was barely audible.

"And after everything I've shared about myself with you!" That's what made it hurt even more, I told him about my past, about Luke and the termination, all the while not having a clue that he had fathered a child.

"I know," Matthew looked anywhere but at me, his shoulders slumping down.

"I don't know if I can get over this, Matthew,"

Matthew's eyes flew up to mine, they were wide with panic and, maybe regret. My words hung in the air between us. I was broken, devastated from the lack of trust he so clearly had in me.

"Please, don't leave me again," he pleaded, his voice small.

"I-1" was all I could manage as the tears stung my eyes, a harsh lump forming in my throat. I didn't want to end things, Lord knows I didn't but, what other choice did I have? The deceit was far too big to be mended. First it was his engagement to Lydia that he kept from me and now this?

Matthew stepped towards me, caution in his eyes with every step he made. I watched him wearily. Suddenly, he dropped to his knees, the same way he did in the shower. He looked down at the floor just in front of him, not saying a word.

"Matthew?" I asked.

"I can't do this without you, Felicity. I won't be able to function or even go on without you, you are what keeps my heart pumping blood around my body," he looked up at me, tears clouded his eyes. "You have opened my heart back up after it was closed for so long. You've taught me to love again, to love you! I love you, Felicity,"

I couldn't talk. I had no idea what to say to him. He has just told me that he loved me. They were the three words that I wanted and needed him to say but, just at the wrong time.

"Matthew, I-I can't see a way past this for us. I really can't,"

Matthews' eyes gave way to the tears that were

building, they flowed down his cheeks. I had broken him, again.

"The reason I never told you about Ophelia was because it's part of my life that I'm not proud of. I was seventeen, in college and high most of the time," Matthew let out a sigh before continuing, "her mother was part of my group of friends. One night, we smoked and had one too many to drink and well, you can guess the rest,"

I didn't say anything, I couldn't.

Matthew carried on, "with all that you've told me about your birth mother, I felt I couldn't tell you about that side of me, I didn't want you to think I was like her, I know how much she hurt you, and it *still* hurting you, "

"Do you still take drugs?" I breathed.

"God, no!" Matthew answered instantaneously.

"Was it just cannabis that you used to smoke?"

"Yes,"

"Then you are nothing like her,"

"It was just a phase,"

I nodded as Matthew met my gaze.

"I promise I haven't touched it since,"

My mind went into overdrive, trying to digest all that he told me. Could we get past this? Could I trust that he was telling me everything? Could I handle a teenager, his *child*? I made the choice *no*t to handle one when I was just a teenager myself.

"Matthew, you have a sixteen year old

daughter, it's a big fucking deal," I stated, still in disbelief.

He nodded slowly "I know it is,"

"A daughter," I breathed. It was like I had to keep saying it outloud for it to sink in.

"Biologically, yes I have a daughter, but emotionally I don't,"

What does that mean?

"She's still your flesh and blood, Matthew," I paused, realising that could be said for me and my birth mother. I shook my head, as if to clear the grim thought.

"What?" Matthew asked, his eyes cautiously regarding me.

"Nothing, I just can't believe you kept such a secret from me, I feel like an idiot, it's almost like you can't trust me," another grim thought popped into my head. What if bitch face Lydia knew all along? Is that why he seemed so infatuated with her, he was worried she would spill his secret?

Keep your friends close but your enemies closer.

"Does Lydia know about her?" I asked.

"No, not her, Sophie or my aunt or uncle,"

I was silent.

"Nor does Dr. Roberts,"

His therapist didn't even know!

"Why have you kept her from everyone?"

"I told you, I was ashamed. I am a powerful man in the business world, everyone wants to work either for or with me," he stopped as he watched my reaction. My mood had shifted and I was trying so desperately not to giggle at his big-headedness, "The press would be all over it if they found out I had a love child from a quickie back in college! My name would be mud!"

I stifled my grin "I'm sure they have bigger things to report on than you!"

"Hey, I'm quite a big deal you know,"

"You're a *big* something alright," I said, rolling my eyes, "are you going to get up from the floor?"

He looked up at me with hope in his eyes.

"Does this mean I am forgiven?" he asked as he pushed to his feet.

"I don't know. It's a lot for me to take in. I need time to adjust to the fact that it's not just you anymore, that you have a daughter who needs you, who will come before me, and quite rightly so too, " I said honestly.

Matthew stood, towering over my five foot three frame. He took a cautious step towards me, gauging my reaction. I could feel the oh-so familiar fizz of energy between us.

"If it helps, I haven't known about her for very long, and you will always be a priority for me, Felicity," he breathed as he stepped even closer, reaching for my hand.

"When did you find out?" I asked as he brushed the back of his hand against mine, trying to hook my index finger with his.

"Only a couple of years ago,"

I gasped in shock, "you've missed out on so much of her life,"

He shrugged as he linked his fingers with mine, closing his palm around mine, "yes, I have and I won't ever forgive her mother for making me miss those years,"

"What is she like?" I breathed as I swallowed the lump that had formed in my throat.

"She's like any teenage girl, rebellious, and thinks she knows it all. She's brunette like me too,"

"I bet she's beautiful," I said as he pressed his other hand to my back, forcing me closer towards him.

"She is, and she knows it," he bent down and pressed his lips to mine. I could feel the saltiness of his tears that lingered on his lips. He knew exactly how to press all my buttons and reel me in. And I was more than willing to be hooked.

"Can I meet her one day?" I murmured against his lips.

"I would like that,"

"Does she know about me?"

"I think so, I'm sure she's read about us in those gossip magazine she buys weekly,"

"Is that the reason you bought LuxeLife?" I asked, leaning back to look into his ocean blues.

"Well, that and the fact you work there," he said, winking at me.

"Ha-ha,"

"Ophelia is coming round Friday, if you fancy

joining us?"

"Yes, I would love too,"

Matthew's expression changed from cautious to elated in a flash. I knew that it would be strange but, if I wanted to carry on being a part of this man's life, then I would have to become a part of Ophelia's too, even if it wasn't quite what I planned.

* * *

My limbs and head are heavy and are aching. My mouth and eyelids are welded shut, unable to open. I am still incapable of communicating with the world.

As I stir from the fog, consciousness is within reach but still so far. I can hear muffled sounds once again that slowly become voices.

"You should go home and get some rest,"

"Nope, I'm not leaving her, Hugh,"

Daddy? My dad is here!

I can feel my hand being squeezed by Matthew. I try with all my might to squeeze back but it's useless, I can't.

"She's fine, Matthew, I've checked over her vitals and chart, she's stable. We just have to let her rest and then she'll come back to us once she's strong

enough. We'll know more then too,"

"Matthew, honey, if anything changes we will let you know,"

The warm comforting voice of my mum fills my ears.

I will myself to wake, but nothing.

"Please, Matthew. It will be a while before she wakes up, and anyway when she does, she will be groggy and confused," my dad murmurs.

"Even more of a reason for me to stay,"

"It's ok, if she wakes up, I've got her, I'm her father after all and not to mention a neurosurgeon,"

I can hear the assertiveness in my dad's voice. I can picture them with both their chests puffed out, trying to prove who is the alpha male. Truth is, they both are, just in different ways.

The room is silent for a split second and then Matthew places a kiss to my forehead, "I'll be back soon, my darling, I promise,"

As soon as he starts to walk away, the fog comes back down and takes me away.

AFTER THE REVELATION ABOUT Matthew's daughter on Saturday, Matthew was more attentive towards me than ever. I think he was worried that I was going to walk away from him, again - granted I was very close. But, I was committed to him, mind, body and soul. He spent Saturday afternoon, evening and most of Sunday with me. It was nice. We spoke more about Ophelia and the more I learnt about her, the more I accepted the idea of her. I would have to tell Heather about her soon, I was hoping that she wasn't going to see it as another nail in Matthew's coffin.

I dreaded going into work on Monday after my 'chat' with Ron and Evelyn on Friday morning. Matthew finally got it out of me on Sunday. He asked me how work was going and I caved and told him. Needless to say, he was not happy.

"She said what to you?"

"I will be speaking to Ron too,"

"No one upsets the woman I love,"

I pleaded with him not to intervene and he agreed not to but I wasn't convinced he wasn't. I kept my head down and kept myself to myself, only talking to Amber when we were in the kitchen or on lunch.

Amber seemed better and stronger day by day, that was until she was told that the monster had denied the allegations against him so therefore it would need to go to trial. Amber was petrified that she would now have to give evidence and stand up in court. Face to face with him.

It approached 4pm and I was returning to my desk with a cup of tea when Matthew came strolling into the office. He strode across the floor with such purpose, his eyes firmly set on his destination.

Shit.

People moved out of his path, practically

driving out of the way. I watched as he barged into Ron's office, slamming the door shut behind him. Even the door wasn't enough to stop his angry, bellowing voice from being heard, although slightly muffled.

"Wow, he is *pissed*," Amber said from behind me.

I stood, gaping at the closed door. "Oh, shit," I breathed.

"What? Do you know what it's about?"

"Possibly. . .,"

Suddenly, a solemn looking Evelyn shuffled out of her office and into Ron's, clearly having been summoned.

". . . Definitely," I clarified.

"Well, I wouldn't want to be her right now,"

I turned on my heels and sat at my desk, trying to ignore the looks and comments I could hear being made. He promised not to get involved. *He promised.*

A few minutes later, Matthew emerged from Ron's office. He marched over to me and spun my chair round so that I was facing him. Before I could react, his lips were on mine. He kissed me with such meaning, his soft lips working their magic. His tongue forced itself into my mouth, teasing and leisurely dancing with mine.

Matthew pulled back, leaving me wanton and breathless. My chest was heaving as I struggled to control my breathing.

Wow.

He straightened, his face suddenly turning serious again as he addressed the room, "that was to confirm to anyone who wasn't sure that I am indeed in a *serious* relationship with Miss. Walker and, in fact, I love her,"

Matthew smiled his boyish, warm smile down at me, "See you later, baby,"

And, with that, he turned and left, leaving the whole office looking at me.

14

“WHAT WAS THAT ABOUT earlier in the office?” I asked as I opened a jar of red sauce. It was Ethan’s birthday so I had been asked to make one of my ‘famous’ Lasagnes.

“Well, I wanted to give the good people of LuxeLife what they wanted - confirmation, it will stop them gossiping and speculating,” Matthew replied down the phone, almost sounding pleased with himself.

“It hasn’t stopped them gossiping, that's for sure,”

“Well, let them carry on, they must have very boring lives to be so caught up in ours,” he said.

“Or they are jealous,” my colleagues were probably green with envy at the thought of Matthew and I. Lord knows, he was a sight to behold and he was all mine.

“What are you doing tonight?” Matthew asked, changing the subject.

“Oh I have a very exciting evening planed, I am cooking a lasagne for Ethan as its his birthday and then we are going to have a movie night,"

"Is it just you two or will Heather be there?" he asked, his voice suddenly laced with a seriousness I didn't like.

"Yes, Heather and Isaac will be here," *what was his problem?* "Why? Would it be a problem if they weren't?"

There was silence down the other end of the phone, I think he was choosing his next words carefully. "No, not at all, I was curious is all,"

I rolled my eyes as I stirred the sauce in with the mince, I couldn't help but want to have some fun with him. . .

"You know hes gay right?"

"Yes,"

"So then he isn't a threat," I paused purposely, "But, there was this one time when we did kiss, we almost went all the way. . .,"

I heard Matthew's sharp intake of breath. He was clearly not amused.

"Felicity, do I have to put you over my knee and spank you until you learn not to dick around with me?"

I gasped. I was shocked at his reply and even more shocked at the reaction it had on me. Before I could stop myself, the words left my mouth, "Do what you think you have to, Mr. Harper,"

Matthew let out a low groan, "don't tempt me, Miss. Walker. I would be round in a flash if I thought you were serious.

"Maybe I am," I whispered, suddenly feeling

breathless from the excitement that had built low inside of me.

"Christ, even your words get me hard,"

I smiled ear to ear, I was still in disbelief that I had the same effect on him as he did on me.

"Well, I have to go now as I'm busy being a domestic Goddess. In the meantime, I would suggest that you become reacquainted with your right hand,"

And with that, I swiftly hung up, but not before I heard his groan down the phone.

I placed my iPhone down onto the countertop and smiled to myself as I let the mince simmer. Just as I was preparing the cream sauce, my phone buzzed.

I am now VERY acquainted with my right hand however, I would have preferred it to have been yours or even you.
Enjoy your night, sweetheart.

I let out a giggle as I read his text. My fingers poised to reply when Heather walked in.

"Hey, girl," she said as she went straight for the red wine I had already opened.

"Hey,"

"What are you smiling at? Message from lover boy?" she asked.

"Yes," I replied, peeling my eyes from my

phone and smiling at her.

"You are one smitten kitten aren't you?" Heather said as she took a sip, "woah, which wine is this? It's gorgeous!" she said as she picked up the bottle to inspect it.

"It's a bottle of Châteauneuf-du-Pape, I picked it up on my way home from work," I shrugged as if it was nothing. Truth is, ever since meeting Matthew I have been spoilt with decent wine. As it was a special occasion I wanted to make the effort.

"I assume Mr. Money Bags drinks this?"

I rolled my eyes at her sardonic tone, "of course,"

"I may still have my reservations about him, but I have to admit, he does have good taste!"

I shook my head, she may not be a big fan of Matthew but I still loved her. "He really is good to me Hev, and besides, my dad gave his approval so he must be ok,"

Heather put down her now empty glass of wine, swallowing what was in her mouth, "you know I am kidding, right?" She looked at me with dismay in her eyes, "he's ok - I suppose. As long as he is good to you and treats you how you should, that's all I ask,"

Her honesty took me aback. Ever since I revealed to her that Luke cheated on me which resulted in our first big fight, she had been asking questions and showing an interest in our relationship - something she never did before.

"He is good to me, Hev. More than good. He makes me feel something I've never felt before - *special*,"

Heather smiled warmly at me, a look that I had not seen her give to anyone before. It was a look that told me Matthew and I had her blessing. Not that we needed it, but it was nice to know we did. She pulled me into a bear hug and kissed my cheek, "I'm so happy you are happy,"

"Thank you," I said as my voice wavered.

"Wassup bitches," Ethan said as he came striding through the front door.

Heather and I broke our hug and turned to face the birthday boy and his partner Sam.

"Hey, guys," I greeted.

"How's your day been?" Heather asked Ethan, hugging both him and Sam.

"Yeah, it's been good! Turns out turning twenty-five isn't so bad after all!"

"You're catching up with Heather and I now," I teased as I put the Lasagna in the oven, "now sit down birthday boy and I'll get you two a glass of wine,"

"You certainly don't have to ask us twice!"

I WAS JUST REMOVING the garlic bread from the oven when our intercom buzzed. Heather set down her glass of wine and eagerly jumped up from the armchair.

"Oh, that's Isaac," she said, rushing over to the

phone next to the front door.

"Hey, babe!" she said into the phone.

I was garnishing the plates with a side salad when I heard what seemed to be an awkward exchange between Heather and whoever was on the other end of the intercom. "Oh. Sorry. Come up," she put the phone back in its cradle and turned to me, her face as red as a tomato.

"Are you ok?" I asked her, amusement laced my voice from her awkward encounter with whoever was at the front door.

"I just called Matthew *babe*," her embarrassment at her blunder was evident.

"Did you just say Matthew? As in my Matthew?" *He was here? Why?*

"Yes. Oh, God I could die right now," she shook her head and walked over to her wine glass, throwing back what was left.

There was a knock at the door and I headed over to answer it. I took a deep breath, suddenly feeling nervous for some unknown reason. I was still dressed in what I wore to work plus my pink fluffy slippers and an apron. My hair had been shoved up into a messy bun with the odd loose strand that had broken free. I was in no acceptable state to see the man who claimed to love me.

I opened the door and my eyes landed on the man who stood before me, looking even more delectable than he did when I saw him at work a few hours previous. He was dressed in a white T-shirt - the logo telling me it was more expensive than the whole of my outfit put together - and dark blue jeans that hung perfectly from his hips. He looked delicious, he made casual look beyond sexy. He beamed down at me awaiting my invitation to come in.

"Wh-what are you doing here?" I stammered, unable to speak properly thanks to his mere presence.

"I wanted to see you, I wanted to tell you that I have to go away for a couple of nights on business. Oh, and to show you how serious I was about taking you over my knee. Are you going to let me in?" he asked as if he hadn't just uttered the last sentence.

I stepped to one side, my legs suddenly quivering with desire as he took a few steps forward, brushing past me as he entered our flat. He stopped and bent down, placing a slow, deep kiss to my mouth. "You look good dressed in that apron. Next time you answer the door to me, I want you dressed in that and nothing else," he said against my lips so that no one else could hear.

Unable to reply due to my dry mouth, he turned and greeted the room. "Gents, Heather,"

"Hi," Heather said, still looking bashful but was saved when the intercom buzzed again, this time it had to be Isaac.

Momentarily forgetting my manners, I composed myself and introduced Ethan and Sam to Matthew and vice versa.

"So, *you* are the famous Matthew Harper, the one who is kindly paying for my chemo" Ethan said as he shook Matthew's outstretched hand.

"The one and only,"

"Cocky - I like it," Ethan said with a small smile playing on his lips.

"So I've heard," Matthew joked, returning his smile, "I also hear that it's your birthday,"

"Yep, the big two-five,"

"Well, happy birthday, sorry I haven't bought anything with me, I came at short notice," Matthew said, turning to me with a shrug.

"Yes, you invited yourself round at short notice. So much so, there isn't enough food for you," I placed my hand up onto Matthew's shoulder blade.

"It's ok, I've already eaten," he smiled.

"Good, come on guys, dinner is served!" I called and everyone made their way to the table.

We ate our meal while Matthew nibbled on some garlic bread that was to spare. It was so nice being all together. It felt like three normal couples hanging out celebrating a friend's birthday. It felt easy, dare I say natural. I watched closely as Matthew interacted with my friends. Asking questions, replying to theirs. He seemed so young and carefree. A far cry from the business mogul he was - it was nice.

Once everyone had cleared their plates of food, the big clean up started. As I had cooked, it was someone else's turn to do the washing up. Heather and Isaac nominated themselves while the rest of us took a seat on the settees. Matthew draped his long arm over the back of the settee, placing his hand upon my shoulder. He was every inch the relaxed man. Ethan and Sam chatted away to each other while Matthew drank his wine.

“I see your sudden taste in wine is similar to someone else's I know,” he said, turning to me and winking, clearly referring to himself.

“Yep, just some guy I know,” I said, nonchalantly.

“Oh is that so, he sounds like a top bloke,”

“Yeah, he’s ok I suppose,”

“Just ok?” he said, cocking an eyebrow at me.

“Yes, the sex is just ok too,” I couldn’t help myself, I was still reeling from the spanking comment earlier.

A look flashed across Matthew’s beautiful face, “Oh, Miss. Walker, I can assure you that he would be willing to show you that he is *more* than just *ok*,” the curve of his mouth drove me crazy, if only the room weren't filled with my friends, otherwise I’d be all over him.

“Well, perhaps he can show me one night this week?”

“Most definitely,” and before I could reply, his mouth was on mine, causing wolf whistles from Ethan.

“Get a room you too!” he gested.

"Oh believe you me, I want nothing more but to use her room right now," Matthew said, with a dark gleam in his eyes.

"Matthew!" I squealed, as I playfully slapped his arm, feeling somewhat embarrassed.

We all had a good laugh and once Heather and Isaac had finished washing up, they joined us in the living room. The night was disappearing from us and all too soon it became 10:30pm. Heather and Isaac made their way to bed and Ethan and Sam headed out to continue the celebration, Ethan was especially making the most of it as he was starting chemotherapy next week.

I was in the kitchen putting away what was left of the birthday cake when Matthew walked over, he glanced over his shoulder checking that the coast was clear.

"So, we are finally alone,"

I smiled as I closed the fridge, "it would appear so,"

Suddenly, Matthew stalked towards me, looking as though any minute he was about to pounce on his prey. *Me.*

I was forced by his movements to retreat backwards, it wasn't until my back came flush with the worktop that I stopped. He was standing millimetres away from me, I could feel the warmth of his body radiating off him. The curve of his mouth drove me wild, along with his smouldering gaze which told me all I needed to know - he *needed* me. He *desired* me.

"Here?" I mouthed, unable to form words.

Without a word, Matthew wrapped his arms around my waist and hoisted me up onto the worktop, he placed himself in between my legs, pushing them apart. *Yep, here.*

Suddenly, Matthew leant forward, his mouth encasing mine. He kissed me with such raw passion. It was like he had been starved and was finally having his fill. As we kissed his hand travelled down to my knee, he then forced his hand underneath my skirt and made his way up to my crotch.

"I can already feel how slick you are for me, your underwear is soaking" he murmured against my lips.

I didn't say anything, I couldn't. I was a hot mess.

"Mine," Matthew breathed as his fingers found their way through the lace material of my underwear and gently skimmed me.

Hearing him claim me by voice made me want him even more. I wanted him to claim *me.* I wanted him to claim me, mind, body and soul. I was his and no one else's. Without hesitation, I pulled up my skirt so that it was bunched around my thighs and spread my legs further, allowing him better access.

Matthew kissed all the way along my jaw, the simple motion spurring me on even more so. His fingers carried on stroking me, sending shivers through me.

"Do you want me inside you?" Matthew ask as he gently bit down on my earlobe.

I wanted to scream 'fuck me, now,' from the top of my lungs but instead I nodded, still unable to form proper words.

Matthew bit my earlobe again, this time harder, causing me to yelp slightly. Every stroke of his long fingers sent me crazy, I couldn't think straight. I was about to have sex in my *kitchen*, which I shared with my two best friends, not to mention the fact that one of them was only the otherside of the wall. But, I couldn't care less at that point. All I knew is that I needed him. I needed him desperately. Not even common decency was going to stop me.

Matthew pushed my underwear to the side with his fingers then thrusted a finger into me, followed soon after by another one. I whimpered at the sensation. The sheer need I was feeling to be connected so intimately with him. I trailed my hands up his strong, muscular back and I clawed at his thick mane of hair as he continued to work his sweet torture. I was on the brink of an orgasm.

"Yes. . .," I panted. "That feels incredible,"

Without warning, Matthew quickly removed his fingers and in one swift move, he buried himself deep inside me, taking me by complete surprise. I moaned loudly, needing to come.

"Shhh, baby," Matthew breathed as he lifted

his hand and covered my mouth, trying to stifle my impending scream.

My orgasm built up once again as I matched his rhythm with my thrusts. Matthew was soon catching me up and was close to his own release, his thrusts getting more and more frantic and deeper. My muscles finally clenched, giving way to a mind blowingly intense orgasm. Matthew followed closely behind, coming hard but silently, the only noise he made was a slight grunt through his gritted teeth.

After we had both ridden out our high and the pleasure subsided, Matthew withdrew himself and grabbed some paper towels from the roll. Without saying a word, he began to clean me up. The very motion took me aback. It was a strange but intimate feeling. He rolled down my skirt and smoothed it down over my legs. He then cleaned himself up and discarded the paper towel into the bin. Clearing the scene of the illicit, intimate act that had just taken place not minutes before.

Matthew placed a kiss upon the end of my nose and grabbed me gently by the waist, lifting me back down to the floor. I clutched hold of his arms as I steadied myself on my wobbly legs. Matthew and I had just let go of one another when Heather came walking into the kitchen. She came to an abrupt stop when she saw the flustered look that was so evident on my face. I glanced at Matthew, who was of course looking unaffected after our recent activity.

"Oh, am I interrupting something?" she asked, stopping in her tracks.

"No, not at all, Matthew was, ah, just leaving," I stuttered, trying to compose myself, but the tremor in my voice was proving hard to control.

"Was I?" He asked as he cocked his eyebrow at me.

"Yes, you were," I said sternly. Truth was I didn't want him to leave, but I was so damn embarrassed from what we had just done.

"Fine, I'll leave but, not before I show you something,"

"Huh?" I asked as he took me by the hand and led me over to the window. I looked over at Heather who looked equally as confused.

Matthew pulled up the blind and I looked down at the street.

"What do you see?" he asked.

Was he taking the piss?

"Erm, a road?" I shrugged.

"Don't be smart with me, Miss. Walker. Look closer,"

I scanned the scene that was in front of me. It was a road, my road where I lived. There were trees, street lights and cars parked along the curb. Then, suddenly I saw it. A car that I didn't recognise.

I pointed at the said car, "that's new? I don't think I've seen that parked there before,"

Why would he want to show me a car?

Was it his car?

But it didn't seem like his usual style.

"Is it yours? It's a tad girly," I said as I turned to face him.

He was staring down at me, his face impassive. I hated that I couldn't read him.

"It's your car," he said, nonchalantly.

Woah, What?

"I'm sorry?" I asked, taking another look at what appeared to be a red coloured car.

"I bought it for you. It's a Volkswagen Beetle,"

I was speechless, I could only blink up at him.

"You bought her a car?" Heather squeaked from behind us.

"I'm worried about you walking or taking cabs on your own. Especially since your friend was assaulted," Matthew said to me as if Heather hadn't just spoken.

"I . . . What? . . . No!" Were the only words I could get out.

Mathew's brow furrowed as he stared down at me, "no?" he repeated.

"You can't be serious? Matthew, it's a car!"

"Eagle-eyed as always I see," He joked, as amusement danced in his beautiful blue eyes. "I wanted to get the car for you, it's my job as your *boyfriend*, or *partner*, to keep you safe," he said firmly.

I rolled my eyes, feeling exasperated at such a gesture. Sure, it was his job to look after me, and I him. But not in this overbearing caveman way. I was a grown woman, I could look after myself. We'd been down this road before, the night I'd got back from seeing Amber. Matthew threatened me with the use of Stanley, telling me that I was not to go out alone without him. Luckily, I had managed to get away with rehashing that subject after we got back together.

"But, but it's so expensive!" I said waving my hands in the air to illustrate the point.

"Felicity, please, I can afford it. Trust me," a small smirk played on his lips. A smirk that for some reason irritated me.

Damn him and his smugness!

And money!

"Well, that's not the point, *Matthew,*" I replied sternly, "I know you are awash with cash but that doesn't give you carte blanche to do with it as you please, especially when it comes to me-,"

"Especially when it comes to you, Felicity," he interjected.

Out of the corner of my eye I could see Heather backing away slowly towards her bedroom, the conversation was clearly making her uncomfortable, hell it was making me uncomfortable!

"I would not be able to live with myself if you were to come to any harm! Especially seeing as I have the power to make sure that doesn't happen!"

"Matthew, you aren't God, you can't control

the future, as much as you think you can if you throw enough cash at it,"

"I've managed to keep you safe so far," Matthew stated, his facial expression indecipherable, not giving anything away.

What did he mean by that?

"What, what does that mean?" I asked, cocking a brow at him.

Matthew stepped away from me, making his way over to the kitchen and helping himself to a glass of wine.

"Hey, answer me," I said, my voice raised slightly more than I intended.

Matthew sighed and ran his hands through his deliciously chocolate brown locks. "Ok, I've hired someone to follow you, to look out for you. To keep you safe when I'm not around. I had even more of a reason to do so after your birth mother showed up and upset you recently,"

I frowned. He actually hired someone to follow me and all because of her and what happened to Amber? My birth mother, Chantelle, was sure as hell not a threat to me, she just turned out to be a threat to our relationship "What, you've hired someone? You've actually hired a bloody bodyguard?"

"Sort of, I didn't want to say anything as I knew it would end up like this," he waved his hand in the space between us, "in a heated discussion, like it always does with us,"

I exhaled. I didn't want to fight, not about

this, not since he was going away on business and I wouldn't see him for a few days. I knew his intentions were good and he only wanted to protect the woman he loved. And besides, it was getting late, I didn't have the energy or fight left in me.

"Well, let's not fight, or have a 'heated discussion' now," I said, extending my arm and offering him my hand. He closed the space between us and slipped his hand in mine, then swiftly pulled me into his arms. I inhaled his sweet scent as I pressed my nose against him. My favourite smell in the whole wide world, Matthew.

"You just need to learn to maybe get me other gifts, you know something like flowers or at a push some nice-not-too-expensive jewellery,"

"I get you jewellery sometimes!" he protested as he kissed the top of my head.

"I know, and I love it when you do."

I hugged him close. As I did, the feeling of unease and something else I couldn't put my finger on flooded me. I couldn't get my head around his wealth. The way he could buy me a car just like that. I knew he wasn't buying my love, but a part of me felt like that was exactly what he was doing.

My brain went into overdrive as he snuggled his nose into my neck. I loved him so much but sometimes he was so overwhelming.

* * *

The haze lifts, and once again I am back in the room. But not completely. I try to open my eyes but my eyelids refuse to budge. I have no sense of time, I have no idea how long I have been in a coma for. Hours, days, weeks?

"As you can see, DC Morgan, she is in no fit state to answer any of your questions. I'd appreciate it if you do what you do best and go and investigate what fucker ploughed into her car and did this to her,"

"Yes, Mr. Harper, our investigation is of course still ongoing. We have a lead which we are following up,"

"Good, you better get your hands on them before I do."

Matthew's voice trails off as his phone begins to ring.

"Harper . . . Hi, hold on one second . . . Sorry Detective, I have to take this call . . . Hello, Ash? Any update?"

My head begins to pound, and I am soon taken away from Matthew once again.

AS I MADE MY way to work the next morning, I was constantly checking over my shoulder, trying to see if I could work out who was following me, or rather 'keeping me safe' as Matthew called it. Matthew left shortly after 11:30pm last night, deciding it was best not to risk sleeping in my bed in case of another night terror, and also because he had to pack for his trip later today. I hated that he worried about hurting me in his sleep. I know he did once, but him not being able to sleep next to me hurt more.

When I left the flat this morning, the car was there, staring me in the face. I had to give him credit where credit was due, it was a lovely car, very me. But, while it was a nice, albeit over the top gesture, he needed to learn to stop being so overbearing. I had parents who managed that quite well. I understood his reasons for wanting to protect me from murderers and rapists, but, if it was going to happen it would be a matter of wrong place, wrong time. Not because Matthew or some sort of bodyguard wasn't there to save me.

My birth mother definitely wasn't going to show up that soon after her last visit. She had a pattern, she would show up, beg for my forgiveness, ask me to give her another chance and then disappear from my life for a good year or so. Or so I hoped. Now that she knew I was in a relationship with an insanely wealthy man, it did give her more of a reason to show up more and more. The thought made my stomach turn in disgust. I chose not to tell my parents that she had shown up recently, I learnt the hard way and it only upset them.

I walked from the Tube station and reached the magnificent building that housed LuxeLife and the new up and coming MWH Group Holdings headquarters. Matthew was getting excited about the HQ, I was told that everything was going to be state of the art. His excitement when he was explaining everything to me made me smile.

I sat down at my desk and switched my Mac on, ready to begin a new day. It wasn't until I sat down that I realised just how tired I was. I had not long fallen asleep after Matthew left, I was exhausted, especially after our shenanigans in the kitchen, but I hadn't slept for long enough to recharge my batteries so I already knew that the day would be a struggle.

After I made my usual morning cup of tea and chatted with Amber in the kitchen, I started on the day's tasks of sourcing, researching and writing articles. I truly loved my job, aside from the chastising I received from Evelyn and Ron. Speaking of which, I hadn't seen either of them, which was strange. Usually they were in at the crack of dawn.

As if on queue, Ron strode into the office, greeting and smiling at people as he passed. He came to a stop next to my desk, "Felicity, can I have a word with you this morning, say 11am?" he asked.

My face fell. "Yes, of course," I replied, my heart

sinking in my chest. *What have I done now?*

"It's ok, you're not in any trouble," Ron said, reading my expression before walking away into his office, and closing the door behind him.

Why does he want to speak to me?

His reassurance did nothing to settle the feeling I had in my stomach.

I busied myself, trying to distract my mind from the meeting that loomed over me and also because I was already missing Matthew. Not seeing him for a few days was going to be hard. I'd sent him a text when I woke up but he was yet to reply.

Janey, one of my colleagues, popped her head up from her desk in front of mine. "Have you heard about Evelyn? Oh what am I saying, *of* course you have,"

"I beg your pardon?" I narrowed my eyes in confusion.

"Oh, you actually haven't heard? Mr. Harper hasn't told you?"

I frowned at her question. *What has Matthew not told me?*

"She's handed in her notice! Rumour has it she was forced to,"

She what?! Shit. *He promised.*

"How do you know?" Where is she getting this information from, she was surely mistaken.

"Ah, you may be sleeping with the Chairman, but I have a little birdie of my own,"

Everything I so desperately tried to avoid

was already happening. People were making assumptions that Matthew was feeding me inside information, which was definitely not the case.

"I don't understand, why would she be forced to quit?" None of this was making any sense.

Janey raised a well manicured eyebrow at me, "isn't it obvious? Mr. Harper came storming in here yesterday, shouting the odds and next, she's gone? It's because of *you*, it has to be!"

I couldn't listen to her anymore, I needed answers. I needed Matthew to straighten this whole misunderstanding out for me before I went insane.

Abruptly I rose to my feet and bolted it towards the ladies. Once I was in the confines of a cubical, I dialled Matthews number. It rang and rang before going to voicemail.

Damn.

I tried again and again but it was no good. He wasn't picking up. He must have been in a meeting and unable to take my call. I decided to send him another text instead.

Matthew, please can you call me, it's urgent! Evelyn has apparently resigned and please are saying it's cos of what happened yesterday x

My heartbeat was rapid as a mixture of

nerves and anger took hold of me. I eventually composed myself and headed back to my desk. The hours passed slowly with no word from Matthew. Colleagues stared at me and whispered to one another whenever I walked past them. It was exactly what I knew was going to happen when our relationship was made public knowledge. I would choose the paparazzi anyday over the looks my colleagues were giving me, and that was saying something.

I walked on shaky legs to Ron's office and knocked on his door. He called me in and I took a seat in front of his desk. Nerves caused me to toy with a ring that was on my middle finger.

"So, Felicity," Ron started, rubbing his chin, "I don't know if you are aware but, Evelyn has given her notice. It seems that her actions while working for the company are deemed *inappropriate* by the powers that be," I may have been wrong, but I could have sworn that I detected a hint of sarcasm laced in his voice as he spoke.

"I've heard rumours," I said, dryly.

Ron nodded and then stood, placing his hands in the pockets of his trousers. "Believe you me, this is just as awkward for me too,"

I looked down at my hands, not sure quite what to say or do . . .

"Felicity," Ron started, removing his hands from his pockets and resting them on the back of his desk chair, "the bottom line is that we need a new Editor. And well, I have been assured that you would be the best replacement,"

I shot my head up, my eyes meeting Ron's. *Was he for real?* Why on earth would I be the best replacement? There were people sitting out there who had been here longer and had more experience than me. This had Matthew's name written all over it.

"Ron, I appreciate the offer, but - but how can I possibly accept?"

Ron now looked as uncomfortable as I felt. He clearly didn't want to be having this discussion. He idolised Evelyn. I certainly wouldn't have been his first choice as her replacement.

Ron pulled out his chair and sat back down, making himself comfortable. "Well, if you don't want to accept the job then that's your call. And I completely understand your reasoning behind it, I can only ask. I've done my bit," he held up his hands in defeat.

Shit, he was going to have to tell *Mr. Harper* that I declined. And Mr. Harper wasn't going to be happy.

Not unless I got in there first.

"Ron, look, if you prefer, I am more than happy to tell Matthew - I mean Mr. Harper myself," I had to put the poor man at ease somehow.

A look of relief flooded Ron's ageing face. He clearly wasn't happy with the situation, nor the thought of telling his boss that I said no. "If it helps, you would be very good at the job, you know. You don't give yourself enough credit. You're a hard worker. I know we were hard on you the other day but, I want you to know that didn't come from me,"

I offered him a polite smile for his kind words, not knowing what else to say. "Thanks, Ron. Is that everything?" I asked, conscious that I had a lot of work to do.

Ron started at me for a moment, computing what I had said and then rose to his feet, "Yes, that's all,"

"Ok, thank you," I scurried past him, feeling like a complete idiot. I was embarrassed beyond belief. How dare Matthew meddle with my career! Who the hell did he think he was?! It was the God complex yet again.

As soon as I got to my desk, I grabbed my iPhone, checking for any messages or missed calls - but nothing. It was very strange for Matthew not to at least send me a text if he couldn't call.

Maybe he knew I would be mad.

That had to be the reason for the radio silence.

Well, I can be silent with him too. I can show him just how pissed off I really am.

IT REACHED 3PM AND my phone started buzzing. I was greeted with a photo of Matthew as it rang. I let it ring out, and then it began again.

Buzz, buzz, buzz.

I rolled my eyes at the screen and silenced the call.

It continued to ring, and I shoved it in my handbag. There was no way I was in any sort of mood to talk to him, the last few hours had done nothing to simmer down my bad mood - which had been caused by him and his domineering ways.

Seconds later, my desk phone began to ring. I stared at it with wide eyes, knowing exactly who was on the other end as I recognised the number. I looked round over my shoulder to check if there was anyone around.

Could I get away with letting it ring out?

There was a three ring policy at LuxeLife and I had definitely gone over that.

Janey's head popped up over her monitor, "Felicity, is that your phone ringing," it wasn't a question, it was more of a statement.

I inwardly rolled my eyes at her, "yes, yes it is," I replied sweetly. *That woman was the definition of annoying.*

It began ringing again. I was left with no choice but to answer the call.

"LuxeLife, Felicity speaking," I said, as professionally as I could muster.

"Why the hell aren't you answering your mobile?"

Oh hello to you too.

"Sorry, Sir, I have been extremely busy," I said, still sounding professional.

"Cut the bullshit, Felicity. When I call you I expect you to answer, I get worried otherwise," Matthew's tone was firm and somehow, even though I was angry with him, he still managed to do things to me that only he could.

"I can confirm that all is well, thank you. We won't be needing your services at the moment,"

Feeling empowered, I rather quickly placed the phone back in its cradle, cutting the call.

Ha!

I knew I was going to be made to pay for that at a later date, but to be honest, I couldn't give a shit, I was equally as pissed off, if not more, as he would be now. Moments later, my email pinged.

YOU HAVE NO IDEA HOW MAD I AM RIGHT NOW.

Kind regards

Matthew Harper
Chairman, MWH Group Holdings.

Seriously? Was this man for real?

Mr. Harper,

You have no right to be mad at ME.

I asked you not to interfere with my situation and yet you couldn't help yourself - therefore, I am the one who should be

MAD!!

Kind regards

Felicity Walker
Junior Writer/Editorial assistant
LuxeLife Magazine

I closed my emails in a fit of rage. I was too angry to even work right now. All I wanted to do was to go home and sleep for a week - or have a large drink. Matthew persistently called and texted me. I ignored them all of course.

I was typing away when I heard the gentle chatter of the office dissipate into silence. I glanced up and saw my colleagues all scarpering back to their desk and Matthew striding down the carpeted walkway hell bent on reaching my desk. His jaw was clenched. He was clearly mad.

I squared my shoulders as he approached me. He came to an abrupt halt next to me and I could feel his glare boring into me.

"Miss. Walker, can I see you for a moment in the boardroom?" he said in a firm voice.

Saving my document, I swivelled around in my chair and gave him an overly sweet smile. "Yes, Mr. Harper, of course."

He stepped aside and let me lead the way to the boardroom. I made my way across the floor, fully aware that all eyes were on me. Once I was in the room, I crossed my arms tightly around my body.

I wanted him to see just how mad I was - that I was furious.

Matthew closed the door and turned to face me. “Baby, I -”

“Hold it. You don’t get to ‘baby’ me.” I said, cutting him off.

Matthew’s jaw tensed.

There was no way I was falling for his charm this time. This was the final straw.

“I don’t want to fight. It feels like that’s all we fucking do.” He ran his hand through his hair.

My heart dropped at his words. Yes, we did have a number of disagreements but we always got past them. Was there some sort of limit to how many one couple could bear?

I puffed air into my cheeks. “I don’t want to fight either, Matthew. But it shouldn’t be this hard, should it?” *Choose your words carefully, Felicity.* “I feel like I’m in a constant battle with you. One minute we are fine and it's the best relationship that I could wish for and then the next, you are buying me cars, hiding daughters from me, hiring someone to follow me and interfering in my career when I explicitly asked you not.”

I searched Matthew’s eyes for some sort of answer as to what he was thinking. But, he gave nothing away. He remained passive and just stared at me as he listened.

“No, it shouldn’t be this hard. But, I don’t know how to do this.” he finally said, not breaking eye contact with me.

“I feel suffocated sometimes.” I whispered. I’d never even realised until I heard myself admit it.

Matthew’s eyes grew larger at my confession. “Suffocated?”

I nodded. “I’m suffocated by your wealth, your power and your love.”

“My love?”

“Yes, I love that you love me and want to protect me but, I’m not some damsel in distress that needs to be rescued by her Prince Charming-.”

Matthew opened his mouth as if to say something but then closed it again.

I continued with what I was saying. “I’m an adult. I’m independant and always have been. I’m not some fragile woman that lives up in an ivory tower. I make my own decisions and work hard for my career.”

“Then what do you suggest we do? Because I’ll never stop loving you and protecting what is mine. I care for the people I love, Felicity.”

“I don’t know what to do, Matthew. That's the problem!” It was true, I didn’t know what I wanted anymore. “Maybe this business trip will be good for us, it will give us the distance and space that we need.”

“No! I don’t want there to be any fucking distance between us.” His voice was laced with desperation and anger.

I could feel my eyes start to fill with tears.

"Sometimes you don't always get what you want, Matthew." *What am I doing? I'm playing relationship suicide.*

"Felicity, please don't do this. Don't do this to us. I can change." he begged.

"Matthew, I'm not saying this is the end, just that maybe we need time apart to think about what we want."

"Bullshit! I know what I want - I want you! It sounds like you are the one who's not sure." he shouted, causing me to flinch.

"I do want you." I whispered.

Matthew shut his eyes as if pained by my words. When he opened them again, they were full of anguish. "Felicity, you know that if I go away and we leave it like this, that's it for us. Breaks never work. It will drive more of a wedge between us."

His words cut right through me. But deep down I knew that he was probably right.

"I-I." I didn't know what to say.

Before I could say another word, Matthew darted towards me and cupped my head in his hands and kissed me. He kissed me with force. It wasn't tender or passionate. It was desperate. He was pleading with me. He forced his tongue into my mouth and he pushed me up against the floor to ceiling window as he ravaged my mouth. I gave into his kiss and kissed him back, my tongue finding his. I reached for his upper arms and gripped them tightly.

I didn't want this to end or for us to take a break but, maybe we needed to for my own sanity? Maybe I was just scared. I was scared at just how much he loved me. Maybe I was scared of getting hurt again. He hadn't cheated on me like Luke did, but nonetheless, he hurt me. The lies and deception hurt just the same.

I managed to fight the need I felt deep down in my groin, and instead listen to my head. I pulled my mouth away from his and pushed him away. I looked at him and placed my hand over my lips. Tears that had filled my eyes before were now emptying down my cheeks.

"Baby, please." He begged. His voice barely a whisper.

"Matthew, I'm scared at just how much you love me." I closed my eyes, trying to blink away some of the tears. "I feel in over my head in this relationship. I need time to myself to think about if this is what I want."

His eyes became glassy with the threat of tears as he listened.

"My last relationship was filled with lies and distrust. I'm worried that this one is heading the same way."

The anger that was building in Matthew was palpable. "I would never cheat on you. I would never hurt or deceive you like that."

"Matthew, you already have! Don't you see that?" I said, raising my voice at him. I was getting angry with him and with myself for not saying this all sooner. "Not telling me about being engaged to Lydia, about Ophelia and now what you have done today with my career is just the same. You *lied*. You hid the *truth* from me. You *betrayed* my trust."

Matthew recoiled from me as if I'd gone to strike him. "I know I've fucked up royally. *Believe me*, Felicity, I know. And if there was a way I could change the past, I would - in a heartbeat. But I can't. I can only learn from my past mistakes."

I stared at him through my tears. "I think you should leave me alone now - please."

He exhaled in a rush and shook his head. "No."

"Please." I whispered, looking down at the floor. I couldn't look at his wounded expression any longer. "Please, go."

"Felicity, I swear to God if you make me walk out of this door, that's it. We're done. We won't be able to recover. I won't be able to recover from it. You have walked away from me one too many times."

"I can't fight with you anymore, Matthew. I'm exhausted."

I squeezed my eyes shut, not wanting to watch Matthew leave.

He sighed and stepped closer to me so that our bodies were inches apart. "Fliss. . .," he tilted my chin up with his finger. "Please look at me."

I opened my eyes and Matthew's wounded, haunted eyes met with mine. "I'm not going to fight for you. I can't. But, I want you to know, Felicity, that I'll never stop loving you." He bent down and placed a sweet, tender kiss on my lips, then he turned and left. He left me without looking back. And just like that, I was alone. Again.

15

THE GROUND SHIFTED FROM underneath me. My world had been turned upside down once again. This time it was from my own making. What was I thinking? I just threw away a man who fucking adored me. But, it was too late for us now. He made it clear before I let him walk away. For so long I was the one running away, now it was his turn. I pushed him away. No. He pushed me away.

I left the office as soon as I managed to peel myself up off the floor. After Matthew left, I sobbed and sobbed. I sobbed until there were no more tears left to cry. I spent the afternoon walking around. Walking nowhere in particular. I just couldn't face going back to my flat. I knew Ethan would be there and I wasn't ready to talk to anyone just yet.

It was 12:15 a.m. when my phone started ringing. I pulled it out of my bag and saw Heather's name. She was probably worrying about me. Then, my phone rang again. This time it was my mum. Everyone called but the one person I really wanted to speak to. *No, Felicity, it's done. You made your bed. You have to now lie in it.*

It was 1am when I stood across the road from my flat. I glanced to my right and saw the car. The car that he bought me.

I'll go for a drive. That will clear my mind.

That's what people do when they are stressed or having an argument, isn't it?

They go for a drive?

Before the sane part of me could kick in, I walked over to the car. I pressed the button on the keyfob and the car unlocked.

I slid into the driver's seat and threw my bag in the back. Taking the key, I inserted it into the ignition and started the car. She purred into life and I glided my hands over the leather steering wheel. I adjusted my mirrors and eased out of the space and into the streets of a sleepy London.

As I drive round London. I decided to take things up a notch. I needed to feel this Goddamn car in action. To see just how good it was for me. I joined the motorway and really put my foot down. *God it feels good.*

I officially left London and was in the next county - Essex. I had no idea where I was going but I just knew I needed to get away from the City. To get away from Matthew. He probably wasn't even in London now. He was going on his business trip after all.

I pulled off the motorway and approached

traffic lights that were red. I brought the car to a stop and waited. I started at the traffic light, willing it to turn green so I could continue to drive, continue to concentrate on anything other than *him*. The light turned green and I put my foot on the peddle and the car began to move forward.

Out of the corner of my eye, I saw something. Something hurtling towards me. As I turned my head, I heard the ear-splitting squeal of tires and brakes. My car was propelled onto its side as the sound of metal screamed and contorted on impact. My body lurched forward as the car rolled, causing glass to shatter and break. The air bags exploded in my face and chest. The sound was deafening. Like a bomb exploding right in front of you. The car rocked before coming to a complete stop. A groan escaped my mouth and I felt something warm run across my face - my body screamed in agony. I was bleeding. I was unable to move. *I'm going to die. This is it. I'm never going to see Matthew again.*

Matthew

MY PHONE VIBRATES ON the bedside table. I wake with a jolt. Where am I? Oh right, a hotel. I frown as I look at the number. It's one that I don't recognise. I glance at my iWatch, it's 03:30am. It's early. Very early.

I clear my throat before answering. "Harper."

"Matthew?" A woman asks on the phone. She sounds worried.

"Yes, Speaking."

"Oh, Matthew!" she cries, she sounds so distraught. The feeling of unease floods my veins.

"I'm sorry, who is this?"

"Meredith, Felicity's mother."

My scalp prickles.

What's happened?

"Meredith, hi. Is everything ok? Is Felicity ok?"

She wails and whatever she says next is incoherent.

I hear a muffling sound in the background and someone takes the phone.

"Matthew, it's Hugh. Felicity has been in a car accident"

Fuck.

My stomach drops.

My Felicity is hurt.

"Where is she?" I ask. I am unable to grasp what he had just said, even though I had just heard it.

"She's just gone into theatre. I think you should be here, Matthew."

The seriousness in his voice sends alarm bells ringing in my ears.

Shit.

Felicity is hurt. She's being operated on right now.

She needs me. I need to be there with her.

"Which hospital?" I ask as I clamber out of bed and onto my feet.

* * *

I SIT BY HER bedside, my hand gripping round hers tightly. "Please wake up baby, please." I plead. As soon as I got the call from her parents I drove miles across the country. I made it just as she came out of theatre. She was in there for five hours. Five hours of having her scalp opened and her brain pulled about.

She's been in a medically induced coma for four days. Four long days. They say she is stable and that she just needs to rest before coming back into the world. She had a Subdural haematoma - a bleed between her skull and the surface of her brain. They had to fucking resuscitate her. Her body tried to give up. It tried to slip away from the world. From me.

I stupidly walked away like a coward. I told her that I wasn't going to fight for her. How could I be so stupid? I caused this. I caused her to get into the fucking car and drive in the early hours, tired and emotional. It was my fault. I know how vulnerable and upset she can get. I've seen the scars on her thighs caused from the hurt of the last man who left her. Sure, he died but he still left her. She claims she is tough but deep down I know she is fragile.

I've been playing the last conversation over and over in my head for the last four days. The more I think about it, the more I hate myself. I suffocated her to the point where she needed to get away from me. She needed time away from me to breathe - to breathe on her own. Without me.

Her parents are here most of the time along with me. I wouldn't ever leave her side if I had my way but the nurses and doctors basically throw me out claiming that I need some rest. I'll rest when I'm dead. Right now, I need to be with the woman I love. The woman who I'd die for. The woman who I wish I could swap places with.

"All her vitals are stable at the moment which is promising but, we will know more when she wakes up,"

The doctor's words echo around in my ears.

"She's going to need a good support system when she wakes up, she'll need a lot of help. She'll most likely need rehabilitation such as physiotherapy to help her with things like movement and muscle weakness,"

Whatever happens when she wakes up. I will be there for her. I will get her the best care and physio that money can buy. I thought I was using my money for good, looking after her by hiring bodyguards to follow her and buying her that godforsaken car. This time, it will be used for good.

Felicity

I OPEN MY EYES. Water. I need water. My mouth is so dry, it's like sandpaper. I look up at the ceiling, almost blinded from the light. I am confused. My head hurts. Everything hurts. I feel like I have been dreaming forever. Why am I in a hospital? What are all the beeping machines for? The sound is piercing through me.

I wince as I try to sit up. The simple motion, causing searing pain to coarse through me. It takes my breath away. I start to panic. I'm all alone. *Help.*

I reach for the button that is beside my bed. I press it over and over again until someone comes. "Felicity!" A kind looking woman smiles. "Welcome back."

She walks over to me and she realises that I'm in distress. "Felicity, it's ok, try to keep still. Everything is ok."

"Water." I mouth, my voice too dry to form words.

"Yes, we will get you some water." The nurse

says as she adjusts my pillow. “The doctor will be here shortly to speak to you.”

Right on queue, a man in a shirt and trousers enters the room. “Hello, Felicity, I’m Doctor Watkins. I’m a Neurosurgeon here at the hospital. It’s nice to finally meet you properly.”

“Dad.” I mouth again. I need my dad. Not this doctor. He is a renowned Neurosurgeon. He’ll know what to do.

“Your father is with your mother, they are getting a coffee from the canteen. They won’t be long.” he says, looking at some sort of tablet device. “Now, I’m going to ask you a few questions and I want you to answer the best you can, ok?”

I nod.

“Do you know today's date?”

No.

I shake my head.

“Ok, when is your birthday?” he asks.

“Water.” I croak.

Where the hell is that damn nurse with my water?

After attempting to answer a few questions. The nurse finally hands me a glass of water. I take it from her and drink the whole glass dry. I have never needed anything quite as much as I needed that.

“Felicity?” My mum squeals as she comes into the room.

“Mum!” I cry.

She comes running over to me and hugs me

tight. I wince as the pain spasms up and down my body.

"Careful, Meredith." My dad warns.

Daddy!

"Welcome back, baby girl." My dad places a loving kiss on my forehead. It is then that I realise that I have a bandage around my head.

God, what happened to me?

Out of the corner of my eye, a large figure fills the door frame. I turn my head and my eyes meet Matthews'.

Matthew.

My heart flutters in my chest at the sight of him. He looks haunted. Worried even.

My mum looks over at him and smiles. "Matthew?" she asks. "Come here, come and greet our girl." She waves him over.

Matthew hesitates before walking slowly over to my bed.

"Hi," he greets

I smiled at him. "Hi,"

"We'll leave you two kids alone," my dad says, ushering my mum away from my bed. "Doctor Watkins, let's have a chat outside."

My parents leave the room along with the doctor, leaving Matthew and I alone.

"Can I have a kiss?" I ask.

Matthew doesn't move, he looks pensive.

"Do you remember what happened before the accident, Felicity?" he asks.

"I remember waking up in the wreckage and

speaking to a fireman."

Matthew sucks in breath.

"Why? Why is it so important that I remember?"

Matthew pauses, as if thinking about what to say next. "It doesn't matter, baby." He shakes his head and his shoulders visibly relax.

"Ok," I smile.

OVER THE COURSE OF the next few hours, I have lots of visitors. Heather, Ethan and Amber came to visit and after they left, I realised just how tired I was. Mum and dad have not long left when Matthew returns back with some chocolate for me to eat.

"All alone?" he asks with a smile.

I try to stifle a yawn and nod.

Just then, Kathy- one of the nurses- walks in. "Someones tired." She says she places a fresh jug of water down on the table.

"I am."

Kathy turns to Matthew, who refuses to look at her. He practically hasn't taken his eyes off me the whole time I've been awake, only to use the toilet, sleep or get food.

"I think she needs to get some sleep, dear."

Matthew frowns and looks up at her, "I'm not leaving if that's what you are asking."

"I'm not asking, I'm telling you. She needs to rest for the physiotherapist tomorrow."

"No." Matthew says firmly.

"Matthew, please. I'm ok." I don't want him to worry about me anymore. He looks like he's aged about ten years through worry since my accident.

Matthew looks at me and his expression softens. "Fine." he huffs. Matthew looks back to Kathy, "please can we have a moment, to say goodbye"

"Of course." Kathy smiles and walks out of the door, closing it behind her.

Matthew reaches for my face and gently cups it in his hand. "I've missed you so much, you have no idea." Tears begin to pool in his eyes as he looks down at me.

"Baby," I breathe.

"I thought I'd lost you forever. I have been through hell and back without you."

I feel a lone tear run down my face. I hate that I worried him, I hate that I worried everyone.

"I honestly can't imagine my life without you, Felicity." he continues. "You are my everything. I have never felt like this before. For years I'd built a wall so high that no one could break it, until you. You broke me wide open. You have seen right through all my bullshit."

"Matthew," my heart is exploding in my chest from his words.

"Please, let me say this, baby." He looks at me with admiration. "It has made me realise just how much I want you. You are my future. I want my future with you. I never thought that I would love someone like this. I never thought someone would love me, like the way you do-"

"Matthew, I lied." I interject.

He furrows his brow in confusion. "You lied? About what?" he asks.

I sigh and look down at my knotted fingers in front of me. "I can remember what happened before the accident." I admit.

Of course I remember that I told him that I wanted space and that I felt suffocated by him, his overbearing ways and his wealth. How could that be something I would ever forget? Crash or no crash. Telling him that hurt more than my brain injury and the surgery combined.

"I remember everything."

"Oh." Matthew says, as his expression falls and his shoulders slump.

"I know you love me, and believe you me, I love you so much more. But -," I sigh, " - I don't think this changes anything. You can't help the way you are, Matthew."

His eyes widened in panic. "Yes, yes it does! This has knocked the sense into me that I needed. It's made me see that life is short. Before we know it, this could all just end. Felicity, this has made me a better man. I want to be a better man, for you. I've always pushed people away when they get close to me. I don't want that anymore. I want to be surrounded by love - your love."

I close my eyes, his words causing my stomach to summersault. "I'm just so scared that we can't get past this."

"Oh but we can, if anything, this will make us stronger, baby. We can do this. We have been through so much already in our lives. I think we've earnt the right to finally be happy."

Matthew sits on my bed, careful not to hurt me and cups my hands in his. "You are well and truly under my skin. I can't do life without you. I can't breathe without you. You are the one who keeps the blood flowing through my veins, my heart would be nothing if you weren't there to make it beat."

Matthew wipes away the tears that flow down my cheeks. All this has brought back memories of losing Luke, and those hours when I thought that Matthew and I were over for good. Maybe he was right, maybe this will make us stronger. Maybe we are stronger together.

A thought occurs to me. I might not be the same after my accident. The doctor told me that I might have changes in my mood or muscle weakness or poor coordination. Will he still love me the same?

"Matthew, I'm worried I might not be the same person you fell in love with. I haven't even got out of bed yet. My brain function is there, but-" I stop, struggling to say the words out loud, "-what if I have trouble walking?"

"Felicity Walker, I would love you if you couldn't walk at all. I love you for you and not for your ability to walk."

I feel a blush creep across my face. *Now I feel silly.*

Kathy suddenly walks back into the room, startling us both. "Mr. Harper, you have to leave now."

Matthew rolls his eyes and gets up off the bed, but not before placing a kiss on forehead. "See you first thing in the morning, baby."

I gaze up at him, looking at him with nothing but love. *God, I really do love this man.*

Three Months Later

Felicity

I'M STANDING IN THE kitchen looking out to the beach and at the sand dunes. I watch as the blades of grass dance in the sea breeze and the waves crash on the shore. It is early evening so the sun is setting over the sea, the sky is a beautiful bloody orange colour. It's a picture perfect view.

I finished my last session with my physio yesterday and having made a full recovery, Matthew and I are celebrating with a long weekend in Norfolk, in one of Matthew's homes. It is a beautiful contemporary modern house, with floor to ceiling windows giving an expansive view over the North Norfolk beach. It is breathtaking and just what we both need.

Matthew has been so supportive of me, even paying privately for my sessions. I wouldn't have been able to do it all without his love and support. He's also learnt to let go a bit, even though I could see it was hard for him, especially when I would get tired from walking. I could see that all he wanted to do was to scoop me up in his big, strong arms and carry me to the chair or bed, but I didn't want him to. I wanted to do it myself. To prove to him that I was ok.

Once I was discharged from hospital, Matthew insisted that I move in with him, he claimed it was so he can help me but, I think he was worried I would change my mind about us.

I'm never going to though - this is it. He's my man. I realise now that I have to take the rough with the smooth. The bad with the good. Living together has been easier than I thought it would be, Matthew even told me that he was looking forward to never having to spend time apart. He gives off such a hard demeanour to the rest of the world, I'm the only one who gets to see just how soft and loving he really is.

I hear Matthew approach me from behind. He places a kiss to the side of my neck and my body immediately tingles in response to his touch. Matthew spins me around and I drape my arms around his neck. He is dressed in a plain white T-shirt which shows off his toned muscles and pecs. He looks delicious. His hair is getting so long, so long that it's flopped over his forehead. My fingers twitch with the need to run my hands through it.

"Hey." I beam.

Matthew dips his head and kisses me passionately, his tongue finding its way into my mouth and joining my tongue in a tango.

"God, I love you." He breathes as he kisses me.

"I love you too, baby,"

"Come with me, I have something to show you." Matthew takes me by the hand and leads me up the stairs and through the bedroom and onto the balcony that overlooks the sea.

My mouth immediately drops to the floor. The large wrap-around balcony is unrecognisable. On the ground are large bouquets of beautiful red and cream roses in vases, there must be at least a dozen, and threaded around the handrail are magical sparkling fairy lights and lanterns that glow softly.

I turn my head round to meet his. Matthew gazes down at me, his expression unreadable. Tugging my hand, he leads me further out onto the balcony. Suddenly, Matthew sinks down onto one knee.

Oh my God.

My heart is in my mouth as tears prick my eyes.

From his jeans pocket he pulls out a black box and I swear to God I stop breathing. His ocean blue eyes are full of emotion and dare I say, nerves as he slowly opens the box.

Never in my wildest dreams did I expect this!

"Felicity Jayne Walker, I love you. And, for the rest of my time on earth, I want to cherish, love you and spend everyday making you happy. I want to grow old with you and raise children with you. Please, would you make me the happiest man alive and marry me?"

I blink down at him as my tears flow down my cheeks. The man, my man who I love so much, wants to share his life with me, and all I can do is nod my response. I am speechless, lost for words as emotion hits me.

Matthew flashes his megawatt grin, clearly relieved. He pulls the ring from the slit in the box and slides it onto my finger. It's the most beautiful ring I have ever seen. It's a large round diamond in a platinum ring and stunning in its simplicity.

"Oh, Matthew," I sob. I am overwhelmed with joy. Matthew rises from his knee and stands. He kisses me and I kiss him back, I kiss him with all my love. He wraps his arms around me and his hands fist in my hair. I know in my heart of hearts that this is right. Matthew William Harper is the best thing to ever happen to me.

We've come so far together in such a short space of time. Overcome so many hurdles and I know we still have so many to go, but we are made for each other. We both have physical scars but our metal ones are diminishing with each passing day. We are meant to be together. Life has finally dealt me a good hand, and I intend to play it.

ACKNOWLEDGEMENT

I am grateful to all my friends and family who has supported me, my dream and my book. It means the world to me.

Simon, you have been my rock and your unwavering support has spurred me on to push myself.

And finally, a big thank you to you - the reader. Thank you for choosing my book, taking a chance on me and with any luck, enjoying it too!

ABOUT THE AUTHOR

H L Potter

Working in an office as a day job, H L Potter had always dreamed of publishing her own novel.
Her passion was to create a real, relatable female lead whom falls in love with someone who the reader can connect to on an emotional level.
She is addicted to reading, alpha males and a good love story. She resides in Essex, UK, where she lives in her own love story with her fiance and dog, Cooper.

Printed in Great Britain
by Amazon

82995621R00281